D0037357

EARLY PRAISE
FOR THE BELLADONNA AGENCY SERIES

"If you're looking for a hot, sexy, emotional read, Virna DePaul delivers!"
—J. KENNER, *New York Times* and
USA Today bestselling author of *Release Me*

"Virna DePaul creates yummy alpha heroes, relatable heroines, and supercharged emotional plots. Run, don't walk, to snatch up one of her stories."
—*New York Times* bestselling author TINA FOLSOM

"A captivating start to a fascinating new series with a hero who's to die for!"
—Nationally bestselling author RHYANNON BYRD

"*Turned* is intense, intricate, and insomnia-inducing (plan to stay up way too late!). Virna DePaul puts the awesome in the awesomesauce of paranormal romance."
—Joyce Lamb, curator,
USA Today's Happy Ever After

"The chemistry between the two was great and made for some very sexy scenes."
—*Fresh Fiction*

"This book has everything you could want and so, *so* much more!"
—*Guilty Pleasures Book Reviews*

"*Turned* is an intriguing story with flawed characters who I connected with immediately. Fans of paranormal romance rejoice, here's a compelling new series to sink your teeth into."

—*Harlequin Junkie*

PRAISE FOR VIRNA DEPAUL

"Seducer and protector—this vampire has it all."
—*Fresh Fiction,* on *A Vampire's Salvation*

"Virna DePaul is amazing!"
—*New York Times* bestselling author LORI FOSTER

"Incredibly well written, different, and hot."
—*New York Times* bestselling author LARISSA IONE

"A gripping tale! DePaul creates the perfect blend of danger, intrigue, and romance. You won't be able to put this book down!"
—*New York Times* bestseller BRENDA NOVAK

"If you have not yet started this [Para-Ops] series . . . you are really missing out."
—*The Book Reading Gals*

"This is my first book by Virna DePaul and it will definitely not be my last. *Deadly Charade* is a suspenseful story full of love, betrayal, and forgiveness."
—*Fresh Fiction,* on *Deadly Charade*

TURNED

TURNED

THE BELLADONNA AGENCY SERIES

VIRNA DEPAUL

BANTAM
NEW YORK

Turned is a work of fiction. Names, places, and incidents either are a product of the author's imagination or are used fictitiously.

A Bantam Books Mass Market Original

Published in the United States by Bantam Books, an imprint of Random House, a division of Random House LLC, a Penguin Random House Company, New York.

BANTAM BOOKS and the HOUSE colophon are registered trademarks of Random House LLC.

This book contains an excerpt from the forthcoming book *Awakened* by Virna DePaul. This excerpt has been set for this edition only and may not reflect the final content of the forthcoming edition.

ISBN 978-0-345-54245-8
eBook ISBN 978-0-345-54246-5

Cover design: Lynn Andreozzi
Cover photograph: © Claudio Marinesco

Printed in the United States of America

www.bantamdell.com

9 8 7 6 5 4 3 2 1

Bantam Books mass market edition: April 2014

For my brother, James.

You take what life throws at you
and you keep fighting.
You amaze and inspire me.
I love you!

TURNED

PROLOGUE

He woke to the ugly whine of a power tool.

Bright lights and shadowy figures hovered above him. His body seemed paralyzed. His mind numb. Caught in that ethereal place between dream and reality.

Still, there was the faintest feeling of unease.

Mental pictures of being with three others—his sister Naomi, Peter Lancaster, and Ben Porter. They'd been on their way to see a movie after work and had been stopped by a group of men. Men who'd turned on them.

Bit them.

Killed them . . .

The sound of the power tool—was it a saw?—grew louder. Sinister.

A scream echoed in the distance, followed by broken pleas for mercy.

So he wasn't dreaming but rather having a nightmare.

No matter. He'd lived with plenty of those, too. It would end soon, though he had to admit—this one seemed particularly brutal.

"He's coming to," a distant voice murmured, but Ty's vision remained blurred. "Should we keep going?"

Another voice answered, but it was muffled. Unclear. Even though Ty couldn't decipher the words spoken, he heard the authority behind them.

Then it happened . . .

Numbness fled. He felt again.

He hurt. More than he'd ever thought possible.

Was he sick? Had he been in an accident? Was that why he kept imagining Naomi screaming and covered in blood? Not just her blood, but his, too.

That must be it, he thought desperately.

He was in the hospital, maybe even in an operating room. They thought they'd given him enough to put him under, but they hadn't. Given how heavily he slept, it was ironic that it took a boatload of drugs to put him out for any length of time; he'd woken up during medical procedures too many times to count.

Pain radiated throughout his body. He was made of agony—excruciating, white-hot misery. It wasn't just his hollow stomach and aching gums and parched throat. His bones were wickedly sharp knives piercing his organs and sawing through his skin. And just when he thought the pain had reached its peak, someone—or something—poked him or cut him or ripped at him, proving he was wrong and making him scream even as he prayed for death.

Help me, he thought. They don't know I'm awake but I am. Can't they see my eyes are open? Can't they hear my screams?

But as more and more time passed, he realized they could hear his screams. And they didn't care.

He wasn't dreaming.

He wasn't in a hospital being operated on.

He was a prisoner. And saving him was the last thing his captors were interested in.

So, unfortunately, was killing him.

Special Agent Ty Duncan's eyes flew open just as a shrill ringing pierced his eardrums. Blinking wildly, he took several seconds to realize the sound wasn't coming from a surgical saw. Nor was it the pitiful screeches of men and women in agonizing pain. It was his phone.

His *fucking* phone.

But the nightmare—no, the *memories* of his captivity—had left him trembling and sweating, gasping for air, barely able to move. His heart slammed against his chest so hard he felt bruised and his stomach roiled with nausea.

It was as if his caller knew what he was going through because the phone just kept ringing.

Ring. Ring. Ring.

When Ty could finally breathe and move again, he picked up his cell. "I'm here."

"Surveillance is a go," his new boss, Carly, stated. "We've set you up next door with all the equipment you'll need. You fly to Seattle tonight. You ready?"

"I've *been* ready," he pointed out, his gaze automatically drifting to the open files scattered around the room. He didn't need to see her picture to visualize his mark's face.

Eliana Garcia, aka Ana Martin.

Former Primos Sangre gang member. Sister to Gloria.

A female with long glossy dark hair and large dark eyes, her beauty straddling the line between ingenue and seductress, tempting a man to alternately protect and challenge her even as the ugly scar on her face warned him not to try.

The woman who just might be able to get them where they needed to go.

Soon he'd have more than her photographs to look at. He'd meet her. Talk with her.

He'd do whatever it took to bring her in.

He'd do his job.

It was all he had left thanks to the vampires who had captured and tortured him.

It was all he had left now that he was no longer human himself.

After a few more perfunctory instructions from Carly, Ty ended the call. Then he couldn't help it. He'd memorized Ana's face but . . .

He found his favorite photograph of her, the one in which she was *almost* smiling. The promise of that smile was as intoxicating as it was frustrating. Next to seeing her smile outright, there were only two things he wanted more.

To fuck her. Hard.

And to drink her blood while he was doing it.

He slapped the photograph facedown on the table. He was shaking. *Shaking* with need for a woman he'd never even met. A woman whose past should have repelled him. Instead, he'd been inexplicably drawn to her since the moment he'd first seen her photograph, and now that he'd gotten the green light to go to her, the dark images from his nightmare had been replaced with unshakeable fantasies of taking her and sucking her blood.

It wasn't going to happen. He couldn't feed from her. Couldn't fuck her.

No, it was more than that—he *wouldn't*.

Six months ago, he'd been turned into a vampire. Afterward he'd been tortured. First by the vampires who seemed determined to test his immortality and his tolerance to pain. Second by his own body. Anytime his captors left him alone, he'd craved blood and sex. Lusting after them to the point where it was all he could think of. All he was interested in. Eventually, his overwhelming hunger had waned. Now he had a strict abstinence policy. No human blood. No sex other than with his own fist. It was the only way to be sure he wouldn't sink to the depths he had before.

If only he knew more about being a vampire. How to

be a vampire. How to *stop* being one. All he knew was what the FBI had told him.

Vampires were born. They breathed and they had heartbeats. They very much *lived*, but they lived in secret, interacting with most humans without giving away what they really were. When they'd been discovered years before, vampire leaders had assured the FBI they were no threat. While they drank human blood, they only drank from a small group of humans who knew what they were and whose ancestors had volunteered for the job for centuries. Moreover, turning humans into vampires, while technically possible, was forbidden as a matter of vampire law and morality. In the end, the FBI had decided it was in everyone's best interests to keep the existence of vampires a secret.

The FBI, however, was also keeping its own secrets from vampire leaders, the major one being that it had disregarded vampire law by employing several vampires—now labeled "Rogues"—to turn human recruits.

Well, surprise, surprise. Even as the Rogues had been turning human recruits in exchange for FBI favors, they'd been running their own operations behind the scenes. Maybe the FBI had suspected as much. Maybe they'd been willing to turn a blind eye to minor infractions. But after Ty, Peter, and Ben had been captured and turned, the FBI had gone into damage-control mode. No more human recruits would be turned—not until the Rogues were contained. Failing to do so would not only put the whole operation at risk, but might alert the general human population about vampires before the U.S. government was ready for that to happen.

That's where Ty came in.

He was still a special agent with the FBI. Granted, he was being hidden away like a dirty secret, but he was an undeniable asset. Like the born vampires, Ty could move as fast as a cheetah. And like the born vampires, he was unable to tell a lie. But the animal blood that weakened born vampires was more than enough to sustain Ty, and he could survive brief contact with the sun while born vampires burned instantly upon direct contact. On the flip side, he could only occasionally read minds, while born vampires could easily and consistently do so.

Now he had one immediate task—recruit Ana Martin for Belladonna, an off-the-books agency formed by Assistant FBI Director Rick Hallifax. *So* off the books that the only people who knew it existed were Hallifax, his right-hand man, Special Agent Kyle Mahone, Peter, and Carly, Ty's boss.

If things worked out the way they wanted, soon she'd be Ana's boss, too.

PART
1

THE JOB OFFER

CHAPTER ONE

Seattle, Washington
A few weeks later . . .

Back in the Bronx, Eliana Maria Garcia's weapons of choice had been a smart mouth, the occasional threat of a knife, and her fists. Now, standing with her back pressed against the brick wall behind Monk's Café, Ana Martin had something even better—a gun. One she was hoping she wouldn't have to use.

Confronting the man who'd been following her, however, was unavoidable. She'd noticed him at the bank yesterday, then the market. But last night she'd seen him outside her house. And moments before? Across the street.

That was one coincidence too many. She'd left Primos Sangre over seven years ago, but if there was one thing the gang had taught her, it was that survival meant confronting danger head-on rather than running from it. Since she didn't trust the cops—didn't trust anyone—her only choice was to handle this herself. Her way.

If only she wasn't so scared. But she'd put her old life behind her, and even though she wasn't happy—could never be happy without her sister—she was often content. Sometimes when she looked in the mirror she even managed to like the person she saw looking back at her. The thought of losing that scared her more than any threat of physical harm ever could. And it scared her enough that she was willing to fight to make sure it didn't happen.

The sun had set long ago. Now and then a stab of light from a passing car pierced the shadows of the alley where Ana was hiding, forcing her to dodge back. Invisible, shrouded in darkness, she waited. When she heard footsteps, she knew it was him.

Forcing her near-numb fingers to tighten their grip on the gun, she watched as he walked past her, then made her move, coming at him from behind, pressing the barrel of her gun against the back of his head.

He didn't even jerk.

From the back, he looked big. Broad. Muscles rippling. Dangerous.

But from the front? Even from a distance, he'd looked more than dangerous. He'd looked deadly. Beyond handsome. Midnight hair and eyes just as dark. Savage and sophisticated at the same time. She'd never seen his equal. Certainly never met anyone that came close.

Part of her knew she'd gotten the drop on him a bit too easily. That perhaps she was doing exactly what he'd been expecting. Hoping.

But it was too late to go back now.

"Hands where I can see them," she managed to get out.

Slowly, he raised his hands in surrender. Only she still wasn't buying it. Her nerves screamed at her to run, but logic kept her feet planted firmly on the ground. Somehow, she knew if she ran, he'd only come after her.

"Why are you following me?"

No answer. No surprise.

With her free hand, she patted him down, the way she'd learned to do in the gang. By the time she'd frisked him from the back, she was the one who was sweating. And not from exertion.

Nothing about him was small. He was tall and buff, more than big enough to overpower her slight frame. Sangre-style paranoia set in, and it occurred to her that this guy might be undercover. She instantly recalled the run-ins she'd had with cops as a teenager. The way they'd often pulled her long dark ponytail, hard enough to make her back arch and breasts lift. The way they'd sometimes copped a feel or implied they'd leave her in peace if she made it worth their while. She'd never given them that satisfaction.

But no, she decided. This guy's vibe was just too different. Not so much cop as outlaw.

His entire body was contoured with interesting ridges and bulges and planes. This close she could smell him, a subtle spicy scent that managed to convey unabashed maleness and warmth despite what seemed to be a rather low body temperature. The man held himself in control. Unlike her. Gritting her teeth, she ignored the rush of heat to her cheeks and moved faster to disguise the telltale trembling of her hands.

"Turn around," she commanded.

Slowly, he did.

Despite the heat in his gaze, his mouth was tipped into a mocking smile, as if he knew how affected she was by touching him. What he didn't know—*couldn't* know— was how confused she was by her reaction. He made her feel . . . restless. Edgy. Vulnerable.

She hated it.

As such, she hated *him*.

Methodically, she frisked him from the front, delving between his denim-clad legs to make sure he wasn't packing more than nature had provided.

He grunted slightly and said, "Keep that up and you might find more than you want, princess."

His accent was clipped and tidy—upper-crust British. Despite herself, her gaze shot to his.

"Don't call me that," she said automatically, just before she found the gun tucked into a sleek holster concealed inside his waistband.

She pulled it out, and the sight of the Luger didn't surprise her. The well-made weapon suited him. Swiftly, she slipped it out of his holster and into the front of her own waistband.

The only other time she'd seen a Luger was when she'd delivered a package to Pablo, the leader of Devil's Crew, another street gang, and he'd insisted on inspecting the contents before he paid. He'd told her the guns had been stolen from some Richie Rich who liked fancy cars as well as fancy guns. When he'd asked her what kind of car she drove, she'd told him the truth. None. She'd only been fourteen at the time.

Even so, her youth hadn't stopped her from fighting the gang leader when he'd decided to inspect more than the package she'd delivered. All she'd gotten for her trouble was a beating and the ugly scar on her face.

To her, big and male was synonymous with power and violence.

"I'm not going to hurt you," the man in front of her said softly, as if he'd read her mind. "If you'll listen to me, I can help you, Ana."

The fact he knew her name shocked her . . . and scared her even more. "Fuck you," she snapped without meaning to. Swearing was an old habit, one she'd fought hard to break, but sometimes it came out. When she was angry . . . when she felt threatened . . . the tough girl inside her lost control, cursing and spitting and speaking Spanish in an effort to protect herself despite the fact it merely revealed how vulnerable she really was.

How weak.

She bit her lip, furious that he'd sensed her fear. Furious that his offer of help made her easily long for things she couldn't possibly have.

She'd gotten soft. Too soft. And once again she was paying the price. The only question was how high the price would be this time.

"Move." She gestured with her gun. "Face the wall." He had her so rattled she was second-guessing herself. She needed to frisk him again. Make sure she hadn't missed anything the first time.

He merely stared silently at her, and she forced herself to snap, "Now."

Unbelievably, he practically rolled his eyes just before he obeyed, cursing when she suddenly shoved him face-first against the brick; Eliana Garcia, gang member, was quickly chipping away at the civilized, respectable woman Ana had been trying to become.

But instead of retaliating, he waited while she frisked him yet again. When she was done, when he failed to make a move on her, she relaxed slightly. "Face me."

As he did, she saw the slight trickle of blood now dripping from a cut on his forehead. She felt a momentary pang of guilt. Along with it came the strange temptation to wipe the blood away and kiss the wound better. To kiss *all* his hurt away. Hurt she somehow sensed was there.

Which was beyond ridiculous. Like one of those tear-jerker movies where the love of a good woman saved some useless son of a bitch.

He didn't need her to wash his freakin' pain away. He needed to know who was boss. Besides, she didn't take care of anyone but herself anymore. It was better that way. Safer.

Instinctively, she gripped her gun tighter while he leaned back against the wall and crossed his arms over his chest, no longer smiling but watching her with an intensity that made her shiver.

"You've been trailing me since yesterday," she said, "and not just because you like my coffee. ¿*Porqué?*"

At her lapse into Spanish and the thickening of her accent, Ana clenched her teeth, then deliberately modulated her voice so it was once again white-bread Americana. "Why are you following me?"

He smiled again, as if her speaking Spanish had amused him.

Embarrassment washed over her and she wavered, accidentally lowering the gun. "Answer me, *bastardo*—"

In a blur of movement, he grabbed her wrist, wrenched the gun from her hand, flipped her to the ground, and covered her body with his much larger one.

Reflexively, she struck out, striking him in the face before he pinned her arms and his body simply weighed her down. Damn it, she'd known it had been too easy. He'd set her up. And the way he'd moved . . . Faster than anything she'd ever seen before.

But oddly enough, he had his body braced so his full weight wasn't on her. As if he wanted her pinned but not hurt.

As if he was taking care of her.

Breathing hard, she stared into his mesmerizing face. His scent would be all over her, she thought absently. When he shifted, rubbing his lower body against her, she blinked at the unexpected warmth that flooded her. He was cold, yet he made her feel so good. So hot. Literally. For another crazy second, she wanted to grab either side of his face, pull him closer, and kiss him.

Ah Dios. She was losing it.

He tsked. "It was your f-bomb that finally got to me, you know. Normally, you hold back. You don't have to. Your cursing. Your use of Spanish. I like it. I *more* than like it. I just had to see if you felt as good as you look. As you sound."

Again, that dazzling smile. The British perfection in the way he modulated his words. Those cold eyes. Danger emanated from him like a flashing red light, while charm oozed from him like honey.

He leaned closer and whispered. "Lucky me. You feel even better than I'd anticipated." When she failed to respond, he raised a brow. "What? I've rendered you speechless? Or are you just holding back again? I told you I'm here to help. That starts with offering you a job."

Now *that* she hadn't been expecting. She snorted and shifted underneath him, working to twist her way out from under his weight. The intoxicating feel of her limbs rubbing against his made her want to move slower. To relish the contact.

Instantly, she ceased her attempts to get away from him.

"I'm not stupid or gullible—" she began.

"No. In fact, Téa believes you're extremely smart. One of the smartest she's ever worked with."

Ana went rigid with hurt. Téa—a woman she'd thought was the closest thing she had to a friend—had sent him here with no warning? "Please get off me," she whispered when what she really wanted to do was scream. Cuss. In Spanish *and* English.

He kept his gaze locked on hers for several seconds, then said, "As you wish." Pushing himself to standing, he held out a hand to help her up.

She ignored him and scrambled to her feet, immediately backing several steps away. "How do you know Téa? Why did she—"

"Ana!"

Ana jerked when she heard Paul, one of her employees at the coffee shop, call her name, but she didn't take her eyes off the man. "I'll be right there," she shouted back.

The man in front of her didn't bat an eye.

She shook her head. "Téa misled you. I don't want anything from you."

"Not even information about your sister?"

Her heart stopped beating and for a moment the world around her blurred. She fought against the wooziness, focusing on the man's face. Excitement tickled the back of her throat and sent a buzzing up her spine.

Ana hadn't seen her sister, Gloria, for seven years, not since Ana had tried to jump them both out of Primos Sangre. Gloria had only joined the gang after returning from living with her grandparents. Ana had barely recognized her. Gloria had been angry. Distant. Wanting her sister's company one minute and hating it the next. After the shooting, she'd written Ana in prison, making it abundantly clear she blamed Ana for her injury and never wanted to see her again.

Had Gloria changed her mind? Had she sent this man to tell her that? A wash of excitement shot through her. Buoyed her. Maybe the stranger that had returned from living with her grandparents had finally turned back into the loving sister Ana remembered. Without even realizing what she was doing, she stepped closer. "You know Gloria?"

"I know about her."

"But did Gloria send you to find me?" she asked, hope reducing her voice to a whisper.

"No."

Disappointment. Suspicion. Dismissal. All cut through the excitement and hope, scattering them to the wind.

Nothing had changed. As such, this man had nothing she needed.

As if he could read her mind he said, "I told you, I'm here to offer you a job."

"I'm not interested in anything you're offering." Slowly, her eyes never leaving him, she retrieved her gun, tucked it into her waistband right next to his, covered them with her sweater, and started walking backward toward the cafe entrance.

"I'm quite fond of my gun, you know," he called out.
"It's mine now."

"It's also a violation of your parole for you to carry a firearm."

That made her freeze, but only for a second. She turned and walked to the coffeehouse door, her steps slow and lethargic. Over her shoulder, she muttered, "So tell my parole officer. Téa always knows where to find me."

Ty sighed as Ana walked back into her coffeehouse. She moved fast and loose, as if tackling a guy in an alley and pointing a gun at him was par for the course. He supposed given her background, it was like riding a bike—you never forgot how, not when your very survival was at stake. But that didn't mean she hadn't been shaken up by their encounter.

She seemed to fit in well with the college crowd she served. In fact, in her uniform of short tees and tight jeans, she could have been a student herself. She worked. She went home. She kept to herself.

But she wasn't happy with her life. Far from it. She'd simply convinced herself she couldn't have more. Sometimes, however, her true nature came through despite her best attempts to hide it.

Soon after he'd arrived in Seattle, Ana had ceased to be a fuck fantasy. The hot ex–gang member with the checkered past turned out to be a woman to admire. She kept her distance, but she was hardworking and good to her employees. He'd also been right about her smile. She didn't use it often, but when she did, her hotness ratcheted into heart-stopping beauty.

His surveillance had also alleviated any lingering concerns he'd had about her refusing to do what they wanted. Because as hard as she tried to keep herself apart from others, she clearly longed for the type of connections she didn't allow herself.

He'd seen how she'd stared longingly at the couple playing footsie in the corner of her coffee shop. How she'd stared at two women at the grocery store, arm in arm, obviously loving sisters. And how she'd helped a frail young man with MS across the street; she had watched him walk down the block until he turned the corner and disappeared from view.

Over the past few weeks, his protective instincts had kicked in. So many times, he'd wanted to go to her. Wrap his arms around her. Comfort her. But of course he hadn't. Because she would have fought him, yes, but also because his hunger had grown almost unbearable.

When she'd confronted and challenged him, he'd managed to hang on to his control, but just barely. He'd known she was waiting for him in the alley and he'd been prepared for her to touch him, even if it was simply to disarm him. Although he'd allowed himself to touch her back, he'd done so with ruthless restraint. He'd led Ana to believe he was just a strong human rather than a hungry vampire lusting after her blood and her body. His sheathed fangs ached the way his dick did, longing to penetrate and take everything from her: her sweet blood and her complete surrender.

Once again he reminded himself it wasn't going to happen. No matter how he admired her, and no matter how she made him feel, she was a job and that was all she could ever be.

He took out his cell and punched in Carly's number.

"You found her?" Carly's voice was husky. Feminine. It was flat-out sexy—deliberately so—and he couldn't help compare it to the gravelly, clipped speech that Ana had used, her occasional melodic slip into Spanish aside. Despite the sentiment behind her words, the flow of them combined with the touch of her body had made him hard, harder than the brick wall he'd been pressed against. The intensity of his desire as well as his decision not to push her too far—yet—had been the only reasons he'd remained against that wall. Despite carrying an illegal gun, Ana had turned her life around. He didn't want to take that away from her. And she had no reason to hurt him unless he gave her one. Besides, it wasn't as if one of her bullets could kill him anyway.

As far as he knew, nothing could.

"She's not going to be as easy as the others," he said in response to Carly's question.

"I wouldn't say the others have been easy."

"She's good. Even managed to get my gun."

"Right," Carly answered, her tone laced with the knowledge that if Ana had gotten Ty's gun, it was because he'd let her do it. Just like he'd let her spot him watching her in the first place. "Did she shoot you?"

"No, she did not shoot me. She cursed me, though. In Spanish. Something that seemed to bother her." It had certainly bothered him, but only because he'd liked it. Too much.

He closed his eyes and replayed her words, enjoying the way it made him think of heat and skin and sweaty, slippery silk sheets. With her golden skin, cinnamon eyes, and dark hair, he could easily picture her spread beneath him, begging him for release as he crooned back to her in her native tongue:

Todavía no. Not yet.

Un poco más largo. A little longer.

Dé a mí. Give to me.

He bit back a groan.

Give to me.

Even now his dick twitched, ready to get busy, ready to immerse itself in Ana's warmth.

He couldn't have her. Not sexually. Not in ways that

might involve her heart as well as her body. And that made him angry.

It fucking made him want to kill someone.

Thankfully, Carly seemed oblivious to his internal struggle. "Excellent," she said. "You're right about that, she hates it when she speaks Spanish. She's trying to deny who she is—who she was—but even after all these years she can't. She's still the tough little girl from the Bronx."

"Yes. The little girl packs quite a punch, too." Raising a hand, Ty rubbed at his mouth, grinning when he saw the blood. She might not be able to kill him, but she sure as shit could make him bleed.

"Was that before or after she got your gun? Pity. I know how fond you are of it."

His silence just seemed to amuse her. True to form, she pounced on it.

"Oh my. Are you saying you can't handle this one?" she purred.

God, he hated Carly sometimes. Hated her bitch-on-steroids act. Hated the necessity to partner with her at all. But she hadn't always been like this. Years ago, as a fellow newbie agent with the FBI, she'd been good at her job but she'd had a gentle side, too. That part of her had long been quashed. And now? Sure, she'd helped Ty and Peter when they'd needed her most, but her assistance had been more about using them than saving them. Carly was doing what she needed to adjust to her new life, part of a team but very much alone. Just like him.

Ty glanced in the direction Ana had disappeared. "No," he said, this time letting a trace of humor leak into his voice. "I can handle her. I'll just have to be a little more direct, that's all."

"You don't have authority to reveal what you are, Ty," Carly snapped. "Not yet. We have one month until the leaders of Salvation's Crossing attend the Hispanic

Community Alliance fund-raiser, and we need Ana fully invested before we show our hand."

"I have no plans to tell her I'm a vampire right now. But she still has my gun, and I have no intention of letting her think she can take anything from me and just walk away."

CHAPTER TWO

Inside the coffee shop she'd built with blood, sweat, and tears, Ana leaned against the closed door, keenly aware of the tension that zipped through her body like an electrical charge. The man had done a number on her, both physically and mentally. She tipped her head back against the door, forced herself to take a deep breath, and focused on the small but well-appointed space with its gleaming wood, plush sofas and chairs, and brightly colored walls, trying to get her mind off the encounter in the alleyway.

Not much luck. The man's heady scent hung about her, as if he was still near. The sensation of his muscular body on hers—his pelvis pressed to hers—still echoed in her bones.

She forced herself to listen to the familiar strains of one of her favorite songs, playing softly in the background. Calming, but not enough to wipe clean her distress.

Handling the gun, holding it to his head, trying to come off tough—it had all shaken her up more than she wanted to admit. Her insides still quivered, both from challenging him and from the way he'd made her feel.

Alive.

And empty at the same time. He'd brought out a rush of feelings inside her, but the moment he'd mentioned Gloria, he'd blasted it all away again, leaving her numb but longing for those few blessed moments of sensation. Longing for things that could never be hers.

She should be used to it by now, but she wasn't. It hurt. It made her want to cry out, *Why? Why me? Why now? Why can't people just leave me alone to live my life in peace?*

Swiftly, she sent Paul home. With no customers in the coffee shop to see her do it, she took both her gun and his and stuck them into a cabinet behind the counter. Then she picked up her cell phone and dialed Téa's number. Cursing softly when it went to voicemail, she left a message asking Téa to call her back right away. A glance at the clock on the wall confirmed she only had another half hour before closing time. She shut off the music then waited, steeling herself for what was coming.

Ten minutes later, the man walked in. Ana was finishing up an order for a last-minute customer, one of her late-night regulars, Bobbie Hernandez. As usual, Bobbie was accompanied by a pretty girl. Even as she tensed, Ana continued to chat with the two of them, refusing to look at her unwanted guest even though she really wanted to. Bobbie glanced at the other man curiously, but he simply stared back, expression inscrutable.

The moment Bobbie and his girlfriend left, Ana snapped around the Closed sign so it was facing out. Moving away from the glass door to the solid wall beside it, she leaned back, crossed her arms over her chest, and turned to him. As she watched, he shrugged out of his jacket and sat down, shirt untucked, legs splayed out in front of him.

"Don't get too comfortable. I'm closed now. You need to leave."

"I'm not leaving until I say what I came to say," he said softly. "You know that."

His voice caressed her, as did his gaze. Once you were able to see past all the mesmerizing angles of his face and body and his slick clothes, he had nice eyes. So dark they almost seemed black. Like dark chocolate. Or a richly decadent espresso. Two of her favorite things. Automatically, her gaze dropped to the bulge in his pants. It was lovingly framed by his thighs, the fabric of his jeans pulled tight against them so it molded itself to the hard muscle.

She'd touched him when she'd patted him down, so she knew he was well endowed. Big and intimidating even when he wasn't aroused. He'd stirred when she'd touched him in the alley and the memory of her fingers on such an intimate part of him made her flush. Given her history, the reminder of his masculinity and vitality should scare her.

Why wasn't it scaring her?

Why had she suddenly grown warm, throughout her entire body but particularly between her legs? Why did she have the sudden urge to kneel in front of him and unzip him, so she could see what she'd already felt—

For God's sake. Stop! Men had never caused her anything but pain time and again. This man wouldn't be any different.

Forcing her gaze away from his body, she focused on his positioning instead. Despite his relaxed pose, she noted how he, too, had placed himself where he could see the entrance, but still remain out of view and out of range of anyone on the street.

"How about I call the cops?" she asked, hoping he wouldn't call her bluff.

"How about we make a deal instead?"

"What kind of deal?"

"I want my gun back. And something tells me you're not just going to hand it over to me."

"So?"

"Let's focus on what happened outside. Do you really believe you would have gotten my gun if I hadn't wanted you to? You're good, sweetheart, but as I said earlier, you were holding back. I did the same."

She'd held a gun to his head. Slammed his face into a wall. And he thought she'd been holding back? "I don't know what you're talking about," she clipped out, even though part of her did.

"You were willing to fight dirty, but only to a degree. You're ashamed of who you were. The way you used to talk. The way you used to fight. That shame hinders you."

His perceptiveness grated at her. He was right. She hated the person she'd been. Resented any necessity to be that person again. But she was never going to admit it to him or anyone else. "And according to this absurd theory of yours, you decided to take it easy on me to keep things fair?"

He grinned. "Don't believe me? Let me prove it to you. Fight me. Fight me with everything you are. Everything you've got. I get the gun back, you listen to what I have to say. All of it. You consider what I'm offering you before you make your decision."

"And if you don't get it back?"

"I leave, but first I'll give you some of the information I have on your sister."

Suspicion flickered through her . . . and temptation. "Why don't you just give me the information anyway?"

He smirked. "Sorry, but it doesn't work that way. Come on, Ana. Give it your best shot. Show me what you've got. Show me what you learned on the streets," he taunted.

"Shut up," she hissed.

He sobered instantly and she could tell he knew. *He knew*. He knew what she'd done in the past to survive— maybe he even knew what had been done *to* her despite the fact that she'd have rather died—and she couldn't hold back the intense shame that washed over her, making her feel nauseous.

"I was referring to your fighting skills," he said softly.

"I know what you were talking about."

"So then?"

"How do I know you won't just retrieve your gun—assuming you are able to retrieve it—and shoot me instead of giving me the information I want?"

"You're a smart girl. I guess you'll just have to trust me."

"I don't trust anyone."

"Like I said, smart girl."

Without another word, Ty lunged out of his chair, not for her, but for the counter behind her.

Ana didn't bother protesting his sneakiness. He wanted her to fight him with everything she had? So be it. This time, as fast as he was, she was faster. Probably because she had the advantage of knowing exactly where she'd put his gun. Vaulting over the counter that separated the work area from the customer area, Ana grabbed what was handy—a couple of heavy coffee mugs—and hurled them at him.

They bounced off his chest. She turned swiftly, but his arms wrapped around her from behind just as she was reaching for the shelf underneath the cash register. "Stupid move," he growled. "You led me right to it."

"Or maybe I just led you to this." She tightened her grip on the small club and, even with her limited mobility, swung it down, aiming for his knee. Just in time, he raised his leg, decreasing the distance between her and her target so it deflected the blow. With his arms wrapped tight around her in a bear hug, he lifted her off the ground and swung her around so they were facing the opposite counter.

With her feet dangling and the air being squeezed

from her lungs, she began to see stars. "So what are you going to do now, little girl?" he taunted in her ear.

What she did was drop the club, plant her feet on the cabinets beside her, and twist her body so she leaned closer to one side. Then she shifted her arm behind her so she could grab his dick in a punishing grip. He bellowed and she shoved herself to the other side so that his arms loosened just a bit—just enough so she could hit him in the gut with her elbow. It wasn't a powerful hit, but it was enough to gain her a bit more freedom. Violently twisting his manhood, she finally managed to cause him enough pain that he loosened his arms. She pushed off the counter, sending him crashing backward, and twisted out of his grip. Breathing hard, she bolted out of reach and turned to face him.

He had paled to a sickly white but the look in his eyes was murderous. His lips were flattened in a tense, thin line. She actually grinned, feeling more alive than she had in months. Hell, years. She danced around on the balls of her feet, waiting for him to come at her. "Oh, come on. Don't be a poor sport. This was your idea, *amigo.*"

"Where is my gun?" he bit out.

She couldn't resist. She glanced down beneath the cash register again, expecting him to dive for it while she went in the other direction. Once she opened the cabinet and had the gun in her hands, she'd have won and that meant—

Unfortunately, she didn't have time to finish her thought. The premature victory was cut short when Ty rushed her, pushed his shoulder into her stomach, and hefted her over his shoulder. As the world spun, she screeched. "You asshole." She pounded at his back and tried to kick her legs, but he wrapped his arms around them like vices, prohibiting her movement. "You bastard. *Yo le mataré. No, usted deseará que usted estu-*

viera muerto! I'm going to cut off your balls. I'm going to—to—"

He actually slapped her ass, making her scream in fury once more.

"You've done quite enough damage to my balls already, thank you very much. Now you're going to have to take your punishment."

The world spun as he lowered her to the ground and himself on top of her. Her ponytail had come loose. Her dark hair was hanging in her face and she could barely see him through it, but she could feel him, all his hard angles pressing into her softest places. He gathered her wrists in his hand and held them over her head. Then he lowered his head until he spoke right into her ear.

"Now," he said. "Just tell me where my gun is. Once you do that, it'll be a fair challenge."

His voice sounded different. Slightly slurred.

"You weren't worried about playing fair when you got a head start on me," she snapped.

He seemed to consider that. "I suppose I wasn't. What does that tell you?"

"That you're an unscrupulous, manipulative bastard that's willing to work any situation to your advantage so you can get what you want."

Finally, he raised his head and his gaze met hers. His expression was hard. "That's right. Now, tell me. What is it you think I want right now?" His hips pressed forward. Even if they hadn't, she'd know he was aroused. His erection hardened and lengthened with each second that passed.

Oh God, had she totally misjudged him? Was this what he'd wanted all along? Was he going to—

"Don't you fucking look at me like that," he clipped out, the curse word sounding as foreign coming out of his mouth as his accent. "I'm not going to rape you. But I don't have to, do I? You want me. And something tells me if I kiss you—just kiss you—you'll tell me exactly where my gun is. What are the odds that I'm right?"

As fear drained from her body, it was replaced swiftly by anger. She felt her face flame and hated that her weakness was so transparent. Worse yet, she hated him for being witness to it. She renewed her struggles, but that didn't stop him from lowering his lips to hers.

"Bite me," he warned, "and I swear I'll bite you back."

She didn't bite him.

She couldn't.

She was too busy trying to stifle her every sound and every reaction to his kiss. The first touch of his cool mouth to hers seared her nerve endings, and although he kept the contact quick and gentle, she was shaking when he raised his head.

"Where's the gun?"

She stared mutely back at him.

"You want me to kiss you again, sweetheart?"

She tried shaking her head. Wasn't sure if she actually did. She said nothing, however, afraid if she did she'd give herself away.

Yes. Yes. Yes.

She wanted him to kiss her again. But damn if she'd tell him so.

Thankfully, he didn't need to hear it. Lowering his head once more, he was neither quick nor gentle. This time, his touch didn't feel cool.

This time, he opened his mouth and penetrated hers with his tongue.

This time, heat swept from him into her so hot and so fast she practically ignited. She whimpered, and the sound shocked her out of her lust-induced trance. No, she thought. I won't let this happen. I can't.

Wrenching her mouth from his, she turned her face to

the side, closed her eyes, and surrendered. "Your gun's in the cabinet under the toaster."

Several seconds ticked by. The only sound was that of their breath being dragged in and out of their lungs. Ana clenched her teeth. "You won, okay? Get off me."

"Look at me." His words were dark and commanding.

Bitterly, she opened her eyes and turned back to him.

His expression was savage. His eyes burned with hunger.

"This isn't a victory, Ana. Not for either one of us. But if you can get over your attitude, you'll find I can be generous. You can also judge this for yourself. I don't lie. Ever. Your sister is alive. She's healthy. She seems happy. You want a shot at the same? You want to be reunited with her? Then listen to me. Just listen before you make up your mind. What do you say?"

She hesitated for a moment then nodded. "Fine. But only if you get off of me. And only if you promise never to touch me again."

He stared at her silently then pushed himself to standing. "I can't promise that. I told you, I don't lie. Now, are you ready to listen?" He held out his hand.

And to her amazement, she took it.

CHAPTER THREE

When Special Agent Kyle Mahone's cell phone rang it was half past midnight and the caller's number was blocked. No biggie. He knew who was calling and why, and even though it technically involved FBI business, he'd been ordered to keep that business as far away from the Bureau as possible. Which was why he immediately packed up his things and left, not just the J. Edgar Hoover building but the city limits.

Doing what he did for a living, paranoia was a way of life, and being paranoid had saved his life more than once. As of four months ago, he and Assistant Director Rick Hallifax were the only two people inside the FBI who knew about Operation Belladonna and its true purpose—to cover the Bureau's ass at all costs.

The real problem?

Mahone was no longer sure whether he *should* be covering the Bureau's ass or exposing it for the entire nation to see. Until he was sure, however, it was going to be business as usual.

Once he determined he hadn't been followed, he dialed Carly's phone number.

When she answered, Mahone asked, "Has Ty made contact?"

"He's talking to her even as we speak," Carly responded. "Just as we suspected, she's going to need some convincing. We'll debrief her slowly. Make sure she's truly committed to seeing her sister again before we introduce her to the others and tell her."

Tell her that vampires actually existed, she meant.

Tell her that Ty Duncan was one of them, but only because he'd been forcibly turned by a group of Rogues who—oh yes, by the way—had once been working for the FBI but were now liabilities the Bureau couldn't afford.

Fuck, Mahone thought as he ran a hand through his hair. All he'd ever wanted was to serve his country and work for the FBI. He hadn't been naive about it, either. He'd accepted long ago that safety and freedom came with a price. That sometimes things needed doing in spite of traditional notions of morality.

But what he was dealing with now?

When had his life become such a nightmare?

He grimaced at his inane mental questioning. He knew exactly when. When the FBI had discovered vampires. When the FBI had assured vampire leaders it would keep their existence a secret. When the FBI had conspired against those leaders by recruiting vampire traitors to work for them in the Turning Program. And most of all, when those traitors—Rogues—had decided to fuck over the Bureau by going out on their own, forcibly turning humans, including several FBI agents, and wreaking havoc in general.

Hallifax was freaking. He was afraid all the work he'd put into the FBI's Turning Program was going to be ruined or, even worse, that the Rogues would reveal the existence of vampires to U.S. citizens. He wanted Mahone and Carly and the rest of the Belladonna team to eliminate that threat. And he wanted it done before anyone, including the Vampire Queen, found out the truth.

According to Carly, the way to accomplish that was by recruiting four human females to help them. Mahone wasn't so sure. Not for the first time, he voiced his concerns.

"Maybe we should think this through again, Carly, before it's too late. We're talking about four women with no common connection except one tragic night. Three of them with no law enforcement experience whatsoever. Let's not get them killed. Could make our mission even more difficult."

"Skip the sarcasm, Mahone. Hallifax expects us—Ty, Peter, you, and me—to accomplish miracles with very little support. You're my only link to the Bureau. We can't do this on our own. We need people in the field that we can trust, who *need* what we can give them."

Mahone rolled his eyes. Not like Carly could see him.

"And these four women?" she continued. "They need. More important, they deserve. The FBI—no, *I*—screwed up their lives by failing to stop that gang shooting seven years ago," Carly said softly. "They were all negatively affected by it—"

"Which is why," he interrupted her, "if they knew the truth, they'd just as soon fuck the FBI over rather than help it—"

"But they *don't* know the truth," Carly insisted. "And they don't *need* to know the truth about the FBI's involvement in that shooting. Not the full truth, anyway. But *I* know the truth. All that matters is I have a chance to make things right for them. Starting with the one woman who can help get us into Salvation's Crossing."

"Ana."

"Yes," Carly confirmed.

Salvation's Crossing was a Hispanic rights organization. But according to Hallifax, under the surface it was actually a militarized cult with ties to the Rogues. Hallifax suspected the cult was helping the Rogues victimize humans, including buying and trading illegal immigrants as blood sources for other vampires.

Given her background, Ana would absolutely be of use to Belladonna in infiltrating the cult. "But the others—"

"Have unique skills we can hone," Carly said. "And even if they didn't, they're beautiful and they're human. We can capitalize on both those things."

"And you really think you can convince them to join us? You think you can trust them even after they find out the truth?"

"I do. I've been watching these women for a long time. The FBI took things from them. Ana spent two years in prison and lost all contact with her sister. Barrett Miles and Justine Maverick lost loved ones. And Collette Parker seems to be paying the highest price of all—her life."

"We're all dying," Mahone said, but only because he was used to playing devil's advocate. Everything Carly said was true. The four women had all been unnecessary victims of a gang shooting the FBI could have stopped but hadn't. The Bureau had been more concerned with gaining favor with the Devil's Crew gang—which ironically turned out to include several born vampires—than with protecting the innocent.

Now Carly thought the four women could help the Bureau take down the Rogues. Big question mark as far as Mahone was concerned.

It seemed risky. It seemed unnecessary. It seemed . . . wrong.

But in the end, what choice did he have? Carly was right—she couldn't bring down the Rogues on her own. And Ty and Peter might have unique strengths as vampires, but they also had undeniable limitations.

"You said you'd trust my instincts, Mahone. Have you changed your mind?" Carly asked.

He *wanted* to change his mind. Didn't want to support the recruitment of four human females who had no idea what they'd be up against. But that's why they needed them. Because no one, not even the women themselves, would suspect what they were going to use them for.

"No," he said. "Bring Ana Martin in. Debrief her. And keep me posted."

CHAPTER FOUR

As Ty walked behind the counter and retrieved his gun, Ana got to her feet and sat at one of the larger tables. It took her a moment to catch her breath, far longer than that to stop shaking. She wanted him gone. Now. But by fighting him for his gun, she'd tacitly agreed to his terms, so she'd do what she agreed to. She'd hear what he had to say. Then she'd kick him out and make sure she never saw him again.

Even as she kept her gaze averted, she tried to wipe her mind clean of the memory of his touch. His kiss. When he stood next to her, however, she had no choice but to look at him. For a second, she swore his gaze dropped to her mouth and her lips actually tingled. She automatically licked them in an effort to drive the sensation away, but all she got for her trouble was the faint taste of him on her tongue. Although she managed to stifle a moan, the darkening of his eyes suggested he knew she'd had to do so. But he didn't say anything. Instead, he extracted a business card from a small polished case that he slipped out of his pocket and held it out to her.

Slowly, she took it.

All it had on it was an agency name and phone number. "I'm Ty Duncan. As you can see from that card, I work for an organization called Belladonna."

She couldn't deny how intrigued she was, any more

than she could deny her body's visceral response to his. "Go on."

"Belladonna is Italian for 'beautiful lady.' It is also a plant whose berry juice was used in Italy to enlarge the pupils of women, giving them a striking appearance. Not a good idea, since the juice can be poisonous."

"Thanks for the history lesson."

He sighed. "I'm trying to explain why I want to hire you, specifically. Someone who is both beautiful and deadly."

She stared at him with her mouth open, then snorted. Right. Like he found her beautiful. Kissing her to distract her was one thing, but she'd bet the women he slept with spent serious money on clothes, wore silk lingerie to bed, and sipped tea out of antique porcelain cups in the morning. Plus they probably used endearments like "dahling" or "poopsie."

"Belladonna is a private intelligence agency," he continued. "Not listed anywhere. We maintain the strictest confidentiality, for both our clients and our employees. We also mainly employ women."

Surprise tickled the back of her spine. Whatever she'd been expecting him to say, it hadn't been this. The only private intelligence agencies she'd heard of dealt in intellectual property—corporate secrets, not national security. Nonetheless, she told herself to play along. To find out exactly what connection this man had to Gloria.

"Why women?" She was relieved that her voice sounded steady, even a little bored.

"Specializing in female agents allows us to maintain a variety of covers. To go where the government can't."

"What kind of intelligence, specifically?"

"Intelligence that bad guys don't want us to have."

Her mouth twisted and she nodded. "Ah, *por supuesto*. You're one of the good guys. Saving the world from criminals and bureaucratic bullshit all at the same time."

He grinned and stretched, raising his arms high above his head as if working out the leftover kinks from their tussle. His sleeves strained to contain bulging biceps and his shirttail lifted, revealing just the slightest glimpse of a ridged, rock-hard stomach.

Oh, God, she silently moaned.

What's wrong with me? I've never been this attracted to a man before.

And it wasn't just her body that was reacting to him. It was almost as if he'd inserted himself in her mind . . .

But then, she'd never met a man like him before. He was a novelty, that was all. Dragging her gaze away and up, she narrowed her eyes at the twinkle in his.

He quirked his lips, then lowered his arms and shrugged. "Does it really matter to you whether we're the good guys?"

She hesitated. "Let's assume for a minute it does."

"In that case, good or bad is a relative term, but yes, I believe what we're trying to do is for the common good."

"Good for the world and good for you," she said.

When he raised a questioning brow, she said, "I'm assuming you get paid well for what you do?"

He tilted his head, his expression almost chiding. "You have a problem with compensation for a job well done?"

She looked away and pressed her lips together, suddenly feeling foolish. Even so, she could still hear the prosecutor's words from seven years ago, echoing in her head as if he was standing right next to her.

"Money. A few measly dollars. That's why she did what she did, ladies and gentlemen. It's why she stole. Sold drugs. Preyed on the weak and elderly. For cold, hard cash. Don't let this young woman's face fool you,"

he'd said with disgust. "She's a mercenary through and through."

"Ana," the man prompted softly.

She shot to her feet. "Don't you know *el dinero es la raíz de toda mal?*"

"That's where you're wrong. Money isn't the root of all evil. Humans and other monsters have that covered all on their own. Money is just money."

She ignored the latter part of his statement. "You speak Spanish quite well. I assume you learned in Europe. And your accent is British. So why aren't you busy protecting England's soil?"

"I'm half American on my father's side. As to why I'm not in England? Because the monsters I'm hunting are here, not there."

"What monsters?"

"Let's just say that's on a need-to-know basis. And until you agree to join the agency, you don't need to know."

"You know I'm not going to," she said softly. "Stop playing games and tell me the information you have about Gloria. Where is she?"

Because Ana had no idea. Despite her sister's clear instructions that she wanted to be left alone after the gang shooting so long ago, Ana had still needed to make sure her sister was okay. She'd worked hard in prison to earn computer privileges, and whenever she got the chance, she'd used her time to search online for Gloria. She'd even put up with one guard's filthy innuendos and wandering hands for a time, just to make sure she didn't lose computer access.

She'd combed through hospital records. Property records. Newspapers and gossip rags. Aside from the news stories that had covered the gang shooting itself, she'd found nothing. It was as if Gloria Garcia had simply vanished off the face of the earth. Ana had been forced to accept the truth. Gloria hadn't just wanted to break ties with Ana—she'd wanted to *vanish*. Somehow, she'd made sure that no one, including Ana, could ever find her.

Just like always, the thought filled her with pain. Now, however, the pain was slightly muted, simply because the man in front of her required her total attention. He took up so much space, mentally and physically. It didn't help that he still looked like he wanted to drag her under him and do all kinds of wicked things to her.

She felt her heart racing, in fear and in anticipation. Finally, his lips tightened and he banked the fire in his eyes. Silently, she let out a sigh of relief.

"Accept our offer," he urged.

"And if I did, my tasks would be . . . what?"

"You'll work missions, but you'll also train other women."

She couldn't help it. Her eyes bugged out. The idea of her training women to be super agents was ludicrous. He'd shocked the hell out of her and she didn't care if he knew. "What makes you think I have anything to teach anyone?"

He looked at her steadily. "The information we gather isn't the sort people give out willingly. In fact, it's the kind people kill for in order to protect."

"So you kill them before they can kill you?" She'd never sign up for something like that. Gang life had been about protection and survival, not war. Not premeditated murder.

Whoa. Scratch that last thought. *She* had never committed murder, planned or unplanned. She'd never wanted to look too closely, but she'd always known how dangerous some of her fellow gang members could be—even to each other.

"Wrong. We avoid using force, and we avoid doing anything that would unnecessarily call attention to the agency. At the same time, our agents need to be pre-pared for any eventuality. They need the skills to blend in. To talk themselves out of trouble. And yes, if it's absolutely necessary, to fight violence with violence."

"What makes you think I'd risk breaking a nail, let alone my life, for some agency I never even knew existed?"

"Because I know more about you than you think. I know you'd do just about anything to see your sister again. Why not work for the right cause in the process?"

She shook her head. She didn't believe in causes. Didn't waste her time with volunteer work and trying to make the world a better place. The world was a minefield. You looked out for yourself or you got blown to kingdom come.

"Even if that's true—and I'm not saying it is," Ana said, "I'm not an expert in any of the things you just talked about."

"You're not giving yourself enough credit. You've assumed a new identity, quite successfully, I might add. And you managed to make me hurt—and bleed—more than once," he pointed out.

True, but still . . . he'd already proven quite thoroughly that anything she'd done to him was probably the result of him having *let* her do it. She chewed her lip, considering him. Considering what he offered. He seemed like he was on the up-and-up—crazy but legitimate.

Téa had told her often enough that she would get tired of rejecting human contact—but as a coffee shop owner-manager, Ana usually had so much human contact that by the end of the day she wanted to rip up her apron and run away into the Seattle sunset.

It was *emotional* contact she could use. And work that meant something. Her greatest achievement to date was learning how to correctly foam skim milk for half-caf double-shot supertalls at six bucks a pop. She still lived week to week. There was never enough to consider quitting and giving the search for Gloria all she had. Sure, Gloria had told her to leave her alone, but if Ana could find her, if they could see each other face-to-face, she knew their sisterly bond would take over, giving her a chance to talk sense into the other woman. They were *family*, for God's sake.

Ana ached to hold Gloria again. To see the dimple on the side of her cheek when she smiled.

And to find out how everything had gone so wrong that day seven years ago, when her formal jump out of Primos Sangre had turned into a shoot-out.

She wanted her sister, damn it. But there was no denying she wanted more, too.

Ty said Belladonna paid well. What else was he offering?

He smiled at her.

Riiight.

Could she really relax enough to let someone in again? Even if it was simply to work with a team, to work with Ty and be treated with kindness and respect, to maybe even explore the sizzling attraction that flared to life whenever he touched her . . .

Her instincts fought against the idea. Her aching heart tugged her forward.

"Ana," he said quietly. He walked toward her, his movements slow. Predatory. Primal. Jesus, he got to her. His strength was a natural part of him, just like his confidence.

"I've answered a few of your questions," he said quietly. "Now I want an answer from you."

What could he possibly want to know? Belladonna seemed to cross so many of the lines she had created for herself. If she accepted the job, what would she be asked to do? Was he going to ask whether she'd ever killed someone and would be willing to do so again? Whether she'd sold her body for money and would spread her legs for information? Whether she'd—

She stiffened as his gaze zeroed in on her face—one specific part of her face. A split second later, he asked, "Why haven't you done anything about the scar?"

Her scar burned under his gaze, a reminder of how much she'd paid because of her past. At the time, the payment had seemed worth it. Now?

She'd simply learned to make the scar invisible when she looked in the mirror. Of course, she wasn't going to tell him that.

This job he offered—this chance to get information on Gloria—could be a chance to finally heal. Or it would scar her more. Right down to her soul.

"*Pobrecita,*" he murmured, and the sound of her native language falling from his lips made her shiver. "You see the scar as penance, don't you?"

Slowly, he raised his hand and ran his knuckles against the unmarred skin of her left cheek.

She shivered, but didn't pull away.

Penance? That implied forgiveness. A fresh start. She wanted it. She was so close to having it.

But as this man's questioning proved, she wasn't close enough.

Ty leaned closer and nuzzled his nose into her hair, nudging the heavy, dark brown tendrils behind her ear. Despite the chill he radiated, her body was infused with sudden heat.

She waited in breathless anticipation for him to kiss her again. She wanted him to. Was close to pulling his face around so she could initiate a kiss herself. This time, she thought, *she'd* use her tongue. She'd sate herself on the taste of him, and let her hands explore the body that seemed capable of both strength and tenderness . . .

As if by accident, his fingertips brushed the raised, jagged line on her left cheek. Her eyes flew open. Like a bucket of ice water, the contact with her scar shocked her out of her trance. "Stop!" She shoved him away, took several steps back, and put a chair between them.

For a second, he looked like he was going to come after her. Like a fool, she wanted him to.

He didn't. Suddenly he was all business again.

"Belladonna can offer you something different, Ana. Something more than the gang ever could. Something more than what you have now."

"Shut up!" She was disgusted by how easily he'd pulled her in then allowed her to back away without even a hint of regret.

Ty waved his hand around the coffee shop. "Technically, you're fine. You immerse yourself in your business and your garden. I'll bet you even shag every once in a while, just to prove you can. But you have no friends to share your highs and lows with, and when you do have sex, you probably never come. Hell, you don't even have a cat for company. Are you living? Or are you just waiting? And if so, who are you waiting for?"

No one.

But it wasn't true.

More than Gloria, she'd been waiting for someone like *him*.

The realization weakened her knees and ate at her belly.

Ty's expression softened. "You know another term for waiting? Dying. What I'm offering you is the chance to be more. To do more. To join in the land of the living again. To have purpose. In doing so, you'll train and be trained in return. You'll learn to stop suppressing the hatred and guilt and anger inside you. Feel them. Control them. Then you'll hold all the power in the world."

Power. Power to feel again.

Power to feel more of what she'd felt today. With Ty.

Power to feel alive.

She was almost convinced, but he didn't need to know that. She had to keep this interview, which was what it seemed to be, on track.

"These other women I'm to train. Who are they? Gang members? Ex-cons?"

Ty shook his head. "That's also on a need-to-know basis. You won't necessarily be working with each other. Not at first."

"So what you said about training them—"

"You'll cover what you know to prepare them for their own missions, if and when it's necessary. They'll do the same for you. Different skill sets. We need them all."

Annoyed, she stopped pacing and frowned. He was actually serious. He truly believed she could make unknown women into badass spies. That *she* could be one. Weren't Bond girls all boobs and no brawn? "What would *I* need to be trained in?"

He thought that over. "As I said before, control to start with. But the other female agents won't be teaching you that."

"Who—" she began, even though she already knew.

He simply stared at her, all traces of lightheartedness gone.

She wasn't surprised. And she didn't miss his message, either. He wouldn't just train her. He'd push her. Far more than she'd want to be pushed.

He moved, stepping right up to her. His gaze wandered over her face. Her scar. Her lips. But he didn't touch her.

"You have the business card, Ana. You know how to get in touch with me." He paused, looked out the window with a slight frown, then met her gaze again before saying, "You're brave. You're strong. You built this coffee shop from nothing. You've fought to survive, but you're still not willing to fight for what you *really* want in life. When you are, I'll be waiting. And I'll help you. All you have to do is call."

CHAPTER FIVE

Ty strode out of Ana's coffee shop and kept walking despite the strong urge to go back to her. To kiss her again. To do far more to her soft lips, her slick tongue, and her warm, fragrant body.

Lust the likes of which he'd never felt before, even during the first two months of his transition, was riding him hard, making him nearly dizzy. When he'd first been turned, his lust had been for sex, regardless of who it was with. Now, his lust seemed reserved for Ana alone.

Shaking, he headed toward the flat he'd rented. It was across the street from Ana's house, so that he could easily keep her under surveillance. Thankfully, the more distance he put between himself and the coffee shop, the calmer he seemed to get. Within minutes, although he still ached to have her, he no longer felt like he was going to die if he didn't. His surroundings, rather than his desire for Ana, became his focus.

Since it was past midnight, the streets were quiet. Eventually, the trendier neighborhood where Ana worked gave way to a seedier part of the city, one where gunshots and sirens weren't uncommon and some streets were virtually abandoned. Ty's flat—*apartment,* he reminded himself—was nothing to brag about. It was on the top floor of an anonymous three-story brick building with a clear view of Ana's little house. Carly had paid the rent in advance for several months, although Ty had no plans to be there that long. The renting agent was glad to take the cash and asked no questions, handing over the keys and assuring Ty that there was no extra charge for the furniture.

One tug on the greasy string dangling from the bare-bulb light fixture in the ceiling and he'd seen why. The previous tenant had left only a beat-up sofa and a rickety table and chair. There was a hot plate. Shabby digs, but all he needed for the temporary stakeout. Dragging cumbersome items from a van into the building would have attracted attention, something Ty wanted to avoid.

He'd braced the table so it could safely hold his surveillance monitors. The rest of his gear—flash drives and micro-engineered spy stuff, including items designed specifically for Ana—weighed next to nothing.

He slouched comfortably into the chair in front of the monitors, touching a few keys to adjust certain settings. A half hour later, she arrived home.

For a second, Ana looked straight into a tiny camera she didn't know was there.

Ty sat up, mesmerized by the catlike wariness in her brown eyes. He was relieved when she looked away. She moved around inside her house, her expression calm.

Ana was a natural beauty. Thin gold hoops were her only jewelry, piercing plump little earlobes that he wanted very much to nip. With flawless light caramel skin, she didn't need makeup and she didn't seem to use any besides eyeliner. Her fine features and dark, wing-like brows had a delicate symmetry, unlike her full mouth. Her lips were luscious, the lower noticeably more full than the upper. Made for kissing.

And that body was made for loving. Ana was petite and slender in an athletic way, with small breasts he longed to caress and a shapely ass that filled out her jeans. All that combined with her long, dark brown hair had him aching for her.

Tough luck.

She went into her bathroom and shut the door. Not that she had a roommate or a lover who might barge in. Ty had satisfied his curiosity on that score after hours of surveillance. Just as she kept to herself at the coffee shop, Ana lived alone and seemed to like it that way. Then again, it made sense that anyone who'd been in prison would come out with a compulsive need for privacy.

After a few minutes, he could just see wisps of steam curling around the edges of the door. Hot shower.

Thinking about what she looked like naked and wet made him a candidate for a cold one.

Frustrated, he leaned back, tipping the chair so that the two front legs rose from the floor. A sharp creak brought him quickly back down. He stood, bending to lift the loose floorboard where he'd hidden a compact nylon zip bag filled with several forms of ID and a reserve smartphone.

Ty was a true believer in backup, especially during a solo stakeout. He took out the zip bag to check on the contents. Even with the high-tech locks he'd installed on the door and windows, it wouldn't do to be too cocky. Not in this neighborhood.

Everything was there. Real and fake driver's licenses and passports, and several government-issued picture IDs.

His British passport was no more than a sentimental token by this point. He hadn't been back in more than a decade. The picture resembled his father at the same age, a secret agent himself, but for MI6.

No one had known about Gil Duncan's double life. He had been born into wealth and its attendant privileges, turning himself into a master of spy craft simply for the thrill of it.

Ty, his mother, and his sister, Naomi, scarcely saw him

for months on end. They lived in luxury, but explanations for the absences were never forthcoming, and depression became a way of life for his mother, with her spending more and more time in bed, barely able to take care of herself let alone her kids. Just before Ty moved from London to the United States to attend university, his father had told him about his double life and advised him to get a desk job. To raise a family and spend time with them. To reject secrecy.

Too little and too late.

One learns what one lives. Ty knew that all too well.

Two months after his mother died, Ty was recruited stateside. Of course, his father hadn't approved. Not that it was any of his bloody business. Ty could have forgiven the way his old man had treated him, but the way he'd ignored his mother's and sister's needs, leaving the burden of their care to Ty? He couldn't forgive Gil for that. They were still estranged. Ty being a vampire simply made it a thousand times more likely they'd remain so.

He put the nylon bag back into its hiding place and glanced at the monitor. The steam was still curling out from around the closed bathroom door.

Ty forced away thoughts of his father, guilt about his own failings when it came to Naomi, and pleasurable fantasies of joining Ana. He went to the window and absently looked through the slatted blinds. When his mind continued to spin with images of death and blood and sex, he cursed. He had to get out—and walk faster than he could think.

On his way out, he took a last glance at the lighted windows of Ana's house. Given how serious she seemed about leaving her past behind, he marveled that she'd chosen such a dangerous neighborhood to live in. Then again, she didn't have much choice. Since she was an ex-felon, it had been a miracle she'd gotten a small business loan to start her coffee shop. After she paid her expenses, there was barely anything left for rent. Even so, she was making a life for herself, one symbolized all too well by the small house she kept well tended and freshly painted despite the punks who frequently vandalized it and the dilapidated shacks surrounding it.

She was trying so hard to be something better than what she'd been; he couldn't help wonder—was he really going to fuck all that up for her?

Carly swore that wasn't going to happen. She insisted that although Ana was going to be risking a lot to help them, she'd get what she really needed in the end—the better life she'd been seeking, but one unhindered by an unhealthy attachment to her sister, who was also living under an assumed name—Helena Esperanza. Ty hoped that would be the result, but despite Carly's optimistic spin on things, he felt that a happily-ever-after probably wasn't in store for Ana any more than it was for him. He'd damn well do everything in his power to protect her and the other female recruits, but he knew better than most that sometimes there were things you couldn't protect against, things far worse than dying.

Unfortunately, Carly was right about the fact that they needed Ana. All their attempts to get inside Salvation's Crossing had failed, including Ty posing as a wealthy man interested in funding Hispanic rights activities. His cover was extensive and airtight. Anyone checking into Ty Nunes would find ample documentation of his birth, privileged childhood, and even more privileged adulthood. There were several articles on the Web identifying him as a billionaire with a social conscience. There were also tons of pictures of him with gorgeous girls on his arm, hanging out with celebs, paparazzi flashing away. As far as Salvation's Crossing should be concerned, Ty the famous philanthropist was a reality.

Even so, he hadn't even gotten a return phone call or thank-you-for-your-interest email telling him politely to go to hell.

Because of Ana's background and—though it was unknown to her—her connection to the cult, she could ultimately be the key to Belladonna getting inside.

One month from now, the public leader of Salvation's Crossing, Miguel Santos, aka Miguel Salvador, the man who'd first introduced Ana to gang life, was going to make a rare public appearance at a fund-raiser for the Hispanic Community Alliance.

An event that Ty hoped Ana would attend as his date. Miguel's failure to respond to Ty's phone calls and emails signaled suspicion. With Ana on his arm, maybe, just maybe, Ty would be able to convince Salvador that not only was he interested in Hispanic rights, but that he was a trustworthy vampire interested in a new food supply line, as well.

It wasn't a foolproof plan, but the only alternative would be full-scale covert ops and forced entry. Given Belladonna's limited numbers and resources, as well as the FBI's instructions to keep their missions—their very existence—on the down low, that wasn't going to happen.

Ana was their best chance of getting what they needed. Ana.

He couldn't help himself. Despite the fact that his body had finally started to calm, he deliberately conjured the memory of the kisses they'd shared.

Kissing her hadn't just been about shaking her up or capitalizing on the attraction he sensed she felt for him. It hadn't been about coercing her into agreeing to work for Belladonna. No, despite his resolve to remain clean—to drink only animal blood and refrain from having sex—he *wanted* her. Wanted her more than he'd ever wanted anything. Wanted her enough to kiss her not just once, but twice. And he'd barely been able to stop himself from doing it again.

Just like that, the memory of kissing Ana caused Ty's lust for her to return with a vengeance. His hands and teeth began to clench as he fought the strong urge to turn around and retrace his steps. He needed to find Ana. He needed to do more than just kiss her. He needed to mark her and make her his.

Mark her by biting her neck and drinking her blood.

Make her his by taking her, over and over again, until no one could deny the truth of their connection.

His primal reaction confused him. Scared him.

Six months ago he'd been a man. A human. He'd understood himself.

Now, he didn't know where the line between Ty, the former human, and Ty, the vampire, was drawn. Was there even a distinction? His brief moments of closeness to Ana had triggered his vampire urges, but apparently being away from her did the very same thing.

His fangs unsheathed. He groaned and staggered, nearly coming to his knees.

His body shook as if he were caught in the throes of a major earthquake, and determinedly, he placed one foot in front of the other, pressing forward.

Instinctively, as he felt the power of the monster within him growing, Ty walked faster. He was crossing the street when a wave of dizziness hit him.

He suddenly felt parched. Starving. His stomach began to cramp, threatening to eat him alive from the inside out. He'd felt this feeling before. He knew what it meant.

His lust for Ana had triggered more than his vampire need for sex. It had triggered his need for blood, as well. *Human* blood.

Damn it, no. He wasn't fully vampire, he told himself. Part of him was still human, and if he wanted to keep that part of him alive, he had to maintain control. He had to hurry . . .

There were several bottles of animal blood in the flat's fridge. He increased his speed. He was almost there when a shout came from behind him. He whipped around. A homeless man reeking of alcohol stumbled down the street. Fresh wounds were visible on his forearms and legs. He was bleeding, and the scent of that blood drifted on the wind and embedded itself in Ty's nostrils.

Ty stumbled back. "No," he whispered. "No." But even as he said the words, he sucked in another whiff of the guy's scent and trembled.

"Hey . . . hey, man," the man called out. "Can you spare some change?"

Ty opened his mouth to say no again. A hiss came out instead.

The man's eyes widened with fear and Ty felt that same fear take hold of him.

Before Ty knew it, he was moving toward the stranger. Not walking. Not even running. But barreling toward him with inhuman speed.

The smell of the man's blood and his dark memories combined with his interaction with Ana, his hunger for her, called forth his deepest primal urges, the ones that he normally kept controlled by sheer force of will. He opened his mouth. Barely managed to choke out, "Run. Get out of here."

Luckily, the homeless man heard him and didn't question the command. He turned. Tried to flee.

But that, unfortunately, only made Ty's predatory instincts kick into higher gear.

Blood. He has the blood you want. The blood you need.

Get it. Get him.

Now.

Before Ty knew it, he'd dragged the man between two buildings and had him trapped against a wall face-first, the same way Ana had trapped him earlier. But instead of letting him turn around, instead of backing away the way she had, Ty punched his fangs into the man's neck and began to drink.

The whimper that escaped Ty was one of despair but it quickly turned into satisfaction. The metallic bitterness of the man's blood was an explosion of nirvana on his tongue.

He drank. And drank. And drank.

With every swallow, thoughts of his human life vanished.

He lost himself in the pleasure of drinking blood how it was meant to be drunk, fresh from the vein. From a warm body. From a human who was weaker than him . . . a human who was meant to serve him . . .

Ty gasped, horrified enough by his thoughts that he somehow found the strength to pull his fangs out of the man's throat. The sound of a car backfiring and distant shouts made him jerk and look wildly around him, but there was no one in sight. Didn't mean someone wouldn't show up soon and discover him. Discover what he'd done . . .

With a shudder, Ty returned his attention to the man he still held. As soon as he'd bitten him, the man had gone compliantly silent and even now dangled in his arms. Ty stared at him, his previous thoughts echoing in his ears. The way he'd thought of the man as a *mere* human, as something weak and existing only for his own benefit, had him stumbling back, his arms falling to his sides.

The man crumpled to the ground, groaning. Blood trickled from the puncture wounds in his neck, but Ty could hear his heart thudding and his blood flowing. He was okay. Ty would leave him here, and the man would never know what had happened. At most, he'd assume he'd been so drunk he'd hallucinated a feral monster attacking him . . .

Shakily, Ty swiped his sleeve across his mouth, noting the light streaks of blood there. He expected himself to throw up, because his thoughts had indeed sickened him. Instead of puking his guts out, however, he felt a renewed energy and vitality zipping through his veins. His senses, already heightened, became even more acute. *This* was what was intoxicating. Addicting. Even more than the taste of the blood itself, how could anyone resist this feeling of strength? Of sheer power?

He could feel the moisture in the air changing, telling him it would rain before dawn. He could see the fleas on the cat that balanced on a Dumpster thirty feet away.

And he could smell . . .

He took a deeper breath.

He could smell someone approaching. His mind screamed at him to run. With a final glance at the homeless man he'd terrorized and a muttered curse, Ty obeyed. Strengthened by the blood, he ran fast. Past his flat. Past Ana's house. Past anything resembling a residential neighborhood until he came upon a remote warehouse. He jumped the fence and found an unlocked door. As he stepped inside, the cool, dark air welcomed him like a mother's embrace. Leaning against an interior wall, he sank to the cold concrete floor. Closing his eyes, he cursed what he'd become.

What he'd lost.

Not just his humanity. Not just his chance to have a relationship with a human female like Ana.

He'd lost the only family he'd had left. His sister, Naomi. She was dead because of him.

When the men had approached them on the street six months ago, Naomi had urged him to walk away. Only he hadn't. Instead, he'd—

A faint shuffling sound came from behind him.

Instantly, thoughts of that night shattered and he was focused solely on the here and now. Ty shot to his feet. Listened.

When the sound came again, this time from somewhere to his left, he stepped toward it. As he did so, his nostrils caught a new scent—something with a hint of mint.

He stiffened when a voice drifted out of the darkness.

"Well, look what we have here, Niles. It's the vampire. The one that left his prey in that alley with puncture wounds still in his neck, but only after he drank from him with all the skill of a newly born babe at his mother's tit. All desperate hunger and no finesse."

Automatically, Ty reached for his gun. Before he could withdraw it, however, something flew out of the darkness and knocked him down.

"Don't waste your time, mate. Guns won't work on us," the same male voice intoned.

Ty scrambled to his feet, body crouched against another attack.

The sound of male laughter came from the opposite side of the room. Ty whirled around, then back again, trying to decipher movement in the darkness just as someone flipped a switch, washing the room with a faint yellow light. Two males stepped out of the darkness to flank him on either side.

Not just two males. Two *vampires*.

Shock held Ty paralyzed. Except for his time in captivity, Ty had never actually seen another vampire aside from Peter, at least not one who wasn't hiding what he was. But these males?

They were both tall and lean, with the same silver hair that Ty now had. But Ty dyed his hair dark. He also wore contact lenses to disguise the eerie silver pupils that went along with his black eyes, which had once been blue. Even from twenty feet away, Ty could see the males weren't bothering to hide their unusual eyes any more than their hair. Why? Because they were concealed in the dark building? Or because they could somehow camouflage themselves from human eyes? How else had they witnessed him leave the homeless man in that alley without Ty knowing they were there?

His curiosity was tempered by caution, but also, despite himself, by the faintest stirrings of hope. In the faint glow of the buzzing overhead light he could see the two vampires wore matching gold medallions—three linked triangles, two on top and one directly beneath the others. Were they part of an organized group? Vampire leaders? Could he get information from them without letting them know about Belladonna's purpose?

He'd already taken a step forward before he forced himself to stop.

No, he couldn't take such a risk. By their words and their expressions, these vampires were a definite threat. So that was how Ty would have to treat them. As if they might be one of the Rogues he'd been ordered to bring down. Facing them squarely, his body tensed for an attack, Ty remained silent.

He concentrated. He tried to read the minds of the vampires in front of him.

Nothing.

Damn it. Peter was much more skilled at mind reading, maybe because he didn't share Ty's misgivings about the intrusive act.

Then a horrible thought occurred to him. He'd tried to read their minds and failed, but what if they tried to read *his* mind? Damn it!

It had always been a possibility—that Belladonna's purpose would be discovered by a mind-reading vampire, one that wouldn't appreciate the fact they were hunting their own, Rogue or not. One that would try to stop them. In the end, the potential risk hadn't mattered. Belladonna needed agents out on the street. It was just as possible a vampire would read any one of those agent's minds, including Carly's, just as much as Ty's. So what to do now?

He could try to outrun them, he supposed. But he wasn't sure he'd be faster than they were.

The one called Niles snorted. "Apparently he's the strong, silent type. But I don't recognize him, Lesander. Do you? Maybe he's visiting from abroad. Maybe that's why he left his dinner for us to clean up. Because he doesn't care if humans in the area begin to suspect our presence here. Only . . ."

He suddenly stopped talking and narrowed his eyes.

"No, wait. He's not one of us. I can—I can still smell a hint of human. From him, not his dinner." Niles looked at Lesander, his expression grim. "He's been turned."

"Son of a bitch," Lesander growled. He came at Ty and struck him before he could even blink. As the force of Lesander's initial blow forced him backward, the vampire flew with him and continued to pummel his face, each blow feeling like a metal spike was being driven through his skull.

Ty hit the wall behind him with enough force that plaster rained down on him. Rained down on them both. Lesander wrapped his hands around Ty's throat and squeezed, cutting off his air. He tried to break Lesander's hold, but despite his own considerable strength, he dangled in the air like a broken puppet and gasped for breath. Clear as day, a vision formed in his head, one in which the homeless man dangled from his own hands. Helpless.

Yeah. Talk about karma.

"You fuck," Lesander snarled. "Who turned you?"

"I—I don't know," Ty gasped, blinking in an effort to

see past the blood dripping into his eyes. Lesander frac-
tionally loosened his grip on Ty's throat and immediately moved on to the next question.

"How long ago were you turned?"

How long ago was it? It felt like years, decades since
he'd been himself. Truly human. Pleasantly oblivious to
the fact that vampires really existed. But no, it hadn't
been that long. "Several . . . months . . ."

"Been having fun since, huh?" Lesander opened his
mouth to say more, but suddenly shook his head. "Oh
fuck it. There's a better way to see what you've been
doing." He stared intently at Ty, and within seconds Ty
felt it—a faint tingling in his mind, as if someone was
sifting through his thoughts . . .

No! he thought, outraged. Get out. Get out of my
head.

"Damn it, everything we've suspected is correct,"
Lesander said. "The FBI has been working with born
vampire traitors—they call them *Rogues*—to turn humans. This explains the increase in vampire deaths and
disappearances. The Rogues must have blackmailed
them. Threatened their families. This one's a fucking
agent, only he . . ."

Ty barely processed Niles's claims of blackmail and
threats. He was more concerned with the secret he'd inadvertently given away. He and the rest of Belladonna
were supposed to be protecting the FBI's Turning Program, which was in jeopardy due to the fact Rogues had
stepped out of line, and now these vampires knew about
it—or at least he'd just confirmed their suspicions for
them.

The faint wail of police sirens could be heard in the
distance but were obviously getting closer. Had someone else seen what he'd done in that alley? Had they
followed him here, just like these vampires had?

"Shit," Niles hissed. "Damn it, they're coming. We need to go. We can't be seen by the police. Not yet."

"We need to take him with us," Lesander said. "I don't know who . . . I don't know *how* . . ."

"Then that means he doesn't know, either. Doesn't matter," Niles said. "We need to disappear fast and we can't teleport with him. Dear Goddess, we have to go to Queen Bianca. Tell her what the FBI is doing—"

"Shut up, you fool," Lesander shouted.

For a second, Lesander squeezed Ty's throat tighter, cutting off his ability to speak completely when all he wanted was to shout, "Wait, don't go. I know you don't like what the FBI is doing, but I need to know more about what you are. What I am. Can I become human again? Can I die?"

But apparently, he didn't need to shout. Not when the vampire could so easily read his mind.

"Why on earth would you want to be human again?" Lesander's lip curled with disdain. "As for the way to kill a vampire? I'm sure you can understand why we don't go around advertising that kind of thing. But tell you what. I'll let you live . . . for now . . . and next time we meet, I'll see if you've figured it out."

Abruptly, Lesander let him go. Then he hesitated, as if weighing his options. Abruptly, he took off the necklace he was wearing and looped it around Ty's neck.

"What the hell are you—" Niles shouted, but Lesander cut him off with a look before turning back to Ty.

"I know what you're trying to do. You're trying to find proof that Rogues are preying on humans. You're trying to stop them. Well, I want the same thing. If you want any hope of completing your mission, then do not remove this necklace. It will prevent another vampire from being able to read your mind. Do you understand?"

Understand? Fuck no, Ty didn't understand, but he nodded his head anyway.

Then Lesander and Niles vanished into thin air.

They didn't even leave behind wisps of smoke or glittery particles in their wake.

Even as he crumpled to the ground, Ty stared in shock while the vampire's words echoed all around him. Automatically, he lifted the medallion hanging around his neck and studied it. Was this a trick? Had the other vampire really given him such a powerful means to protect his mind?

He mentally noted the other details he could catalog about the encounter: the vampires' names were Lesander and Niles. They'd worn matching medallions. Lesander, unlike Ty, could wield his mind-reading power with precision, and both vampires had been able to teleport themselves away. Lesander had implied there was a way to kill vampires. And despite his disdain at the idea, Lesander *hadn't* denied there was a way to become human again, as well.

While Ty couldn't do anything with all this information now, it was more than he'd ever had before. He now had several leads to follow. And renewed hope.

As the sound of sirens became almost deafening, Ty stood, tucked the necklace inside his shirt, and forced himself to start moving. He ran to the same door he'd used to enter the warehouse, but had traveled only several yards when the sound of screeching tires behind him made him curse. Within seconds, shouts of "Police" and "Freeze" made him do just that. "Bloody fuck," he muttered, putting up his hands and slowly turning around.

He wouldn't risk harming the police or chance making a spectacle of himself, which could later be traced back to Belladonna. Better to let them arrest him and break out of jail when they weren't looking. But one thing was for damn sure—he wasn't going to let them take the necklace around his throat.

The older of the two cops approached him, and Ty relaxed slightly. His partner, who lagged behind by a few feet, was young. An obvious rookie. It was always better to deal with an experienced veteran who had less to prove. Reduced the chances of things unexpectedly going bad.

The cop, whose name tag read Southcott, stopped just in front of Ty. Instead of ordering Ty to turn around and present his wrists in order to be cuffed, he took a quick scan around the area. Then he raised his gun and took aim, his intent to shoot plain on his face.

Swiftly, Ty's hand shot out to knock Officer South-cott's gun away, but it was too late. The other man fired a bullet that hit him squarely between his eyes.

CHAPTER SIX

From his hiding spot behind an abandoned cargo container, Bobbie Hernandez barely flinched when he heard the cop's bullet hit bone. After all, Bobbie had instigated the hit by telling his boss about the dark-haired man who'd been hassling Ana. What he hadn't known then was that the man was a vampire. He did now. The cop's bullet couldn't kill him. But it would cause Fang Face a shitload of pain.

Ducking his head, Bobbie stifled a grin. Delight rippled through him. Even as a kid, he'd loved the mingling of blood with pain. Whether it was the sight of it, the smell of it, the sound of it . . . whether it was his own or someone else's . . . didn't matter. He'd cut himself and cut up others, animals and humans, enough times to know what floated his boat.

His mother had tried to make him feel bad about himself. She'd always told him he was a freak. Twisted. And for a while there, he'd started to believe her. He'd even let her commit him, and had undergone weeks of treatment by doctors who'd prescribed handfuls of pills. The medication had clouded his mind until he'd found the strength to fight back. Until he'd finally understood the truth.

Until he'd joined the Devil's Crew gang and learned that vampires weren't just myth, but joyful fucking reality.

In the end, he'd realized his instincts weren't wrong, he'd just been *born* wrong. How many times had he heard about men who felt like women trapped in men's bodies? So much so that they'd willingly cut themselves up to change their gender. Well, Bobbie sure as shit hadn't been born the wrong gender, but he had been born the wrong *species*. He should've been a vampire, and now he was going to have his own shot at reassignment surgery.

But only if he played his cards right.

Vampires. Damn, he knew for a fact they existed. He'd seen them for himself. Still, sometimes doubt reared its head. Sometimes he expected to wake up in an insane asylum. But having just watched this dark-haired one drink from a homeless man's throat, Bobbie knew that no, he wasn't crazy, just lucky. Lucky to be in the know when ordinary fools didn't have a fucking clue. When so many were still operating under the delusion that humans were at the top of the food chain.

As the cop got back into the squad car with his partner and drove off, Bobbie shook his head with awe. His boss's efficiency was impressive as hell. All it had taken was a phone call from Bobbie saying a strange male was sniffing around Ana and that he'd gotten rough with her inside the café—though from Bobbie's hiding spot outside, their tussle had seemed more like foreplay than actual violence. He'd been immediately instructed to follow the guy and make sure the hit went down as planned.

When the guy had freaked and attacked the homeless man, Bobbie had been surprised. Mesmerized. And undeniably excited. When the vampire had run, Bobbie had lost him. He'd been panicking when he'd heard the sirens and decided to follow them. And his hunch had paid off. He'd seen the cops pull up. Knew from prior experience who'd sent them.

And knew what Officer Southcott didn't—the man the boss had wanted dead wasn't. Wasn't a man. And wasn't dead.

But just to be sure . . .

Bobbie walked toward the wounded vampire and crouched beside him. Instinctively, he felt a shiver of pleasure at the bloody hole in the man's forehead. He was still breathing, however, his chest rising and falling with his jerky breaths.

God, how awesome it would be. To be that strong. That indestructible.

But despite his capacity to heal, this vampire hadn't been as strong as the other two.

Why? Did vampires come with varying degrees of strength? If that was the case, Bobbie would have to make sure that when his time came he was turned into the best of the best. Unfortunately, he wasn't a vampire yet, and that meant he had to hurry before this one woke up. Even if he was the weakest vampire, chances were he could crush Bobbie with a flick of his little finger.

Sure enough, the wound was already starting to close, pushing the bullet out of the man's skull. Bobbie quickly patted down the man until he found the silver case with the cards inside.

Belladonna. There was only a phone number. No email or nothing.

Per his boss's instructions to identify the man, Bobbie took the card as well as the guy's license. As soon as he left, he'd call his boss and tell him what he'd discovered. He'd report that this male was a vampire, something Officer Southcott had failed to notice. The boss would be pleased and Bobbie hoped he'd finally be rewarded.

Although it was difficult for him, he didn't take the wad of cash in the guy's wallet—the boss might not approve. He was about to stand up when it occurred to him to take the guy's cell phone, too. Maybe there'd be useful information on the SIM card that his boss could use. He was searching for it when he caught sight of the gold medallion around the man's neck. He couldn't help himself—he picked it up.

Shit, it was heavy. Was it real gold? And what did the three triangles symbolize? 'Cause they looked a little like fangs. A genuine vampire artifact. He started to lift it, but felt the buzz of a mosquito at his temple. Frowning, he swatted it away.

Don't take the necklace.

Forget you ever saw it.

Leave the necklace alone.

Take nothing else from me. Go.

The words echoed inside Bobbie's brain, but surely he was imagining them.

He slapped at the mosquito again.

Then abruptly he released the chain and stood, slightly woozy.

He wasn't going to take the necklace. Was going to forget about the necklace. Would leave the necklace alone. He would take nothing else from the man. He would leave.

He turned, swayed a little on his feet, and headed out.

He had a phone call to make.

As the man dropped the necklace, Ty's tense muscles relaxed. He'd been preparing to fight if the man had actually tried to take it, but frankly, Ty hadn't been sure he'd be able to lift his arms, let alone overpower anyone. He struggled not to scream with pain. Fuck, it was bad. He felt like his skull was going to blow off but he forced himself to remain silent. To not give himself away.

Distantly, he listened to the man who'd searched him walk away.

The man's scent carried on the wind long after his footsteps faded. Ty recognized it. A kick of adrenaline numbed his pain and had him feeling faintly satisfied.

The young guy who'd been in Ana's café with his girlfriend. Ana had called him Bobbie. Bobbie Hernandez.

He'd obviously followed him. Did Bobbie have anything to do with the cops who'd shown up and shot Ty? He was betting that was the case. Unfortunately, that was all he could do. Although he'd tried to read the kid's mind, a lot of blood and ugly visions had gotten in the way. Bobbie was a wannabe vampire. His brain was crowded with violent fantasies.

Besides that, Ty had picked up two images. One of Ana. And one of two men talking about turning humans into vampires. One of those men had been Miguel Salvador, the very man they were hoping she could influence in order to get them inside Salvation's Crossing. The same man who knew exactly where Ana's sister was—right by his side.

What he'd read of Bobbie's thoughts was just further confirmation Belladonna was on the right track. That Salvation's Crossing was indeed more than it appeared to be and that by getting inside, they'd be able to eliminate the Rogues.

Ty caught a whisper in the air and listened carefully. It was a distant echo of Bobbie's excited brain, he realized with no small amount of amazement. Leftover mental energy oozing with Bobbie's desire to be a vampire.

Shit, if it didn't already have one, the FBI should print a recruitment brochure:

Join us! Openings at all levels! Human? Become immortal. Who cares if you need to drink blood for the rest of your life? Natural vampire? Turn humans for fun and profit. Opportunities for advancement at major government agency.

Ty snorted.

It was frustrating as hell, the fact that he could sometimes read minds, sometimes couldn't. And now he'd discovered his psychic ability worked on lingering mental thoughts. And the fact that Bobbie hadn't taken the medallion around Ty's neck, when he'd clearly coveted it? Ty couldn't help wondering if Bobbie had obeyed Ty's silent commands to leave it alone. Had Ty somehow been able to use *mind control* on the other man?

The questions were stacking up quickly, and would likely continue that way.

About twenty minutes later, when Ty didn't feel like vomiting from the pain, he opened his eyes and forced himself to a seated position. Bobbie's scent had faded, so Ty knew he was long gone. Standing, he thought once again of the homeless man whose blood he'd feasted on.

The vampire named Niles had implied he'd cleaned up Ty's mess to prevent humans from learning about vampires. How? Had he closed the man's puncture wounds by licking them, as Ty should have done? Had he somehow erased the man's memory? Or worse, had he killed the man? That would make sense if the point was to ensure vampires remained a secret.

Renewed guilt washed over him. "I'm sorry," he said quietly, and God knew he was. He wondered about the man's family, if he had one. Maybe a wife or kids who'd long ago stopped wondering where he was. Whether that was the case or not, he deserved better than what had happened to him tonight.

He took out his cell phone. "I've run into some trouble," he said when Carly answered. "Real trouble. I was attacked by two vampires. One read my mind. And according to them, their queen suspected what the Bureau was doing. And I've just confirmed those suspicions for her."

For a few seconds, Carly didn't respond. Then she merely sighed. "I'll contact Mahone. Anything else?"

"I need you to look into an Officer Southcott with the Seattle PD. And send agents to the area of Wilcox and Booth. Advise them to be on the lookout for a body."

"Whose?" she said coolly.

That was Carly. Someone was dead but she didn't waste time with unnecessary words or emotions. "A homeless man who probably has my DNA all over him."

That made her pause for a second, but just barely. "You drank from him? Damn it, Ty, I thought you had yourself under control!"

"I did. I just—I just waited too long to drink." *It won't happen again.* He tried to say it, but of course he couldn't. Because he didn't know if it was true.

Her voice softened, but only slightly. "Are you hurt?"

It didn't escape him that her question seemed more practical than caring. After all, his lapse tonight notwithstanding, she was already short-staffed. And as a turned vampire he did have a special skill set. "I should be dead, but I'm fine. At least, I will be. But someone tailed me tonight. Someone with a connection to Ana and Salvation's Crossing."

"And?"

"He's identified me." Of course, he'd done it using Ty's Belladonna-issued fake ID, which would merely confirm Ty Nunes was a wealthy philanthropist with a yen to give money away. But the identity check hadn't really been about him. If Bobbie was indeed working for Miguel Salvador and Salvation's Crossing, then the man had been keeping tabs on Ana.

And he hadn't been happy that Ty had contacted her.

CHAPTER SEVEN

Ana was tired. Truth be told, she'd been tired for a long time. Unfortunately, Ana hadn't gotten a full night's sleep since . . .

Well, since she could remember.

Every night was a struggle not to drag her bedding into her closet and sleep on the floor, praying that would give her the extra few seconds she'd need to escape if someone started to shoot up the house or tried to break inside. The same was true now. Granted, thanks to Ty Duncan's visit earlier that night, she was more distracted than usual.

He made her mind spin. He made her *feel*. She was jumpy as a cat.

She threw back the covers and got out of bed, snapping on the light on her way to a recent acquisition: a thrift-shop vanity with a mirror the size of the moon. She sat on its matching chair and yanked open a little drawer to find a hairbrush.

With long, slow strokes, Ana drew the brush through her dark brown hair, something that usually soothed her.

Not tonight. She set it down, looking at herself in the mirror. Her brown eyes were troubled. She rubbed at the dark circles under them, then sat back, pulling up the frayed strap of her tank top.

Ana Martin, secret agent. Hah. Big fat fucking hah. What did Ty see in her?

How badly she wanted to trust him and reach out for all that he'd offered. His help. A sense of purpose. A team to belong to, on the side of the good guys this time. That would be interesting. It was even more interesting that Ty thought she was perfect for it. He didn't seem to doubt that she could be what he and Belladonna needed her to be.

Maybe he was right, she thought wistfully. Maybe she *could* teach Belladonna's female agents something and prove to Ty that she was worth trusting. But he seemed to know far too much about her dirty past.

It hadn't stopped him from kissing her, though. It hadn't stopped him from looking at her like he wanted her. Needed her. Like maybe, given enough time, he could even come to love her.

You really think a man like that could love someone like you?

It was possible. Ty had kissed her like he meant it and didn't seem to care about her scar, but that didn't mean the guy wanted anything from her but sex. Story of her life.

Ana pushed back the chair and flung herself into the tangled bed. She knew she'd toss and turn for hours.

She reached for the alarm clock, running her hand down the cord to pull the plug from the outlet. The last thing she needed was to watch the digital numbers change until the sun came up. She'd stare at the ceiling. She slept and dreamed instead.

After making it back to his flat, Ty dragged himself into the bedroom and collapsed on the bed. Several hours later he woke and breathed a sigh of relief. The pain had finally receded. He gingerly poked at his forehead to confirm that the bullet wound had completely healed. He'd kept the slug as a fucking souvenir.

Ty was still a filthy mess, though. He was covered in dried blood and sweat, and the bitter taste of the homeless man's blood in his mouth was enough to make his stomach roll. The digital clock beside his bed told him it was 3 a.m. Shakily, he pulled himself to his feet and into the bathroom, where he brushed his teeth and spent almost an hour in the shower. Then, feeling remarkably better, he dried off, threw on some sweats, and headed for the surveillance equipment that took up one corner of the room.

As good as the shower had felt, it was nothing compared to the curious sense of peace that washed over him as soon as he saw Ana. Peace, however, looked to be the last thing she was feeling. Her restless, sleeping image was crisply displayed on the monitor, just as it had been for the past few weeks since he'd bugged her house. For all her street smarts, Ana still had a lot to learn about sweeping a room and making sure the enemy wasn't spying on her. That, of course, was to be expected.

She was a tough girl, but not trained in covert operations. And despite what she wanted to believe, she was still gullible.

He'd never tried to read Ana's mind, and even with what he'd discovered tonight about his ability to read lingering mental energy and possibly control minds, that wouldn't change. Though he knew he was invading her privacy right now, he was doing so by garden-variety covert means, not the paranormal. He refused to stoop that low. Anything he needed to know from her, he could damn well use his other skills to get.

Unless mind reading became absolutely necessary. Then he'd play as dirty as his talents allowed him to. But right now, she was pretty much an open book to him. Far more than she realized.

As Ana muttered something and rolled to the other side of the bed, Ty winced. The speakers transmitted her low moans as her dream got worse. The images that plagued her in her sleep might be different from his, but seemed no less painful.

Cursing, he rubbed his eyes and got up to get a bottle of animal blood from the fridge. He chugged it down, almost gagging. Compared to the human blood he'd swallowed earlier, it tasted flat. Barely palatable.

But he hoped he never drank anything else for the rest of his vampire life. He didn't want to remember the blood lust that had overcome him before any more than he wanted to remember his lust for Ana. Deep down inside, he knew he'd feel both again. The question was whether he'd act on either one.

After putting the bottle of blood back in the fridge, Ty sat at his dining table and dropped his face in his hands. Even so, he could still envision the amber specks in Ana's brown eyes and the way the scar contrasted with the softer, silkier skin of her face.

With a muffled curse, Ty rose and returned to the surveillance station. Ana was still moaning. It didn't surprise him that he had to fight the urge to go to her. It did surprise him that rather than wanting to fuck her or drink from her, what he really wanted to do was comfort her. Hold her.

And be held and comforted in return.

CHAPTER EIGHT

In the cold, hazy mist of her dream, Ana was transported from the bedroom in her Seattle home to the shadowy streets of the Bronx. For a moment, she simply looked around, trying to push back the memories that threatened to overwhelm her.

It was odd the way she dreamed. As if there was always two of her: Ana, the objective observer, and Eliana, the girl who was swept away by the events of the dream. Somehow, it was possible for her to be in the heads of both of them—both of her selves—at the same time. Even more odd was the fact that being in Ana's head was the most frightening, because while Eliana was often carried away by the violence around her, it was Ana who knew the eventual outcome and the depths to which she'd sunk.

On this particular night, Eliana slammed the door as she escaped her mother's house, her disgust palatable. Ana cringed in sympathy.

Theresa Maria Sanchez Garcia, Eliana's mama, was a whore of the worst kind—the kind who didn't bother collecting her money before she let men fuck her; the kind who passed out drunk, leaving her daughters—half sisters Eliana and Gloria—alone with strange men who considered them part of the deal their mama had struck. Thankfully, now that Gloria was living with her father's family, Eliana had only herself to worry about, but that still meant carrying the knife that her friend Miguel had given her, and using it if she had to. So far, she hadn't had to use it, but Ana knew that was about to change.

"I'm not gonna use that," she'd scowled at Miguel when he'd first held it out. "What? *Son usted loco?* You wan' me to kill someone? I'd go to jail!"

"Jail would be better than being raped by some pervert!" Miguel had shouted.

"I've always escaped before. Me and Gloria—"

"Gloria's gone now. You're alone. It's just you and me, and when I can't be there to protect you, you need to protect yourself. Please. I care about you."

And that was that. That was why eleven-year-old Eliana Garcia, who had a nasty mouth but secretly wished she could be like the Disney princesses she sometimes saw on TV, had reached out and taken the knife. That's why she'd started to carry it with her. Because now someone besides her absent sister and her drunken, whoring mother cared about her.

She'd been such a fool, Ana thought, wishing she could reach out and tell Eliana that, but of course, she couldn't. All she could do was watch as the dream fast-forwarded through more days, Miguel playing a major role in all of them.

The fifteen-year-old boy had been an anomaly to eleven-year-old Eliana. Protective of her when she'd always taken care of herself. Tough but completely willing to crack a joke to cheer her up. Insistent that Eliana was more than her mother, that she should get good grades in school, that there were plenty of good people who cared about her and would protect her and give up their lives for her if only she was willing to let them.

"Didn't I save you in that drive-by? Didn't I risk my life to pull you to safety?"

"*Sí, pero*—" Eliana began, but Miguel shushed her.

"No, Eliana, no 'but.' When you're part of a gang,

that's what you do for each other. *Usted hombre arriba.* You man up. You protect one another. *Eso es familia.*"

Family. It was what she longed for. It was what she missed most now that Gloria was gone. "But I wasn't in your gang, Miguel. I'm still not."

"That's okay, *mija*. Don't matter to me. You belong to me. Only I can't be everywhere at once. If you belonged to the gang, you'd belong to all of us. And that means we'd all die to protect you, *chica*. You'd never have to be afraid again."

But Eliana hadn't been convinced. She was as afraid of the gang members who ran the streets as she was the men her mother brought home with her. She knew they dealt in drugs and firearms and stolen cars. To her, that seemed far removed from what a Disney princess should want out of life.

Over the next few months, however, the closer Eliana got to Miguel, the more she became resigned to the hard truth—she was never going to be a Disney princess and, if she wanted to live, she was going to have to accept that.

Ana had finally quieted. Unable to resist, Ty zoomed in on her face, wondering at the difference sleep made.

Awake, Ana was all snarling, snapping energy, triggering an intoxicating rush of adrenaline that kept a man on his toes and fearing for the safety of his balls—he certainly knew that firsthand.

Asleep, she was captivatingly feminine, with dark lashes fanning her cheeks, her plump lips slightly parted to expose the tip of her pink tongue and strong, white teeth. She didn't exactly look vulnerable; more like someone a man could be vulnerable with. A woman strong enough to lean and be leaned on. A warrior prin-

cess who'd be as fierce in bed as she was on the battle-
field.

It was when she was quiet that her true strength came
out; the rest was all show, and anyone could see that. If
she joined Belladonna, he would teach her that hiding
the monster within was your best chance at unleashing
it and destroying your enemy.

He should know. He *was* a monster, after all. She'd
figure that out, too, eventually.

But for now . . . for right now . . . he wanted to release
his firm hold on reality.

He wanted to pretend that he was human again. That
his future didn't involve coercing and endangering and
using this intriguing woman in front of him, but rather
pleasuring and giving to her. That she could give him all
that she was, fierce fighter and tender lover, and that he
could do the same, with no fear of repercussions or regret.

In a way, it was his own dream, but one he gladly entered while awake. One awash with vibrant color, intoxicating smells, and luxurious texture. He should have
died multiple times now, but for once he was glad he
hadn't.

Because he wanted Ana.

And in his dreams—in *this* dream—he could have her.

One minute Ana was dreaming about herself as a pow-
erless child and the next she was dreaming about sex,
not just for the sake of having it, but because she craved
it. Because for the first time in her entire life, a man was
making her crave it.

That man was Ty Duncan.

They stood mere feet away from each other. Instead of
the pitch-black hair and dark eyes he'd had back at the
coffee shop, his hair was lighter and his eyes were now

a sea-swept blue. The difference in coloring made him appear younger. More approachable. So did the look of yearning in his eyes. He stared at her as if he needed her to breathe. To feel. Quite simply, to exist.

Had anyone ever looked at her like that? As if she was everything to him?

He might cherish every part of her, if only she'd let him.

He remained silent, though. Watchful.

"Afraid I'm going to hurt you?" she asked, thinking of how she'd smashed his face into a wall and grabbed his balls. But that had been in real life. This was a dream. Perhaps he didn't remember. Or perhaps for this dream-Ty, none of it had actually happened.

"I *am* afraid you're going to hurt me," he said quietly. Yet somehow, they both knew he wasn't talking about her hurting him physically, but on a deeper emotional plane.

She didn't wake up. The slow burn of arousal continued to coil through her body. She raised her hand, cupped his neck, and tugged his head down.

Though his eyes widened slightly, he pressed his forehead against hers.

"You're cold," she said, noting again how low his natural body temperature was. It was simply an observation, not a complaint, and his features relaxed.

"Maybe to you. But I feel anything but cold right now."

"I know what you mean," she confessed, relishing her ability to talk freely for once. "Me, too."

"You're hot," he agreed. "But I'm wondering where you're the hottest."

"You know curiosity killed the cat, right?"

He laughed and she jolted slightly, awed by how much his entire demeanor softened. Dear God, she'd thought he was amazing when he'd been in full badass mode.

When he let down his guard and laughed? Hell, it was entirely possible she'd climax right then and there. Instead, she instinctively squeezed her thighs together, trying to dull the empty throbbing in her core.

He took a swift breath, his eyes heavy-lidded. Slowly, ever so slowly, he reached out and trailed his fingertips lightly against her hip. "Doesn't matter. I'm willing to take my chances."

She couldn't speak. She quivered as his fingertips shifted to her outer thigh.

"So will you?"

"Will I what?" she breathed, not taking her gaze away from his fingers.

"Will you let me find out where you're the hottest?"

Swallowing hard, she asked, "Don't you know?"

She was stunned by her own daring. She was actually teasing him. Flirting. Encouraging his sexual attention. She'd never done that with a man. At least, not so naturally. On occasion, she forced herself to go to a bar and find a man to have sex with, but to her those interludes had always been about proving something. Not sexual anticipation or pleasure. This way was so much better, she realized.

"I could guess," he said reluctantly. "But I'd rather take it step by step. Unless you want to just tell me."

Tell him and end this, he meant. Even in her dream, he was being a gentleman.

"No," she said. "I don't want to tell you."

He grinned. "Good. So let's get started—"

His hand moved, and she suddenly panicked and grabbed his wrist. "Wait! When—when will you stop?"

"Whenever you want me to."

She must have looked as dubious as she felt because his expression went completely serious. Despite her death grip on his wrist, he turned his hand over and entangled their fingers.

"You never have to fear that I'll take things where you don't want to go, princess. All I want is to please you."

"Why do you keep calling me princess?"

He looked uncomfortable for a second. Odd for a dream. She'd thought he'd answer that question just as easily as he had the others.

"You said you never lie," she reminded him.

He hesitated awhile longer. Then said, "I used to read to my sister, Naomi, at bedtime. Her favorite fairy tale was *Sleeping Beauty*. Remember I said you weren't living, but waiting? I call you princess because you're asleep. You don't know how beautiful you are. How much the world needs you. And I want to be the man who kisses you and wakes you up."

His words stunned her. Made her melt inside and yearn to be cradled in his arms. Instinctively, she tried to protect herself, shooting back, "So you see yourself as a prince?"

He grew even more somber. That look of need came back, but along with it were hints of things she didn't want to see. Not from him.

Defeat. Resignation.

"No, I'm no prince." Releasing her hand, he pulled away. Automatically, she let go, too. He took several steps back, his gaze hardening. "In fact, I'm more devil than anything. You should remember that."

He turned to go and another feeling of panic hit her, this one far stronger than the first.

"Wait," she called out. "You promised you'd stop when I wanted you to."

He paused, and she forced herself to keep speaking so that this odd but lovely dream wouldn't end yet. God, please don't let it end yet.

"And I—I don't want you to stop," she confessed. "I want you to find where I'm the hottest."

He walked up to her again. "You going to give me any hints where to start?"

She took his hand and led it to her breast. Swiftly inhaled when he gently cupped her aching flesh.

"Nice," he said just as his mouth lowered to hers.

She expected him to plunge his tongue inside her mouth, but he kept his lips closed. Gentle. Respectful. He kissed her the way a young boy courting his first girl might, his body vibrating with excitement even as he forced himself to go slow.

No one had ever treated her with such care.

Miguel had loved her, of course. He'd sacrificed much to protect her; she'd ended up hating herself for it, and in some ways hating him. Every time she'd seen him, she'd seen the life that she could never escape. With Ty, she saw the type of life, the kind of *man,* that she could never have.

Except here . . . in her dreams. Here, she could enjoy his touch. And because he made her feel safe with his gentleness, she didn't need it so much.

Opening her mouth, she licked his lips, urging him to give her more. Groaning, he angled his head and rubbed his tongue against hers. The hand that he'd placed on her breast began to move, kneading the small globe. Soon, his thumb rubbed her hardened nipple. The contrast of that firm, confident touch and the warm, increasingly eager but still silky-soft pressure of his mouth made her whimper. The sound was fraught with need, and she instinctively pulled her mouth away from his, ashamed.

One look at Ty made her embarrassment vanish.

If she'd sounded needy, he looked it.

He watched her intently. His cheeks were flushed. His breathing broken. His gaze dropped to his hand, which was still playing with her breast. She inhaled swiftly at the sight of his big hand cupping her and she immediately imagined *both* his hands on her. On both breasts. All over her body. In her hair. On her hips. Between her thighs.

With his free hand, he grabbed her hip and tugged her slightly closer so his beautiful blue eyes stared into hers. "I want to taste your breasts. Will you let me?"

She hesitated. He was being so *good*. Asking her permission before taking things further, as if he didn't want to scare her. In response, she pulled away completely. His face reflected his disappointment.

When she peeled off the tank top she wore to sleep in, he was on her.

His hands on her hips. His mouth on her breasts. His tongue on her nipples. His smell all over her. Inside her.

And somehow, he went straight to the place that mattered most.

Her heart.

After watching Ana sleep for several more minutes, Ty took a shaky breath and turned away from the monitor. He'd already taken several steps when she moaned again. This time, her moan was different. She didn't sound haunted, as she often did when she dreamed. No, this moan had a distinct tone of arousal to it.

And that caused him to whip around so fast he almost lost his balance.

In all the days he'd watched Ana sleeping, she'd never given any sign of having sexual dreams. Until now.

Another breathy, trembling moan echoed out of the surveillance equipment, but as much as it jacked him up, that wasn't what held Ty transfixed. No, it was what Ana was doing to herself that rocked his world. She cupped both of her breasts and gently massaged them. At the same time, her hips began to twitch underneath the sheets as she sought some kind of relief from her arousal.

Ty immediately felt his cock lengthen and his mouth start to water. As he watched, her movements grew bolder. More frantic. She pinched her nipples. Caressed her face and thighs. And . . . Oh, God, there she was, cupping herself and then pushing her panties aside to slide her fingers inside herself. He leaned as close to the monitor as he could, but even though he knew she had to be soaking wet, he couldn't see the shine of her juices on her fingers. Couldn't smell her arousal. Couldn't feel her.

And damn it, he wanted to feel her. Wanted all those things.

Instead, barely able to stop himself from racing to her house and taking what he wanted, he unzipped his pants and began stroking his painfully swollen cock, feeling guilty. He was jerking off to a woman who was asleep and on whom he was spying and he didn't have enough strength to stop.

He kept his rhythm consistent with hers, imagining that he was inside her. That it was his cock and not her fingers that were pleasuring her. Finally, however, as he neared his release, he closed his eyes, not wanting to lose the fantasy that they were together by seeing her come alone in her bed. With no other visual stimuli to distract him, he let his imagination go wild and slowed things down.

He was no longer inside her, but as much as he mourned that loss, something wonderful had taken its place.

In his mind, he saw them. Interestingly enough, he saw himself as he had been, with the same brown hair he'd had before he was turned. The same blue eyes. For a split second, that outward countenance seemed to be a stranger rather than the original deal, but those details quickly became unimportant.

They touched, but they also talked.

Bantered. Flirted. She trusted him enough to ask whether he'd stop touching her if that's what she wanted. He trusted her enough to reveal why he called her princess. Both of them were disclosing their fears and revealing bittersweet memories. Soon, however, the time for talking was shoved aside by physical need. By his determination to do all that he'd promised—touch her everywhere until, step-by-step, he discovered where she was hottest.

For a panicked moment, he thought she was going to end it, but instead, she removed her nightshirt, baring her body to him. He sucked on her nipple and the taste of her made him dizzy. Immediately—because this was all in his head, after all—he nipped at her skin, not enough to hurt her but enough that a drop of her blood hit his tongue. It was so good, and by her excited gasp of pleasure, she agreed.

She tasted nothing like the blood sources his captors had brought him. And more important, tasting her blood didn't have him thinking about her "mere" humanity or how she was meant to service and feed him. Rather, it had him thinking that there might be more of his humanity left inside him than he'd believed. And that maybe she was the one who could make sure that didn't change.

He shook his head, automatically rejecting any notion that Ana could somehow save him. Right now, being saved wasn't what he wanted anyway. Her body, the pleasure she was bringing him? That was a different story.

To get his mind back on track, he stripped Ana and himself, then carried her to a bed. He covered her body so his face hovered just above hers.

"God, you're beautiful," he whispered. She was drenched between her thighs and he wanted to go down on her. Wanted to suck her blood and taste her pussy juice until he was drowning in each one. He wanted to make her come. But first . . .

He looked up at her, silently asking for permission.

With a beautiful blush, she nodded, leaned back, and spread her legs even further.

He buried his face in her core.

She gasped when he licked at her moist slit, flattening his tongue to get at all the best parts. She groaned when he sucked on her clit, humming against the hardened pearl to increase her pleasure. She screamed when he penetrated her with one finger, hooking it until he found that spongy patch of nerves she probably didn't even know existed.

And she came when he added another finger to the mix.

He didn't let up, though. Instead, he continued to play with her, prolonging her release until she was pulling at his hair and begging him to stop. He growled, not wanting to obey, but he finally raised his head. That's when he felt his fangs unsheathe.

Her eyes widened with fear.

"No," he said. "Don't be afraid. This is me, just wanting you."

For a moment, she remained silent, then said, "You want my blood?"

"I want all of you," he answered the only way he could. Honestly.

To his shock, she opened her arms wide and said, "Then take it. Take me now." She arched her back and offered her throat to him. Part of him wondered if this was some kind of trick.

So be it.

In a second, he was on her, his fangs piercing the delicate skin at her throat, taking everything that she'd offered him. Her body tensed, not with pain or fear but because she was about to find release again, and this time, before she could, he plunged his aching cock inside her. He thrust. He hammered. He let the animal take control of him as he took her blood. It felt so good to be with her. In her. It felt unreal.

Somewhere, an engine backfired and someone shouted. The sounds pulled him out of his daydream with stunning brutality.

His eyes popped open.

That's when he realized none of it had been real.

He was standing in his flat, with the image of Ana on the surveillance monitor in front of him. She was still touching herself, still writhing as she struggled to find the release he so badly wanted to give her. In that moment, it didn't matter what was real and what wasn't. She was caught in the manacles of pleasure, the same pleasure that had taken hold of him. He squeezed his cock tighter and felt the tingling at the base of his spine as his orgasm came barreling down on him. His balls tightened. The tension within him gathered and grew until every minuscule space within him was filled by his desire for her.

Oh, Jesus, he thought. It's never been this good. I'm going to die from the pleasure.

In her bedroom, Ana moaned again, longer and louder than ever.

Only she didn't just moan.

She moaned *his name*.

And when she did, he shouted, coming in violent spasms while she did the same.

CHAPTER NINE

Ana's orgasm jolted her out of her dream so suddenly she could still hear the faint echo of her cries around her. Chest heaving with her effort to catch her breath, she desperately tried to ground herself in reality. Instead, all her mind could do was play back images in shocking detail.

Had she really just dreamed about sex with Ty? More important, had she dreamed about him having fangs and drinking her blood and making her come so hard as a result that she'd just about blacked out? She wasn't into weird, kinky fantasies like that. She didn't even like sex. And she'd never liked reading books or watching movies or, hell, even talking about vampires. Lord knew Bobbie Hernandez was fascinated enough with the subject, always bringing it up when he visited the coffee shop.

Maybe it was just her mind's way of warning her that Ty was dangerous. That he was going to use her. Take from her. But deep inside she didn't believe that. No, she'd been thinking of Ty last night. Thinking of joining Belladonna and him falling in love with her. More likely the dream was just her mind's way of telling her to stay real. To trust him, but not too much. Not *that* much.

Ten minutes later, still reeling from the entire experience—the inescapable knowledge that her body could actually find pleasure through a sexual connection, let alone one that involved the exchange of blood—she could still do nothing but lie there and stare at the ceiling. Eventually, she realized the sheet beneath her was drenched with sweat and clinging to her skin.

Wincing, she forced herself to her feet, stripped the bed, and tossed the linens into the washing machine. Then she took a shower, occasionally bracing a palm against the tiled wall because her knees trembled. As she washed, she was alternately hesitant to touch herself and tempted to linger at those special places that still tingled with the memory of Ty's attention.

Why? What in the world had made her dream about Ty? Not the real Ty she'd sparred with, but one far more relaxed. Sensual. Sexual. More important, why had dreaming about him gotten her off so fast and so hard? Why did she want to close her eyes and fall asleep so she could dream of him once more? So she could come again. Why did the thought of never feeling his cock or his imaginary fangs inside her leave her with a feeling of utter despair?

Finally, she was pissed off enough by her continuing desire for him that she wrenched the temperature of the shower to cold. The blast of freezing water on her skin made her jump and screech, but she gritted her teeth and forced herself to stay where she was. Only after she was sufficiently cooled down and the last vestiges of her arousal vanished did she turn off the water, towel dry, and get dressed.

Her physical languor had worn off. So had her mental cloudiness.

She wouldn't be able to go into work and pretend nothing had happened. The memory of Ty's visit and the memory of her dream wouldn't leave her alone. As much as she wanted to hide from both, she couldn't.

She booted up her computer and proceeded to run

several searches for Gloria. She used every search term she could think of, but like always, she came up empty. For some reason, her failure to find any trace of Gloria this time didn't leave her sad as much as angry.

It was just weird to think about how Gloria had totally abandoned her. Ana had been willing to let the gang beat her up, for God's sake, just to give Gloria a fresh start in life.

Despite her determination to see her sister again and convince her how wrong she'd been to abandon her, Ana always circled back to the cold, hard truth. Her sister must not give a damn. So why did she continue to bother?

With a frustrated cry, she grabbed her wireless keyboard and threw it against the wall. Several keys popped off and the keyboard bounced before landing on the floor. Covering her face with her hands, Ana dropped to her knees and struggled not to cry.

No tears, she told herself. No tears.

They won't change anything.

They won't bring Gloria back.

Besides, now that Ty knew about her, her life here was over. Ana Martin was no more. Whether she ended up signing on to work with Belladonna or not, she could never return to Seattle, taking the chance they wouldn't leave her alone but would continue to ask more and more from her. Sooner or later, they'd stop asking and figure out a way to make her do what they wanted.

After several minutes of deep breathing, Ana finally calmed. Slowly, she got to her feet, picked up the keyboard, and retrieved the scattered keys. Then she headed straight for the garage and the flattened moving boxes she kept there. One by one, she rebuilt them, then started to pack.

By 8 a.m., she was done.

She owned very little that was important to her. Some

photographs. Clothes she simply didn't want to have to buy again. And some dolls she and Gloria had played with as children . . .

Dolls she'd put in storage during her stint in prison.

With a small smile, she picked up the baby doll with yellow yarn braids and a faded gingham dress. It had once been Gloria's prized possession, mostly because it had been a gift from their mother, who'd for once remembered one of her daughters' birthdays and had made some effort to celebrate the occasion. By evening, they'd been alone again, but they'd had the doll and the leftover cake and each other. They'd spent the entire night taking care of their "new baby."

Ana still remembered how eight-year-old Gloria had crooned to the doll, promising that her life would be wonderful. Vowing that she would never let anything happen to her. Promising to protect her the way eleven-year-old Ana protected Gloria.

Months later, when Gloria's grandparents had arrived to give her a better life, Gloria had given the doll to Ana, blinking back tears, saying, "So you won't be lonely. So you can protect each other while I'm away."

And years later? After fifteen-year-old Gloria had returned from her grandparents, quiet and broken?

She hadn't wanted the doll anymore. In fact, she'd threatened to burn it, only Ana hadn't let that happen. She'd kept the doll hidden, because it reminded her of a rare moment when their mother had been something like sober. And she'd held on to it since then because she had needed a reminder of her sister, whatever it was worth.

Ty Duncan had promised to give her information about Gloria . . . *if* she came to work for Belladonna. Despite her despair and loss of control earlier, there'd never been any question of what she was going to do—if there was any chance of her finding Gloria, she'd do what it took to make sure that happened.

Ana placed the doll into a box and taped the lid shut.

She'd have to go into work and start packing there, too. Put her business up for sale and have the funds transferred into a secure account. Maybe—

A knock on her door made her jump. She immediately thought of Ty. Annoyance or anger should have been her first response. Instead, she felt a jolt of excited anticipation.

Warily, she approached the front door. "Who is it?"

"Seattle PD, ma'am."

"What do you want?"

"If you open the door, we can talk about it."

"What's your name? Your badge number?"

"Officer Southcott." He recited his badge number and rattled off the number of his station.

With a quick phone call to Seattle PD, she confirmed his visit to her house as official. Only then did she open the door and allow him to cross the threshold. But she didn't ask him to sit down. He could say what he'd come to say standing up.

"Ms. Martin." He gave her a curt nod. "I'm here to ask whether you know Téa Montgomery."

Téa? Why was he—? A feeling of dread hit her and she automatically thought . . . Ty Duncan. He'd said he'd spoken to Téa about her. Had he hurt her?

He couldn't have. She was far more suspicious of this cop than Ty. "Téa's my parole officer, but I'm sure you already know that. What's this about?"

"Ms. Montgomery is dead," he said baldly, holding nothing back. "She passed away almost a week ago."

Shock punched Ana in the stomach and was followed swiftly by grief. Even so, she deliberately kept her face blank and her breathing steady.

But, God, how it hurt.

Téa hadn't just been her parole officer, she'd been a friend, at least as much of a friend as Ana had allowed herself. Téa had cared about her. Encouraged her. Told her she was more than her past. Now she was dead.

Something was wrong, really wrong. It was possible that Ty Duncan had killed her. Ana had no real reason to trust him at all.

Seated in front of the surveillance monitors, Ty cursed when he saw Officer Southcott—the same bastard who'd driven a bullet between his eyes—stroll up Ana's front walkway to knock on her door. Last night, he'd assumed the cop had been sent to the warehouse to go after him by someone wanting to protect Ana. How wrong he'd been. Now Southcott was going to kill Ana before Ty could do anything to stop him.

Shooting to his feet, he was about to run over there when he realized it was broad daylight. Sure he could withstand the sun for a short time, but he'd be seen. Identified. Maybe even questioned. Southcott had parked his patrol car in front of her house, which didn't exactly scream nefarious intent, so he paused. Waited. Heard Southcott give Ana the phone number of his station house. On another screen, he watched Ana pick up the phone and confirm the officer was actually supposed to be there. Further proof that Southcott wasn't going to harm her.

Still tense but no longer panicked, Ty sat back down.

So why was Southcott there?

He watched and listened, then cursed.

He'd already known Téa Montgomery was dead before Ana had confronted him in that alley. He'd also known it was only a matter of time before Ana learned the truth. But now? After everything he'd put her through? After the way she'd thrown that keyboard, then slowly and methodically packed up her things?

The expression on Ana's face when she heard the news made Ty wince. She hid her grief so damn well. Too well.

Ty had guessed why she'd packed her stuff. And why she'd thrown that keyboard. Even worse, he knew things were only going to get harder for her.

"How—how did she die?" Ana asked the cop.

Southcott was watching her carefully, as if he thought she was going to break down and weep. He seemed somewhat surprised when she didn't.

"A car accident."

What a mundane way for such a vibrant woman to lose her life. Téa's family—her parents, the sister she often talked about—had to be shattered. *Madre de Dios . . .*

"That's terrible," Ana said, because he clearly expected her to say something.

He held out a piece of paper. "This is a transcription of a text on Téa's phone. Just a draft, never sent. I don't know if the accident is the reason she never finished it, but . . ." The police officer shrugged.

Ana took the paper and read Téa's incomplete text: *Ana. Stay away from Belladonna. Too dangerous. Gloria—*

It stopped there.

Téa had truly been her friend to the end. She'd tried to warn Ana to stay away from Belladonna because she'd wanted to protect her. Yet the text confirmed what Ty had already told her—that Belladonna and Gloria were somehow linked.

"Any thoughts?" Office Southcott asked. "Do you know anything about Belladonna? Or who Gloria is?"

"Gloria is my sister. I haven't seen her in years. And Belladonna?" She shook her head. "I don't know. I've never heard of it."

She felt a twinge of unease at the lie, but didn't let it influence her. She was used to lying to the cops. Since she didn't know whom to trust, she wasn't going to confide in this one. Suspicion still nagged at her. All she wanted was to get Southcott out of her house as soon as possible.

But first she had to ask all the right questions. It was the least she could do for Téa. "Are you investigating her death? Is it being ruled a homicide?"

"No. We've apprehended the man who hit her. Drunk driver, multiple violations. I just wanted to follow up and make sure you got her message. And her warning." Southcott smiled tightly. "I knew Téa Montgomery. Smart lady. If she's telling you to stay away from someone, even your sister, I'd listen to her."

The guy's condescending grin and know-it-all attitude set Ana's teeth on edge. "Thank you. I will."

It was another lie, of course.

Southcott gestured to the boxes she'd packed. "You moving?"

"Yes," she said. "Not far. I'm buying a place closer to work," she said.

Southcott just stared at her for a few seconds, then nodded. "Well, you know where to find me if you need me."

She didn't reply. Simply walked him to the door and said good-bye, then locked it behind him. Shakily, she leaned back against it and looked around at all the boxes that were packed and ready to move into storage. This sealed it—she was going to find out what Belladonna really wanted from her.

And if Téa's death had anything to do with it.

With determination, she picked up her phone and

dialed the number on the card Ty had given her. She wasn't surprised when he answered, his voice low and somber. "Hello," was all he said.

Ana took a deep breath. "Téa Montgomery is dead."

"I know. I'm sorry."

"How could you not tell me that? Did you know when you came to see me yesterday?"

"Yes." He hesitated. "I didn't tell you because I thought you were already suspicious of me. I thought it best to let you find out when you tried to contact her. Which I knew you'd do."

"Did you—did you have anything to do with it?"

"No."

This was it. She had to decide whether she could trust him enough to take the next step. But she'd called him, hadn't she? In spite of that weird dream she'd had. That proved on some level she'd already made up her mind, even after hearing about Téa's death.

Her intuition told her that he was waiting for her to confirm that. Ana didn't want to give him the satisfaction of a definite answer just yet.

"Listen, Ty. Right now I'm not making any promises except this. If I find out you're playing me, if I find out you had anything to do with Téa's death, you'll regret it."

"I wouldn't expect anything less."

"So if I join . . . what happens next?"

"We have to get you to Belladonna without anyone tailing you."

"Why would anyone want to?"

"Lots of reasons," he said.

Though she was annoyed by the nonanswer, Ana figured he would fill her in on those later. He'd better or she wouldn't come in.

"You always have to assume people want something

from you," he continued. "And that they're willing to do whatever it takes to get it."

"Does that include you?" she asked, remembering what he'd said in her dream about being more devil than prince.

"It especially includes me."

CHAPTER TEN

After leaving Ana Martin's house, Officer William Southcott finished the second half of his double shift. As he did, he couldn't keep the little hottie out of his head.

He'd delivered the message as instructed, but damn, he'd wanted to give Ana Martin a whole lot more. She was fine, with a hot little body he had no trouble imagining naked, spread out and helpless. He'd love her to fight him. He'd force her to come for him and punish her if she dared to fake it. His imagination supplied the juicy details. What a sick mind he had, he thought happily.

By the time his shift was over, Southcott was in a state of painful arousal and intent on dealing with it. Not with the woman, of course. She belonged to the boss, whether she knew it or not. It was Southcott's second job to mete out punishment for anyone who messed with her, and that had even included the lady parole officer with the big mouth. The boss didn't call on him often, but when he did and Southcott completed what was asked of him, he was generously paid. He wanted to keep getting generously paid.

He also wanted to stay alive.

That, more than anything, made his fantasies about Ana Martin exactly that.

But still . . . he'd never actually been that close to her before. Had never actually talked to her. There was something about her, something that had made keeping his hands off her damn difficult, even though he'd recently shot a man between the eyes for failing to do just that.

With a shake of his head, Southcott unlocked his apartment door, secured his weapon, and showered. There, he took his desire for Ana Martin in hand, spilling his seed in a pathetically short amount of time. He was about to go at it again when his shower door was abruptly and violently yanked open.

"Jesus Christ," he shouted, body jolting and eyes widening when he saw who loomed in front of him. Fear didn't even begin to describe the sensation that shot through him. His bladder released, combining urine with the semen and water swirling down the drain, but he managed to sound fairly commanding when he said, "What—what the hell are you doing here?"

His boss was normally calm, cool, and collected, but now looked feral. Crazed. Why?

"I came for an update on your visit with Ana Martin."

Despite his fear, Southcott forced himself to frown. To maintain a strong front even in the face of someone so much stronger. "And you couldn't wait until I was out of the fucking shower?"

"Not when I knew what you were doing. Who you were doing it to. You're psychotic, Southcott, which sometimes suits my purposes just fine. I don't care about the others you've hurt so long as you follow my orders. But this is different. I saw your thoughts. I saw what you were doing. You were hurting her. You were defiling her."

Southcott's mouth went dry. "That was all in my head. I didn't actually touch her."

"You don't get to have fantasies about her!"

The vampire stepped into the shower, eyes menacing. Intent clear.

Despite himself, Southcott trembled and took several useless steps back. "It wasn't real. You can't kill me for thoughts I can't control." He was shaking, his words pitched high with fear. His gun. He needed his gun . . .

"You're not thinking clearly, Officer Southcott, or you'd remember your gun won't do you any good. And to the contrary, I *can* kill you for any reason I deem fit. You jacking off to thoughts of Ana while you hurt her? That's a good enough reason for me."

As pain ripped through Southcott's body, his last thoughts were of the man he'd shot between the eyes. And the knowledge that his death wasn't going to come as quickly or as easily.

PART
2

THE TEAM

CHAPTER ELEVEN

Two days after he had confirmed Téa Montgomery's death to Ana, Ty was back in his suite at the Belladonna compound. He'd just finished showering and was getting dressed. As usual, his thoughts were filled with Ana— the way she'd pointed a gun at him in that alley, the way she'd felt beneath him as he'd kissed her, the look in her eyes when he'd caressed her scar, and most of all—yes, most of all—the way she'd moaned his name during that crazy-ass masturbation session in front of his surveillance equipment. He was so lost in his thoughts, in fact, that when someone knocked on his door, he jerked.

"Yeah?"

"It's Peter."

Peter Lancaster was Ty's friend and another special agent-involuntarily-turned-vampire.

But he had actually known about vampires before he'd been turned and, as such, had known whom to contact when they'd escaped—Carly.

As fucked up as the whole situation was, at least Ty knew he was in good company.

"Come on in."

As Peter entered the room, Ty hoped his expression—

and his body—didn't betray who and what he'd just been thinking about.

"So," Peter asked. "Have you heard from your gang girl again?"

"Ex–gang girl," Ty responded.

"Right. Like she can ever really escape that part of her life."

Ty's mouth twisted. "You're right. She has as much chance of doing that as you and I have of escaping what we are now."

Peter snorted. "Jesus, Ty. We might be vampires of one sort or another, but so far, *we're alive*. We still have our minds. Our memories. We're still the same men we've always been. When are you going to get over your shit and remember that?"

Never, Ty thought, but he didn't say it. Still, Peter's words, his obvious ability to adjust to a situation that Ty couldn't, made his control slip. Other memories flooded him. Ones he usually managed to lock down tight. Memories of Naomi. "Maybe when I stop wanting to drink other people's blood," Ty shot back. "Or stop thinking about Ben, the guy who helped us escape but didn't make it out himself, or my sister, *the girl you were dating*. She's dead. Do you remember that?" He usually kept his grief at bay by focusing on his mission and his own fucked-up situation, but sometimes it threatened to overpower him, especially when guilt was added to the mix.

To be fair, however, Ty had always felt guilt where Naomi was concerned, even when she was alive.

Peter flinched. Turned away. Slammed his palm against the door hard enough that it dented inward and cracked the doorjamb. For several seconds, he stared at the floor. When Ty said nothing, Peter finally turned back toward him. "Ben was one of us. He was a good man who knew the score, and the score was if we hadn't run when he told us to, we wouldn't be here right now. As for Naomi . . . I miss her, too, you bastard. But I knew her a lot less time than you did, and even I could tell the chances of her living to a ripe old age were nil. She didn't deserve what happened to her, but . . ."

Peter didn't finish the sentence, but Ty knew where it was going. Despite their life of privilege, Naomi had always been troubled and she'd loved to seek out even more trouble.

Ty said nothing, but Peter wouldn't let the matter drop. "She was addicted to heroin and sex, Ty. She was always attracted to the wrong type. Dangerous people. I don't know how, but it was obvious she knew the vampires who attacked us, and they knew her. So yeah, we went out a few times, but she didn't love me and I didn't love her, not that way. I'm sorry."

"Do you—do you blame her for what happened to us?" Ty choked out. "Do you blame me?"

"No and no. But you? I'm betting you're blaming a lot of people. Me and Carly for working with the Turning Program. For keeping the existence of those bastards a secret. But also yourself. Am I right?"

He wanted to say no, but he didn't. He couldn't. Part of him did blame Carly and Peter and every other person who'd had a hand in the FBI Turning Program. They'd made the Rogues think they were untouchable. The least they could have done was warn humans, especially their own fucking agents, about the danger vampires presented.

But Ty also blamed himself for what had happened.

The last time he'd seen Naomi's face, she'd been scared, frightened of the street thugs who'd called her name and blocked their way on the street. She'd urged Ty to walk away, but Ty hadn't listened. He'd threatened the guys. He'd even shoved a few of them. He'd been so damn pissed at learning Naomi was consorting with what appeared to be thugs again, and so damn cocky because he was a badass FBI agent, and he was with Peter and Ben, two other badass FBI agents.

Just plain stupid of him.

Ty had been stunned when things went crazy, firing his gun only to discover that the bullets were no help.

All he'd felt after that was pain, and that pain had only magnified tenfold when he'd woken, strapped to a table and at the mercy of his captors. The true shock, however, had been discovering what those men thought he was—a vampire. One they'd created to serve them.

For nearly a full day, he'd told himself that help was coming. That the FBI would find him. That he'd escape. Those feelings had intensified when he'd realized Peter and Ben were also captives. At the time he'd figured his sister had been taken, too. She'd be terrified, he'd thought, but that had simply made him more determined to save them all.

Then his own body had turned against him, and he'd witnessed his crazed behavior in those around him. How nothing mattered but getting more blood. More sex. He'd been certain he'd kill to get whatever he needed, thinking he might even slaughter Peter or Ben or God forbid Naomi, if they asked him to, if only they'd give him another taste of blood or another female to fuck.

When he'd come back to himself and they'd told him that Naomi was dead, he'd screamed until his throat was raw. For a while, his sanity had completely left him.

But then things changed. Their vampire captors had herded a bunch of them into one room—including him, Peter, and Ben. The vampires had been freaked out, whispering that their location had been compromised, that maybe the FBI had found out they were double-crossing them, and that they had to transport everyone to another facility immediately, regardless of whether it was daytime or not.

That's when Peter had revealed a huge secret—that he'd had a role in the FBI's Turning Program and therefore had some knowledge about vampires, including the fact born vampires couldn't survive direct contact with the sun; as such, it was a pretty safe bet the vampires transporting them would be turned vampires and thus easier to take down. The odds would be against them, especially given the torture they'd endured, but Ty, Peter, and Ben were hoping their extensive combat training would give them an edge. It had. As soon as they'd been shepherded outside the building, he and Peter and Ben had worked together to overpower the two turned vampires transporting them. Peter and Ty had managed to get away.

Ben had not. The last time Ty had seen him, he'd been pinned to the ground and shouting for them to run.

Peter had contacted Carly, another special agent working in the Turning Program, who got Mahone to arrange their transfer to a safe house. Eventually Ty and Peter had recovered. His freedom and the prospect of continuing his work as a special agent hadn't miraculously fixed things, but it had eventually brought him back from the edge.

"It's okay, Ty," Peter said. "I know you loved her. That's all that matters."

When Ty again remained silent, Peter stared at him, long and hard, then sighed, obviously choosing not to pursue the subject. "Carly heard back from Mahone. Doesn't matter if the queen knows about the FBI's Turning Program; we're to proceed as planned."

Ty grunted. No surprise. The fact that he might have confirmed the Vampire Queen's suspicions didn't necessarily open up many new options for her. She was the leader of a hidden race, one that wanted to remain hidden. That meant she didn't have a public forum to object to what the FBI had done behind her back. She could still, however, take matters into her own hands. All they could hope was that she concentrated her resources on the Rogues rather than the FBI.

"Well, I've done my job recruiting the others. Collette, Barrett, and Justine are scheduled to arrive," Peter continued. "You really think Ana will be able to teach them anything useful? I know they haven't been assigned to any specific missions yet but—"

"She needs training herself. But I think Ana can demonstrate the finer points of street fighting."

Peter was fully briefed on their first mission and as such he knew exactly what they were going to be asking of Ana. It wouldn't involve her fighting anyone so much as fighting her own demons, which was often the more difficult challenge.

"So what's going on with her? She coming in?"

Ty thought back to Ana's phone call. She'd been upset. Grieving the loss of her friend Téa. She'd asked him if he'd had anything to do with it, and he'd been honest when he'd said he hadn't, but *someone* had killed Téa. And it hadn't been the pathetic drunk driver who'd been blamed for the car accident, either. Had it been Bobbie? Miguel? Officer Southcott? Someone else entirely?

One thing was for sure—Southcott wouldn't be providing answers. The morning after he visited Ana, Southcott's housecleaner had found him dead. The means of death had been a gunshot wound to the head, supposedly the result of a random home invasion. Ty wasn't buying that, but he didn't have a clue as to who had actually killed Southcott, or why, either.

He needed to talk things out with Peter, but suddenly Ty didn't want to stay in this room. "I don't want to sit on my ass," he said abruptly. "Let's get in some target practice and I'll fill you in."

Five minutes later, the wind whipped harshly across Ty's face. The day was overcast, but even so, their skin would eventually mottle and burn from the little sun that was shining through. If they stayed in the sun, they'd just keep burning. He wasn't positive how much sustained exposure would actually kill him. In the past, he'd only managed to stand two hours of direct sun and the third-degree burns he had suffered had been excruciating.

Maybe the fact that they could survive even that much sunlight had something to do with their body temperatures. That was another trait they'd shared since being turned. On the other hand, their core body temperatures seemed to rise with each passing month. Eventually, he and Peter suspected they'd maintain a body temperature similar to born vampires, which was about five degrees warmer than human. What would happen then? Would they still be able to walk in the sun, or would they be confined to the dark, like born vampires? If so, that would be just one more reason to end things.

He gestured to Peter and they both lay down on the damp forest floor, their long-range rifles at their sides. As he did, Ty felt the gold medallion he'd been given by Lesander press against his body, still hidden beneath his shirt. He'd told Peter and Carly about his encounter with the vampires but he hadn't told them about the medallion.

And he hadn't been sure why.

Until now.

He turned to Peter.

"Read my thoughts."

His friend looked at him as if he'd lost his mind.

"What?"

"You've been able to do it more consistently than I have."

Peter looked insulted. "I've never tried to read yours. If you think otherwise then fuck you." He started to get up, but Ty stayed him with a hand on his arm.

"No. I don't think that. But tell me this. When you have tried to read minds, how many times have you been successful?"

Peter relaxed slightly, though he still continued to frown. "If I had to guess, eight out of ten."

Ty nodded. "That's a pretty good record. And that's why I'm asking you to read my mind right now."

"Why?" When Ty just continued to look at him, Peter rolled his eyes. "Fine." The other vampire's eyes grew more intense as he stared into Ty's. Thirty seconds passed. A minute. Ty felt no tickling sensation.

Peter shrugged. "Nothing."

Ty hummed. So the necklace actually worked. Unless this was just one of the rare times when Peter's mind-reading powers failed him.

"You gonna tell me what that was about?"

Just testing this necklace that I got from another vampire. He said it'll stop any vampire from reading my mind.

That's what Ty was about to say. But he didn't. And again, he didn't know why.

He just knew his gut was telling him to keep quiet. And for now, he was listening to it.

"Nope," he said smoothly.

Of course, Peter appeared less than satisfied but he dropped the subject.

Ty pointed at a pine tree a ridiculous distance away, far enough to be a challenge to even two vampires with supersharp, extraordinary eyesight. "The challenge is to shoot the pinecone right where it joins the limb. There's a one- to three-inch shaft, and if you hit it just right, the pinecone drops. Ten points for each dropped pinecone. Five points for every pinecone you obliterate on the tree. Zero points for hitting the tree. Negative points if you have to use a scope."

"You're on," Peter said, hefting his rifle up to his shoulder and aiming.

They'd downed five pinecones each before they took a break to reload. Ty finally told Peter about Ana's phone call and what she'd learned about Téa Montgomery. "So what do you think?"

"My bet's on Miguel being behind it," Peter said. "He probably used Bobbie or Southcott as his hired gun."

Ty shifted, aimed, and shot, only to destroy the pinecone while it was still on the tree. Damn.

"But why kill Téa Montgomery?" he asked. "And why now?"

Peter proceeded to execute several successful shots before turning to Ty. "You think Bobbie Hernandez tried to pop you to protect Ana, right?"

"Yeah. He wasn't around when we were in the alley, but I continued to smell him after he left the coffee shop. He was close by. Maybe just outside. He probably saw me wrestling with her."

"You sure that's all he saw you doing?"

Ty remembered the way he'd kissed her and his silence was a deafening admission of guilt.

"Anyway, Téa and Ana were friends."

"But she hadn't seen her since her last parole check-in a couple of months earlier. Why would Miguel move on her when he did? Why at all?"

"You talked to Téa about Ana, didn't you? Used her to fill in your research?"

"Yes."

"Téa gave you answers because she knew Carly and trusted her. It wasn't part of her job. In fact, what she told you was probably illegal."

Peter handed him a thermos of animal blood. Ty took a swig, then wiped his mouth. Drinking animal blood settled the unease that ate at his gut every day, but it never seemed to satisfy like a good steak or fish-and-chips had when he'd been alive. He'd never had enough to know, but he'd bet if he drank human blood on a steady basis, the hollow feeling in his gut would completely disappear.

But since that wasn't going to happen, he forced himself to focus on what Peter was saying.

"So Téa betrayed Ana by giving us info about her, and Miguel offed her. But how would he even know?"

"The same way he knew you and Ana had 'wrestled.' Maybe he had her office wired," Peter replied. "Or had someone watching her. You ever check Ana's prison records?"

"She was a model inmate."

"How about the records of her cell mates? Of anyone who'd talked to her? Given her a bad time? Maybe even a guard."

"No. Why?"

"What's to say Miguel didn't have eyes and ears in prison, too? In two years, somebody had to have harassed Ana. And chances are they probably paid for it. You should see if you can find proof."

"Jesus. You really think so?"

"It's a long-shot theory, but if it's true, what does that tell you about how our man Miguel feels about Ana?"

Ty pondered the question for a few seconds. "He not only loves her, he's obsessed with her. He's watched over her for seven years. And he'd hurt or kill anyone who hurts her and not think twice about it."

"That's right. And a man obsessed with a woman is the most dangerous kind there is. And yet the plan is for Ana to catch his eye so he'll invite you into Salvation's Crossing. You really think she can handle something like that?"

"Maybe not now, but when we're done with her, yes. Besides, it's entirely possible that Miguel's not as dangerous as he thinks he is. He had a chance to kill me and he failed," Ty pointed out.

"Something in your tone tells me you regret that. You would rather have died?" Peter asked. "That day? Six months ago?"

"Damn right," he gritted out. "Dying was supposed to happen. Just like it was supposed to happen when Officer Southcott shot me. And numerous times before that."

"Hmmm," Peter intoned, neither agreeing nor disagreeing with him. "Well, I for one am glad I didn't die. If that makes me some kind of sick fuck, so be it."

"You've also been a vampire for six months. Let's see how you feel in a few decades. Maybe in a century. Something tells me living without really being alive's gonna feel a lot like trying to eat a hologram of a slice of cake. There, but not there. I am not looking forward to it."

"But you're looking forward to catching the bastards responsible for all this, aren't you? 'Cause I certainly am. When you start thinking about wanting to die, force yourself to think of that instead."

"Vengeance won't bring back my sister. Or my humanity. But—you're right. It's something," Ty agreed. Right now, it was everything.

He fired again and dropped several more pinecones. Peter did the same.

"Score's dead even. You want to keep going or call it a day?"

Peter grimaced. "My skin's starting to burn. Let's go in and you can tell me more about your girl."

Your girl. That was the second time that Peter had referred to Ana in that way.

Despite Ty's misgivings, the words sounded right.

CHAPTER TWELVE

Deep within the recesses of Building T, Mahone watched from behind a one-way mirror as Mike Polanski, a twenty-five-year-old army vet who'd had his legs blown off in Afghanistan, ran around the track of a full indoor gymnasium. The guy was grinning from ear to ear, and for a moment, Mahone wanted to grin with him. He didn't.

Mike Polanski was now a turned vampire.

Just like the turned vampires that had come before and after him, no one knew how he'd been turned, just that he'd been delivered that way by the Rogues that had been doing the FBI's bidding.

Turning Polanski into a vampire hadn't made his legs magically grow back, but what it had done was give him amazing strength and speed. The fact that he had to use prosthetic legs was irrelevant. Even with the prosthetics, he still moved faster than any human. Was stronger than any human. And for a man who'd been on the verge of suicide when Mahone had found him, that was an amazing accomplishment.

This was why he'd supported the FBI Turning Program from the beginning. Because it was achieving some incredibly positive things.

And when the program had been threatened, he'd agreed to act as the FBI's liaison to Belladonna. So that the Rogues didn't mess everything up.

Only lately . . .

Mahone couldn't deny it. He was starting to have doubts about what they were doing and whether they should be doing it at all.

Polanski was running again because the FBI was tampering with forces it knew nothing about. His speed and strength were the equivalent of playing with fire.

Hell no. Not even that. They were the equivalent of playing with an atomic bomb.

The program was based on experimentation and on keeping secrets from the Vampire Queen. Now two vampires had attacked Ty Duncan. They had probably already told their queen about the FBI's duplicity.

Would she go to the Bureau director? Would she seek out the president himself?

Unlikely, Mahone thought. She'd have to admit her spies had read Ty's mind against his will, something she claimed vampires were honor bound not to do. She'd also have to admit there was such a thing as Rogue vampires in the first place.

The door to the gym opened and Mahone watched as Malcolm Creeley entered. He was a turned vampire, had been one for about two years now.

Creeley joined Polanski on the track, clapped a hand on his back, then picked up the pace. Mahone reached over to the bay of control knobs and turned on the speakers, listening in on the vampires' conversation as they ran full-out around the track.

"How many miles have you done today?" Creeley asked Polanski.

"Fifty and counting."

Fifty miles in about thirty minutes. Again, amazing stuff, but it ramped up Mahone's worry. Hallifax seemed to think containing the Rogues would be enough, but Mahone wasn't so sure anymore. What happened if the Vampire Queen, infuriated by what the FBI was doing, decided against anonymity and peace, and launched a full-scale attack against humans? The U.S. certainly wasn't ready for it. FBI Turning Program or not, they might never be.

On the track below the one-way mirror, Creeley continued the conversation. "You done any sparring yet?"

Polanski shook his head. "Later for the fighting. They say they'll train me after I've overcome the worst of my—"

"Urges?" Creeley finished Polanski's sentence, grinning as he did so.

A newly turned vampire had to feed. And fuck. Four months past his turning, Polanski's feral instincts were fairly manageable but they were still very much there, under the surface. Sparring could cause a rush of adrenaline and bring out his latent violence. "If you can control them," Creeley said to Polanski, not even panting, "you can really start to have fun."

Together, the two vampires raced around the track, leaping over hurdles and other obstacles. Polanski whooped and pumped his fists in the air.

Like all the vets who had been recruited into the FBI's Turning Program, Polanski was a gung-ho soldier, sworn to fight Uncle Sam's enemies. Ethnicity, race, political bent—none of that mattered to him. As far as the FBI was concerned, it was a win-win all around.

Anyone with half a brain would know it wasn't that simple.

Mahone watched as the vampires slowed to a stop.

"You know," Creeley said, casting Polanski a sidelong glance, "we train you to be the best. Better than a mere vamp."

"How so?" Polanski asked.

"Born vampires are losers," Creeley sneered. "They hide who they are, posing as humans."

"So we're an improvement?"

"Yeah," Creeley insisted. "We combine human ambition and vampire power. Those of us who've been turned are now the ultimate predators."

Tension shot up Mahone's spine.

Talk about proving his fucking point.

This wasn't the first time he'd heard a turned vet diss full vampires. He'd heard them refer to "mere" humans in the same way. The FBI had wanted to create supersoldiers in order to fight its human enemies *and* an inhuman race. But now that he was hearing turned vampires identifying themselves as a distinct group, accountable to no one . . . He had good reason to be scared shitless.

Mahone's attention was suddenly riveted on the track. Creeley had just punched Polanski in the shoulder. Polanski didn't look happy. Mahone turned the volume up.

"What the fuck was that for?" Polanski asked.

This time Creeley shoved him, both hands on Polanski's chest. "Wanna spar?"

Polanski backed up a step.

"Come on. I want to see what you've got." Creeley swung a fist at Polanski's face. The other man blocked the punch and threw a roundhouse, connecting with Creeley's jaw.

And the fight was on.

Mahone was transfixed, as if he was watching a horror movie. The kind where you knew someone was going to die in a really bad way and the monsters were going to get away with it. Fists cracked against bone, skin split, blood spattered.

Polanski seemed to be giving as good as he got.

God damn Creeley. What was the turned vamp trying to do? He was taking a risk, calling out Polanski's vampire instincts like this. If Creeley kept this up, Polanski would go feral. Granted, as the older vamp, Creeley should have the strength and training to take Polanski out if the other vamp lost control—and whatever damage Creeley did to the man, Polanski's body would regenerate. No harm, no foul. But still, sparring with another turned vampire until they'd both been cleared went against the guidelines.

Mahone had no power to stop the fight. He was here to observe, nothing else. Hands off. His role was to report to Hallifax alone.

It wasn't lost on him that most of the world, including most of the FBI, was being kept in the dark about vampires. What, then, was *he* being kept in the dark about?

Hell, if vampires existed and lived hidden among humans, who was to say that other paranormal creatures didn't exist, too? Werewolves. Mummies. Ghosts. Assuming they did exist, did the FBI have some other grunt observing them, too? Or were they still managing to conceal their existence? Because they'd certainly be smart to.

Could be that the worst thing to happen to the vampire race was being discovered by the FBI. Mahone just hoped that discovery didn't end up being the worst possible thing to happen to the human race as well.

In the gym below, Polanski lost it. Howling, screaming gutturally, he ripped into Creeley, who kept that fucking grin on his face and danced away. The main doors to the gymnasium opened and Ross Newton, another agent, rushed in.

"Get him under control!" Newton yelled.

Creeley just shook his head, still smiling. "Can't. He's gone too far. Only thing to do now is let him feed . . . and fuck."

Newton stopped in his tracks. "Fine. I'll get him something to eat."

"Bring me a feeder, too. I'm hungry," Creeley said.

Newton stormed his way out of the gym, flicking his gaze over the blood-spattered floor in revulsion.

"That's right, human," Creeley said to the closed door. "Better do what I say when I say it." He ducked as Polanski swung at him and laughed. "Hold on there, man. Soon we'll be drowning in blood and pussy."

So Creeley had forced Polanski into a frenzy that only blood and sex would satisfy, and wanted his share of the feast. Selfish asshole. Mahone's cell phone rang. The number on the screen didn't surprise him. He'd been half waiting for this call ever since Carly had told him that a vampire had read Ty Duncan's mind.

The caller was Rhonda Locke. The woman who, along with her husband, headed up the FBI's Strange Phenom Unit. They'd discovered the existence of vampires, and today remained in close contact with the Vampire Queen. Locke was the equivalent of an ambassador, keeping peace between humans and vamps, which was why she'd never been told about the Turning Program.

Until now, he suspected.

"This is Mahone."

"I need to ask you a question." Locke's voice, clipped and angry, sounded in his ear. "You get one chance to answer me, so think before you do."

"Go ahead." He kept the phone to his ear as he kept his gaze on the gym and on Polanski, writhing on the floor, screaming for blood.

"Is the FBI turning humans into vampires?"

"Yes," he answered, with no hesitation. She knew. That meant the Vampire Queen knew. There was no point in lying.

A quickly indrawn breath.

"You're part of the program." She said it as a statement, not a question.

"Yes." For now, Mahone thought. He wasn't sure if the program would survive the Vampire Queen's inevitable fury.

"Why wasn't I told?"

The door to the gym opened again. A man—strong, young, Hispanic—was shoved into the room. The bile Mahone had tasted earlier now surged into his mouth. "Why are you asking?"

"You know exactly why. The Bureau has been dealing with born vampire traitors. Now those vampires—Rogues, I believe you call them—are out of control and the FBI's trying to cover its ass."

"Correct."

Mahone leaned in close to the one-way mirror. Had this feeder been provided to the FBI by Salvation's Crossing? After all, they believed Salvation's Crossing was supplying vampires with migrant workers to feed on, workers willing to do anything to provide a better life for their families. Why wouldn't the Rogues have used some of those same immigrants to fulfill its obligations to the FBI?

In the end, it didn't really matter who'd brought the man here. The way he stared, open-mouthed and unmoving, at the frenzied and blood-soaked Polanski told Mahone all he needed to know. Didn't matter what race this man was or what lies he'd been told. What he saw wasn't something he'd signed up for.

Polanski caught sight of his victim. Mahone fought the urge to close his eyes. If he interfered, his superiors would be notified, and he'd never be let back inside Building T. He couldn't risk that.

"This can't continue, Mahone," Locke said.

As soon as she said the words, Mahone's misgivings about the Turning Program solidified. Belladonna would have to see its mission through. But once the Rogues were out of the equation . . .

"You may be right, Rhonda," Mahone said, his voice flat. "And we do need to deal directly with the vampire leaders eventually. Hallifax believes the Rogues can be contained and somehow, eventually, the Turning Program can resume. My team's supposed to make that happen."

He watched as Polanski charged, racing faster than humanly possible, his prosthetic feet a blur. The man he ran toward let out a high-pitched scream. It was the cry of someone who feared death, but Mahone knew from past experience the man wouldn't be allowed to die. Newton would allow Polanski to feed and then intervene, pulling out the feeder before he was drained of too much blood. Standard protocol.

Mahone still didn't want to see it go down.

Turning away, Mahone reached over and turned down the volume. So Locke couldn't hear the screams, he told himself.

"The Bureau thinks it's choosing the lesser of two evils," he said to her. "Give me more time. Let my team hunt the Rogues and figure .out exactly what kind of threat they've become. If I get proof that the FBI is in over its head, it would help."

"Have the turnings been authorized by the president?" Before he could answer, Locke sighed. "Of course they have," she said.

Something thudded behind him and Mahone automatically turned around. A spray of blood had hit the one-way mirror, obliterating his view. But he knew what would follow. The feeder—the man used to satisfy Polanski's blood lust—would be dragged out to be treated. Then a woman, a prostitute, one who bought into the whole vampire fantasy or the notion of serving her country no matter what, would enter. And Polanski would fuck her until he was spent.

Like the feeders, like the males who had been turned, all these people had supposedly volunteered to do what they were doing. But in his heart, Mahone knew that even if that had been true in the beginning, it wasn't the case anymore.

Not a godddamn thing he could do about it.

Most of the born vampires they knew about followed rules and customs long established. They respected the authority of their queen. But there were rebels. Anarchists. Rogues—the born vampires the FBI had connected with, somewhat at random. They didn't seem to follow the same law as the vast majority of vampires. They were the immediate problem. But so was the Vampire Queen's refusal to provide the Bureau with crucial information about her race.

Even if Belladonna contained the Rogues, continuing peaceful relations between vampires and humans depended on humans believing that vampires in general weren't a threat.

"Do you think Queen Bianca will meet with me?" he asked Locke.

"Why?"

Just listen, he wanted to scream. Because humans and vampires need to come together, *work* together, to fix this. It was the only way.

"To exchange what information we have. To see if there's a way we can stop this crazy crap from going any further."

"You'd do that?" Locke asked, her voice tense. "Even if it could mean your job? Your life?"

The blood spatter on the one-way mirror trickled down. Mahone cast a glance below before quickly looking away, sickened. "Yeah. Yeah, I would."

A minute later, he ended the call. Thought things through. Then dialed a number.

When the man on the other end answered, Mahone took a deep, silent breath, then said, "Hallifax. This is Mahone."

"So talk." The assistant director of the FBI sounded less than thrilled to hear from him.

"I just got a call from Rhonda Locke. Queen Bianca knows the Bureau has been working with rogue vampires."

Hallifax's response was short and curt. "And?"

"And I've set up a meeting with her."

"To what end?"

Mahone hesitated a moment again. He obviously wasn't going to tell Hallifax everything, but he had to tell him something. "I'm hoping I can convince her to do what we originally asked. Work with us so our need for the Rogues is eliminated."

"You're a fool, Mahone. It'll never happen. The Vampire Queen isn't interested in playing nice. She's waiting for a chance to strike first. In the meantime, we're doing what we can in the way of preemptive measures."

Mahone waited for an explanation. None was forthcoming. "Are you saying you don't want me to meet with her?"

"What if that's exactly what I'm saying, Mahone?"

Mahone hesitated, not liking the hint of a threat in the man's voice. He forced himself to respond calmly. "I understand, sir. I just thought this could be another way to get what you want."

After a tense silence, Hallifax chuckled. "Good to know where your loyalty lies, Mahone. Go ahead. Meet with the Vampire Queen. Feel her out . . . or feel her up, for all I care. Doesn't matter to me. Like I said, I think you'll find she's not prepared to play nice. But do let me know if I'm wrong."

CHAPTER THIRTEEN

Two weeks after Ty had delivered an offer of employment, Ana sat in the back of a plush sedan, wondering if she'd lost her mind. Even if she had, she thought, there was no going back. Not now.

To maintain her precious anonymity, she'd sold her coffee shop—the one thing she'd built for herself after years of having nothing—at a loss. She'd given up her little house, too, the one she'd rented the same day she saw it, simply because she'd loved the big backyard and the garden that grew there. And for what? Because Belladonna wanted her to teach wannabe female agents what she knew—how to act tough so people respected you. Not liked you, but respected you, because they were too scared not to.

Ty was right. If there was one thing she knew—one thing she might be able to teach a woman—it was the ability to stay alive.

Siga adelante conlo ya, Ana. Get on with it.

How long was she going to sit here blindfolded before she worked up the courage to do what needed doing? The blindfold, she was sure, was more to cow her than anything else. Ty and the mysterious Carly wanted to see how serious she could be about cooperating with the agency's security. Knowing that, she'd played along simply because she had no reason not to. Blindfolded or not, she could find her way out of anywhere.

"Ma'am, are you ready to go in now?"

The voice of her driver, the well-mannered gentleman who couldn't make a smooth lane change if his life depended on it, asked the question for the thousandth time.

"One minute," she said, then mentally listed the reasons why taking this job would be insane.

Fact: The top-secret stuff was getting a bit tiresome and things hadn't even started yet.

Fact: She didn't know what the hell she was getting into besides teaching other women some of her "special skills"—but only after she underwent Ty's brand of anger-management training. Ana snorted at that one.

Fact: The women she trained might have to kill, which meant she'd have to teach them how. There was no guarantee the women wouldn't turn around and try to kill her.

Okay, that last one pretty much covered it, she thought. To be fair, she then listed the reasons she should take the job.

Fact: She'd be working for the good guys.

Fact: She'd have a purpose again.

Fact: She'd get to spend more time with Ty.

Fact: Gloria.

That alone substantially overrode every negative.

She wanted a new life. For a while there, she'd thought she could be satisfied with the one she had. She'd been fooling herself. All it had taken was a gorgeous man teasing her with information about Gloria and Ana was willing to sacrifice everything.

So be it.

She had to see Gloria again. Just one more time. To see for herself that Gloria was okay. To apologize for hurting her. And then to say good-bye forever, if that's what her sister still wanted.

With a sigh, Ana felt for the door handle and wrenched

the door open. Before she could hesitate, she scrambled out. She heard the driver's door open and shut, then felt a courteous hand underneath her elbow.

Despite being blindfolded, Ana walked with her arm through the driver's, her back straight, chin up, and gait smooth, with just enough natural sway in her hips to appear relaxed but not trashy. Just in case she was being judged. She had no idea who was watching. Soon they entered a building and she felt the air-conditioned coolness wrap around her.

The driver withdrew his arm from hers. "If you'll allow me to remove your—"

"No need. I'll take care of it."

As soon as she heard the voice, Ana's body tensed. She knew that voice. Knew him. And, if she was honest with herself, he was the reason she'd stalled for time outside. She'd told herself that her physical connection to Ty on the night they'd first met hadn't meant anything much. It'd been a one-time thing that was unlikely to happen again.

Just hearing his voice now, she knew that she'd been wrong.

He turned her on. No matter how inappropriate her reaction was, given where they were, what they were doing, or what they were talking about, she couldn't help it. Her body responded to Ty, and even worse, her foolish heart beat faster. "Good day, ma'am," the driver said before she heard the sound of his retreating footsteps.

"No, wait—" she began, then pressed her lips together. What was she going to say? Please don't leave me alone with him?

In the tense silence, she felt his eyes on her. She also smelled him—that same delicious, intoxicating smell that had been all over her in Seattle until she'd scrubbed it off. Ana maintained her cool for several minutes before she was unable to bear it any longer. She raised her hands to remove the blindfold herself.

His hands caught her wrists and gently lowered them to her sides. "I said, I'll take care of it."

In the dark, his voice was even sexier. Harder. Hotter. Ana felt her body respond with a rush of moisture between her thighs. Her nipples tightened underneath her shirt, and she imagined they stood out like little soldiers at attention. Years of faking arousal, and after one meeting this man made her want things she'd prayed she never would.

Smoothly, he lifted the blindfold from her. Ana blinked. She immediately took several steps back and shook out her hair. She looked around her, taking in the classy foyer that broke off into a huge great room and two hallways; anything to keep her gaze from locking with his. Unfortunately, everything she saw—the thick carpet, the dark velvet curtains, the wrought iron banister, and fancy mirror on the wall—only served to make her feel small and out of place. "So, this is it? My home away from home?"

"That's going to be up to you. Want to see it from the outside?"

"Yeah. Just to make sure there are no bars on the windows." She wasn't really joking.

Ty led her back down the steps, going slowly. Her shoes crunched over a graveled driveway until he stopped and turned her around.

Ana sucked in a breath. Wow.

The Belladonna mansion was a classic example of southern architecture in the grand style. The towering white columns on either side of the mahogany doors were taller than her whole house back in Seattle. Above them rose a second story with its own colonnaded veranda.

Ana lost count of the windows. Most likely those

were the bedrooms, situated there by the original builder to take advantage of every breeze.

It almost looked like a movie set. Old magnolia trees with large trunks and huge dark leaves dotted the beautifully landscaped grounds. Flowering shrubs brightened the stone foundation of the mansion. Set well back from it were other, much smaller houses and outbuildings. Ana recognized one as a stable. A horse draped in a blanket was being led out, stepping high, on its way to a white-fenced paddock.

"What do you think?" he asked.

"Nice."

He seemed amused by the one-word answer. "Look between the trees—there, to your right. That's the Potomac."

"How about that." The river seemed wider than she'd imagined, even from this partial view. Its flowing water had a dull gray sparkle.

"I'm glad you're so impressed," he said dryly. "I'll tell you more about the house later. Right now I'll show you to your room, you can have some time to yourself, and then the orientation will begin."

"When do the other women arrive?"

"Soon enough."

Something in his tone made her freeze. "When—?"

"I told you, Ana," he said patiently. "First you talk with Carly. You decide if Belladonna's for you. And then you turn yourself over to me."

"You never said—"

"What's wrong? Afraid to be alone with me?"

She lifted her chin. "That cuts both ways. Aren't you the tiniest bit afraid I'll murder you in your sleep?"

"Not at all."

When she shook her head at the confidence in his voice, he smiled.

"Believe me, Ana, if you and I ever end up alone in my

bedroom together, the last thing I'm going to be doing is sleeping. I'd advise you to remember that. Now, I'll show you to your room."

She was flushed and thrown off, especially as she remembered the power of that erotic dream she'd had about him. "Fine. I could use a shower," she said as she began to follow him.

"Is that an invitation?" he murmured.

She stumbled slightly. Her heart sped out of control. She hadn't meant it as an invitation, but she suddenly wanted to pretend that she had. She wanted to grab Ty's face and kiss him. Hold him. Love him.

And the sad truth was, that word was slipping far too easily into her vocabulary where he was concerned.

Yes, she was hoping to enjoy more time with Ty, but she had to be realistic. Him loving her? It was never, not in a million years, ever going to happen. She was here to do a job, that was all.

Narrowing her eyes, she stopped, kept smiling, loosened her clenched fists, and stepped up to him. "Of course it's an invitation." She trailed her fingers up his chest, then abruptly dropped her hand along with her smile. Her gaze dipped down to his crotch, then back up again. "If you want me to finish what I started in Seattle, take me up on it. This time, I promise I won't stop until your balls are in a box."

"Careful, princess. Remember what happened the last time you went after me. Or do I need to remind you?"

She stiffened at his threat. At the reminder of the way he'd beaten her—with the simple caress of his lips against her. And he knew she was reliving that moment because he lowered his gaze to her mouth and smiled. Then, quietly, gently, he stepped back and started walking again, leading her upstairs. Within minutes, he stopped at a heavy wood door and opened it. "Enjoy your shower," he said before walking away.

She walked into the spacious bedroom, taking in the antique canopy bed, stone fireplace, comfy armchair, and small antique desk topped with a potted orchid. Gingerly, she pulled back the heavy duvet and ran her fingers over the white, crisp sheets that felt heavenly. And then she cursed herself for imagining herself covered in nothing but those sheets . . . and Ty.

Twenty minutes later, the water streaming down on Ana in the shower began to cool. Even so, she was reluctant to leave the marble sanctuary that was bigger than the bedroom she and Gloria had slept in growing up. Doubts assailed her as she thought back over her recent encounter with Ty.

Had she done the right thing by coming here? Did she really think she could hide her attraction to Ty long enough for him to train her? And who the hell was Carly, anyway?

She supposed she was about to find out.

With a sigh, she shut off the water, got out, and dried herself off with a towel. Maybe she should forget all this. Leave and start over yet again. But . . .

Naked, she sat on the bed, her head lowered in defeat.

She had nowhere to go. No place she belonged. That had never been truer now that she'd sold her business and given up her lease in Seattle.

Her eyes stinging with tears she refused to shed, Ana got up to pull on her clothes. As she turned, her gaze caught her reflection in the mirror above her dresser. Quietly, she backed up until her entire body was visible. This far away, she couldn't see the scar on her face, or those on her body, but she knew they were there. With her fingers, she tracked them: the one across her belly that she'd gotten when a rival gang member had jumped her; the ones on her right arm caused by trying to hop over a barbed wire fence; and the worst, the ones across her thighs, the raised, mottled, ugly burn scars from when her own mother had taken a pot of boiling water and thrown it on her to shut her up.

She'd only been four at the time, but she could still remember the pain, physical and emotional. The emotional had been the worst. She hadn't been able to comprehend how her mother, the woman she loved despite the fact that Mama had no kind words for her, could do that to her.

But she understood it now.

Her mother had hated her because every time she'd looked at Ana, she'd seen Ana's father, the man who'd left her. She'd hated Gloria for the same reason, despite the fact that their fathers had been different men.

And she'd hated them both until the day she'd died, naked and filthy and bleeding, left by some john for Ana to find.

Ana was getting dressed when a piece of paper on the floor caught her eye. It looked like it had been slipped under the door when she'd been in the shower.

Hell, someone might've put it there when she'd been examining herself in the mirror. Swiftly, she stepped over it, unlocked her door, and jerked it open.

She looked right and left, but the hallway was empty.

Shutting and locking her door, she stood next to the paper and looked down at it.

Her body trembled. Slowly, she bent, picked it up, and turned it over.

Then, Ana Martin did something she'd never done before. She smiled, a huge, genuine, heartfelt smile of joy that had Eliana Garcia's memories all over it. Until she looked at the photograph more closely. Then her smile dimmed.

It was a picture of Gloria.

She'd grown into a beautiful adult, but she had the same light brown hair and dark eyes she'd always had.

Yet despite what Ty had said, she didn't look happy.

She looked sad. Desperate. As if she was the Disney princess that Ana had always wanted to be—one that urgently needed rescuing.

Ana's heart squeezed with regret. She'd seen that expression on her sister's face before. It was one she'd perpetually worn after she'd come back to Ana, a shadow of the young, happy girl she'd been. As it had turned out, her grandparents had given her a home of privilege, but not safety. While Gloria had always managed to avoid being molested by their mother's "friends"—Ana had seen to that—she hadn't escaped her grandfather's wandering hands.

"I couldn't take it anymore," Gloria had said when she'd shown up back in the Bronx at fourteen. "Not even for all the wealth he provided. I knew you'd protect me. You always protect me."

And so, even though she was only seventeen herself, she had done her best to protect Gloria. She'd brought her into the gang, thinking that safety would come in bigger numbers. And then when she'd realized that she and Gloria would be better off on their own, that they needed to start fresh, she'd tried to leave the gang and take Gloria with her.

Instead, the "jump out" had turned into a bloodbath, with members from the Devil's Crew coming in, guns blazing. Ana had ended up grabbing a fallen gun and shooting her own sister in the shoulder in order to propel her body to the floor, away from lethal shots.

Yes, she had tried her best to protect herself and Gloria, but she'd made one mistake after another. In the end, she'd failed them both.

This time, I won't fail again.

Ana finished dressing.

When Ty knocked on her door, her doubts were gone. She was here. She was staying. And she was finding Gloria.

CHAPTER
FOURTEEN

As Ty led Ana through the Belladonna compound, Ana's nerves got the best of her. Normally at ease with silence, she found herself gesturing to the stone hall and mullioned windows and blurting, "This building is really something. It's so old."

He smiled slightly, as if he understood why she suddenly wanted to make small talk. "The main house is part of an old plantation. Over the years, the property has gone from a timber farm to a tobacco farm to a rich family's vacation estate. We've added on. There's an Olympic-sized pool. An airplane hangar we'll be using to train in. Even a parlor for, uh, soirees. I think that's what they're called."

"I wouldn't know. So do I have to learn to walk with a book on my head? Am I going to play the ignorant gangster girl to your Professor Higgins?"

"I want you to walk with a book on your head? Yes. You'll do it. Remember that when you're having your conversation with Carly, will you?"

Fury swelled within her, but before she could retort, he'd let her into a large office off the foyer and pointed at some fancy phone equipment.

"Sit down and we'll start the conference call."

She snorted in disbelief. "You're joking. So what is this? Your take on some cheesy seventies drama about three women and a guy named Charlie that they never get to meet?"

"Three *hot* women," Ty said mildly. "Don't forget that part of it."

"Even more reason why I don't belong here."

Ty tsked. "Now, now. That's not fair. Throw a challenge out like that and I have no other recourse but to prove exactly how hot I find you, do I?"

"I wasn't challenging you," she said quickly. "But come on. I don't get to see Carly face-to-face?"

"No."

Ana cocked a brow at him. "Do you?"

His face remained impassive. Too impassive. "Yes."

"Then why can't I?"

"Because, Ms. Martin," a seductive female voice spoke from the intercom box on the table beside them. "Ty's proven his loyalty both to me and to Belladonna's cause time and again."

Ana hated the woman instantly. Carly's voice, like Ty's, conveyed money and good breeding, although Ana couldn't place Carly's accent. Unlike Ty's, Carly's also dripped with condescension. Ana's emotions must have been all over her face. When she looked at Ty, he dropped his gaze, the faintest hint of a smile on his lips.

"I thought this agency just opened," Ana replied for lack of anything better to say. "So how could Ty have proven his loyalty already?"

"Ty and I knew each other before this agency was even a thought in my mind."

The depth of that knowledge was obvious from Carly's tone. Fine. The two had fucked one another—so what? Irrationally, it just made Ana madder. "So when I prove my loyalty, I see your face. Must be *un maravillosa* display."

"It is. And yes, when you prove your loyalty, you might get to judge that for yourself. Until then, if you saw my face, I'd have to kill you." Carly waited a beat before her laughter overrode Ty's sigh. "That last part's a joke, by the way."

Ana gritted her teeth. "Not a good one. And I don't like playing games. The blindfold was bad enough, but—"

"Please don't blame the blindfold on me. That was strictly Ty's decision."

She shot a wary glance at Ty. "Does he often do things you haven't approved of?"

"All the time. But I try very hard not to interfere with my employees' freedom of expression, especially when they're bringing in a new operative. Hopefully you'll discover that for yourself."

"I'm not an operative."

"Of course not, Ms. Martin. Not yet. But you will be. And you'll be asked to teach others to be operatives."

"Will I be asked, or am I being asked?"

"This one's slippery, isn't she, Ty?"

"Not really," he said. His voice was neutral but his implication clear, at least to Ana—that he'd managed to grab hold of her at least once. She glared at him and he raised his brows at her as if to ask: What?

Ana suddenly felt like a puppet being yanked between two very careless kids. "I was told I was being offered a job. I wasn't aware I had to interview for it. If that's the case, then *olvídese esto*."

"Excuse me?" Carly asked.

"Forget this," Ty clarified.

"Oh. Well, you are being offered a job, Ms. Martin. If you'll sit down, I'll tell you the basics and you can ask questions from there. How does that sound?"

It sounded like she could see her, Ana thought. She glanced around but saw no signs of cameras. She glanced at Ty, hesitated, and then finally, remembering Gloria's photo in her bag, slowly sat in one of the wing chairs beside the table. Ty, she noted, remained standing.

"Go ahead," Ana said to the box.

"A wealthy Colombian's wife and daughter have been taken captive by a cult—Salvation's Crossing. For various reasons, the FBI will not intervene at this time. Mr. Montes has asked Belladonna to take the case and go where the FBI refuses to. Your mission will be to infiltrate the cult and remove Ramona and Becky Montes from their grasp."

So all this was about a man looking for his wife and child? Not that she didn't understand the desperate need to be reunited with one's family, but . . .

"How do you know this man's wife and child didn't leave on their own? How do you know that the thing they have to fear most isn't Montes himself?"

"We've done our homework, Ms. Garcia. Ty, show her the photos of the Montes women."

He reached for a folder and slid out several photos, enlargements from smartphone snapshots, on the blurry side. Ana studied the photos and gave him a dubious look. She mouthed a reply for his benefit.

Best you can do? Are you kidding?

Ty shrugged and returned the photos to the folder as Carly continued.

"You don't need to worry about Mr. Montes's truthfulness or intentions."

"And I'm just supposed to take your word for it?"

"Considering that between the two of us, Ty and I have twenty-five years of covert ops experience—yes."

"Uh-huh," Ana said in a voice edged with disbelief. "You two are badass spies. So what makes you think I can get some rich woman out of a cult when you can't? I'm a former gang member and barista. Not a cult member."

"You're Hispanic. And Salvation's Crossing is publicly known as an outreach group dedicated to promoting Hispanic culture and diversity. But that's a false front. Instead, the group preys on illegal immigrants and holds them at a compound in a California valley, using the members for slave labor, and even selling people on the black market."

Again, bad shit, but did Carly really think her revelation was going to shock her? After all she'd seen? Ana fought growing frustration. "Are Mrs. Montes and her daughter in the U.S. illegally?"

When she answered, Carly's voice echoed the frustration Ana was feeling.

"It doesn't matter if she is or she isn't. Do you understand the concepts of captivity and cults? Or are you not as smart as Téa said you were?"

Ana's first instinct was to tell Carly to go take a flying leap off a tall building, but she didn't. Asking questions about things that didn't make sense was one thing, but she couldn't forget she was here because of Gloria. And Téa.

"I still see nothing I can bring to the table here," Ana snapped. "Cut the bullshit and tell me what you want from me."

Carly let out a sharp laugh. "She *is* a hothead, Ty. You'll train her on that, I take it?"

"Among other things," Ty said.

Ana folded her arms across her chest. Yes, she wanted info on Gloria, wanted to know for certain her sister was happy or help her become so, but exactly why she'd been recruited just wasn't clear. "You just said it yourself. Maybe I'm stupid when it comes to cults. So why do you want me?"

Carly continued smoothly. "There are certain similarities between cults and gangs. Both depend on a culture of fear that is covered up by a false sense of family and belonging. Both types of organizations exploit their members, often in heinously cruel ways. Because you belonged to a Hispanic gang, you bring an insider's skill set to this operation."

Something shook loose inside Ana. She sucked at the air, suddenly unable to breathe as memories of gang life pounced on her consciousness. She gave time for the oxygen to settle in her system before answering. So cults and gangs were related. Made sense.

But why use a former gang member to go in? Why wouldn't the U.S. government get the rich Colombian's wife out of the cult?

"Is the FBI afraid of another Waco?" she asked, naming a failed FBI raid on a cult that had occurred many years in the past. "Are they scared they'll screw up the rescue?"

"We have our suspicions as to why the FBI refuses to rescue Mrs. Montes. Bad press might be part of it," Carly conceded. "The links to the Crossing are weak—there's not much of a paper trail for the FBI to lean on. In addition, we suspect the FBI may be reluctant to infiltrate in case something goes wrong. This is an election year, and it fears the ramifications of targeting a minority group."

"So the FBI is being pussy-whipped by the politicians," she snapped out.

Next to her, Ty snorted again.

"An interesting term. Not one I'd use, but still . . . Now that you know more and understand what's at stake for innocent people, will you join Belladonna?"

"I—I don't know," Ana hedged. "What you want of me doesn't make sense. And when things don't make sense—"

Ty interrupted. "Carly, for God's sake, she's not buying any of this and I for one don't want to spend the next few hours talking in circles. You need to tell her."

"Tell me what?" Ana focused her attention on Ty.

"Why you're our best bet for infiltrating the cult."

Something sunk within her stomach. "Spill it," she demanded.

"You won't want to hear it," Carly responded.

"Just fucking tell me!"

"Temper, temper," Carly cooed.

If Ana could punch the woman, she would. Instead, she tensed her whole body, hands clenched into fists, glaring at Ty as the woman's voice continued to penetrate the room.

"Ana, all the reasons we gave you for wanting you to join Belladonna are true. You have what we want— street smarts, knowledge of the Hispanic culture, an understanding of the mentality of a cult, and above all, high intelligence. But we also want you because you will be driven to do your absolute best for us. Even if training wipes you out, frustrates you, drives you nearly insane, you will persevere."

"Why would I?" she asked.

Silence suffused the room. Ty's gaze never wavered from hers.

Then Carly spoke. "Because the cult has your sister."

CHAPTER FIFTEEN

Ana slowly turned toward Ty. "You told me she was healthy and happy. You lying piece of shit!" She moved toward him and Ty caught her with an arm around her waist and a hand around her wrists so she couldn't hit him. As she struggled, he nearly groaned at the feel of her body against his.

"I told you," he gritted out. "I don't lie."

"Oh, so she's a prisoner of a cult and that's a good thing?"

"She's using an assumed name. Helena Esperanza. That's why you haven't been able to find anything about her. Even if you search for her now, you won't find much. But you'll find a few articles about Salvation's Crossing that mention her name. From everything we know, your sister is with the cult of her own free will."

"Right," she spat. "Just like Mrs. Montes, huh?"

"That's what we need to confirm." Ty released her, not missing how quickly Ana backed away. She was breathing hard. They both were. And he'd be a fool not to recognize that fear of her response to him was driving her retreat almost as much as anger was. Momentarily, his mind shot back to that night and the way she'd looked while she'd been masturbating. The way she'd looked when he'd imagined himself going down on her.

"And what if Gloria or Mrs. Montes have been brainwashed?"

"It depends. Were you brainwashed when you were with the gang? Were you in danger before you tried to jump out?" He knew she'd been both on some level, but he was curious what she'd say. If she'd admit it. If she was in denial about her past, as determined to punish herself for the choices she'd made as he suspected she was.

She hesitated, as if reluctant to make excuses for herself. "Some would say I was brainwashed. Maybe not from my gang, directly, but—"

She'd walked the line, both admitting more than he'd expected and taking responsibility for her choices all at the same time. "But did you need saving?" he pushed.

"I wanted it," she whispered, not just surprising him now but shocking him. "Whether I needed it, who knows? But if Gloria's brainwashed, if what you say about this cult is true, then what?"

"Then we rescue her," he said simply.

"I'm sure it'll be that easy," she sneered. "The prince charging up on his white steed rescues the damsel in distress. Too bad you're more like the devil."

He frowned at her. Prince. Devil. The words echoed in his brain. Reformed.

He suddenly pictured himself and Ana, just the way he'd imagined them when they'd been "getting it on," so to speak—with her wearing a thin T-shirt and him with his light brown hair and blue eyes. Fragments of a conversation between them that had never actually happened filtered through his mind.

I used to read to my sister, Naomi, at bedtime. Her favorite fairy tale was Sleeping Beauty. *Remember I said you weren't living, but waiting? I call you princess because you're asleep. You don't know how beautiful you are. How much the world needs you. And I want to be the man who kisses you and wakes you up.*

So you see yourself as a prince?

No, I'm no prince . . . In fact, I'm more devil than anything.

He knew they'd never actually had that conversation outside of his own mind in Seattle, but the insult she'd just delivered . . .

Was it possible he'd somehow inserted himself in her mind, the same way he'd done with Bobbie Hernandez? He frowned, unsure what to think. "What did you just say?"

"I said, you make it sound so easy."

"No. Not that part. That part about me being more devil than prince."

Her eyes widened and he swore he heard her heart start beating faster. Briefly, she glanced at the intercom, as if more embarrassed by the fact that Carly could hear them than by his actual question. Of course, Carly, likely intrigued by the turn of the conversation, remained silent.

Ana's expression cleared and she shook her head. "You heard me. Did I insult you?"

He was tempted then. Tempted to try to read her mind. To see if what he thought was impossible was actually true. But he resisted. A man, he thought. To her, I'm just a man. Just another human. It wasn't true, but he wanted it to be. So he didn't try to read her mind. Instead, he shrugged. "Look," he said. "I never said rescuing anyone would be easy. Far from it. Salvation's Crossing is heavily guarded. Even so, if I'm the devil, I'm one that's going to help you find your sister. If she needs help, then you have the power to help her. The question is, will you?"

"What choice do I have? You waited to tell me what you know because you needed to hold something over me. You've been manipulating me since the second I met you."

"Did it work? Because if it has, once you're done with

your temper tantrum, you might want to start reading the information we have on Salvation's Crossing. Given your history, I think you'll find the reading material quite interesting."

"Because Gloria's there?"

At her question, Ty hesitated then looked at the intercom that had remained noticeably silent. As if she knew it, as if she could see him waiting for her to speak, Carly said, "Gloria's there with other members of Primos Sangre. That includes the cult's leader, Miguel Salvador. You knew him as Miguel Santos."

Stunned, Ana stumbled slightly and caught herself on the table as images of Miguel's face flashed before her. "M—Miguel? The leader of a cult?"

"That's right," Carly said.

Automatically, Ana shook her head. Miguel had been a survivor. He'd done bad things to protect himself— and protect Ana—but he'd always been her friend. He'd known how much Gloria meant to Ana. How much Ana wanted a better life for her sister. He'd even sworn to watch over her when Ana was taken away. "You must be mistaken."

This time, Ty answered. "He's the acknowledged leader of the group even though he rarely makes public appearances. Occasionally, he meets with investors. Solicits funds. I've tried to meet with him myself, posing as an investor who shares the group's mission to support Hispanic rights. So far, he hasn't taken the bait."

When she remained silent, he walked up to her. Grasped her chin and tilted her face up so he could stare into her eyes.

"You want to know why we chose you to help us with this mission, Ana? It's because you're a survivor. You did what you had to in order to survive, and when it comes to protecting your sister, you'll do the same. Another reason? The gang you belonged to has grown. And while you might have walked away from it and never looked back, the same isn't true for the rest of its former members."

"You're saying Primos Sangre joined Salvation's Crossing?"

"I'm saying Primos Sangre *is* Salvation's Crossing. It's being led by a man you know. A man you befriended. A man you once had an intimate relationship with."

She jerked her chin out of his grasp and shook her head as she backed away. "Who gives you your intel? Because whoever it is sucks."

"You're denying you once had a relationship with Miguel Santos?"

"I didn't have a relationship with him. He fucked me. Once. To jump me into the gang."

Ty shrugged, seemingly unconcerned by Ana's revelation, not giving away whether he'd known that little fact or not. "Let me ask you this. The fact that he only fucked you *once*. Was that his choice or yours?"

"What—what do you mean?"

"I mean, I have reason to believe he cares for you. Deeply. That if you'd let him, he'd have fucked you far more than once."

Her eyes flickered with the knowledge that he was right. That Miguel had loved her. That he would have, if Ana had been interested, wanted more from her than friendship.

Belladonna wants to whore me out, she thought. And even though she'd been fully prepared for that possibility, somehow this all seemed like a betrayal on Ty's part.

To torture herself, Ana played back that moment he'd kissed her, not in a dream but for real, when they'd been wrestling in her café. He'd kissed her twice, and though they'd been fighting and he'd simply been proving his power over her, that kiss . . . that kiss had *felt* real.

It had made her feel alive, in a way she hadn't felt in her entire life. And as much as she wanted to deny it, she'd wanted him to kiss her again. And she'd wanted to kiss him back.

You're a fool. You always have been and you always will be. This man was never interested in you for himself. He just wants you to spread your legs for someone else.

He knows, just like you do, that you did it once. And he knows that you'll do it again.

But even with that knowledge, she couldn't go down like this. Couldn't let him see how devastated she was. She wanted to cry. Instead, she simply turned on her heel and left.

"She took that better than I expected," Carly said over the intercom.

Ty cursed. "Life's always thrown her shit. Maybe she's simply used to it. Little does she know the worst is yet to come."

"You sound upset by that fact."

"Of course I'm upset," Ty gritted out. "She doesn't deserve this. None of it. Least of all the games we're playing with her."

"Whether she deserves it or not, we can't just blurt out what's really going on here. We decided the best strategy was to get the women here, assess their talents, and evaluate what they're willing to do—all before we drop the mother of all bombs—that you and Peter are vampires and, oh yes, by the way, will you help us prove Salvation's Crossing is turning humans into vampires and trafficking in human blood slaves?"

Pacing, Ty swept his hands through his hair. "You

don't have to remind me why we're doing what we're doing, Carly."

"No? Because it certainly sounds like you need to be reminded. It sounds, God forbid, like you're getting soft."

"Soft? You think? I almost bled a homeless man dry; the fact that I left him alive didn't matter. He still died because of me. Believe me, I'm not going soft."

She hesitated for a moment, but when she spoke, her voice was gentler. "You fucked up, Ty. You caught the attention of two vampires and one was able to read your mind. Bad luck for us, but as far as the homeless man is concerned? You didn't kill him. They did."

"He was killed because of me. Same difference." He closed his eyes. "Just like you think Ben was killed because of me. Because he was trying to help Peter and me escape the Rogues. You do think that, right? And if that's the case, then I'm just as much responsible for the homeless man's death as I am for Ben's."

This time Carly's lapse into silence was longer. He pictured her stricken face—a sickly white, her features pinched, grief and anger flashing in her eyes because of the way Ty had mentioned Ben, a man who had been Carly's lover. But when she spoke, her voice was measured and controlled. "We don't know if Ben's dead. Even if he is, I wouldn't blame you for that, Ty. He was trying to escape, too, remember? He was just in the wrong place at the wrong time. Just like you and Peter. Just like that homeless man. But I'm not going to argue with you. Right now, we need to focus. Ana knows enough. She knows we need her to get into Salvation's Crossing. She knows about Ramona and Becky Montes. She'll learn the rest later."

"Right. The rest. Like the fact that the Rogues turned humans into vampires for the FBI? And that even though the FBI wants those Rogues dead now, it also wants to find a way to continue the Turning Program? God, everyone wants a part of the immortal pie. But what they can't know is that it sucks. It *sucks* being a vampire!" he roared as he swept a table free of books.

The silence in the room was deafening. Then Carly laughed. Not one of the mocking, arrogant laughs that he hated, but a genuine, I'm-trying-to-stifle-it-but-I-can't laugh.

And to his shock, after hearing his own words echo around him, Ty laughed, too.

"Fuck," he said when he could finally catch his breath. "I can't believe I actually said that."

"Screamed it at the top of your lungs, more like it. Let's hope Ana didn't hear you. Or maybe that was the point. You've never liked deception, not when it comes to someone you consider an ally. If that's going to be a problem . . . if you feel it's imperative that you tell Ana about vampires now . . . then maybe you should. She's going to learn it soon, after all, and—"

"No," Ty said tiredly. "You're right. It's too much to spring on her at once. We need her invested in Belladonna first. Committed to doing whatever it takes to find her sister. Only then can we tell her."

"You're that sure she'll fall into line? Because proving that she's committed to doing whatever it takes? That's not going to be easy."

"We need her," Ty said.

"We need her in control," Carly corrected. "But I suppose if anyone can tame her, you can. You've had to work to control your wild side, too. As a human and a vampire. Your tirade a few minutes ago aside, Ty, I want you to know I have confidence in you. You'll be able to get her where she needs to go. So what now?"

"Now, we test her. Train her. And hope that in two weeks, she'll be ready to attend that fund-raiser with me and, more important, get us inside Salvation's Crossing."

Twenty minutes later, Ty knocked on Ana's door then entered without waiting for her to give him permission.

She sat cross-legged on the bed, arms folded over her chest, glaring at him.

She probably hated him right about now, assuming she hadn't already felt that way before. He couldn't blame her, but he couldn't afford to go easy on her, either.

"Have you made a decision?" Ty asked Ana.

"About whether I'm going to join Belladonna or whether I'm willing to fuck Miguel in the process?" she snorted. "I don't have a choice."

"We all have choices. And I never said you have to actually fuck him."

She shot him a look of disbelief and he scowled darkly. "I'm not saying it's not a possibility, but do you think I want that? After the way I kissed you? The way you almost kissed me back?"

Her eyes widened. "I didn't—" she whispered.

He leaned down, getting right in her face. "You're attracted to me. Just as attracted as I am to you. And believe it or not, I'm not dragging you into this situation for fun, Ana, but because something very important needs doing. We're giving you options. You have a choice whether to be involved in all this. And you'll obviously have a choice if and when it comes to . . . that. Doesn't mean you'll like it and it doesn't mean I will, either. Never think that. Never think that anything I ask of you, I ask lightly."

Her eyes were even wider now and she looked away. "I obviously have a history of making the wrong choices. I've been trying to change that. I thought—I thought I was going to be able to rewrite my past, but . . ." She shrugged. "I can't change my past. Not until I can be certain Gloria has moved past it herself."

He straightened, giving her breathing room so she'd look at him again. "That's why you want to find your sister so badly? So you can write her off as happy and healthy, and in doing so, write off your past? Or how did you put it—*rewrite* your past?" So he'd been right about her tendency toward denial; he just hadn't realized she was conscious of it, as well. "No one can rewrite the past, Ana. We have to face it. Accept it. Move on."

At his words, his conscience tingled.

Was he being a hypocrite, telling her that? No, he reassured himself. He wasn't denying he was a vampire. He just accepted the fact that being a walking science experiment wasn't something he wanted. That didn't mean he was in denial. Ana, however, still had her entire future in front of her. She just needed to accept what had happened in her past, move on, and stop caring more about her sister's well-being than her own. Of course, he couldn't tell her any of that because it was her connection and her loyalty to her sister that they were counting on for this mission.

"Easy thing to say when you obviously grew up on easy street," she retorted.

"And you know that how?"

"Your clothes. Your accent. You reek of old money. Why? Am I wrong?"

He pressed his lips together. "No. You're not wrong about my privileged childhood. But you think that made my life easy?" He shrugged. "You're obviously not as smart as Carly and I gave you credit for."

"Obviously not. Because I have made my decision. I'm going to work with Belladonna. And I'm going to save my sister," she said. "No matter what it takes."

So it was done, Ty thought. Ana Martin had agreed to work for Belladonna, only she had no idea what they were going to ask of her.

Just like she had no idea what Ty was.

Soon she would.

And when she did, she'd look at him differently, he knew.

He angered her now. Frustrated her. Annoyed her. Confused her.

But despite all that, she wanted him. Craved him, just like he craved her.

Soon, she'd crave nothing but getting as far away from him as possible. All he could do was enjoy what little time he had left with her.

As if she sensed what he was thinking, she narrowed her eyes on him suspiciously. He didn't smile. Didn't give away by word or expression anything that he was thinking. But his gaze took her in. Every detail. His nostrils took in her scent. His skin absorbed the thrumming of her pulse as his ears heard the rush of her blood through her veins. No, he didn't react to her suspicions, but like an animal being stalked by a predator, she stiffened, as if she could read his thoughts.

Then again, she probably just noticed the stiffness of his erection, something he wasn't bothering to hide. Why should he? He was perpetually hard whenever he was around her. If he tried covering it up, he'd spend his time doing nothing else.

She cleared her throat and spoke first, which was exactly what he wanted. She already held too much power over him. It was best he didn't give up any more to her.

"So, what now?"

"In two weeks, your old friend Miguel will be making a very rare public appearance at the fund-raiser for the Hispanic Community Alliance. It's a black-tie affair. We're going to attend the fund-raiser together and re-

mind Miguel what made him fall in love with you in the
first place."

"What's that? I was eleven when we met, fourteen
when I joined the gang. I wasn't any more of a femme
fatale then than I am now."

"No matter. He loved you for your strength. Your
bravado. Your determination to survive. That's still an
inherent part of you. In preparation for this fund-raiser
and your overall mission, however, we're going to train
you in a variety of other things. Weapons. Surveillance.
Social etiquette. Even what shoes to wear with what
dress."

She cocked a snotty brow. "So you match shoes and
dresses. Tell me, what's your go-to outfit?"

He had the insane urge to twirl just to make her smile,
but he didn't. Instead, he thought of the menagerie that
was soon going to invade the Belladonna compound
and shot her a sympathetic glance. "Afraid fashion's not
my expertise. For that, we're bringing in the big guns—
the rest of the team. You'll meet them in a few days. For
now, however, you're mine."

CHAPTER SIXTEEN

When Ana opened her eyes, it was still dark outside. She stretched, turned onto her side, then froze when she saw the man sitting in the chair beside her bed.

It was Ty. Her dream Ty, with light hair and blue eyes.

Slowly, she sat up. A sense of unease passed through her only to be chased away by the electric thrum of excitement. She licked her lips, and his eyes narrowed and followed the path her tongue took. Seeing the heat in his gaze caused a conflagration to spread throughout her body.

He smiled slightly, but there was nothing humorous in his expression. Instead, he looked like the very devil he'd previously admitted to being. "Be careful about teasing me, Ana," he said, his words edged with a dark intent that made her shiver. "I'm barely hanging on to my control as it is."

Then give it up. A sense of self-preservation stopped her from voicing the thought. She should take his warning seriously. Yes, some crazy part of her wanted to prod him until his control shattered, wanted to revel in the knowledge that she got so deeply under his skin. But was she really ready for that? In their last dream encounter, he'd been gentle. Giving more than he took. How would she react if he took his fill of her? If he took without asking? Would his urgency call forth her fear and ugly memories? Unwilling to take that chance, she pulled the sheet tighter around herself and asked, "Why are you back? Why now?"

She didn't clarify what she meant, but she could tell he already knew. Why hadn't he visited her dreams since that one time in Seattle?

"I've been fighting it. Fighting you. Fighting this. Just like you have. But something's changed. You want me tonight. You need me. So tell me. Do I stay or do I go?"

Ana bit her lip, praying for guidance. Sure, this was a dream, but Ty had already invaded her waking hours. Inviting him to be intimate with her, even if in her dreams, could only bring trouble.

But it would also bring intense pleasure.

Pleasure she'd experienced just one time before. Pleasure she wanted to experience again.

As Ty stood before her, he looked right but . . . not right. She'd gotten used to seeing him with dark hair and eyes, and the difference in his physical appearance emphasized that he wasn't real.

So if he isn't real, a voice tempted her, it doesn't matter what you do together. No one will know. Hell, *he* won't even know. You might never get this chance again. Remember what they're asking of you. Remember why you're doing it. Take this for yourself.

Take him.

"I want to take you," she blurted out, her chin held high. "I want you to lie on your back and let me do whatever I want to you. Will you do that?"

He held out his hand. With a small frown, she slipped her hand in his. He pulled her to her feet but didn't kiss her as she'd expected. Instead, he took her place on her bed.

Lying back on the crisp white sheets, he folded his hands behind his head so his biceps bulged and his abs rippled. The light dusting of hair on his chest arrowed down his torso and disappeared into the waistband of his sleep pants. At his groin, his cock pushed against the cotton seam as if straining to reach her, and her mouth went dry at the evidence of his girth. As she continued to watch, his hips arched, tempting her to action.

Her gaze shot back to his face. She expected him to be smiling again. Maybe even watching her with an arrogant look of triumph. Instead, he looked hungry. Famished. Ready to break down and beg if she didn't touch him.

She knew exactly how he felt.

With more bravado than actual confidence, she stepped closer to him and pressed her palm against his chest. The strong thud of his heartbeat echoed the throbbing need between her legs. A slight hiss escaped him as her hand made contact. "Yes," he groaned. "Touch me. Please."

"I—I am touching you," she whispered.

"Touch me with both hands. With your mouth. With your body. I need you, Ana. I need you so much."

The naked vulnerability of his pleas made her breath catch. *He* needed *her*?

"Yes, I need you," he said, making her wonder if she'd voiced her thoughts or he'd somehow read her mind. "And once we begin training, once you learn more about your mission, things are going to change. The way you feel about me is going to change."

"Why? Are you going to be mean to me?" She pouted, skimming a nail across his nipple as if to punish him for any future transgressions against her.

He jerked. "I'm going to push you, and you're not going to like being pushed. But more than that, you're going to see me for who I really am. What I really am. And you're not going to want me any longer. Not the way I want you."

Instinctively, she pulled back at his pain-filled words. She had no idea what he meant, but when she opened her mouth to question him, he shook his head wildly. "Don't ask me to explain because I can't. Just know that I want you and need you, Ana. Here. Now. I need you to take me, just like you said. Do what you want to me. Do anything. Do everything."

Anything. Everything.

Most of the time, sex had always been about what someone else wanted to take from her. On the rarest of occasions, it had been about what she'd been willing to give up. She'd never thought of sex in terms of taking for herself. But now here was Ty, every luscious inch of him, begging her to do just that.

Her fears. Her insecurities. Her questions about what he'd said. They all disappeared as a maelstrom of desire overtook her. For once, she was in charge. For once, she had the power to take what she wanted.

She wanted him. She wanted to take from him.

Anything. Everything.

And she was going to.

Faster than she'd ever thought possible, she stripped them both naked. His gaze devoured her bare flesh, but he kept his hands pinned behind his head, giving her total control.

"Your fangs," she said suddenly. "You had fangs before."

He was trembling. Closing his eyes, he swallowed hard. "I don't have to use them again. I don't have to drink your blood."

She remembered the sensations of fear that had overtaken her when he'd drunk from her before. How quickly that fear had been dispelled by fascination, then acquiescence, then mind-boggling pleasure. She shook her head. "I want you to. I want you to drink my blood, but not from my throat."

His brows crinkled with confusion. "Then where?

Where do you want me to drink from you?" he croaked out.

"Anywhere I tell you to," she said before climbing on top of him, flesh to flesh.

Heart to heart.

Ty moaned with delirious pleasure as Ana pressed her breasts against him, opened her thighs, and, with one soft, feminine hand guiding him, pressed his cock inside her.

He slipped in, her folds instantly closing around the head of his dick. Slick. Tight. A velvet glove that had been warmed by a fire.

Above him, her eyes were tightly closed and her head was thrown back in a paroxysm of agony, but it was pleasure that had her thighs clasping him tighter and her core taking him deeper. Bit by bit, she engulfed him while her fingers gripped his biceps, the bite of her nails a sweet sting that made his gaze lock on her throat in sudden hunger.

She wanted him to bite her again. She'd said so herself. But she hadn't told him where, and suddenly he was cataloguing all the wonderful possibilities in his mind. Her throat. Her breasts. Her ass. The warm crease of her thigh.

Any and all would be nirvana, but even as his mind spun with the memory of how sweet her blood tasted, the feel of her body fully enveloping his made him groan. He was buried to the hilt inside her. Right now, this was what he wanted. This was enough.

It was everything.

As if she could read his mind, her eyes flew open and she began pumping him inside her, rising and falling, her hips undulating with ever-increasing speed, swirling and circling him like a joystick under her complete command. One made solely for her pleasure. And that was fine with him.

A soft sheen of sweat coated her body, making her skin glisten. He reared up, anxious to have one of her tight berry-red nipples on his tongue. When it filled his mouth, he sucked softly, then harder, and without conscious thought he began pumping his hips up, urging her to greater speed and stronger thrusts, taking control away from her without quite meaning to.

She gave it to him, wrapping her arms around his head and pulling him closer, feeding him more of her breast. Her hitching breaths and soft moans were sweet music to his ears, and, God, it was glorious—the sound of her, the feel of her. The taste. The smell. It surpassed anything he'd ever experienced as a mere human and made him feel like the damn luckiest vampire to ever exist.

She was the best sex he'd ever had.

"Now," she moaned. "Bite me. Take blood from my breast," she begged.

At her plea, Ty felt himself swelling inside her. He could feel his balls tightening with his impending release. He was going to come and he wanted to take her with him. Every single way she'd let him, he wanted to take her.

When her orgasm started and he could feel her vaginal muscles fluttering around him, he gave her what she wanted, plunging his fangs into the soft upper globe of her breast. She screamed, the sound rife with skyrocketing pleasure, and the gush of her blood mimicked the gush of his semen as it burst out of him and into her.

Liquid pleasure. Their life's essence. From her to him and then back again.

Nothing had ever been so wonderful and yet so sad. The intense pleasure and emotions that swirled through him quickly receded and were replaced with the cold, brutal truth.

When his eyes snapped open, he cursed.

She was gone. His arms empty.

Once again, the best moments of his life had been a dream.

And no matter how hard he tried, no matter how much he wanted it, further sleep eluded him, taunting him with everything he could never have.

CHAPTER
SEVENTEEN

Ana was going to kill Ty. Somehow, she was going to end his miserable life in exchange for all the sadistic hell he'd been putting her through. It had been seven days since she'd arrived at the Belladonna compound and no sooner had she had her first team meeting with Carly than Ty had begun her training. At least, that's what he maintained he was doing. Only it felt more like torture.

Not that she'd ever cop to that. She'd die before she asked him for mercy.

And based on how she felt at the moment, death wasn't too far off.

Her recent shower had done little to relieve her sore muscles. She supposed that when one had bruises upon cuts upon sprains, only heavy-duty pharmaceuticals could bring relief, but she wasn't allowed those. No, she had to make do with ibuprofen because otherwise her senses might be muddled and her reactions slowed. And then what kind of pseudo agent would she be?

What she wouldn't give right now to have her senses muddled with tequila and fresh lime juice on ice.

With a wince, she pulled on some clean clothes before face-planting herself on her bed. God, it felt so good to lie down. To clear her mind of countersurveillance tactics and proper gun-handling techniques and self-defense moves and body-language clues and all the other shit that Ty had been shoving down her throat.

According to him, when the rest of the team arrived she'd be learning social etiquette. How to walk. How to talk. What to wear. What wine to pair with what food.

Truth be told, she dreaded charm school FBI-style far more than her next training session with Ty.

Truth *really* be told, she'd enjoyed every brutal minute of her time with Ty and feared the moment their solitude would end. True, their time together had been as far from romantic as one could get. No matter how the air sizzled when they were in the same room, no matter how her skin sparked when they touched, Ty had kept things purely businesslike once her training had begun. But she'd still loved every second of it.

He pushed her, physically and mentally. He pissed her off and sometimes he made her want to cry, although she never did, at least not outside the privacy of her own room. But he also treated her with respect. As someone worthy of being taught. As someone who was going to accomplish great things, like . . . saving her sister and other innocent women and children from a cult.

And that's why, even though part of her really, really wanted to kill Ty, she was never late for training and more times than not, fell asleep smiling because she was thinking of him.

So far, she hadn't dreamed of him again. Not since the dream she'd had right after her arrival at Belladonna. But that just made her hunger for him during the day all the more unbearable.

When a knock sounded on her door, she mentally groaned and stayed silent, hoping her visitor would take the hint and go away. No such luck.

"Ana. It's Ty. Meet me in the airplane hangar in ten. We're going to work on your knife-throwing skills."

She smiled in spite of herself. Yes, her time spent with Ty was as far from romantic as one could get. But it was certainly turning out to be fun.

An hour later, after Ana had thrown knife after knife at dummy targets while Ty stayed by her side, giving her tips on aiming and technique, she accompanied him to Belladonna's giant lap pool. She scanned the area around it before turning to Ty. "I don't have a swimsuit."

To her surprise, he shook his head. "You don't need one. Just take off your clothes and get in."

"Excuse me?" Ana stared at Ty as if he'd lost his mind.

More like he thought she'd lost hers.

"You heard me," he said, his expression blank. Almost cold. Completely the opposite of the subdued yet friendly one he'd been wearing ever since she'd first arrived. "I said take off your clothes and get in the pool."

Maybe this was some kind of training in itself, she thought. Gamely, she asked, "And why would I do that?"

"Because staying alive on these missions is about doing whatever needs to be done."

Okay, she was beginning to understand where this was going. Still, that didn't mean she was just going to prance around nude in front of him simply because he demanded it. "Except I don't have to strip naked at the moment. If I need to, I will."

"No, you'll hesitate, just like you're doing now. You'll search for an alternative."

"I won't."

"Prove it."

He was still looking at her with that cold expression. As if what he was asking was completely reasonable. As if he'd feel absolutely nothing if she stripped naked in front of him right now.

She felt a surge of disappointment at that.

One by one, she stripped off each article of clothing she wore. And even though this wasn't about him getting his rocks off, even though he didn't seem to care that she was naked and vulnerable in front of him, that didn't mean he took any pity on her. He took his time looking at her, making sure he started at the top of her head, stopping and paying particular attention to her key parts—her throat, her breasts, her flat stomach, and the mound between her legs.

As he did, Ana felt his gaze like a caress.

And to her shame, she trembled.

She yearned.

She wanted him naked. She wanted him pressed against her.

She wanted him inside her.

And she wanted to urge him to give her more.

More. More. More.

Until the world disappeared and nothing existed for either of them but the pleasure of being in each other's arms.

As Ty admired the beauty of Ana's body, he tried to remain detached. He told himself he was doing this merely as part of her training, which she'd been excelling at. She was smart, hardworking, an eager pupil. He'd admired and respected her before, but those feelings had only grown. He'd pushed her, but he'd also kept things strictly friendly between them. Not just for her peace of mind, but his own. It was hard enough to wrestle with her and gaze into her eyes without losing his shaky grip on control; if he reacted to the desire he saw in her eyes, he was afraid he'd have her stripped and nailed to the floor before either one of them could blink.

But a half hour ago, when he'd been watching her gleefully throw knives at man-shaped targets, he'd realized he wasn't doing her any favors. By not forcing her to deal with her own insecurities or the possibility of sexually charged situations, he could very well be placing her life in danger when she was in the field.

What he'd said was true—if for whatever reason she needed to strip buck naked at a moment's notice on a mission—she had to be able to do it without hesitation. Fear, modesty, insecurity—none of it could get in the way.

Now, as he stared at her naked body, detachment and practicality and training were the farthest things from his mind.

He'd seen her like this before, and not just on his surveillance equipment. He'd seen her exactly the way she looked now, down to the mole next to her belly button, when they'd both been naked and touching each other. He'd licked that mole when he'd paused while going down on her to look up at her face. She looked exactly the way she had in the dreams he'd had of the two of them. The damn dreams that he couldn't get out of his head.

But he had to. And he certainly couldn't dwell on his suspicion that she might be sharing the sexual dreams with him. So he continued his inspection of her, moving from the best parts of her body to the worst—the burn scars across her thighs.

He knew how she'd gotten them and if her mother wasn't already dead, he'd kill her himself. And it had nothing to do with his being a vampire. Even if he'd been fully human, he'd have felt the same way.

Maybe he'd spent too much time staring at her scars or maybe she read his mind, because she snapped, "Don't pity me."

His gaze locked on hers. "Why would I?" he asked, careful how he chose his words. Because the truth was he did pity her, but no more than he pitied himself. "You're a survivor. I admire you." And *that* was the honest truth. "Now, show me how well you can swim."

With a muttered curse, she jumped into the pool and proceeded to do one lap after another. Eventually, after what seemed like hours but was probably only twenty minutes, he called out, "That's it. You can get out and dress."

Then he took a deep breath, vowing to hang on to his control long enough to do what he had to do next.

Ty had his back turned to her and appeared to be reviewing paperwork. Relieved, Ana climbed out of the pool. Her muscles were shaking with exhaustion and she shivered with cold. Hurrying, she dried off, then started yanking her clothes back on.

She'd just zipped her pants when Ty grabbed her by her arms, held her body against his chest for a brief moment, then backed her up against the wall. Even with their clothes between them, she was acutely aware of his chest sliding against her breasts. And how the sensation made her shiver with pleasure even as she shook with fury.

He pressed his mouth against her ear. "You're too easy," he complained. "I told you to never let down your guard around me. Don't turn your back on your enemy, especially when you're vulnerable. You have to be aware at every moment or you risk being overtaken."

"Fuck you."

He smiled faintly. "You also have to be able to stay calm when someone touches you sexually. You can't let the past control you. You have to accept it and control it, so you can manage the situation and come out on top. No pun intended."

Despite his attempt at humor, she struggled in his grip, the harsh brick of the building scratching her hands where he held them against the wall.

"I'm a threat to you. I want to take you down, Ana. What can you do to get away?"

"You're bigger than me. Stronger. I don't know what to do," she snapped out. She twisted, hitching her hips, pulling against Ty's hold. Nothing.

"I'm not giving you that answer. Figure out how to get away from me on your own."

She would have kneed him in the nuts, but Ty clearly anticipated that move since his legs were firmly between hers. No way was she going to be able to get a knee between his legs. And his strength overpowered her. She couldn't pull away.

He held her close, his heart beating almost painfully against her chest, his scent filling her nostrils. Too male. Too close.

Panic set in and her mind went blank, leaving her a reactive mess, a body twisting against the bondage of a man. *This* man.

Not because she was scared or feared he'd truly hurt her, but because she wanted him.

"Think, Ana." Ty's voice came through to her consciousness. "Think."

She focused on his words, remembering she wasn't really fighting Ty. She was fighting her feelings for him. He wanted her to prove she could let a man touch her sexually without freaking out, but little did he know that she only cringed from his touch because she wanted it too much.

She needed to turn the tables on him.

And suddenly she knew how she was going to do it.

Slowly, she softened her movements, replacing twisting with writhing, struggle with acceptance. She turned her face to his and let her breathing slow, opening her lips so that each breath caressed his cheek. Startled, he turned his face to hers. And then she kissed him. Licked his lips. Thrust her hips against his, then angled her body to rub her breasts against his chest. Let a gasp escape her throat and deepened the kiss, going limp in his hold.

Yes, she thought. This was what she'd wanted all this time. And funnily enough, he'd given her the means to get it. Because she pretended it was all part of her training. That she was only giving him what *he* wanted, not what she needed.

Ty let go of her hands and groaned, but the sound wasn't of pleasure. He sounded like she was torturing him. Teasing him with something he couldn't really have. He swept his tongue through her mouth, toying with hers, then quickly ripped himself away.

Breathing hard, he stared at her. His eyes were heavy-lidded, his face flushed, his lips red and swollen. His fists opened and shut several times before he seemed to deliberately relax his fingers. He nodded. "Good. That's a good start. You can fake sexual interest to get away from a man."

But she hadn't been faking, she wanted to say. She did desire him. She wanted him. And suddenly, despite the fear that had been driving her to get away from him before she revealed too much, she wanted him to know it.

Before she could say it, however, before she could even open her mouth, he was gone.

CHAPTER
EIGHTEEN

The next day, in Belladonna's formal dining room, Ana let her fingers drift down the smooth, polished hardwood table that could seat at least twenty people, aware of her own reflection in the sheen. She'd used makeup to cover the dark circles under her eyes, evidence of the restless night she'd had after that incident with Ty by the pool. She'd spent half of her waking hours alternately trying to imagine more intimacies with him while berating herself at the same time for her attempts. She'd spent the other half wondering about the team she was supposed to meet today.

What were they like? What had brought them here? What had Carly promised them?

In the end, however, it didn't matter. They didn't need to understand each other. They didn't even need to like each other. All they needed was to be able to work together.

She'd been living a lie these past few days. Enjoying her time with Ty as if this were some kind of vacation. But if Ty walking away from her by the pool hadn't been enough to drive that point home, there was the fact that she'd spent a sleepless night in her bed, aching with her need for him. Everything Ty did was a means to an end, not a genuine display of affection for her. So he could get an erection around her. Big deal. Right now, she was the only other woman on the premises. It was to be expected. He didn't truly want her. He didn't care for her. She meant nothing to him. She had to focus. All that mattered was finding Gloria.

She might not mean anything to Gloria, either. Not anymore. But given what Ana had been told, she was beginning to hope that wasn't true.

It was now possible to believe that Gloria had cut off all contact with Ana not of her own free will, but because she'd been under the influence of cultish mind control. If that was the case, Ana had the chance to regain the most important person in the world to her.

She took a deep breath and looked around the semi-circular library. Leather-bound books lined shelves that ran twenty feet high. Three sliding ladders hung from iron rungs. Leather club chairs in deep hunter green crowded around small tables with reading lamps, and in the middle of the room was a larger table with a speaker, Carly's preferred method of communication. Either the woman was seriously paranoid, or she truly had enemies. And with the type of work Belladonna seemed to be conducting, Ana was betting on the latter.

"Like what you see?" A man's deep voice came from behind her.

Ana whipped around, staring at the stranger who'd entered. Like Ty, this man was tall and broad with dark eyes. His hair, however, was slightly lighter, a tawny brown.

"No weapon," he calmly observed, looking at where her hand was.

She realized she'd grabbed at her waistband out of habit. Once upon a time her switchblade had always been there, a vital accessory to her daily outfits. Part of her, when you got right down to it. She'd always gone for it when members of other gangs entered her turf.

But she hadn't worn a knife in years. And when she'd first arrived, Ty had insisted she leave her gun in her bedroom safe. "For everyone's safety," he'd said, acknowledging that he was probably going to piss her off more than once in the coming days.

"What were you reaching for? A knife?"

Ana just continued to stare at him, which made his lips twitch, as if he was suppressing a smile. "You know how to throw them?" he asked.

Thanks to Ty, she did now. But for some reason, she didn't tell him that. "In the hood, you don't throw away your weapon."

"A bit different than Covert Ops. We had two knives— one for throwing, and the other for stabbing our enemy in the guts. Or slicing across the throat. Why not carry two?"

She suddenly got who he was. "You must be Peter Lancaster."

"Avoiding my question?" he asked, his eyes twinkling and the corner of his mouth rising up in what she guessed was a smile.

"No. Why didn't I carry two knives?" Ana shrugged. "I only wanted to protect myself. Pulling out a knife quickly was usually all we needed to stop an enemy. You, on the other hand . . ."

He nodded. "Had been instructed to kill the enemy." He crossed the room and stuck out his hand. "And you are right. I'm Peter."

She shook his hand, aware of how small hers felt in his.

He was attractive, but not as attractive as Ty. Not to her, anyway.

Madre de Dios. She did not need to be thinking about how handsome Ty was. She commanded her body and mind to let go of images of the man who'd brought her into this whole mess and focused on the voices she now heard just outside the library doors.

"That'll be Ty and the others," Peter said, watching her closely.

The library doors opened, revealing three women . . . and Ty.

She practically devoured him with her eyes, then made a point of ignoring him when the woman he was with, the one with short brown hair and glasses, arched a brow at her.

Five minutes later, introductions had been made. The average-size woman in her early thirties with the glasses was Collette Parker. She was an ex-cop, but in her nicely worn jeans and button-down paisley shirt with sleeves rolled to the elbows, she looked more like a soccer mom. The woman with dark skin and darker hair and an unmistakable air of sensuality was Justine Maverick. And the slim, elegant blonde with sophistication and prestige and wealth stamped across her forehead was Barrett Miles.

Ana was as curious about all of them as they seemed to be about her; each of them studied the other with thinly veiled suspicion. She had to stifle a half groan, half chuckle.

Let the games begin.

"Carly's already briefed you to some extent on Salvation's Crossing," Ty said, directing his attention to Ana. "It's supposed to be a public outreach program for Hispanic culture, but we believe it's actually a false front for a cult." When she nodded, he turned his attention to the others.

"Illegal immigrants are being used by the cult for slave labor and for . . . well, let's just say they're being sold on the black market. Miguel Salvador finds illegals and welcomes them in to Salvation's Crossing. He's seeded the streets of San Diego and Los Angeles, and even

Tijuana and Mexico City with hucksters he pays to spout the word of Salvation's Crossing."

Collette—the ex-cop, ex–blackjack dealer who'd had extensive training in body language and could morph into anyone she needed to be, be it ingenue, femme fatale, or hooker—spoke up. "So when the illegals make it across the border, they think Salvation's Crossing is *their* salvation."

Ty nodded, looking around the room to ensure Ana, Barrett, and Justine understood as well. Barrett was sitting staring out the window, her knees held together at a perfect angle, the silk skirt she wore skimming her thigh and riding up just enough to be sexy but still classy. No one would guess she'd graduated from West Point Academy at the top of her class and had served overseas.

Next to her, Justine sat more relaxed. A former dancer known for blowing men's minds and making them blow a wad of cash on her when she pole danced, Justine had an innate sensuality. She was also an ace when it came to anything with an engine, particularly cars.

The two of them seemed uninterested in his lecture, but Ty could tell they were on alert, absorbing, filtering, and processing his words. Good.

Ana, though—he cast his gaze to her. As he'd expected, she was looking at him with chin raised, eyes challenging, a woman ready for a fight. That bravado, which he fully knew she could back up with fists or a knife, stirred something deep inside him just the way it always did. Desire, he reminded himself, as his cock went to half-mast. Ana stirred up his sexuality in a truly visceral way. After their little lesson at the pool, he'd been on the verge of losing it. Before he could rip her clothes off and plunge his fangs into her neck, he'd practically run away.

"Any questions on Salvation's Crossing?"

"What's the next step?" Ana asked. Despite her calm demeanor, he sensed her vulnerability. It hit him then— how much a young Ana would have benefited from an organization that purported to do what Salvation's Crossing did. How different her life would have been if she'd been given a home instead of a place in a gang.

That's what was really driving her. Ana didn't want to go back to her childhood home, but she wanted *a* home. One that looked like her place in Seattle, but where she didn't live alone. She wanted to find her sister, make sure Gloria got out safe. And she wanted to stay with her sister. She wanted to have a family again.

Just like he did.

Fact was, however, she still had a chance of getting what she wanted. He didn't.

Still, her complete love and loyalty to her sister moved him. Had he loved Naomi to such a fierce degree? He'd like to think so, but he wasn't sure. Maybe because he'd suspected Naomi hadn't loved him with that same fierceness, either.

Never mind the sisters, his or hers.

What he wouldn't give to have Ana love him that much. To know she was his and would be in his bed every night, freely, enthusiastically, despite the fact that she knew exactly what he was.

A vampire.

His cock strained against the soft fabric of his jeans, no longer at half-mast. Images of ripping Ana's jeans off her ass and plunging himself into her warm depths raged in his mind. He'd take her, and hard—from behind, up against a wall, sideways. Bite her neck—

Suddenly he realized the rest of the team members were staring at him, silent. Barrett raised an eyebrow at him, the hint of a smile quirking at one side of her mouth. Bollocks. Had she realized how much he'd been hungering for Ana? He shifted in his seat, hoping his straining erection was sufficiently hidden behind the folders he held in his hand.

"We continue with your training. Collette, Barrett, and Justine will teach you a few things that can help you with your mission before they train with Peter."

"Such as?" Ana's question wasn't rude, just direct.

"Your mission isn't an extraction or surgical strike. It's intelligence gathering. The only way we're going to get in, get the evidence, and get out with it is if our cover is believable."

Ana frowned. "What cover?"

"We'll be posing as lovers," he said smoothly. "That means you're going to have to be a social butterfly. You know, someone who's accustomed to the best in life and who's also a free spirit. Also, it can't bother you if I touch you—however that might happen." He watched understanding flicker across her face and saw the bitterness that twisted her mouth.

Just like during your training, he wanted to say. It was really best if she thought that, he told himself.

But he still wanted to shake her and insist that she see the truth: she was beautiful and he wanted her and he'd want her regardless of how they'd met. Her mind, however, was already on the mission and everything she'd learned so far.

"But I thought one of my roles was to seduce Miguel into letting us into the cult. How am I going to do that if he—if he—"

"If he thinks you're mine?"

She scowled. "If he thinks we're sleeping together."

"Can you really be that naive about men, Ana?" That came from Barrett.

Ana rounded on her. "You don't know me at all. And who asked you?"

Ana was more innocent about the desires of men than

she could ever realize, Ty thought. Mainly because she didn't give herself the freedom to feel her own.

"What Barrett is saying," Justine chimed in, "is that thinking you're with Ty isn't going to put off a man who's truly interested in you, Ana. In fact, if Miguel believes you're lovers, he's going to want to win you over even more."

A few hours after she'd learned she'd be posing as Ty's girlfriend, Ana entered the stable behind Justine. Collette and Barrett were already inside. The blonde spoke softly to one of the mares, stroking the blaze on her forehead and slipping her a baby carrot.

The warm smell of fresh hay and old timber made Ana stop and take a deep breath, just to enjoy it. She glanced at Barrett again. There was an apple half in her hand.

Ana hadn't thought to bring treats. She doubted they had been told to meet here to pal around with the horses, although she didn't know the reason for Carly's order.

Show up at the stables. Collette has my instructions.

"Hello, ladies," Justine said, sidestepping a sticky green-brown clump that rolled out of the straw. "Eww. Where are all the stable hands? They need to tidy up in here."

Collette laughed. "I believe that's our assignment."

"The hell it is," Justine retorted, pushing back a wavy lock of black hair. "Who told you that?"

The ex-cop took a piece of paper out of her shirt pocket and unfolded it, showing it to Justine, whose eyes widened with horror as Barrett laughed.

"Collette already enlightened me," the blonde said. She didn't seem in the least upset.

Ana wasn't sure what to do or say. The other women already seemed comfortable with one another, and despite Barrett's tendency toward snootiness, Ana could see herself liking all of them. And despite the shitty bonding assignment Carly had given them, she liked the stable, too. It was a down-to-earth place where real work got done; and though she'd never ridden a horse, Ana had always suspected she'd love them. One whickered in her direction, as if he seconded that thought.

Collette went to a rack on the wall that held tools. "Take a rake, Justine. Pick an empty stall and muck it out."

"I'm not dressed to deal with horse shit," Justine wailed.

In jeweled flip-flops and tiny shorts, Justine wasn't wrong about that. The other two women were in gingham tops and worn jeans, and Collette's short brown hair was covered by a bandanna. Ana had opted for knee-length cutoffs and a T-shirt, pulling her hair sleekly back into a single thick braid.

She spotted a row of rubber boots in different sizes under a bench, and then noticed that Collette and Barrett already had theirs on. Feeling awkward and uncertain—two feelings she absolutely *hated*—Ana sat down and selected a pair that looked likely to fit, took off her sneakers, and pulled them on.

"Get over yourself, Justine," Collette said briskly. "Whistle a happy tune or something."

"Fuck that."

Justine stomped over to the bench and changed her footwear, then grabbed one of the rakes Collette was holding out.

"Where should I start?" Ana asked, standing up.

"First you take out the water bucket and the manger," Collette said. "And then the hay."

Ana headed toward the chestnut.

"It's also a good idea to remove the horse," Colette called after her, her tone clearly good-natured.

Despite herself, Ana found herself relaxing and fought back a smile. She went in a different direction to an unoccupied stall, thinking it had been a long time since she'd indulged in "girl time." Trying to do so, even getting closer to Téa, had always reminded her of how she'd lost Gloria. Now, with these three larger-than-life women, she suddenly found herself hoping they'd learn not to just work together, but to like one another.

Justine entered a nearby stall, the horse next door watching her with interest as she began to pitch sodden straw into the main aisle.

"You have to separate the manure," Barrett told her. "It goes in the wheelbarrow."

Justine looked at the contraption with disgust when Barrett pointed.

"Gee, thanks for the tip, Miss B. Where'd you learn that? You don't look like you ever get your hands dirty."

Justine's mouthy comeback earned her a sharp look from Collette. She quit talking.

"You'd be surprised," Barrett replied calmly.

Ana had to admire her for not losing her cool. And for the advice. She wouldn't have known to separate the, uh, stuff from the straw.

The other two women got to work with them.

Three hours later, they were gathered around an outdoor table with cold beers in hand.

Justine popped the cap off her bottle with a long-nailed thumb and took a deep swig.

"Ahhh." She set the bottle down with a thump on the wooden table. "That was so much fun. Let's do it again. Every day."

"That can probably be arranged. So shut up already." Collette took a sliver of ice from the small cooler on the table and rubbed her forehead with it.

Barrett sipped from her bottle, but Ana rolled hers between her palms, enjoying the coolness. All four of them had worked up a sweat, and smelled stronger than the exercised horses now getting rubdowns, but the job had gotten done.

Justine rested her elbows on the table and propped her chin in both hands. "Ana, you okay? You're awfully quiet."

"I'm fine except for the blisters on my hands."

"Let me see."

Barrett's soft-voiced request surprised Ana but she extended her hands, palms up.

"I have some balm that I use. I'll give it to you when we get back to the main house."

"Okay. Thanks."

"*I* might not make it that far," Justine said dramatically. "Bury me here."

"Ana worked harder than you and she's not complaining," Collette pointed out. "I'm pretty sure she worked harder than any of us."

"No way," Ana protested, but despite herself she felt a tingling of pleasure.

"Oh, hush. And drink that damn beer before I do it for you," Justine said to her.

Collette raised hers in agreement. Ana drank as the ex-cop, who seemed to have naturally fallen into the role of leader, finished hers.

"Okay, ladies," she said. "Before we all crash in our bedrooms, has anyone figured out why Carly the Invisible picked us for Belladonna?"

"She must have her reasons," Barrett observed. "Plus a bizarre sense of humor."

"Two good guesses." Collette clinked her bottle against Barrett's, then Ana's.

Justine held on to her second beer, not joining in. "Ya think? I'm not getting the humor part. I don't think Carly is all about fun."

Wasn't that the truth?

"Forget her. Let's talk about us," Collette said. "Who we are, what we have in common, what we don't. You start, Justine."

"Not me. I hate sharing."

"Okay then. You can go last." Collette set down her beer. "You all know my name. Don't play cards with me. I used to deal blackjack. And I used to be an under-cover cop. Actually, you never stop being one, even when you quit." She paused.

Ana wondered why but Collette didn't add anything more.

"Don't look at me," Justine said. "I pay my outstand-ing parking tickets on a quarterly basis."

Barrett shook her head but she smiled. "My last gig was overseas. Army. Eastern Europe, working with ref-ugee women and children. Pick a conflict. I probably was there."

Ana took that in. Nothing she'd done compared. She had a new respect for the cool blonde.

Collette's intelligent gaze rested on Ana.

She fought her natural resistance to talking about her-self. To sharing anything that could possibly and proba-bly be used against her. "Ah—I had my own business. A coffee shop in Seattle."

"Ooo," Justine said. "Now we're getting into the rough stuff."

Ana felt her face grow warm and automatically thrust out her chin. "There's more to it. But some other time."

To her credit, Justine let it go at that. There was some-thing to being quiet and patient and letting other people make the mistakes, Ana thought.

Justine set down her empty bottle with a sigh. "Okay. I started my glorious career as a roadhouse hostess and figured out quick that I could make more money as a dancer. Please don't hate me because I worked in a thong."

The others murmured to the contrary, but all Ana could think was that Justine working in a thong would probably drive men crazy. Would *her* working in a thong do the same to Ty?

"I'm totally done with that," Justine continued. "But I met a lot of interesting people and had a lot of fun. Oh, and somewhere in there I learned how to fix cars. You don't ever want to show up late at Angels from Heaven because your beater threw a rod."

Barrett blinked as if she was trying to figure out the last sentence. So she didn't know what a beater was, Ana thought. Well, that wasn't a crime.

She was cutting the blonde slack, she realized. Cutting them all slack. Had she already started to bond with these women?

Over manure. With aching backs.

It was a start.

Looked like the mysterious Carly had accomplished what she'd wanted.

The other women nodded and Ana automatically did the same.

"I say we reconvene for group mani-pedis in a week," Justine piped up. "Show of hands?"

Ana looked at her short, uncolored nails. Plain. Simple. Boring.

When she looked up, the other women were watching her with different expressions. Gentleness—Collette. Amusement—Justine. Challenge—Barrett.

The vote was unanimous.

"I know a red that will look fabulous with your coloring," Justine said as they all left the stable. Feeling slightly dazed, Ana simply nodded.

But when she was alone in her room, she showered and fell into bed with a smile.

CHAPTER NINETEEN

Two days after Carly had Ana bond with the other women over horse shit, Ty stood on the upper story of the Belladonna training facility and looked down at the paddock, watching as Ana got dumped off the gray horse yet again. She cussed first at the horse, then at Barrett, who was teaching Ana to ride. Barrett responded with a cool smile, and gestured for Ana to get back up on the horse. Although she hesitated at first, Ana gathered the reins, and apparently her courage, and launched herself back into the saddle.

When Ty's cell phone rang, he answered it.

"How's our ghetto girl doing?" Carly's sultry voice queried.

"Don't call her that," he snapped out even as he kept his gaze on Ana, who'd gamely pressed the horse into a canter. She bounced a bit in her seat, but held on.

"Sticking up for the masses?" Carly taunted. "So magnanimous of you, ignoring class."

"There is no class system in America," he responded, hitching in a breath as the horse took the jump.

Carly laughed bitterly. "So goes the lie. So how's Ana's training going?"

"Quite well. She's handled everything we've thrown at her. Before today, she'd never ridden a horse, but she's getting the hang of it."

"Why the hell does she need to ride a horse?"

"The compound has a few horses, so riding just might come in handy. Plus, the lessons are another team-building experience more than anything else," he said.

"Ty, we need to push forward," Carly said. "We have less than a week left before the fund-raiser. If Miguel takes the bait, things could move quickly. We need to tell her."

Ty stiffened. He understood what Carly was getting at.

Tell her what I am. A freak of nature. A monster.

Instinctively, he resisted. "I don't want to tell her. Not yet."

"She's done everything you've asked of her, Ty, and that's been plenty. She's proven she's invested in the mission. Peter and I will be talking to the others. Tell Ana or I will."

As the line went dead, Ty cast his gaze below, focusing again on Ana. She'd dismounted, and stood next to the horse, stroking its shoulder as she spoke animatedly with Barrett. And smiled.

After Carly's little bonding exercise, he'd put Ana through hell all over again, but she'd done everything he'd asked without complaining. More than that, she'd started to take pride in her own achievements and the small connections she was making with the rest of the team. She'd been smiling more and more easily. And, God, but Ana smiling was something to look at.

Too bad he had to wipe that smile right off her face.

Fifteen minutes later, Ty leaned against the paddock fence and watched Ana exit the barn. She was still smiling, her expression soft, her chin tipped up so the afternoon sun stroked her cheeks. Happy.

Once again, her visible joy took his breath away.

Then she caught sight of him, leaning against the whitewashed boards, and she frowned.

"So, I pretty much sucked, didn't I?" she asked, gesturing with a thumb over her shoulder to the barn behind her.

"You looking for a phony compliment?"

She frowned. "No. I was looking for agreement."

He kicked off from the paddock fence, and with his hands still dug deep into his pockets, came to stand a bare two inches away from her. "Won't get that from me. You actually have a good seat."

Now her frown turned to a scowl. "Stop blowing smoke up my ass. That's the first time I've ever been on a horse. Of course I sucked. What you're doing is patronizing me, and I don't like it. Don't want it."

A smile edged its way across his lips, slow and steady. "As I told you before, I never—"

"Only a liar says they never lie."

"And only a fool won't face the truth. Were you perfect on the horse? No. You held your shoulders too high and didn't dig your heels down deep enough. Were you good? Yes. After getting dumped a few times, you ended up with excellent balance, and you kept control over the horse. Now get that chip off your shoulder and stop acting as if I'm your enemy."

He expected her to say, "Everyone is the enemy," but she didn't. No matter. All of a sudden, he *felt* like her enemy.

Her neck was exposed, her heartbeat thrumming through the visible vein there.

Aching, his fangs reacted along with his cock. The scenery—the red barn and its white trim, the lush willow trees lining the long paved drive, the green grass of the meadow and the golden brown sand of the paddock—grew dull and gray . . . a roaring in his ears sounded . . . hunger ate at his belly, gnawing, clawing, screaming, demanding . . .

Feed.

Suck.

Drink.

Blood. Punctured skin. Throbbing veins opening up under his fangs.

He jerked backward. Their surroundings slowly swam back into focus. In front of him stood a perplexed Ana.

"Ty? What's wrong?"

He worked to calm his breathing. To reduce his heart rate. He hadn't given himself away. She hadn't seen him for what he really was. Hadn't seen the beast that lived inside him. The thing he hated.

"There's quite a few things wrong at the moment, but we need to focus on what's important."

"And what's that?"

"The truth. The full truth," he said. "There's more that you need to know, Ana. A lot more."

"What is it?"

He didn't want to tell her. He truly didn't.

But his reasons were selfish.

He wanted her to continue looking at him with desire. He wanted to hold her and kiss her again. But he'd known this day would come.

So he told her the truth. Starting with what he was.

She didn't believe him, of course. She laughed.

"You're a vampire. Right," she said.

She moved to walk past him, and he gently took her arm.

"I'm not joking, Ana."

"Of course you're not. And of course I believe you. Did I ever tell you I'm a fairy? At night, I fly around sprinkling fairy sparkle dust over the world."

Ty shook her, not hard enough to hurt, but hard enough to get her attention. "I'm a vampire. I wasn't born one, but I was turned into one. Six months ago. By born vampires called Rogues."

"Rogues? As opposed to what? Lawfully abiding vampires?"

"That's right."

She threw her arms wide, breaking his grip. "Of course. And does everyone know about vampires—that you are one—but me?"

"No. Hardly anyone does. Just us—"

"Us?"

"Carly. Peter and I. And a select few people in the FBI."

"Oh, so it's a government conspiracy. Kind of like UFOs?" Her expression was still mocking. Her tone still laced with disbelief.

"No conspiracy. Not like UFOs. Just . . . just a discovery the government's not ready to share yet."

"Okay," she said, nodding and backing away. "Well, thanks for telling me. I'm just going to go up now and—"

Ty sighed. Then he proved he wasn't lying. He opened his mouth and showed Ana his fangs.

An hour later, a pale Ana sat in a chair in the Belladonna library.

She'd seen Ty's fangs. In her dreams and in real life. As much as she wanted to deny it, she was beginning to believe what he was telling her.

Vampires existed. And the U.S. government knew about them.

So what the hell was Belladonna's agenda and why were they trying to get into a cult that the FBI was refusing to infiltrate? Was it really to bring a woman and her daughter back home? She knew now that there had to be more to it than that.

Across from her sat Barrett, Justine, and Collette. Peter and Ty stood next to Carly's intercom.

"Did you—did you all know?" Ana whispered. Because it sure seemed like they had. The rapport they'd managed to form seemed to be a thing of the past. None of the other women would look at her.

Justine appeared bored, staring out the window, tapping her short fingernails against the crystal goblet of red wine she held in her hands. Barrett sat prim and proper, her knees and feet together, hands folded in her lap, staring at a spot of nothing across the room. The epitome of class. As always, Collette looked composed and slightly sympathetic, but she kept her gaze on Carly's intercom.

Carly spoke first. "Collette has been aware for some time. I just recently spoke with Justine and Barrett. Neither of them knew about real-life vampires until then."

"And Peter?" she asked, turning to him. But he simply stared back at her, letting Carly answer for him.

"Ty and Peter are both recently turned vampires."

Of course he was, she thought. And here she'd thought Peter was relatively harmless.

Ana stood suddenly, kicking the antique chair behind her, reveling in the sound of it crashing to the hardwood floor. "And none of you care? None of you are freaked out?"

"Oh, calm down, Ana," Barrett said. "It's not like the world is ending. We've simply been informed of a separate species living among us."

"Yeah, one that *sucks human blood* to survive."

"Personally, I don't care who or what I'm battling against," Barrett said. "I simply want what Carly's promised me. And I'll do whatever Belladonna needs me to do in order to get what I want."

"Whatever it takes?" Ana snapped. "Be careful what you say. Or have you forgotten that I'm being asked to fuck, hurt, or kill someone *to get what I want*. No, to get them what they want," she said, pointing at Ty and Peter. "They've kept things from us up to now. What makes you think they're not keeping more?"

For the first time since Ana had met her, Barrett looked uncomfortable. When Ana turned her glare on the company around her, Justine and Collette looked affected, too. Peter and Ty, however, did not. She supposed that was their badass superagent training coming out.

Ana turned to Ty. "Exactly how many vampires are there?"

"Many. They live among humans secretly. As far as we know, they always have."

"You—you said you were turned. Not born. So some are? Born, I mean?"

"Yes."

"Do all vampires look human?"

"Yes. They disguise their unique external traits. Their silver hair. Their black eyes."

"Do you have those?"

"I dye my hair. Wear contacts. Same as Peter."

"What else can you do?" she asked.

A flicker of something flashed across his face, but he answered readily enough. "I can move faster than any human. We thrive off human blood but we can survive off the blood of animals. When we're done feeding, we lick the puncture site and it heals. We—at least Peter and I—can go out in the sunlight but for a limited time. And we can't lie."

"Vampires can't lie," she repeated, then quickly asked, "What happened to you? You said you were turned. How?"

"The three of us—Carly, Peter, and I—were all recruited by the FBI around the same time. They, however, had security clearance that I didn't. Apparently, when the FBI learned about vampires, they immediately sought to exploit the discovery. They found vampires willing to turn humans for them. I knew none of this. Not until Peter, my sister, Naomi, and another agent and I were attacked. I was turned. So was Peter. My sister didn't make it. We don't believe the other agent did, either."

He said it with no grief in his voice or in his eyes. He could just as easily have been saying *I can't find the tomatoes I bought at the store*.

But she knew better. His sister's death bothered him. A lot. He just didn't feel safe revealing how much it hurt him. Totally understandable. But would he feel the same way if just the two of them were here?

Unlikely, she thought sadly.

"Who did it?" she asked.

"Can't you guess?"

"The Rogues you told me about."

He nodded. "We're looking for evidence of why, of exactly who's involved and what they're involved in. When we have that information, we'll shut them down."

"And protect the FBI in the process," she added.

No one replied, but they didn't have to. As a former gang member, Ana knew all about blowback. If one person in a gang messed up, it reflected on the gang as a whole. And once it was lost, street cred wasn't something easily earned back.

She remembered when she'd first talked to Carly and had speculated that the FBI didn't want another Waco on their hands. It was obviously a lot more serious than that. Imagine how much credibility the FBI would lose if it came out that they had been playing with vampires they couldn't control. So yes, this was about the FBI wanting to cover its ass. But for Ty it was about something far more personal. He wanted revenge. For himself and for his sister. She'd bet her life on it.

Feeling her own chest swelling with emotion, she forced herself to keep asking questions. "And Carly?"

"Peter and I worked in the Turning Program together," Carly responded. "That's how he knew to contact me after he and Ty managed to escape."

"Do you and the FBI know how to kill vampires?"

Her question immediately caused a tense silence to fill the room. She suddenly felt the need to apologize, as if she'd somehow insulted Ty and Peter, but that wasn't the case at all. If vampires couldn't be killed, then the FBI's chances of hunting down the Rogues were less than zero. More to the point, how were ordinary humans like her supposed to protect themselves from . . . *them*?

"We're compiling information about the vampires, but no, we don't know how to kill vampires, born or turned. Not yet," Carly admitted. "We don't even know how the Rogues turn humans. Ty and Peter had already been turned by the time they regained consciousness. And when the Rogues were working for the FBI, they always insisted the actual turning process be performed in private."

"Is that the type of intel you're hoping to get from Salvation's Crossing?" Ana asked. "And if so, what makes you think anyone inside has it?"

"If we somehow got that information, it would be a miracle, but it's not one we're counting on. We want inside Salvation's Crossing for a specific purpose. We believe Salvation's Crossing is in league with Rogues who are selling illegal immigrants as blood slaves."

Ana frowned. "Does that include Ramona Montes and her daughter, Becky?"

"According to our intel, they're on site, serving some specific purpose."

"And exactly where does Miguel fit into all this? Are you trying to tell me that he—or for that matter, my sister—*know* these Rogues and what they're doing?" She glanced at Ty, wanting to see his expression, but her stomach dropped when he refused to look at her.

"It's more than that," Carly said. "We believe that Miguel is running the blood slave program for a group of Rogues. And that he's doing it with your sister's help."

"My . . ." Ana shook her head and horror filled her voice at what they were implying. It couldn't be true. It was impossible. More impossible than vampires being real. "You're wrong. You have to be. Gloria would never do something so vile."

"We're not wrong," Ty said, forcing her attention back to him when that was the last thing she wanted. "I know she's your sister and you love her, Ana, but—"

"*Pero nada!* Gloria would never do that. Never!"

"People change."

"Yeah, no kidding," she snorted. "But you're wrong. *Acerca de Gloria y acerca de Miguel.*"

"I'm certainly not wrong about Miguel. And your friend Bobbie agrees with me."

He couldn't have shocked her more than if . . . than if . . . well, than if he'd sprouted wings and turned into a bat. A bloodsucking vampire bat. "Bobbie? Bobbie Hernandez? From my coffee shop?"

"That's right."

"But he's just a kid."

"They grow up fast in your neighborhood. He wants to be a vampire. And he's been keeping tabs on you for Miguel."

"What? You're crazy!"

"Am I? Because I grant you, I was a little skeptical when Peter raised his theory, too. Until I started looking into it. Do you remember the name Greg Flick?"

"Greg—Greg Flick. He was a prison guard."

"You accused him of getting too handsy with you, re-member?"

"Yeah, so what?"

"Do you know what happened to him?"

"I never saw him again. I assumed he was fired. Or transferred."

"He was neither. He was killed. One week after you filed your complaint, he was shot during a home inva-sion. The intruder, however, was never caught."

"So what? That doesn't prove anything."

"After you were released from prison, you rented an apartment in Florida. You had some trouble with the landlord, didn't you?"

Ana swallowed hard. She reached out to steady her-self. Shakily sat down. Then shook her head. "How do you know all this?" she whispered.

"Didn't you, Ana?"

"Yes, I did."

"What happened?"

"He claimed I hadn't paid him rent for two months when I had. He tried to shake me down for more and when I refused to pay, he kicked me out. I—I had to sleep on the streets until I earned enough to get back on my feet."

"How long was that?"

"Couple weeks."

"During that time, your landlord was mugged and killed. You want me to continue?"

"Yes," she said defiantly.

"Okay. How about this? After we wrestled in your coffee shop, I was shot by a cop. An Officer Southcott. Name sound familiar?"

"Oh, God. He came to my house. Told me about Téa."

"Téa, who died. Téa, who gave us information about you that she wasn't supposed to give. We think Officer

Southcott paid her a visit, right before he was eliminated himself."

"He's dead? But why? How?"

"We think he went behind his boss's back by visiting you. Everyone who has ever hurt or betrayed you has paid for it, Ana. If I wasn't a vampire, I'd be dead, too. And I think the man responsible is Miguel. Hell, he probably played a role in getting your prison sentence shortened. Even made sure you got your business loan, despite the fact that you're an ex-con. I tried checking into it, but the bank gave me the runaround. That in itself was enough to tell me someone had intervened on your behalf. Why not Miguel? He loved you. He still does."

"Then why hasn't he come to see me? Why play all these games?"

"Because he made a mistake. One that as a result ensures you'll never be with him. Not the way he wants."

"What mistake?"

"He became your sister's lover."

The world had gone crazy.

It was all becoming too much for Ana to deal with.

She was vaguely aware that everyone in the room had left. Everyone but Ty.

She looked at the intercom on the table.

"It's off," he said. "It's just the two of us."

"You say that like it should reassure me," she said.

He smiled but said nothing, letting her assimilate what he'd told her. Letting her take the lead.

She shook her head. "What you're saying—I'm sorry, but I don't believe you. I know you think it's true, but you're wrong. I know them."

"Then prove me wrong."

She threw up her hands. "How?"

"Help me get to Miguel. If we don't find anything to back up our intel, I'll admit defeat."

"And you'll leave him and Gloria alone. And me as well."

The heat in his gaze intensified. "If that's what you really want. Yes."

She looked at him. Thank God that even if he couldn't lie, she could. They were two different people. Two different *species*. She couldn't trust him. Not when he was so determined to take down what little family she had left. "That's what I want."

Ty nodded. "The fund-raiser is in a few days. It all hinges on that. We fly to California this Friday. You want to be left alone? Finish up your training. Help us get what information we can on Miguel. Then convince Miguel we're legit and get us into Salvation's Crossing."

CHAPTER TWENTY

Ana thought she had been handling the news about Ty and Peter being vampires remarkably well, but apparently Ty had other surprises in store for her.

"You want me to what?" Ana asked.

She and Ty had just finished sparring on the mats. She was sweaty and tired and cranky, edgy from having Ty's hands all over her and imagining what he could do with those fangs of his that would hurt only in the best ways possible. Then he'd told her what he wanted and she had to fight the sudden urge to pin him down on the floor again and knee him where it would hurt most.

Ty's gaze didn't waver. "I want you to accompany me to a bar where Primos Sangre members hang out."

Ana couldn't help it. Her throat went dry, making it difficult for her to speak. In truth, she hadn't had as much trouble speaking yesterday, when she'd learned vampires were real. What Ty was asking of her now was tantamount to making her confront every miserable mistake she'd ever made. And she wasn't sure she could do it.

"Members . . ." When her words came out as a croak, she cleared her throat and tried again. "Members that have joined the gang since I left, or members that were part of the gang when I was?"

"Both. But obviously, we're hoping for more of the

latter. That way, you can capitalize on old acquaintances to get what we need."

"Which is what?"

"You know that we're going to the fund-raiser to try and convince Miguel that we're lovers."

She nodded.

"He's dodged my attempts to meet with him but he trusts you. He'll trust your prior relationship and the fact you want to see him again, separate from anything having to do with me. If you really wanted to see him again, what would you do? Wait for the fund-raiser or track him down yourself?"

"So you want me to go to this bar and pretend to be looking for Miguel? And you think people are just going to lead me to him?"

"Not at all. But if one of them saw you and talked to you, knew how close you and Miguel had been and that you were looking for him, maybe they'd tell him."

"There's one problem with what you're saying. I know it's hard to believe now, but I haven't always been so . . . likable. Not everyone in Primos Sangre would want to do me any favors. In fact, they'd just as soon hurt me than help me."

"This wouldn't be about anyone wanting to do you a favor. It would be about someone wanting to do *Miguel* a favor. And you're not going to be alone, Ana. I'll be right there with you. Do you really think I'd let anything happen to you?"

As she stared into his eyes, she knew he'd do whatever he needed to do to protect her. He'd use his vampire powers, and if he had to, she knew he'd even risk his life for hers. The knowledge that he'd go to such lengths had been there all along. It had been what had enabled her to come to Belladonna in the first place. It had been what allowed her mind to open up and let Ty into her dreams.

She couldn't deny it. She'd come to Belladonna for Gloria, but she'd also come because of Ty. If she hadn't trusted him so instinctively and so thoroughly, she'd have left Seattle and disappeared completely. And none of that had changed now that she knew what he was. In fact, his vampire nature made him all the more intriguing to her. Alleged vampire nature, she thought. *Alleged*. What a way to put it. Was she turning into a lawyer? Some people would say that was worse than a vampire.

She just hadn't seen any compelling evidence of Ty's vampiric nature. Yes, he had fangs. And super speed. But neither overshadowed what Ty was. A good man. Vampires were supposed to be ruled by their lust for blood, but Ty seemed to keep that well hidden. Just like his lust for her.

She mentally winced. Okay, Ana. Like that doesn't sound too bitter. Remember, you keep your desire for Ty hidden, too. It's still there. So is his. Tightly controlled.

Why couldn't they have been just a man and a woman who were allowed to act on their feelings for one another? Why did cults and vampires and estranged sisters and the FBI and a hundred other issues have to get in the way of what might have been something special between them?

Ana knew why.

Because that was her life. It always had been. Fate had denied her anything she'd ever truly wanted. And deep inside, she had a feeling that was going to continue to be the case.

She sighed. "When do we do this?"

"How soon can you get dressed?"

An hour later, Ana glanced around the darkened bar. Ty hadn't brought her to a complete dive, but he hadn't brought her to some swanky nightclub, either. She took in the bar patrons, noting the mix of young, preppy businessmen, probably out for a drink to take the edge off of work, and the few college kids from the local university.

A couple of older men sat at the bar, their backs hunched, their arms circled on the polished wood in front of them, clearly defining their personal space. Locals. Regulars. Not a place she'd expect to see Primos Sangre members. Maybe Ty's intel was wrong. Maybe—

She spotted a familiar face at the bar and stiffened.

It was a man named Louis. He was obviously older than the last time she'd seen him. The ragged wife-beater tank top that had shown off his sleeve tattoos was gone. This Louis looked respectable, with his hair neatly trimmed, a short-sleeve Tommy Bahama shirt, dark jeans, and boots.

He hadn't been a good friend of Miguel's, but he'd been a senior member of the gang nonetheless. She couldn't say she'd liked him, but she hadn't been afraid of him. He'd been polite to her, probably because he'd known she had Miguel's protection. If anyone would have information about her old friend, Louis would.

Ty was sitting to her right at a small table. Making certain he could see her, she sidled up to the bar and wedged her way toward Louis. The instant Louis saw her, his eyes widened. "Eliana Garcia?"

She smiled tentatively, as if unsure of the welcome she'd receive. "It's just Ana now. Louis?"

Louis stood and held out his arms to her. "Si. Come here! *Dé Louis viejo un abrazo.*"

And just like that she was enfolded in the other man's arms. Within an hour, she was surrounded by other members of Primos Sangre, new and old alike. Aware of Ty's eyes on her, she bided her time. She slugged back a shot of tequila and forced herself to make meaningless, cheerful chitchat, about the old days as well as her time in prison. Instead of treating her time behind bars as a joke or something to be envied, the others looked at her with expressions of compassion, making her wonder how much they actually knew about what had landed her there and what had happened afterward. No one actually mentioned Gloria or Miguel.

Another shot of tequila appeared in front of her and she threw it back, then allowed Louis to lead her to the dance floor. The band was playing a fast number and she danced wildly, letting the slight buzz of the alcohol go to her head, growing more aware of her body's reactions. She danced three more songs with Louis until he excused himself to get more drinks.

Awkwardly, she stood on the dance floor, unsure whether to go back and join the others. But without Louis by her side, she was reluctant to do so. With no other choice, she danced by herself for a while, enjoying the music, not making eye contact with onlookers. With her friends around, no one would dare to grab her and grind.

She didn't even glance at Ty. Didn't want to give herself away in case someone was watching them. But she knew without a doubt that he was watching her.

She felt his gaze caressing her.

And she responded in kind. She let her inhibitions go. She swayed to the music, not with cheesy overt gyrations meant to titillate, but in a restrained, undulating dance meant to seduce. Communicate that she desired him. She'd never said it out loud. She might never be that brave. But in this way, she could tell him, and hope that he understood what she was really saying. She desired him in spite of what she knew about him. Body and soul.

I want you. So damn much, Ana.

Ty's voice echoed in her head and she stumbled, just barely able to keep her gaze from flying to him. She swore she'd heard him but he was too far away. The music was too loud. She had to have been imagining it.

The air around her seemed to sizzle and vibrate.

Somehow, she knew. She *knew*.

It was him—it was *them*—that she was feeling.

Was she going crazy? How was it possible to feel so connected to another person?

Her movements became less restrained. More urgent. More desperate. She could practically feel the molecules in the air now, clinging to her body and caressing her in place of his hands. Her nipples tightened beneath her shirt and her core wept for him. She wondered if he could smell her or if he—

She heard a loud crash coming from Ty's direction. Automatically, she looked up and just caught sight of his back as he was striding away. The table where he'd been sitting was leaning to the side, and part of the edge had been broken off, sharp pieces of wood jutting out at odd angles.

She stared at the table with her mouth agape before Louis came back and took her in his arms once more.

Despite Ana's seductive dance—which had caused Ty to break the table he was sitting at and rush outside to get some air—he wasn't gone long. He was acutely aware of the promise he'd made to protect her, just as he'd been aware of what she'd been telling him with that erotic display on the dance floor. Swiftly, he made his way back in and headed to the bar, positioning himself on a stool.

He was harder than an iron spike and all he could think about was striding toward the dance floor, ripping her from that man's arms, stripping her naked, and taking her right then and there, for everyone to see. So everyone could witness that she was his.

His, damn it. To fuck. To feed from. To love. For all eternity.

The thought of what his eternity was really going to look like, however, sobered him instantly. Ana was human. Even if somehow she truly did still desire him and could give herself to him as he was, she was going to die. So was everyone in this bar. Every human currently on the planet. That was what was supposed to happen. What was natural.

Ty wasn't. He couldn't forget that.

As an unnatural being with unnatural urges, he had changed mere seconds before he'd attacked that homeless man. Worst-case scenario, instead of protecting Ana as he'd promised, he might somehow lose it and end up taking her blood, or her body for that matter, against her will.

The very thought made him nauseous, and he closed his eyes, taking in deep, dragging breaths. When he finally opened them again, he searched the dance floor for Ana, relaxing slightly when he saw she was still there, smashed up flat against the Hispanic man's chest.

He didn't like it. Of course, she was only doing what she was supposed to. The man was obviously someone she knew from the gang, and she was getting close to him for the sole purpose of getting word to Miguel that she was looking for him.

But Ty still didn't like it. He hated it, in fact.

The drumbeat picked up, intensifying the rhythm of the music. The wild crowd on the dance floor surged to the beat, merging to form a wall between Ty and Ana until he could no longer see her.

Shit.

Seconds ticked by.

Where was she? Why wasn't she pushing her way toward him? She knew she wasn't ever supposed to lose sight of him.

But she'd knocked back five shots of tequila while socializing with her old pals. Was she too drunk to remember what she was doing? Why they were there?

Fuck.

Ty moved toward the dance floor where he'd last seen Ana.

He froze when he heard Ana scream.

CHAPTER
TWENTY-ONE

Control. Ty knew he needed to maintain control. But adrenaline coursed through his body, his instincts triggered by Ana's scream. He moved through the crowd. Shoving people out of his way, heading in the direction of the scream, he paused at the edge of the dance floor. A narrow hallway with a blinking neon sign for the restrooms, ran to the left. A red emergency exit sign at its end marked it as the back exit.

He grabbed a burly man who'd stepped into his path, lifted him off his feet, and tossed him aside. No one was getting in his way. He had to protect Ana. He could hear her screams so loudly, so clearly.

Why were none of the other patrons doing anything? Was this what being human had been reduced to?

He reached the exit and shoved the metal door open so hard it flew off the hinges and clattered to the ground. There was no sound in the air, except for Ana's continued screams.

Only she wasn't screaming.

In the dimly lit and cluttered alleyway, he saw her, up against a brick wall, a distance away from the bar, next to a Dumpster and a pile of rubble. Her arms were wrapped around the same man she'd been dancing with and she was kissing him.

So why the hell could he *still* hear her shrieking the

word *no*? Was he going insane, imagining Ana's cries of fear and pain?

The man reached down and palmed Ana's breast. *Then*—with Ana's mouth fused to the man's, her cries turned bloodcurdling.

The sound was so loud and terrifying it ripped Ty's mind and heart apart.

Her screams were silent.

I'm reading her mind, he realized. I can hear her thoughts. I can hear how much she doesn't want this. He roared then, flying into action.

Fast. Ruthless. Merciless.

Exactly like the vampire he was.

Ana had her eyes closed, gritting her teeth even as she kept kissing Louis. The guy wanted her, and because he thought he was going to get her, he'd been answering her questions when she could get a word in. He was about to tell her how she could get in touch with Miguel when he squeezed her breast. Even though her body and mind rejected his touch, she let him do it. Just a few more seconds and she'd get the information she needed.

Then she could go back inside to Ty with something that could really help him. Maybe with the information, they could go see Miguel together. Maybe they wouldn't even have to infiltrate Salvation's Crossing.

A roar sounded, loud and angry and not quite human. Her eyes flew open in time for her to see Ty ripping the man off her and throwing him to the ground. She stared, shocked, at Louis, then whipped her gaze back to Ty.

"Ty, wait. What are you doing?" she said even as she moved to help Louis.

Instead of letting her help him up, however, Louis tugged at her, throwing her off-balance and tumbling her to the ground, knocking the breath out of her. She lay there, in the muck and grime that littered the alley-way, clutching her bruised ribs and gasping for breath, panic setting every nerve in her body on fire.

Louis scrambled to his feet and grabbed an iron bar lying next to the Dumpster. He held it in front of him, then thrust it in Ty's direction. "She wants it," he sneered at Ty. "Just like she wanted it years ago. I'm just giving the slut what she wants."

A guttural sound came from Ty, as if ripped from the very depths of his being. In a flash of a second he was right up close to Louis. He threw an uppercut, his fist connecting with the underside of Louis's jaw, and Ana gaped as Louis went flying. He landed a good ten feet from Ty.

No human could punch that hard but Ty wasn't human. He'd told her that. So had Carly. Now she was seeing more evidence of what that really meant.

"Ty!" she shouted, trying to get him to calm down. "Stop!"

Shakily, Louis got to his feet and dropped the iron bar. For a moment Ana breathed a sigh of relief.

Until Louis reached behind his back and pulled out a pistol. And aimed it straight at Ty's heart.

"You still planning on fucking with me, *hombre?*" Louis spat out. He took a step forward. "I'm the one with the gun. Walk away and let me do this bitch in peace or you get a big hole blown in your chest."

"Get the fuck away from her. From both of us," Ty said, his voice deep and haunted and eerie. Hollow.

Louis let out a caustic laugh. "Why don't you make me?"

Ty moved then, faster than Ana could even comprehend. He made it to Louis in under a second. He grabbed Louis and threw him in the air—five, ten, fifteen feet. Twenty feet. Higher than the roof of the bar. And then Louis fell.

On his way down, a gunshot exploded.

Ana saw it happen as if in slow motion.

Louis had shot Ty.

Directly in the heart.

"No!"

Thud. Thud. Thud. Thud. Ana heard the heartbeats coming from her chest. Counted them. Focused on them. She wanted to close her eyes, but she couldn't.

She'd known. They'd told her that a vampire couldn't die, but part of her hadn't believed it. Hadn't truly believed any of what they'd said. Not until now.

Ty had been shot. In the chest. In the heart. She'd seen him get hit. Blood had sprayed everywhere when the bullet entered, and now was spattered across his white dress shirt. Dots of red clung to her. Dripped off her face. And yet Ty still lived. Even now, he was getting up from where he'd fallen back on the ground.

He grimaced. Then hissed, baring his teeth.

But where she should have seen ordinary teeth, she saw his fangs. And the murderous look in his eyes.

"Ty?" she whispered.

"Puta," she heard Louis groan out. He'd hit the ground and lay moaning, his legs immobile but his head whipping back and forth between her and Ty. His body seemed paralyzed.

Not entirely. Ana noticed movement, and realized Louis still held his gun. He lifted it up and pointed it at her.

This is it, she thought.

She was dead.

She'd never get to prove anything to Ty or kiss him again.

Never get to see Gloria again.

She was going to die in a back alley and—

The shot cracked and she closed her eyes.

Waited.

And waited.

And opened her eyes to a horror far more bloody than anything she'd ever seen. Animalistic. Ferocious.

She saw Ty, bent over a struggling Louis, tearing into the man's neck with his fangs.

She stifled a raw, rough scream, but it blasted through the alley anyway.

The sound hadn't come from her. It wasn't Louis. It had come from within the nightclub. People had heard the gunshot and were shouting as they ran down the hallway to the back entrance toward them.

"Leave! Now!" She flinched at Ty's raw command. Her gaze snapped back to him and focused on his blood-soaked clothes and face. Her knees gave out but before she hit the ground, Ty was there, sweeping her up into his arms before she had time to react.

"Stop!" a male voice commanded.

A woman, maybe two, shrieked without stopping.

But though she looked, Ana couldn't identify any of them. Ty, with her in his arms, was moving too fast, so inhumanly fast she knew no one would have clearly seen them, even if they had been able to take their eyes off Louis's gruesome corpse.

CHAPTER
TWENTY-TWO

Ana was as scared as she'd ever been. Considering the path her life had taken, that was saying something. Her heart thudded in her chest and her breaths came far too fast. In her mind, she could still see Louis and the man who'd killed him. Violently. Viciously. But not, it would seem, easily.

After carrying her away from the nightclub for what had to be miles, Ty had finally stopped in what appeared to be a deserted parking garage adjacent to the local mall. He'd set her down—gently, oh so gently—then scrambled away from her.

Crouched down on his heels, his arms wrapped around his head as if to hide or protect himself, his face turned away from her to the wall next to him, he looked . . . tortured. Even from where she huddled herself, she could see he was shaking.

Like a wild animal who'd fought past a herd of predators, he'd collapsed right when he was about to reach safety. As if he'd given up. As if the same horror she'd felt at watching what he'd done was eating him alive. He was whispering something she couldn't hear, clearly in tremendous pain.

It had nothing to do with the bullet Louis had shot him with.

The thought of him suffering so made her feel as if her

own heart was being ripped out. All she wanted to do was hold and comfort him.

Hesitantly, she started crawling toward him.

"I'm sorry. I'm sorry. I didn't mean to scare you. I'm sorry."

He was saying the words over and over again, until she was right beside him, calling his name.

"Ty! *Ty!*"

He seemed oblivious to her presence.

Gritting her teeth, she reached out and touched his arm. "Ty."

His head snapped up at her touch. His mouth was closed and she couldn't see his fangs, but the lower part of his face was still smeared with blood. Louis's blood. The feral look in Ty's eyes terrified her. But as she stared at him, she saw the intensity of his regret. She saw his humanity.

Her fear and panic didn't go away but it did subside.

Swallowing hard, she felt him shake even harder. She squeezed his arm in what she hoped he'd interpret as a reassuring gesture. "Ty, *está bien,*" she said. "It's okay."

"No," he choked out. "This is what I am now. A monster. A freak."

It was exactly what she'd thought about him, but she protested anyway. "You're not a monster. Louis came after us. And you saved me. You saved both of us."

He didn't say anything more. Turning his face toward the wall again, he shook and shook. Somehow, before she knew what she was doing, she had her arms around him to comfort him.

And he let her.

Slowly, his shaking lessened.

She started to pull away. In response, Ty wrapped his own arms around her, pulling her even closer into his embrace. "No. Please. Don't go."

He sounded so vulnerable, though he wasn't. Still, his

raw plea awakened long-ago emotions in her, ones she had never wanted to relive. The memories were unbearable.

Gloria had clung to her when she'd crawled into Ana's bed at night, begging her to keep her safe from the monsters—the ones in the closet, the ones on the street, the ones that their mother brought home with her.

She'd always told Gloria she'd protect her. That she'd keep the monsters away. She wanted to tell Ty the same thing, but she couldn't. In the end, she hadn't been able to protect Gloria. Ty knew that. He would come to his senses, ashamed of his moment of weakness.

He was the strong one. Not her. She pulled away again.

"I have to go," she insisted. "*Debemos ir,* Ty. Back to Belladonna."

Ty heard what Ana was saying and forced himself to release her. Together, they stood up. Every barrier that had come between them, plus a few new ones, crashed back into place.

Taking a deep breath, accepting what she'd said about having to leave, he fought for self-control.

"I need to call Carly. Explain what happened so she can do damage control. Listen to the police radios."

She nodded. "Tell her to send a car for us," she said.

Right. Because they couldn't very well go back to the nightclub to retrieve the car they'd driven there. Police would be all over the place, doing what they could to find the man's murderer.

Him.

Revulsion crawled up his spine and he fought back waves of self-hatred.

His actions as a vampire sickened and infuriated him. Why couldn't he control what he was? How he acted?

He'd been proud of his position in the FBI, proud of serving a country that wasn't even his. He could lose it all.

Quickly, he called Carly and explained what had happened. As always, she was cool. Calm. Detached.

"The car will be here shortly," he said after hanging up, then forced himself to look Ana in the eye.

To his surprise, she stepped closer to him.

She smelled good, musky and real, but underlying that was the scent of . . . what? Disgust? Fear?

At least she wasn't running from him or fighting him off. Ana was strong, he'd give her that.

"Why did you attack him?" she asked, her voice tremulous.

"I heard you screaming."

She shook her head. "No. You couldn't have. I definitely wasn't screaming. I was letting him kiss me. I was trying to get information about Miguel from him."

He noticed spatters of dried blood across her face and raised his hand as if he could wipe them away, then dropped it. "I lost sight of you on the dance floor."

She winced. "It all happened so fast. He pulled me outside, but I was making progress. I was close, so close to getting him to talk—"

"I heard you scream," he said, his eyes haunted. "You kept crying out the word *no,* over and over again."

"Ty," she whispered, "I don't understand. He wasn't raping me. I never screamed. I never said the word *no.*"

He stared into her eyes. In the split second before he'd thrown Louis off her, he'd *felt* how grateful she was that he'd come out when he did, but her lips hadn't moved. He sighed. Nodded.

"I read your mind," he said. "I didn't know it at the time, and I didn't mean to do it, but . . . you wanted it to stop. That's what I was hearing. Your thoughts."

"You can—you can read my mind?" Her expression

and voice were horrified. Her knees gave out and her body buckled. "You never told me that was one of your powers."

He caught her, and held her upright. Once again, he was surprised when she didn't pull away from him. "Would you have wanted to be around me if I had? Besides, I can only do it on occasion. If I really try. But I don't try. I've never tried to read your mind, Ana. I promise." Of course, he didn't tell her what he suspected either. That he'd most likely inserted himself into her dreams and had sex with her. He hadn't forced her. Hadn't controlled her thoughts the way he had with Bobbie. Everything they'd done had been consensual. But right now, especially with the memory of Louis's hands on her, it was the last thing he wanted to discuss. "I didn't mean to read your mind tonight. It just happened. I swear."

"Okay, I believe you." But she pulled away from him. Crossed her arms over her chest.

"You're scared of me now," he said.

"I—" she began, but his cell phone rang.

He waited for her to finish speaking. When she didn't, he answered, then clicked to end the call.

"That's the car. The driver is just around the corner. Let's go, princess." He strode forward and brushed past her, knowing she'd follow.

After all, where else could she go?

CHAPTER
TWENTY-THREE

The luxury town car was driven by a quiet man with what Ana suspected was a deliberately forgettable face. Seated in the back, she and Ty didn't speak on the drive to Belladonna. That was just fine with her. Her stomach was roiling, and she was afraid of what would happen if she dared open her mouth.

Ty's phone rang and he answered. The call was once again brief, with him listening and replying only, "Thank you," before disconnecting.

"That was Carly," he explained. "She put out some feelers. Looks like witnesses at the club saw two people in the alley with a man identified as Louis Corazon before they somehow disappeared. Their descriptions are vague and conflicting. Some said it was a man and woman, some said it was two males."

"That's . . . good?" Ana murmured.

She almost rolled her eyes at her questioning tone. Of course it was good. She was a parolee, for God's sake, one who hadn't notified the parole department of her change of address before leaving Seattle. If someone connected her to Louis's death, she could end up back in prison. Somehow, given the events of the evening and everything that had happened in the past week, she'd forgotten that. She was risking not just her freedom but her life by being here.

In a short time, the car pulled up to Belladonna. Without a word, Ty escorted her into the main house and to her room. As they walked, he seemed to take particular care not to touch her. When they reached her bedroom, he wouldn't meet her gaze.

After what he'd done, she shouldn't be surprised. Unless he was avoiding looking at her because she'd let Louis kiss her.

Seconds passed and she realized he was ashamed of what he'd done. Ashamed of what he was.

And dear God, she could relate to that. Even before she'd been sent to prison, long before that prosecutor had picked apart her life in front of a jury, she'd hated what she'd done to survive. Most of all, she'd hated what she was and the life to which she'd been born. It broke her heart to know that Ty was struggling with those same feelings because he'd been turned into a vampire. That hadn't been his choice, any more than her own misfortune had been.

"Ty—" she began, but she didn't know what else to say. How could she comfort him when she knew so little about what he was? His vampire side was fully capable of taking over. Yet as violent as he'd been with Louis, as viciously as he'd hurt him, Ty had never abused Ana. Hell, the most damaging thing he'd done to her was kiss her, and she couldn't deny that even after tonight, even knowing what he was, she wanted him to kiss her again.

His gaze had snapped up when she said his name. They stared at one another for long moments and he reached out to stroke her cheek. But even as she held her breath, he lowered his hand.

"Good night, Ana."

As he walked away, she blindly opened the door to her bedroom and turned back to close it. He hesitated at the end of the hallway and glanced back at her, giving her one last glimpse of his pale, tortured face. His blood-splattered clothes. And even when he turned and disappeared around the corner, she kept seeing him.

She tried to mold her image of him into a monster. Tried to envision him as he'd been less than an hour ago, fangs bared as he went for Louis's throat. Instead, she saw him as he'd been crouched in that parking garage, arms covering his face, horrified by what he'd just done. She saw him as she had in her dreams, communicating with every word and touch that he yearned for her. Just as she yearned for him.

In other words, try as she might, she saw all of his humanity and none of his vampire side.

Unbelievable, she thought, and leaned her head against the doorjamb.

Despite everything, despite the fact he'd killed Louis in a few seconds of lethal violence, consumed by unnatural rage, she still wanted him. With all her heart.

Ty stripped off his clothes and stepped into the shower, utterly exhausted. He didn't even bother taking off his contacts—he didn't have to. Apparently a vampire could wear contacts 24/7 with no ill effect. He let the water beat down on him, thinking that exhausted wasn't the right word.

He was soul weary.

Something that would only get far worse over the next several decades. This, he thought, is what I have to look forward to. Years upon years of seeing my human side diminish more and more. More violence. More loss of control.

More loss, period.

Bracing his hands on the shower wall, he let the water wash away the blood of the night's kill and swirl down the drain until the tub was white. The horror stayed with him.

He'd killed before. Several times. But before, the kills had been fairly controlled. Foreseeable results of targeted missions, where he'd had time to prepare himself with method and means. He'd never killed with his bare hands—with his *teeth*—in such a vile display of primal rage. He'd never killed as a vampire rather than a man.

He wasn't entirely sorry. The man, Louis, had shot him, but more important, he'd been about to shoot Ana. Despite her shock at witnessing the violence tonight, she had kept things together. Instead of running from Ty, she'd comforted him. Held him. And even now, the memory of her embrace spiked his desire for her.

He tensed with frustration, wanting only to run his hands over her body and confirm that the bastard he'd killed in that alley truly hadn't hurt her. The need to mate with her, possess her, claim her body once and for all hit him hard. Then no one she ever tried to seduce again would dare touch her for fear of what he'd do to them.

Instinctive jealousy kicked in. His fists clenched on the tile wall as he fought to control himself. Unwillingly, he imagined her with Louis.

She had let another man kiss her when she belonged to him. He *had* taken her, if only in his dreams.

In his mind, she was his and always had been.

He growled, overwhelmed by rage and possessiveness. Yet he managed to hold on to his self-control. He managed not to exit the shower, storm down to her room, break down her door, and cover her body with his. He didn't want to scare her any more than he already had.

To her, he was a monster.

The pure white wall in front of him faded to black. Ty stared into the abyss. Slowly, ever so slowly, he was becoming like the vicious, unthinking creatures that had slain his sister. The terrifying ability to perceive his transformation as it happened was about to shatter his mind.

Something snapped him out of it. Instinct again.

He had smelled her . . .

His head snapped up and he took a deeper breath.

Was he imagining it?

No, he could smell her close by. In his room. Here and now.

And he could hear her. Faint footsteps edged closer to the bathroom door.

What the hell was she doing?

His fangs elongated. His dick was already hard. Throbbing for her. Ready to claim her.

He watched as the doorknob to the bathroom door turned and the door pushed open slightly.

He heard her call his name. "Ty?"

Was she asking for permission to come in? Did she really think he would deny her?

He had to. She had no idea what was waiting for her. No idea what he was thinking. He wasn't sure he could do it, but he took a deep, shaky breath, and tried.

He really tried.

"Don't," he gasped out. "Don't come in, Ana."

The door didn't open any further as she hesitated. "Why?" she asked.

"I want you too much. I—I don't want to hurt you."

He waited for her to close the door and leave. He prayed he could let her.

Unbelievably, she stayed where she was. "I know you won't hurt me."

He closed his eyes, trying to block her out along with his spiraling need. "Ana, please listen to me. I'm on the verge of losing control. We'll talk tomorrow. Just leave. Now." He snapped the last word as his control began to shred. But he had to breathe, and when he did, a new, deliciously female scent aroused him even more . . .

He groaned when he realized she was wet for him.

He could smell it on her, and he wanted to taste those juices. Take them down his throat. Bathe himself in them until the day he died. "Go. *Go.*" His voice was almost unrecognizable now. Inhuman.

Fuck, it even scared him.

She didn't leave. Instead, in a voice that was barely there, soft and a little shaky, she said the one thing guaranteed to snap his control in half.

"No."

As Ana pushed the bathroom door open all the way, she saw Ty do the same to the shower door. She stopped cold for a breathless moment when he stepped out of the shower, wet and huge and marvelously naked except for the peculiar gold medallion he wore. She was rooted to the floor as he stalked toward her, his expression as dark and dangerous as she'd ever seen it.

Holy fuck, she thought, as her gaze swept over him. He was incredible. He was exactly as she'd envisioned in her dreams, right down to the birthmark on his left hip. She stared at the mark, which she'd already stroked and tasted in her mind, and instinctively reached out to touch it now. Knowing that her dream might have been prophetic made her shake. Ana instinctively lifted her hand to ward him off. "Wait—"

But then he was on her.

Chest heaving, he pressed his large body against hers, grasped her chin, and brought her gaze up to his. Though he didn't hurt her, his touch was far from gentle. Ana gasped, not with fear, but with anticipation.

He looked ready to eat her alive and lick the plate clean afterward.

"I told you to leave. I gave you a chance. Why didn't you listen?"

His gaze was focused on her mouth. The fingers gripping her chin loosened to stroke her jaw and the scar he'd touched only once before.

This time, she didn't flinch from his touch. She arched into it, more than ready. She'd known perfectly well that entering his room would make this happen.

Fascinated, she watched his fangs grow even longer. They were sharp. Deadly. Capable of ripping out a man's throat—she'd witnessed it happening.

She fought against the sensual languor of her betraying body, feeling as if he had entranced her. Yet she wasn't scared. All she could think about was the intense pleasure his fangs had brought her before, in her dreams, when he'd plunged them into her soft flesh and drunk from her.

She craved that intensity. Felt the first stirrings of love—and respect—for him. He was willing to kill for her. He thought she was beautiful, despite—or maybe because of—the hidden scars she bore. And he cared enough about her to tell her to go, even though he looked as if he'd starve to death without her.

Ana didn't care if he was a vampire or not.

She wanted Ty.

Ty didn't consciously try to read her mind, but he could hear her thoughts now. She was convinced she wanted him. He refused to allow himself to believe it.

His brain ordered his fingers to let go of her and told him to step away but his body wouldn't obey. If he lost contact with her skin, he would shrivel up and die.

The abyss in his mind had vanished when she'd come to him.

The darkness was still there . . . yet he could fight back. He didn't have to die. He wanted to fully live during whatever time he had left on earth and—

She swallowed hard, and his gaze followed the graceful, undulating movement of her throat.

And then he snapped.

He didn't pounce on her. He didn't shove his fangs into her the way he longed to. But he knew in that moment there was no hope of her leaving. He would take her first. He had to.

"I warned you," was all he said before he picked her up in his arms and carried her out of the bathroom and to the bed. There, he laid her down and covered her body with his.

"God, I've dreamed of this. I've dreamed of loving you, princess."

At Ty's words, Ana's eyes widened. "Wh—what did you say?"

"I said I dreamed about you. Does that surprise you?"

"N-no. I just—" As she stuttered and flushed, his eyes narrowed.

He took a deep breath and closed his eyes, savoring the smell of her ever-blossoming desire. "You've dreamed of me as well," he said. "You've dreamed of us. Well, it wasn't just a dream, Ana. I didn't know it at the time. I didn't mean to do it, I swear. But I was really there. In your dreams. In your body. I didn't force—"

She shook her head. "Of course you didn't. I—I wanted it. Wanted you. But those were dreams. Ty . . . what you're saying. It's impossible."

His gaze dropped to the hand that cupped her breast. Gently, he smoothed his thumb across her nipple, making her gasp and arch into his touch. "As impossible as vampires?"

"I don't know," she gasped.

"Never underestimate the power of desire. In my mind, you saw me the way I was before I was turned. You saw me when I was fully human." He lifted his gaze to hers. "When you saw us together, what color eyes did I have?"

"B—blue."

"That's right. Blue. Now, what else do you know about me? Do you know how I kiss when I let myself go? How I feel and how I touch? How I loved sucking your breasts and licking you between your thighs?" As he spoke, he moved his hand to that very spot and rubbed at the tiny pearl hidden there.

She hissed and thrust her hips upward with a moan.

He laughed darkly, loving how the sound made her shiver. "Yes. You're going to come. Just like before. Isn't that right, Ana? You touched yourself in your bedroom and called out my name."

"How—?"

"I was watching you."

Her reply was faint. "I thought so."

"I enjoyed the fact you called my name when you got off. Have you ever orgasmed with a man?"

Her silence was a loud admission.

"Do you know how fucking sexy that is? That just by thinking about me, I gave you something no one else has."

"Don't be so proud of yourself," she said, even as she raised her hands and stroked his hair. Her touch was gentle, yet firm enough to tell him this was real. "I never really wanted the others."

"Which is why you slept with them in the first place. So you could stay in control. And now," he murmured, "you're going to lose it. I want to make you come again. And again."

"Ty . . ."

He stroked her hair, meeting her heavy-lidded gaze. "I'm not going anywhere. And neither are you. Say yes, Ana. But only because you want me."

She stared, brow furrowed, expression somber.

Fearing her rejection, Ty suddenly closed his eyes and buried his face in her neck. Ana smelled heavenly. Her neck was creamy and soft, open and vulnerable. His fangs automatically began to lengthen as he reached out for her—

She stiffened slightly then buried her hands in his hair. When she spoke, he felt the word throughout his entire body.

"Yes."

CHAPTER
TWENTY-FOUR

Ty stiffened, wondering if he'd imagined the word, spoken in Ana's strong, husky voice. Raising his head, he stared into her eyes, seeing no hint of indecision.

She looked certain. Aroused. And the joy that spread through his body was beyond anything he'd ever experienced. Even his dream orgasm while he'd been watching Ana masturbate paled in comparison. Because this was real. She was real.

She wanted *him*.

"Oh, Ana," he said shakily, lowering his head to kiss her.

She shook her head. "Wait. I—I have one condition."

Unease caused him to frown and lift himself up, not entirely away from her.

"Your eyes," she said. "You wear contacts."

He nodded warily, thrown by the unexpected topic.

"Take them off."

He immediately recoiled, shoving himself off her and backing away. "No."

She pushed herself up on her elbows, still fully clothed while he was naked. She'd already seen him for what he was. Why did she want to see more?

"I want to see you, Ty. All of you. Nothing you show me will detract from how much I want you. God, after tonight, don't you know that?"

It made sense. She'd seen him at his worst. What did

it matter if she saw his weirdly colored eyes? Only there'd be no hiding from her then. Eyes were said to be the windows to the soul. If he uncovered his eyes, if she stared into them, what would she see?

She balanced on her knees and inched her way toward him, her hand held out. "Shh," she said, and he realized he'd been making a soft moaning sound. Wordlessly pleading with her, like a child not wanting to take his medicine. "It's okay. I'm sorry. Just come to me. Come to me, Ty. I want you."

He hesitated at first, wondering if this was a trap. But then relief flooded through him and he took her in, his beautiful Ana, finally asking for something she wanted. Something he could actually give her, if not easily, then at least without guilt.

"I'll take the contacts off," he said, and she froze, her eyes widening before she smiled. "But then you have to do something for me. Look into my eyes as they are, and if you still want me after that . . ."

"What?" she prompted when he hesitated.

"If you still want me after that, take off your clothes. All of them."

"Deal," she said quickly. So quickly he actually smiled.

With a curse, he turned and stalked to the bathroom, gripping the basin with white knuckles. He stared at his reflection, then took a deep breath. First, he took off the gold medallion he'd worn since Lesander had given it to him; nothing could come between him and Ana now. Then, with one last hint of hesitation, he took off his contacts. As soon as he could see his eerie silver pupils contrasted against the pools of his pitch-black irises, he winced. He looked like the freak he was. Alien. Monstrous.

He couldn't do it. He couldn't let her see him like this. She thought it wouldn't matter but it would, and once she flinched from him, he'd be—

"Ty."

At the sound of Ana's soft voice, Ty's head turned instantly toward the door.

He gasped, forgetting all thoughts about his eye color or what he was going to do or not do.

She was naked, her scars visible and her copper nipples soft and pouty in direct contrast to her mouth, which was pinched tight with what was obviously insecurity. She'd pulled her hair back into a tight ponytail and he wondered why . . .

Then it struck him. She was making herself completely vulnerable, even to the point of exposing her facial scar. Exposing every hurt she'd ever suffered—and had hid behind her clothes and hair and hostility.

She was doing that for him.

"Ana," he whispered and started toward her. But as he moved to take her in his arms, she held him back again and said, "I want to see. Let me see."

He tensed and a frustrated growl rumbled in his throat, but he forced himself to stop. Under the harsh bathroom light, she tilted her head as she studied his eyes. Then she scanned down his body, taking in *all* of him, including his dick. She stared as it hardened and lengthened, eventually poking her in the stomach, steel hard to her silky soft. But she didn't back away.

She lifted her gaze back to his even as she wrapped her fingers around him and started a gentle pumping motion.

He kept his arms by his sides but tipped his head back, closed his eyes, and groaned. Her touch was delicate and warm, when he'd been cold for so long. She comforted him and ratcheted him up at the same time, and it was such a mind-boggling combination that he almost thought he was dreaming again.

Then he knew he was—*he had to be*—when his cock was enveloped in a tight, wet heat.

Holy fuck, he thought, his eyes flying open and his hands automatically reaching out to tangle in her ponytail.

She'd knelt in front of him and had him in her mouth. She didn't start off soft or hesitant. She started sucking him off, using her lips and tongue and fingers to drive him absolutely crazy.

His ears were ringing. His blood pumping. His senses went into overdrive, so that even as she was on her knees and touching only one part of him, she surrounded him. She was inside him. Her scent was in his lungs, her taste not just on his tongue but coating his throat, her touch *everywhere*. On his cock, but also in the tiniest, most innocuous place. His toes. His ears. And yes, his eyes. The silver pupils that he hated became something bearable because she was there.

No, he thought, and ripped himself away from her.

She gasped and he could see from the expression on her face she thought he was rejecting her.

It wasn't that at all.

He just couldn't stand the idea of her being on her knees in front of him.

She was good. Strong and worthy. He?

Ty dropped to his knees in front of her and cupped her face in his hands.

He opened his mouth, wanting to say something profound and beautiful. Something resembling a sonnet or a love song. Instead, all that came out was, "Need you. Now."

Her relief was obvious. She stood and held out her hand. When he took it, she guided him out of the bathroom and back into his bedroom. Yes, he thought. This is perfect. This is what I want. I need to know she's with me every step of the way. That she wants this, without any fear.

But yet it wasn't right. Because her focus was on him,

and convincing him she wasn't afraid. She desired him, yes, but she wasn't dripping with desire. She wasn't nearly as crazy to have him as he was to have her.

And that was going to change.

As soon as they were both naked on that bed, where she was leading him, he was taking over.

He was taking her.

Ana wasn't stupid.

She knew what was coming, and she'd braced herself for it.

Ty wasn't naturally submissive. He wasn't one to be led. He was allowing it now because he needed to be sure this was what she wanted. And that she wasn't scared.

But as soon as he was convinced of both those things, he was going to take her. She'd heard his intent in those three words he'd spoken to her while he was on his knees, his voice rough and masculine and intense despite his supplicant position. His body was shaking under the strain of holding himself back. It was obvious in those eyes—those strangely mesmerizing eyes. Pools of liquid silver.

She lowered herself to sit on the bed then scooted her way back until she was positioned dead center on the mattress. Fighting back nerves and embarrassment as her bare body jiggled, she lay back, raised her arms above her head, and positioned her legs so they were slightly bent and ready to welcome him in between them. The entire time, he watched her. His face flushed. His eyes heavy. His breathing a rough staccato.

Still, he didn't do what she thought he would. He didn't immediately cover her with his body. He stood there, looking tortured, jaw clenching, temple throbbing. "Sure?" he asked, as if even the effort to string two words together was now beyond him.

How could he even ask? All she wanted was for him to be the type of lover he couldn't help but be, even before he was a vampire. Dominant. Aggressive and rough.

Well, as she'd told him before, she was willing to do whatever it took to get what she needed. She knew how to drive him to the edge. He'd admitted he liked it when she talked dirty. She'd also sensed how turned on he'd gotten when she spoke Spanish. So . . .

Arching her back slightly and parting her legs just a bit more, she said, "Fuck me, Ty. *Le deseo. Dentro de mí. Jódame duramente.* Please. *Tome mi cuerpo entonces toma mi sangre.*"

His eyes flared as he took in her words.

I want you. Inside me. Fuck me hard.

Take my body, then take my blood.

He growled. His fangs sprang out but she barely got a glimpse of them because he was moving too fast. Her breath whooshed out of her as he covered her, pushed his body between her thighs, wrapped her hair around his hands, and lifted her up to meet his marauding mouth.

Ty pushed his tongue into Ana's mouth even as he managed to not plunge his dick into her core or his fangs into her throat. For now, kissing her was enough. He wanted to commit to memory every single thing about her. The texture of her sweet tongue. The slick heat of her mouth. The tangy sweetness that left a hint of something dark and mysterious, something he was determined to capture. He opened her mouth wider, moved his tongue deeper, and caressed her face with his thumbs.

His body was screaming for him to touch more of her, to suck her nipples and finger her pussy and lick his way down to that hard pearl at the apex of her thighs.

But he kept kissing her anyway. Couldn't seem to tear

himself away from the lovely mouth that had spoken such dirty, dirty words, blowing his control to shreds.

Ana, however, didn't seem to have the same problem. It was as if she heard his body's pleas and set out to answer them. Even as her mouth gave right back to him, her hands stroked down his arms, back, and ass. And her body . . . Fuck! Her body.

She writhed and twisted, smashing and rubbing her breasts against his chest, gripping his hips with her thighs and using them to pull herself up and rub herself against his aching cock. He wasn't quite in the juncture of her thighs, but she kept focused on her goal until . . . yes! . . . his length slipped between her thighs and was immediately covered with her creamy arousal.

She moved back and forth, riding his cock, driving the head against her clit only to send it sliding back toward her ass then back again.

He ripped his mouth away from hers and groaned, "Oh, God. Oh, Ana. You feel so good. So fucking good."

She had a pained expression on her face, as if the pleasure she was feeling bordered on too much, but she smiled. "I love the feel of you, too."

He kissed her briefly, then couldn't resist her sweet breasts for a second longer. He sucked one nipple into his mouth, gently, then harder, even as he rolled the other between his fingers. She whimpered, gripping his head with one hand as if to keep him in place. He wanted to tell her he wasn't going anywhere, but he didn't want to give up the morsel in his mouth, not even for a second. He hummed and purred and told her what he needed to with his hands.

She was still grinding against him, but he lifted up slightly, then pushed her knees up and out so she was open to him. He slid his hand between her thighs. With two fingers, he stroked through her wet folds, immediately noticing the hitch in her breath and the way she tensed up.

Given she hadn't had a problem with his cock rubbing against her, it surprised him. Carefully, he watched her face as he penetrated her with both fingers, slowly but thoroughly.

She was really tight and he had to work to even get his fingers inside her. She didn't protest, but she trembled. And he saw the flash of fear on her face.

"What's wrong? Why does this scare you?"

She swallowed hard and he waited for her to deny it.

To his surprise, she didn't.

"I was raped when I was sixteen. He used his fingers. His—his hand. He pinched and scratched. I—I usually don't let men—"

He withdrew his fingers only to slide them inside her again.

Her face grew even redder and she bit her lip. They seemed to be signs of her ratcheting arousal, but . . .

"Do you want me to stop?" he asked.

She shook her head.

"Do you want me to be gentle? Go slow?"

She hesitated. Shook her head again.

"Say it," he commanded. "Because you asked me to fuck you hard. Have you changed your mind? I don't want there to be any doubt."

"No, Ty," she said. "I want everything you can give me. Don't hold back."

He thrust his fingers inside her again, testing out what she was saying. She gasped, but arched up when he pulled back, clearly not wanting him to stop.

So he gave it to her again. And again, eventually hooking his fingers and bumping up against her pleasure spot. Her eyes widened and she shouted out, clearly surprised by the influx of sensation.

"Good?"

"More. I want more."

"You want my tongue on your clit? Because that's what I want. So bad, Ana."

"Do it," she whimpered.

He shifted position. A second later, his fingers still working inside her, he used his tongue to lap at her, groaning at the familiar sweetness of her juices. She was the best thing he'd ever tasted. Better than all the human blood he'd drunk since he'd been turned.

"This is what feeds me," he said. "This is what I want. This is—" His words became muffled as he pleasured her.

She was thrashing around, forcing him to hold her hips down. He wanted to push her over the edge, but her body grew more and more tense, and even though she was into everything he was doing to her . . . it didn't happen. She didn't come.

He sensed she couldn't.

Or, whether she knew it or not, that she wasn't letting herself.

He surged up and was momentarily blinded by the sight of her fingers caressing her own breasts. Taking her hands in his, he pinned them above her head and nudged his cock head against her opening. Her eyes widened at being restrained, but she didn't fight him. "I'm going to take you now. Your blood and body, just like you asked. And you're going to give them to me. No holding back. You're going to take the pleasure I'm going to give you. Only for you."

Before she could respond, he pushed into her even as he pushed up on his arms so he could watch her swallowing him up. Her tight muscles fought him, not making it easy, but he kept going, pushing strongly and steadily into her, feeding her more and more of himself as her eyes became more and more dazed with pleasure.

Finally, he was buried to the hilt and his arms shook

as he tried to fight back his own orgasm. He was close. So close. But his own pleasure didn't matter. Not until she had hers.

She wanted it, too. She was going after it, without any more urging from him. She was shoving her hips up then down, riding him with a look of wonder on her face. Every move she made jacked up his own bliss, forced him closer and closer until he had to reach down and pinch the base of his dick tight, to stop himself from exploding.

Her eyes met his, and as she continued to work against him, she caressed her throat and whispered, "Please."

Softly. Politely.

"Oh, baby." He lowered his face and inhaled, as if he could actually smell her blood along with her arousal.

He licked her throat, teasing her and himself. Once. Twice. Then he plunged his fangs into her.

That was all it took. The first drop of her blood on his tongue, and he was coming, spurting his seed inside her. Shouting out.

And relishing the fact she was coming and shouting, too.

CHAPTER
TWENTY-FIVE

Bobbie cowered in front of his boss. Shadows crossed the cramped office where he sat. His boss strode from one end of the room to the other, the pacing a clear indication of irritation. The male human in the corner, shuddering and bawling like a baby, still had blood trickling down his neck from where Bobbie's boss had drunk. The room smelled acrid and bitter—blood and piss and fear and vomit. And shit.

Not how Bobbie had thought a vampire feeding would smell. Where was the glamour? The allure?

Weeks had gone by since he'd reported on the man/vampire who'd been messing with Ana Martin, and he'd heard nothing from his boss. So why the sudden visit?

"Are you absolutely certain the vampire you saw with Ana was attacking her? Harassing her?" his boss asked.

Bobbie sucked it up.

"He was harassing her, like I told you."

"I hired you to spy on the woman. To report back to me immediately if anyone messed with her. I have something you desperately want. And now I need to know the truth. Not just a repeat of what you think you saw, but the truth. Was this vampire harming Ana? Or was something else going on?"

In the corner, the man who'd served as a human drinking fountain gurgled and flailed about. Bobbie's boss ignored him. With one wet sigh, the man lurched upward, then collapsed back to the polished wood floor, his eyes open. Staring. Unseeing.

Dead.

The way Bobbie would be unless his boss could find it in his heart to forgive him for whatever mistake he'd made. An irrational giggle burbled in his chest and he fought against it. He'd do better to throw himself on his boss's mercy. Death was next, unless he gave his boss exactly what he'd asked for.

"Maybe I misunderstood his, uh, his intentions," Bobbie babbled.

"Meaning?"

"She coulda liked it. I mean, kind of. Like, how some guys get all testosterone-filled and come on to a babe by getting in their face. Some girls like being manhandled and stuff. You know, like those S&M freaks."

His boss hiked a hip against the wooden desk and stared down at Bobbie. "Are you saying that my *friend* Ana is into that shit?"

Fuck! Frenzy tore inside Bobbie's chest, his heart pumping so loud people in the next county over could surely hear the beats. How deep of a hole could he dig for himself? "No! Just that I had this, uh, this sense, that maybe she liked it. Like he was, I dunno, coming on to her in some weird way."

"You mean the vampire was *flirting* with Ana?"

Bobbie nodded, his head bopping up and down like a yo-yo. What else could he do? The vampire in front of him had wanted his opinion. Not just the facts, but his feelings on what had happened. And what he'd just said was the truth. There was something odd about how the weak vampire had acted with Ana. Something almost erotic. "Maybe. I think in a way she liked it. Liked how he held her down."

"So you told me a lie."

Oh, crap. He'd fucked up, hadn't he? Completely

screwed his chance of becoming a vampire. He cast a quick glance at the corpse in the corner. Maybe he'd even screwed up his chance to come out of this meeting alive.

Desperately, he grabbed the neck of his shirt and pulled it down, exposing his jugular vein to his boss. He fell to his knees. "I fucked up. I get it. Go ahead, feed from me. I don't deserve to be turned into a vampire. I'm nothing." He cast another glance at the human in the corner, pale and lifeless.

If this was the end for him, so be it. He only hoped he didn't shit in his pants like the dead dude. At least he'd die doing something worthy. Feeding a vampire.

"Get up," his boss snapped out, then kicked him. "You're worth more alive than dead. For the moment."

Relief flooded through him. Bobbie stood, uncertain of what to expect.

"So do you think she liked the vampire?"

Wanting more than anything to be helpful, Bobbie nodded forcefully. "She wasn't disgusted by him, at least."

"And she knew he was a vampire?"

"I—I don't know. I'm sorry." Stupidly, Bobbie glanced at the door.

His boss came closer. "Stay there."

Bobbie nodded, then waited, standing with shaking knees until the vampire pulled out a photograph from a drawer in the wooden desk.

"Look closely. Is this the vampire you said was flirting with Eliana Garcia?"

Carefully, Bobbie examined the photograph. He nodded. "That's him. Same guy—I mean vampire."

"In that case," his boss said, voice gentle, "this changes everything. He killed a former acquaintance of mine. A man named Louis. I want to know if Louis deserved it. He was a hothead."

Bobbie shrugged nervously.

"He was there with several friends," his boss continued. "Members of the gang. Find those men. Talk to them. Tell me what they know about Ana and the man named Ty."

CHAPTER
TWENTY-SIX

The next morning, Ana woke to an empty bed, fully aware of everything that had happened the night before. Of course, the main event wasn't Ty sprouting fangs and killing a man, but the two of them making love.

Now didn't she just have her priorities straight?

Stretching, she winced at the tiny aches that twinged through her body, the feeling of being thoroughly used but in a good way. The sensation was very interesting. And as foreign to her as some of the acts she and Ty had engaged in.

Adorar Ty había sido celestial. It had been the most amazing experience of her life, and she didn't even feel guilty about obsessing about it . . . until she heard the voices. Loud voices.

Someone was arguing, and though she couldn't make out exact words, she heard Ty's British accent added to the mix. Swiftly, she jumped out of bed, dressed, and followed the voices to the Belladonna library.

Collette, Barrett, and Justine were there, but they were quietly sitting in various chairs. Peter stood grim-faced next to the table that held the intercom box.

Ty stood in the center of the room. He wore a crisp button-down shirt and slacks and a blank expression. When he saw her, heat flooded his expression, but he quickly banked it and looked away.

Carly's voice filled the room, setting Ana's teeth on

edge, but she forced herself to walk into the room and take a seat.

"—screwed up time and again, Ty. If you can't control yourself now, what the hell are you going to do if Miguel decides he wants a little piece of Ana before he'll let you into Salvation's Crossing? Are you going to forget why you're really there and rip him apart, too?"

What a wonderful feeling. Ana was topic A and she hadn't been invited.

So much for girls sticking together.

Ty glanced at Ana again, and this time his gaze was as cold as ice. "She's not going to give Miguel anything," he said quietly.

"Can you guarantee that?" Carly scoffed. "You know he wants her. And that's why we're bringing her in—"

"He might want her but he's not going to have her. I know that with absolute certainty."

"But . . ."

As Carly's voice drifted off, Ana took the chance to think.

Ty couldn't lie, and Carly had to know that. Which meant she now knew that something had changed between Ana and Ty. That Ty meant what he said—he wasn't going to let Ana sleep with a man even if that was the only way to get them what they needed.

Ana smiled at him but he looked away again, as if he was afraid he'd revealed too much of himself. To others? Or to her as well?

The atmosphere in the room was strained and heavy. No one was talking but him.

"All we have to do is convince Miguel that Ana and I are lovers," Ty insisted. "Once I'm inside—well, I'm a goddamn vampire, for Christ's sake. If I can't get the information we need, no one can."

He strode toward Ana and held out his hand.

What he'd just told everyone communicated that Ty

now thought of Ana as his, but he wasn't taking any chances. He was making sure there was no room for doubt.

With only a slight hint of hesitation, she reached out and took his hand. Only then did she see his body relax slightly. In front of everyone, they walked out of the room. Together.

As soon as they were back in his room, however, Ana tugged her hand out of his.

He watched her warily. Then frowned.

Had he read her mind? Or was she simply that easy for him to predict?

"Don't," he warned.

"Don't what?"

"Don't tell me you're still going to do whatever you need to do to get Miguel to do what we want him to do."

He was normally so articulate, so unflappable, that she smiled at the convoluted statement. He didn't smile back.

She got it. Of course she didn't want to sleep with Miguel. And she was overjoyed that Ty didn't want her to, either. But if she *had* to . . . "Ty, you said it yourself. An agent has to be willing to do whatever it takes to get a mission done."

"You're not an agent. Not really."

Where had *that* come from? Apparently Ty was two different vampires in public and in private. She'd had to inadvertently eavesdrop on him and their colleagues to find that out. She was reminded of how little she really knew about this man. This vampire. And although the sex had been amazing between them last night, that didn't mean that in the cold light of day anything had changed.

She crossed her arms over her chest and tilted out her hip with attitude. "Oh? Then what have I been doing here for the past two weeks? Providing naughty entertainment? That's Justine's game."

"Cheap shot. She has nothing to do with this." He gestured toward his bed. "In case you've forgotten, things changed for us last night."

He was right. Things had changed drastically. Being with him had been the best experience of her life. She wanted more. She wished the world would disappear and they could ride off into the sunset together. But they couldn't. He'd brought her here for a reason. Her past. She'd come for another reason. Her future. Her future with *Gloria*. She couldn't let her growing feelings for him get in the way of that future. She was human, he was vampire. He was going to live forever. She'd once more be left behind.

Unless she left him first.

With that thought strengthening her resolve, she forced herself to say, "Why? Because we had sex? We were due, Ty. I wanted you, and though I can't believe how lucky I am that it's true, you wanted me."

He groaned. Strode up to her and cupped her face. "Ana. I'm the lucky one. Don't you get that by now? In your arms, I'm a man. You make me feel the way I did before I was turned."

She reached up and patted his cheek. "I'm so glad. So, so glad. But you brought me here to work, not to fool around. Maybe it's best if we both remember that."

"Ana—"

She interrupted him. "And I do have my own agenda. Sneaking into Salvation's Crossing isn't just about getting you and the FBI what you want. It's about saving my sister, remember?"

His mouth flattened and his expression hardened. "I remember. But how far are you willing to go? Would you seduce Miguel, let him touch you just like you let

Louis touch you when I'm giving you a way out? I'm trying to tell you I'll take care of things for you."

"Who asked you to? Carly?" The sneer on his face when he mentioned Louis touching her irked her. He didn't get to tell her what to do just because he'd gotten between her legs. "Gloria doesn't know you from Adam. Why would she trust you?"

Ty didn't seem to have an answer for that.

"Yeah. So don't tell me what I can and cannot do," she insisted. "Whatever it takes. That's the Belladonna way, right?"

His head inclined in an almost invisible nod.

"You taught me that."

"Don't remind me," he growled softly.

"Let's keep our priorities straight and get back to work. We had one night together, Ty. Sure, it felt great. Sure, it was fun. I certainly wouldn't object to having more. But did you really think because you made me come I'd just let you take over? Trust something as important as my sister to a man I barely know—to a *vampire*?" She hadn't meant it as an insult, not exactly, but that's obviously how he took it.

His face darkened and he stepped away from her. "Right. So in the end, that's all I am to you. A means to your sister. A vampire."

"You are those things, Ty. I can't let a—a good fuck—get in the way of my ultimate goal. And neither can you."

He stared at her for several seconds, his expression blank. Even so, she couldn't shake the feeling that her words had hurt him. Understandable, since they'd hurt her to say them. But she had to be realistic. Practical. It's what had kept her going all these years. She couldn't pretend Ty was her prince come to rescue her from some lonely tower. If life had taught her anything, it was that she had to depend on herself to get the important things done.

Still, something compelled her to reach out her hand to him. "I'm sorry, Ty, I—"

He stepped back before she could touch him. "I guess there's nothing more to say right now. You want to do things your way, then you can do without the physical pleasure I gave you last night."

"Okay. If that's what you think is best," she whispered, even as her heart felt like it was being squeezed in a vise. But she couldn't back down. She'd had him. She'd enjoyed him. But there were limits. When it came to Gloria, that was where she drew a big, thick line.

He walked out of the room without answering.

So. She'd woken up all pink and glowing, and less than an hour later, got demoted from lover to coworker simply because she wouldn't play things the way he wanted her to. Life went on.

Ty wasn't more important than Gloria.

Unfortunately, the thought did nothing to ease the pain of his absence.

PART
3

THE MISSION

CHAPTER
TWENTY-SEVEN

The rolling hills of the Napa Valley were clad in golden grass growing thickly under dark, gnarled grapevines in orderly rows belonging to countless vineyards. The drive up from San Francisco Airport had taken them over the Golden Gate Bridge and through Marin County, a wealthy coastal community that was nowhere near as rustic as it looked. Ty had told her that dozens of multi-millionaires and several billionaires resided there and in Napa as well.

It took fifteen minutes to get to the end of this so-called driveway. The Hispanic Alliance fund-raiser was taking place on an estate that was well hidden from casual visitors. It was also open to the public—assuming one was prepared to pay a grand a plate.

Their driver left them near the main house, an enormous adobe structure with a roof of curved Spanish red tiles and walls punctuated with the round ends of viga beams. Antique doors that looked like they came from some ancient Mexican hacienda had been flung open. The low, semicircular tiled stairs leading to them held terra-cotta planters bursting with unusual plants and small trees.

Ana looked to the left as the luxury car moved into a slot among others, guided there by a bow-tied valet.

"Did you forget something?" Ty asked. "I can have the car brought back."

She shook her head. "No. I was just looking at all the others."

Ana barely knew one make of car from another, but the different vehicles gleaming under the brilliant California sun looked expensive to her, even from here.

Ty didn't seem particularly impressed. But then he was a blueblood and used to all that. Ana straightened up and smoothed her dress.

"Ready?" He offered her his arm.

"I think so."

Ana and Ty made their entrance. She touched a hand to the carved wooden doors for good luck as they passed through them. The gala was in full swing, but a lot of the guests weren't in formal wear. They could have been in Seattle, what with all the natural fibers, artisan jewelry, and hair au naturel. Still, Ana had a feeling that the understated look didn't come cheap.

She felt like she'd stepped into another world. It had nothing to do with the existence of paranormal creatures and everything to do with the unseen power of privilege and wealth.

Unlike Los Angeles, rich people in Northern California weren't in your face with it. But in their own politically correct way, it took about five minutes for this crowd to let you know that they had it all and you didn't.

Ana's radar picked up on the quiet condescension—and a few approving glances. Her classic white linen dress didn't raise any eyebrows. She saw a longer version of it sweep by on a redhead. Probably couture.

This *was* a gathering of the country's philanthropic elite. People who had so much money they could generously give it away to help the less fortunate.

People like her. People who needed help no matter how much they wished they didn't.

The decor was beautiful. The people were beautiful.

Even the trays of champagne glasses and little appetizers were beautiful.

Everything was so frigging beautiful that she suddenly wanted to knock the silver trays out of the hands of the tuxed-up waiters circling the room. At the same time, she wanted to kick her own ass because she couldn't deny that resentment and jealousy were driving her.

For many of these people, this was just a special evening, an occasion to get dressed up. For others, however, it was a way of life. Ty, for example, had probably gone to parties like this all the time. He looked so comfortable, so right in his tux.

If not for Barrett and Justine, she could have looked like a hobo trying to pass herself off as royalty. Both had told her to go for elegant simplicity and be herself. Collette had bowed out of the discussion, saying fashion scared her. Barrett had taken Ana shopping, and Justine had tried out several hairstyles until settling on loose curls. The style softened her scar, which had virtually disappeared under expertly applied makeup anyway.

She'd felt a little like Cinderella, but with much nicer stepsisters.

Afterward, the four of them had stared somberly at one another. They'd all agreed to talk when she got back.

So this was the ball. There wasn't anyone dancing at the moment, even though there was a small orchestra playing soft music under a pavilion tent on the other side of a vast patio.

She forced herself to be honest. She was not Cinderella and she wasn't going to be marrying the prince when this was all over. The best she could hope for was an invitation into a cult to determine whether her sister and her former best friend Miguel were enslaving humans for the purpose of making them feed vampires.

"I don't see Miguel or your sister. Shall we circle the crowd?" Ty murmured into her ear. Although his words were bland, the warmth of his breath and the rough timbre of his voice made her shiver with memories of their night together. Instinctively, she shoved those memories away and stepped forward. As she did, her ankles wobbled underneath her.

Damn, she hadn't trained enough for this at Belladonna's headquarters. She should have worked more on dressing and walking like a lady. She thought back to what Collette had taught her about appearing relaxed when she was anything but: focus on her core. She took a steadying breath, closed her eyes, and tightened her abs, trying to remember what Barrett looked like as she glided around the headquarters in her spike heels, oozing rich-girl attitude.

Chin up. Balance between her heel and the ball of her foot. Shoulders down, face relaxed.

"You're doing beautifully," Ty said. "As beautiful as you look."

This time she did more than wobble. She stumbled. He caught her arm to steady her. His dark gaze burned into her.

"Thank—thank you," she managed to choke out.

"No, thank *you*. For coming to Belladonna in the first place. For flying all the way out here. But most of all, for letting me make love to you."

Her joy was tempered by confusion. For the past several days, he'd treated her just like the other female agents. He hadn't betrayed by expression, word, or touch that what they'd shared had meant anything to him. Even in her dreams, he'd remained distant from her.

She'd dealt with the pain of that distance by telling herself over and over again it was for the best. But her heart had never believed it and his polite comments now caused a flood of inconvenient emotions to rush through her—regret, affection, anger, hurt, desire. He made her feel them all, and it weakened her resolve to keep herself safe from him.

"Despite everything, I think of our time together as a gift. I always will. I should have told you that before now."

She felt tears fill her eyes and quickly blinked them away. Nodding, she tilted her chin toward the large bar in the corner. "How about we get a drink?"

Ty smiled slightly, acknowledging her failure to respond to what he'd said, but he simply nodded and led her toward the bar.

"What would you like?" he asked when they reached the front of the line.

Her mind went blank. She'd just suggested they go to the bar as a distraction. But now . . . "A shot of tequila," she said defiantly, knowing it wasn't something most would order here.

He raised a brow.

Her embarrassment just made her voice sound snotty. "What? You afraid I'm going to get hammered?"

"Maybe. I remember the last time you went to a bar and drank tequila. I remember what you did and how I almost couldn't protect you."

"Well, let me assure you, I have no intention of leaving your side."

"How about instead of a drink, I offer you something else?"

"What's that?"

"A dance."

Her face stiffened with insecurity. She'd undergone basic dance training at the compound and every time she'd felt like a horse wearing roller skates.

"Come on," he urged, grinning. "It'll be fun."

As she looked at him, his expression and words seemed genuine. As if he really wanted to dance with her because he'd enjoy it and not because it would be a means to an end. Of course, that wasn't true, but it didn't change the fact that she very much wanted it to be. Now that their night of passion was over, she wanted to be in his arms again, and if dancing with him was the only way to make it happen . . .

She nodded. "Lead the way."

They walked past the other couples on the dance floor and faced each other. He slid his hand beneath her hair and cupped her nape. Just cupped it. Whatever chill had clung to him when they'd first met was completely gone now. She couldn't help wondering if the fact he'd drunk her blood had something to do with it. The warmth of his hand was like a fiery brand, instantly heating her and making her quiver with anticipation. She stared at his mouth, willing him to press it against her own, but he didn't move, didn't pull her closer. He simply held her, lightly but with an unmistakable air of possession that had her biting her lip to keep from moaning.

She wanted him again. Wanted his mouth on hers. His hands all over her. His body inside her. Here. Now. What came afterward didn't matter.

Only it did. And as she stared into his eyes, that knowledge stared back at her.

He wanted her, too. He wanted to do everything he'd done to her before and more. He wanted to push her, make her once again accept the kind of pleasure she'd never allowed herself before. The kind she hadn't even believed existed until she'd met him.

But he was content with touching her, just touching her, because he knew what happened next *did* matter. Not just to them, but to the countless others whose lives he thought might be made better if they could successfully complete their mission. And whose lives would be lost if they couldn't.

With great sex comes great responsibility, she thought, then had to fight the urge to giggle hysterically. What a joke. She'd never had great sex, not until Ty, but her life had always been about responsibility, whether it had been to her sister or to the gang. Their time together was the first time she'd had one without the other. She wanted it again. But it wasn't going to happen. Not with him. Not now.

With a sigh of regret, she closed her eyes. An instant later, he made the same shaky, puffing sound, pulled her into him, pressed his forehead gently against hers, and began to sway in a gentle, barely there dance. The hand at the back of her neck moved, massaging her muscles in a distinctly soothing rhythm at odds with the tension coursing through his body and her own.

"I still want you," he said, his breath caressing her lips the way she longed for his tongue to do. "Don't think for a second that I don't."

"I know," she answered softly. "I—I still want you, too."

His eyes blazed and a sense of certainty filled his gaze. "Fuck it. I don't care about our pasts and I don't care that our futures are uncertain. I will have you again," he vowed. "We'll have each other. But . . ."

His voice trailed off, and she whispered, "But I'm a nice human girl who should stick to her own kind."

He didn't dispute what she'd said. Ana desperately wanted him to. Hope was a stealthy specter, overwhelming her before she could stop it.

She warned herself to get real.

"Maybe not," he said slowly. "If you want more, I'll show you that what I gave you was only the beginning."

In other words, he wasn't promising her anything beyond the pleasure he could give her during the night.

Why would he? She'd told him sex was all she'd wanted. She knew he couldn't lie, but part of her wished vampires could smell lies uttered by others, too.

They danced for a little while, as close as they dared. Eventually, she couldn't help herself. She leaned forward and kissed him.

His lips on hers were like coming home, or at least what coming home should feel like. Pleasure and contentment and familiarity. She opened her mouth, urging him to take her deeper, and he did. He took things from her she didn't even know she had to give.

When he finally pulled away, she looked off to the side, feeling too vulnerable. Gently, he held her chin and turned her face until she had no choice but to meet his gaze.

She licked her lips. Wanted to cry out that she wanted him. Needed him. Not just for sex or for a night or even until their mission was over. She tried to imagine her life without him in it and she couldn't. Somehow, she knew that when he left her, he'd leave a bigger hole in her heart than even Gloria had when they'd been separated.

And that scared the shit out of her.

Once he adjusted to being a vampire, he'd probably go back to his privileged life. He'd forget about her. Hell, he'd probably forget about Belladonna and Rogues on the loose. She had yet to meet one of those, but they were out there. Using and torturing humans.

Pathetic, helpless, inferior humans, which was all *she'd* ever be.

"What are you thinking?" he asked her.

She raised her chin. "You don't know?"

He frowned. "I told you. I've never tried to read your mind. And I won't."

"Unless you need to. For the job. For some other reason you think justifies your actions."

"It's hardly a power I can use at will. Most of the time

it doesn't work, no matter how hard I try. But what's your point?"

"The point is, you can read minds. You're a *vampire*, for God's sake. We need to keep things professional between us. Get the job done. Get into Salvation's Crossing and get out. And then move on."

"Okay." He nodded and far too easily seemed to dismiss her. As they continued to dance, his gaze swept the room.

"Do you—do you see Miguel yet?"

"No," he said grimly. "I don't. And something tells me he's not going to show. Damn it."

"Why do you say that?"

"He's supposed to be here checking out potential investors. The net worth of the people in this room reaches billions."

"Maybe he's just trying to exercise a little finesse. Miguel was never the brash type. He worked his charm. Moved in for the kill nice and slow." She frowned, wondering why she'd described Miguel more like a predator than the friend she remembered. Belladonna's suspicious mindset must be influencing her more than she'd thought.

"You're right. We'll stay. Assuming you can stand my company for another few hours, that is." He smiled at her. "Are my fangs showing?"

Did he really think that's why she'd retreated from him? "No. And I never said I can't stand your company."

His tense expression relaxed slightly and he shrugged, the careless gesture tearing at her heart. "Great. So we'll drink. We'll dance. We'll get where we need to go, and at the end we'll go our separate ways. Right?"

"Right."

So they drank. And they danced. But unfortunately, it was all for nothing, since Miguel never showed up.

Or so they thought.

* * *

Once they were back at the Belladonna compound, Ana saw very little of Ty. Her days were filled with getting to know her teammates better and teaching them skills she'd learned on the streets or in prison. Every night, however, she dreamed of her dance at the ball with her devilish prince. Even more than she'd thought possible, she missed him.

So much so that when someone knocked on her bedroom door and she opened it to see Ty standing there, she was ready to tell him she'd made a mistake. That she'd take whatever time with him she could get. But as soon as she looked in his eyes, the words died in her throat.

He nodded formally, distantly, as if they'd never held each other. As if he truly planned to never hold her again and was completely fine with that.

"I've been contacted by Salvation's Crossing," he said. "We did it, Ana. They're sending a private jet to fly me back out to California in a few days. Carly and Mahone listened in and okayed it."

"Who's Mahone again?" she asked, more for something to say than anything else. She was still stunned by the news that their ruse had actually worked. That all it had taken to give Ty what he wanted was wearing a fancy dress and dancing with him. It couldn't be this easy, could it?

"The FBI's liaison to Belladonna."

She should have felt proud. Relieved. Instead she felt only dread that Ty had obviously been right about what it would take to get them inside Salvation's Crossing. What else was he going to be right about? "Miguel saw us together? Why didn't we see him?"

"He saw us. We didn't see him because he didn't want us to. Bottom line, you were the key to getting us into

Salvation's Crossing, just like we thought you'd be. He trusts you, he trusts me. Even if he doesn't trust me, he's decided to play the game. And he's going all out. He said he wants my help, to provide funds for Hispanic rights—but also to help those of Hispanic descent become vampires."

"What?" she whispered, shocked yet again despite herself. "He actually said that? He admitted he knows about vampires?"

"He knows. And he knows I'm one."

"But how?"

"Because as I told you, he's been watching you. Watching both of us, apparently. And because he's been turned into a vampire himself."

The shock should have killed her by now, but perhaps she was getting used to it, because she just stared at him. "For real?" she asked softly.

Ty shrugged. "We circled the subject at first, but when I asked him straight out—"

"He couldn't lie."

"He could have evaded my questions if he'd really wanted to, but he didn't. He was upfront about wanting my money. And about wanting to see you. He's going to be very disappointed when you don't show up."

She wasn't sure she'd heard him correctly at first. "What are you talking about?"

"I'm going into Salvation's Crossing but I'm going alone."

He said it so calmly. As if it was a done deal and she had no say in the matter whatsoever. "Ty, we talked about this. You can't—"

"I can. Because as I said before, things have changed. And—and there's more, Ana. I'm sorry, but there's more."

"Tell me," she whispered.

"Your sister is a turned vampire, too."

CHAPTER
TWENTY-EIGHT

This is it, Ty thought. This is where she breaks. But I'm here. Just like she was there for me in that parking garage after I'd shot Louis. I'm not letting her come with me, but I'll help her through this.

Only Ana was even stronger than he gave her credit for.

Although she went white and swayed on her feet, she quickly composed herself. "How?" she asked.

He was struck by how similar she sounded to Carly at that moment. Pushing aside all emotion to ask for only the necessary facts. That ability to distance herself emotionally had been learned the hard way, and the habit would only become more ingrained the longer she stayed at Belladonna.

He'd been right to question himself when he was in Seattle. When he'd wondered if he was doing the right thing by dragging her into all this. He should have left her alone.

Yet in his heart, he knew if he had to do it all over again, he would.

Especially if he'd known Miguel and her sister were turned vampires; it was only further confirmation that Hallifax was right. That the Crossing was a cover for a human blood slave distributor.

No matter how much this information hurt Ana right now, it was imperative that Belladonna shut it down.

He didn't say any of this, of course. He didn't have to. She'd remember it on her own after her shock wore off.

"According to Miguel," he said, "after you went to prison, new gangs began to form in your neighborhood. Devil's Crew and Primos Sangre agreed to merge in order to combine their collective strengths. Not all of the gang members agreed, and those in opposition were rooted out."

"You mean hurt," she said tonelessly. "Or killed."

"Yes. Well, those that were left learned that Devil's Crew was comprised largely of vampires. Not turned vampires, but born vampires. Rogues."

"Rogues. The vampires that were helping the FBI with its Turning Program."

Ty nodded. "Apparently, once they were deemed trustworthy, Miguel and your sister were told the truth and were offered the chance of a lifetime—to be turned."

"And they agreed? To be turned into—into—"

"Monsters?" he asked softly, seeing the revulsion on her face.

"No! *Not* monsters. You're not a monster. But you're not what nature intended, either. If what you're saying is true, neither are they anymore. What made them want that?"

"Because from what Miguel says, the basic premise of Salvation's Crossing is legitimate. They want to help those of Hispanic descent. To become stronger. To live longer. To gain an 'in' with the government they didn't have before."

"My sister was so gentle," Ana murmured. "I guess she got goddamn sick and tired of being used. Can't blame her."

"No. Not really."

Ana sighed. Ty could practically see her thought process. Yes, it made sense. Gloria, a victim of poverty, abuse, and sexual deviation, had lost everything, including the only family she'd had left to count on when Ana was sent to prison. Left alone, she'd been given an opportunity for a new life. To be stronger than any mere human. And to help *la raza* do the same.

"I know what you're thinking, Ana, but the intel is solid. This isn't just a benevolent organization trying to help the disenfranchised. Someone in Salvation's Crossing, be it a human or a vampire, is kidnapping migrant workers and selling them as blood slaves to other vampires—"

"You don't know that. Not for sure."

"No," he answered bluntly. "But that's why I have to go in. I need to be sure."

She narrowed her eyes and raised her chin. "I'm going in, too. Just like we planned."

He scowled. "You can't. It's too dangerous now."

"It's always been dangerous."

"Not like this. Going in covertly, when I thought I was dealing with *mere humans*"—he almost snorted at the dreaded phrase that had left his lips so naturally—"was one thing. I'd have the edge. But now, with at least two other vampires, maybe even more—"

"What? I'm just a liability now? You still need me. They might let you in, but like I said, there's no way Gloria will trust you. For one thing, just about every male in her life treated her like dirt."

Ty took that in. "Maybe the Salvation's Crossing ones don't."

"That's a theory. Your best chance of infiltrating is if I'm with you."

Ty threw his hands up in frustration when what he really wanted to do was smash them through the nearest wall.

She was right. He knew she was right. And it wasn't so much that Ana's presence would make Miguel or her sister automatically trust him. But she would be a major distraction, one he could take advantage of. Problem was, whether he wanted to or not, he cared about her. He didn't want her hurt.

"You seem to forget, vampires can read minds," he pointed out.

"Not all the time, Ty. You can't always. If they're turned, odds are they can't, either."

"And you're willing to take that chance? What if they read your mind and see what you're up to?"

"I'll set my brain waves to True Believer," she said mockingly. "Let them read that. They're going to be a lot more interested in what *you're* up to—"

"I'm not briefing you."

She blew out a disgusted breath. "By this point in my training, I can take an educated guess."

"Supernatural black ops aren't pretty. But, if you're worrying about me—"

Ana glared at him. "Would it make a difference if I was?"

"Don't lose sleep. I doubt they know how to kill their own kind any more than I do. And even if they did—" Ty shrugged. "Maybe it wouldn't be the worst thing in the world for me to die."

She seemed startled by his offhand comment. "That's what you want?"

He grasped her arms and backed her up against the wall. "Not really. Since we made love, what I want is more of you. More of your body. And I want your blood." He raised the hand he'd pressed next to her head and pounded it into the wall, causing her to jump. "I crave your blood. Every second of the day! Knowing that, you think you're tough enough to walk into Salvation's Crossing, where other vampires will want the same thing? Do you really want to spend any more time with me—"

"Yes," she said, pulling his face down to kiss him. Her mouth opened and ravaged his. Startled, his defenses down, he groaned and took what she was offering.

He lost himself in the slickness of her mouth and her intoxicating taste. He touched her. Smelled her. Sucked her essence into himself. He felt his fangs unsheathe and he pulled his mouth away from hers to bite her throat—

He tore himself away from her. He stumbled back, his eyes glued to the sweet, pulsing vein where he wanted to plunge his fangs and feast on her for days.

Without knowing it, she'd again brought him from the edge of an abyss. He didn't dare tell her that she made him *want* to keep living. Despite the ease with which she seemed to be adjusting, Ty knew he was running out of time. She'd seemed to accept his vampire status with aplomb, but he suspected that was because she was running on autopilot. Her world had been turned upside down and she was focused on getting to her sister. Eventually, she wouldn't need him. Eventually, she'd look at him differently. Instead of craving his touch she'd fight him off.

It had been bad enough when she'd pulled away from him on the dance floor. If he saw fear or disgust in the beautiful brown eyes that had looked at him with such passion, he'd be lost for sure.

Right now, he could still find his way. And wherever that road led him, he knew it couldn't lead to Ana. Not if he wanted to keep them both safe.

"It's not going to happen. You're not coming with me. And that's final."

When Ty turned away and left, Ana stared after him in astonishment. She couldn't believe his gall. Once again he was actually *forbidding* her to go into Salvation's Crossing with him. That he'd left her there, shaking against the wall, her mouth missing him, her body yearning for him, was utterly infuriating.

She closed her eyes. God, her heart ached for him.

She loved him, she realized.

Somehow, Ty had slipped past all her defenses, and the fact that he was hurting so much, the fact that he was trying to protect her, made her feelings impossible to ignore anymore.

What he'd said—that it wouldn't be the worst thing in the world if he died—had to have been triggered by a rush of hate. For himself. Wherever it had come from and why, she had to intervene.

And she couldn't let him go into Salvation's Crossing alone.

He was wrong about Miguel and Gloria, at least about them preying on others. They were vampires who were trying to do good. She'd help prove that . . . and then what?

Ty Duncan was entitled to make a few mistakes if he was willing to risk his life for others. He was her kind of man. No. Her kind of *vampire,* she thought defiantly.

She'd lived her whole life longing for someone who cared enough to not neglect her the way her mother had. Someone who cared enough to not use her the way Miguel had. Someone who cared enough to not leave her the way Gloria had.

So far, Ty was all that and more. If she took a chance on him, on *them,* maybe when this was all over, she'd have more than she'd ever hoped for.

Love. Rock solid and blazing hot.

If he had what it took, then she was in. All the way.

She was his. But . . .

First things first.

She had to find out whether he could ever see himself as *hers.*

CHAPTER
TWENTY-NINE

Portland, Oregon

Mahone didn't know what he'd been expecting from his formal introduction to the Vampire Queen. A grand hall? A matronly female weighed down by robes, sitting hunched over in a gold-plated throne and surrounded by somber-faced, looming guards armed with archaic swords or javelins? Or maybe something a bit more austere? Rows of coffins? Furniture resembling the stuff one would find in a torture chamber?

Whatever he'd been expecting, it hadn't been this.

Instead of being ushered into a cavernous room surrounded by her loyal subjects, Mahone had been escorted into a lushly appointed office, with wood paneled walls, a travertine fireplace, and jewel-toned upholstered chairs. The room had a decidedly feminine quality without being over the top, and it smelled of . . . He inhaled and closed his eyes, savoring the delicate floral and mint scent. Beside him, a crystal candy dish held caramels, and although the blackout drapes were drawn, giving no hint of the sun shining outside, the various lamps around the room twinkled with invitation.

But even as beautiful and luxurious as the room was, it was drab and pedestrian and utterly boring compared to the woman—no, the female vampire—who walked in and greeted him.

"Good afternoon, Mr. Mahone. I'm Bianca Devereaux." She smiled with what appeared to be modesty. "I believe you know me as the Vampire Queen."

She held out her hand, as if she expected him to take it and kiss it as he bowed, and . . . Who would have guessed it? That's exactly what he did.

Holy. Fuck.

She was stunning. Beyond stunning. She was the most gorgeous thing he'd ever seen. She put cover models to shame. Her very presence made it impossible to even remember the faces or names of any cover models, let alone any woman he'd ever been intimate with.

Her pale skin actually glowed and she had long silver hair that should have looked ridiculous on a female clearly in her thirties. Silver, hell. It shone like platinum, heralding what a treasure she was.

Though nothing about her screamed arrogance, she exuded vitality and confidence. She was tall and slim, with perfectly symmetrical features, and a regal posture that in no way inhibited her sensuality. Mahone could just as easily picture her wielding a sword to protect her people as reclining in bed, her body cushioned by cashmere and silk, as she opened her thighs and beckoned him to top her.

To fuck her.

He gasped, appalled that he'd thought such a scandalous thing about vampire royalty, but at the same time something startling happened. She gasped, too. Her cheeks went pink. Her mouth dropped open. Her eyes grew slumberous. As if she was picturing the very thing he'd been—as if she'd been aroused by it.

Her reaction snapped Mahone back to reality. Eyes narrowing, he took a step away from her, and blurted out, "Are you reading my mind?"

At his words, her blush dissipated and her expression went smooth. She laughed, an inviting, tinkling sound.

"Why would I need to read your mind when your desire for me is so obvious?"

Again, she spoke without arrogance or disdain. It was merely a fact, one he couldn't very well deny with his erection standing at attention inside his pants. Somehow, he managed to speak without sounding like a babbling idiot. "That doesn't answer my question," he said.

He just wanted her to know that he knew vampires couldn't lie and thus were usually masters at evasion.

She smiled approvingly. "You're right, of course. I apologize. It's habit. But no, I wasn't reading your mind. My people don't read minds as a matter of course. We consider it rude. But I could read your mind anytime I wanted—if, for example, I felt you were lying to me or were a danger to my people."

"We both know that between the two of us, I'm hardly the dangerous one here."

She sighed. "Yes. I understand only too well why humans fear us. It's natural. It's why we've stayed hidden for so long. And why we want to stay concealed, despite the dissatisfaction that causes."

"Who's dissatisfied?" It seemed impossible. Not with her for a queen.

Her brows furrowed. "You can't be serious, Mr. Mahone. Living in the dark? Hiding who we are? Suppressing our natural abilities? All so we can stay safe. You must know how unnatural and tedious that is. It's certainly not our first choice."

"Huh. Must be why some vampires no longer follow your rule. But a lot of laws are a pain in the ass."

She politely ignored his second comment. "I assume that by 'some vampires' you mean the ones you call Rogues. I understand they're causing all sorts of problems."

"You don't know the half of it."

She tapped her platinum-tipped fingernails together

for a thoughtful moment. "All societies have those who refuse to follow the law. We can only police them a little and that from a distance, unfortunately. Maintaining our secrecy is our chief concern."

"Of course."

She smiled again. "Well, Mr. Mahone? Is that why you wished to meet with me? To ask for my help with the Rogues?"

He was having a hard time remembering why he was here, given the all-consuming lust that was riding him. With effort, he crossed his legs and pretended to brush a speck of invisible dust from one of his wingtips. He needed to focus on bigger things. Not necessarily more important, just bigger. For now.

"Yes, Your Majesty. In part. But also because I know things can't continue like this. The reason the FBI went to the Rogues is because you refused to give us any real information about your people. Information that would take away the mystery, and thus maybe the fear, of vampires."

She pursed her glistening lips for a fraction of a second. Fascinated, Mahone stared at her. *Do that again, honey.*

She didn't.

"And maybe the reason I refused is because any information I give will only highlight what a threat we would be. *If* we were so inclined. We're not, but despite the fact I've assured your people of that time and again, you don't believe me. There's nothing I can do to change that."

"You're wrong," he said, obviously surprising her. He got the distinct feeling she didn't hear those words very often.

She sat down on the chaise next to him, crossed her legs under the gown she wore—that, at least, resembled something a queen would wear—and said, "Tell me more."

"You tell us the truth about your powers and we devise ways to reassure humans about them." He cleared his throat, unsure if he could actually say the words out loud, but he had to. It was the only way FBI Director Hallifax would even consider negotiating with this female.

The queen obviously sensed his discomfort and narrowed her eyes. "Continue."

"Right now, part of the problem is the fact your people *are* hidden. We have no way to police you. What if vampires agree to wear some kind of emblem or monitoring equipment—"

She pushed to her feet, her sudden anger all too apparent. "Like a scarlet *A*? Or ankle bracelets? We are not in-home-custody defendants. My people are a sovereign nation."

"A sovereign nation existing within another sovereign nation," he pointed out.

"Don't waste my time, Mr. Mahone."

With that, she strode toward the door, obviously ready to end their meeting when it had barely begun. No wonder. He'd known she'd never go for such things. But he'd tried. And now he'd try again. His way.

"Wait. Please. You must realize the position I'm in. I'm trying to do the right thing here."

She paused with her hand on the doorknob, then turned back toward him. "I know. But that won't be accomplished by treating my people like pariahs or criminals or victims. We'll fight before we'll allow that to happen, and you can take that to the bank, Mr. Mahone."

Mahone wondered for a second if the vampire community had its own kind of money. *One nation, under blood*—

He realized she was staring at him.

"Sorry. Zoned out for a sec. Hey, how about helping me help you?"

"I beg your pardon?" Her tone was elegantly frosty.

What a voice. He felt hotter.

"Help me bring down the Rogues. The longer they run amok, the more havoc they create. Which will lead to more and more problems between your people and mine."

Queen Bianca took a step toward him. Just one.

"You're asking me to help you silence Rogues so that . . . what? The FBI can find others to turn humans in opposition to our laws?"

"Strengthening the Turning Program by eliminating the Rogues is definitely what the FBI wants. It's why I wanted them captured initially. But I know now it's much more than that. Avoiding or ignoring you will only postpone the inevitable. The day is coming when our nations either turn against one another or unite. I think we should get a head start on our unification—by working together to defeat our common enemy."

"Just to be clear. You want information that will enable you to easily defeat the Rogues."

"Yeah."

"But that would mean sharing vampire secrets that will place those loyal to me in peril if humans are informed."

She was considering what he was asking, but she was far from convinced. Mahone thought about Belladonna, and the news he'd just received that Salvation's Crossing had invited both Ty and Ana inside its walls.

He'd okayed the trip. So had Carly.

Mahone pondered the issue of his loyalty to the FBI and its mission to use the vampires to its best advantage versus his duty to humans in general, which included keeping peace with vampires so no one got unnecessarily hurt. He thought about the very real possibility that if the FBI continued to do what it was doing, vampires would fight back in a big way. And he thought about this female, who would no doubt lead the vampires in their fight against humans, and the way he still wanted to fuck her.

Before he knew what he was going to do, he said, "I need your help, but I know I'm asking a lot of you. You have to trust me, when you have no real reason to. So I'm giving you permission to read my mind and find out exactly what I'm thinking and planning. And you'll see that I sincerely do want to help my people—and yours."

She gasped again. Okay, so he'd shocked her. But he could see he'd also impressed her.

"Don't make an offer you don't want me to take you up on, Mr. Mahone. Because, frankly, the only way you'll get help from me is if I do read your mind, and if I like what I find there."

"Do it," he said, his voice loud. Challenging.

And before he could even blink, she did.

He felt her probing his thoughts. Gently but thoroughly.

The unusual sensation should have horrified him, but it didn't.

Somehow it brought him great pleasure instead.

CHAPTER THIRTY

Two days after Ty had decreed Ana was staying put, it became glaringly apparent he was going to be outvoted. He pointed a finger at her, ignoring the rest of the Belladonna team seated in their preferred spots around the library. The room was uncomfortably warm and not only because the late afternoon sun streamed in through mullioned windows. The air was thick with tension.

"I told you," Ty said in a low voice, "you're not coming with me."

"Not your decision." Carly's voice shot from the intercom before Ana could speak. "She has to accompany you tomorrow, Ty. You know perfectly well the only reason you got an invite to Salvation's Crossing is because of Ana. Miguel is in love with her. That fact should tell you she isn't in that much danger."

"It's still danger," Ty gritted out. "I can do this by myself."

"We all take risks, Ty. Ana didn't sign up for a desk job. And you don't get to grab all the glory," Peter said. "Unless that was your plan all along."

Ty whirled on him. "Keep the hell out of this!"

Peter's eyebrows rose into his hairline. "Like that's going to happen. We're a team, man. That means I get to call bullshit when I see it."

Ty strode toward Peter and got in his face. "I'm in this

fucking mess because of you. At least let me handle it the way I need to."

"What the hell are you talking about?" Peter snapped.

"You and Carly knew about vampires. You supported the FBI's Turning Program, and what's worse, FBI collaboration with Rogues, *vampire criminals*—and you kept the rest of us in the dark."

The other man was silent but visibly nervous.

"You continued to be my friend, continued to date my sister, knowing what kind of shit you were mixed up with. And when the inevitable happened, and the Rogues turned on you, we got caught in the crossfire. You caused that. You and Carly. You fucked up my life just like you're about to fuck up their lives."

He swept out his arm in a wave that encompassed Ana, Collette, Barrett, and Justine, then stopped to catch his breath.

The ex-cop shook her head and began to rise from her armchair. "Ty, listen—"

He held up his hand and gestured her to back down. "I know I don't speak for all of you."

"Damn right," Ana muttered.

Ty shot her a glare. "Keeping you out of trouble may be too much work."

She caught Barrett's steady gaze. The blond woman shook her head ever so slightly as if to say *don't argue*.

Ty looked around the room at his silent colleagues. "Well. Awfully quiet in here."

No one said anything.

"I'd like to thank you all for coming in," he said acidly. "And thanks for listening. Please sign the guest book on your way out and exit to the left. Jesus. Why should I kill myself for any of you?"

"Don't make idle threats." Carly's voice held a note of irritation.

"At this point, it's not a threat. It's my plan B. Save the world and drop dead."

The rawness in his tone got everyone's attention.

"All right. Enough," Peter said. "You blame us—well, Carly and me—and not without some justification. But turning this assignment into a suicide mission for reasons you seem disinclined to explain—"

Ty's dark eyes flashed with fury. He didn't look at Ana.

"You may be burned out. Or suffering from PTSD."

Barrett spoke up before the intercom could crackle. "That's enough, Peter. You're not his psychiatrist."

He turned to Ty without responding to her. "If you've been seeking a way to kill yourself, then get help."

"Good advice," Ty said. "But fuck it. And fuck you. Why is it that you don't seem to be suffering?"

Peter finally cracked. "I never meant for it to happen, Ty. If I could, I'd give my life to bring Naomi back."

Seeing the other man's agony, Ty's bluster left him as if it had never been. Control was an illusion. None of them had it. Some things they simply didn't have the power to fight. He couldn't stop Ana from doing exactly what she'd been trained to do. Trying to was making him crazy. She wouldn't meet his eyes.

All he could think was that she wasn't his.

And she never would be.

He had other things to think about at the moment. Ty reached out a hand and placed it on Peter's shoulder. "I know that. Sorry. Guess I lost it."

Peter muttered assent.

Ty turned, surprised by Ana's lifted gaze. Her brown eyes seemed brighter than usual.

"You win," he said with finality. "If you want to go in, I'll do my best to protect you. Just be sure, Ana. Be very sure."

With that, he walked out of the room.

* * *

After Ty left, none of them spoke. Finally, Carly asked, "Do you need time to think about your decision?"

Ana stared at the intercom for a minute, then let her gaze wander around the room. She still didn't really know the people who were supposed to be her team, though they were connected in a way that couldn't be denied. Their training, individual and group, had made that happen.

Everyone who'd heard Ty had to have identified with his rage. That shit came from helplessness. Where he was concerned, she knew it was more than that. She knew it had to be.

"I'm going into Salvation's Crossing with Ty," Ana said firmly. "But first, I want you to tell us the full truth, Carly."

Carly let out an exasperated sigh. "You know about vampires and the FBI's Turning Program, Ana. What do you think I'm keeping from you?"

"Why us? Why did you bring in the four of us to help? Because I know there's something that ties us together. My sister was turned into a vampire after she got involved with Devil's Crew, the same gang that tried to kill her at my jumping-out ceremony. It all goes back to then. Seven years ago and that shootout. Doesn't it?"

They all stared at the intercom, even Peter, which told Ana that even he was curious about what Carly was going to say.

"I'll do more than go into Salvation's Crossing," Ana said. "I'll get you the information you need, no matter what I find out. Even if you're right, even if Miguel and Gloria are involved in what you're saying, I'll do my part. But first I have to know the truth."

A minute ticked by.

Then finally, Carly spoke.

"You weren't the only one affected by that gang shootout, Ana. You all were."

Ana's brows knitted. "I don't understand."

Justine raised her hand. "Seriously. You're not the only one."

"What are you talking about—" Barrett said.

"Just hold on a second. Let me back up for a moment," Carly said.

A stern look from Collette got them to chill. The women quieted and let Carly continue.

"You asked to be jumped out of the gang, Ana, but they didn't want to let you go, correct?"

"So what? That wasn't unusual. They considered me family. And Miguel wanted to keep me safe. He thought the best way to do that was with the gang. But after I told him I was resolved, that leaving the gang was the best thing for Gloria, he relented. He made sure the jumping-out ceremony was scheduled."

"It's an ugly ritual. For the rest of you, let me explain: she got beaten twice—once for herself and once for Gloria."

Ana shifted uncomfortably when she felt the eyes of her teammates on her. "That's right."

"But Miguel insisted that Gloria be there. To see what you were willing to suffer for her. And the beating had already started when gang members from Devil's Crew broke in. Had you seen them before?"

"Yes. Especially the one named Pablo. He's the one who gave me this scar. He and several others came in shooting. Someone next to me dropped his gun. I had a split second to act, and I chose to shoot Gloria myself, in the shoulder, so she'd fall to the ground."

"You mean gangbangers wouldn't shoot someone who's down?"

Ana answered Barrett's question. "Depends. Sometimes they don't. But she had a greater chance of survival if she was down rather than standing up."

More shots had been fired after that. She still remembered the screams. People ducking for cover. Blood. She'd lost track of time and space and what was real and what wasn't. Her last clear memory was cradling Gloria's blood-soaked body in her arms, rocking her sister, begging her to live.

Miguel had stood protectively over them.

Then they'd heard the sirens.

Helmeted cops burst in, wearing bulletproof vests, heavy weapons cocked and blazing. A deafening firefight broke out and she'd been arrested. She'd fought them at first, panicked about who would care for Gloria, but Miguel screamed that he would watch out for her. The memory was painful.

"What are you getting at, Carly? Because I know for a fact none of you were there," she said to the other women in the room.

Barrett spoke again, jolting Ana out of her memories. "I was in New York seven years ago, but I wasn't anywhere near a gang shooting. You've been misinformed, Carly."

"I agree." Justine came to standing, one hand firmly on her hip, the other clutching a glass of wine she must have sneaked into the room. "I happened to be in New York around then, too. As a rule, I'd have to call myself a not-so-innocent bystander, but nothing like that happened to me. I'm sure I would've remembered."

Ana turned to Collette. "What about you?"

Collette nodded. "I was close by when the shooting occurred, but I want to hear what Carly has to say. I want to know how she knows all this."

"Because I was there. At least I should have been," Carly confessed. "I was a junior FBI agent attached to a secret unit, and had infiltrated a gang—the Devil's Crew—when I learned of a hit about to go down on a member of a rival gang. I warned my superiors, but they demanded I stand down. The hit was to continue as planned."

Ana gasped. "Why?"

"Let's just say that even before vampires were officially discovered by the FBI's Strange Phenom Unit, the FBI was acting on information about them coming through Devil's Crew. And they were already putting things in motion to work with them. Collateral damage—as in human life—was deemed worth the cost to get what the FBI wanted from them. But more than one life ended that day and that's why you're all here."

Carly gave them the specific date. Understanding began to dawn.

"What I did and didn't do mattered terribly," she said. "In my own way, I'm trying to make up for it."

"My mother . . ." Justine whispered.

"When the shoot-out happened," Carly said, "one of the gangbangers tried to flee in a car. He crashed into another driver, a teenage girl, killing her mother instantly."

Across the room, Justine gasped, and sank back into her chair, her face pale.

Carly continued. "Another girl was out with her older brother, having insisted he take her for an ice-cream sundae before returning to his military post. Innocent enough, right? Until he collapsed in front of her with a massive heart attack. He was only twenty-eight but he had an undiagnosed cardiac anomaly. The ambulance dispatched to rescue him got caught in the traffic snarl caused by the shootout. He died before EMTs could even reach him."

"And that would be me," Barrett spoke, her voice

calm and cool. Only the way she gripped the armchair, tight, her hands in claws, betrayed her emotion.

"I was there. I'd tried to help the wounded," Collette said. "My father was a pastor. I was serving in a soup kitchen run by the church when I heard shots."

Ana asked, "Was your dad killed? Is that how you're linked to Justine and Barrett and me?"

Collette shook her head, her lips in a tight line. "No. I tried to help one of the injured gangbangers. He was scared. He had a knife. I lost a lot of blood. Needed a transfusion. The blood was clean. Everything should have been fine. But I'm sick. I get weaker every day. The doctors don't know what I have. Or how long I have until . . ."

Barrett gasped.

Justine cursed.

"You're dying," Ana said flatly.

So many lives destroyed. Her story had just been the beginning—and not as bad as the others. She couldn't have known what suffering she'd cause by asking her gang, the people she'd thought of as her family, for a fresh start.

Gangs were not family. They pretended to be, tried to act as protectors, providers.

But in protecting their members' lives, gangs took their souls.

She'd known all this before. And nothing had changed, she realized.

It didn't matter that vampires existed, that Carly had hired four women connected by a gang shooting, or that Ty was a vampire himself, bent on self-punishment. Or revenge.

Bottom line, Ana was still going to do what Belladonna wanted her to do for one reason and one reason only: Ana was going to save her sister.

She summoned up the nerve to back Carly into a corner. "So you knew there'd been a hit ordered. Was I the target?"

"No. Your sister was."

The shock was a one-two punch to Ana's system. "*Gloria?* But why? *Who* ordered the hit?"

"Your friend Miguel."

CHAPTER THIRTY-ONE

You're wrong, Ana wanted to say. No way would Miguel do such a thing. Not in a thousand years.

But by now she knew the futility of arguing with them. Carly had her intel and contradicting her wouldn't make an iota of difference.

"Fine," Ana said, standing up. All she wanted to do was get out of there. Forever. "Sounds like everything's tying together all nice and neat. And maybe there is actual evidence to back up your information. Hope we find it."

She walked toward the library door and froze when Ty suddenly appeared.

He stared at her but spoke to the intercom. "I got your text, Carly. You've heard from Mahone?"

"Yes," she said softly. "This information just in, people. Special Agent Kyle Mahone has information that will help us. Or hurt us, depending on how you choose to use it."

Ana ripped her gaze from Ty's and took her seat again.

Carly then told them three critical facts Mahone had learned. First, the secret to stopping a vampire from reading a mind or being able to persuade it was wearing pure gold. Remembering the medallion Ty wore under his shirt, Ana's gaze shot to him, but his expression remained impassive. She understood immediately. He hadn't mentioned the thing to anyone else. Maybe he didn't trust them after all.

The question fled her mind given her shock at what Carly said next. Mahone's second discovery was that a vampire died when he turned a human. That was why it hadn't happened very often before the FBI had messed things up. Ana wondered why it would have happened at all. Why would the Rogues have agreed to work with the FBI, turning humans for them, if doing so meant sacrificing their own lives? It made no sense.

Unless, of course, they hadn't been doing the actual turning themselves.

But there was more. Moving right along, Carly conveyed Mahone's most important information: only a stab to the heart with a blade dipped in subzero liquid nitrogen would kill a turned vampire.

Nice to know, Ana thought dismally. It was unlikely she or Ty would be let into Salvation's Crossing with a couple of long, sharp knives tucked into their bags. Or better yet, with a canister of liquid nitrogen they'd ask to be placed in the freezer.

"Got it? Memorize everything," Carly said. "And there'll be a briefing on our satellite photos and infrared drone images of the compound before you go. It should be obvious that this information is strictly confidential. Ty, as I'm sure you've figured out, Ana has decided to—"

Ana couldn't take it anymore. She bolted out of her chair and raced out of the library. In fact, she fled as if the devil was chasing her. It wasn't the devil, though. It was the realization that Ty now had a way to do himself in if he was so inclined. He didn't have to be diagnosed with PTSD for her to know how fast he could spin out of control—and how much agony it caused him.

Extreme stress could trigger suicidal thoughts. If he ended up alone somewhere without anyone to talk him out of it, he could kill himself—kill the monster inside—anytime he wanted. And that made her want to weep.

If things went wrong, how could she protect herself, her sister, Miguel, and Ty all at the same time?

She loved them all, she admitted to herself.

Gloria.

Miguel, who she couldn't believe had ordered a hit on her sister.

And, yes, Ty, vampire side and all.

She wished like hell she didn't. She'd lost everyone she'd ever loved in one way or another. Would this turn out the same way?

An hour later, she was sitting by Belladonna's huge lap pool, staring at the water. She sensed the moment Ty crossed the surrounding flagstones, even before he stepped beside her, kicked off his shoes, rolled up his pants, and sat down with his feet in the water next to hers.

Neither of them spoke for several minutes.

"Having second thoughts about coming with me?" he finally asked.

She smiled bitterly and shook her head. "Sorry. No such luck."

Ty was silent for a few moments. Then he leaned back to take something out of his pocket.

Ana was surprised when he handed her a necklace, a more delicate version of the one he'd been wearing. "Here you go. Courtesy of Mahone," he said.

Carefully, she took it from him. She slipped it on and tucked it under her blouse.

"Yay," she said flatly. "They won't be able to read our minds. And now we know how to kill a turned vampire." She snorted. "Who knows? Maybe we'll find some liquid nitrogen, too."

"True," he agreed. "But then what? You'll grab a knife, dip it into the liquid nitrogen, and do what with it? Kill your friend Miguel? Kill your *sister*?" He shot to his feet with incredible ease, leaving her to stare up at him.

Slowly, she got to her feet, as well.

"I told you before, I'll do whatever I have to do," she said fiercely. "But I don't believe that's going to be necessary. I don't believe what you do about Gloria. Maybe Miguel, but I'm not even sure about that."

"It doesn't matter whether you believe it or not. If your life needs protecting, I'll do it, Ana. I don't care if it's Miguel or your sister or whoever else—no one is going to hurt you. You come with me, you come knowing that."

Instead of answering him, she looked away, which prompted him to gently grab hold of her chin and tilt her face up toward his.

"They're not saints, Ana. At the very least, Miguel and Gloria are working with vampires to turn humans for the FBI. Thanks to Mahone, we now know that in order to turn a human, a vampire has to die."

"So I heard."

Ty scowled. "But maybe you didn't *understand*. Rogues aren't doing the turning. Neither are Miguel or your sister. So how do you think they get other vampires to do their dirty work for them?"

"By threatening those they love," Ana said. It was what made the most sense. Gangs, solo criminals, abusers all did it. Just how they rolled.

"Yes." He let her go.

"But Gloria and Miguel could be totally ignorant of the consequences of turning a human," she insisted. "You were. And I guess Carly and Peter and the rest of the FBI Strange Phenom people were, too."

Ty opened his mouth to reply, but Ana held up her hand, forestalling him.

"*Maybe* I can believe that of Miguel. If he wanted my

sister killed, I believe he could do anything. But that's a big *if*. And I'm sorry, but I'll never believe it about my sister. No matter what anyone tells me. Not without proof. That's the only reason I'm going with you, Ty. To save Gloria. This—me being here with you—has *always* been about Gloria."

She guessed his thoughts before he spoke them. Fire blazed in his eyes and his fists clenched, as if he was barely stopping himself from reaching for her. "No. When I held you in my arms, when I was *inside* you, it was only about the two of us, Ana. Remember that."

His hand lifted and he stroked his knuckles across her cheek. Ana's lips parted slightly. She didn't want to kiss him.

But she did.

CHAPTER
THIRTY-TWO

Ana went back into the mansion without Ty, going quickly up the stairs but pausing on the landing when she heard Collette's voice below.

"Before you go . . ."

She turned to see all three of the other women standing in a group on the marble floor, looking up at her.

Oh no. Ana didn't have the energy for some weird little bon voyage party.

"I really have to pack." Her tone was barely polite.

Justine started up the steps. "Let us help. Carly said you would need a few extra things that you probably don't have."

Ana noticed the small bags each woman was holding. She couldn't tell what was in them from where she was, but there weren't any ribbons and wrapping paper. Obviously, she'd left the conference in the library a little too soon.

"Okay. Come on up."

Collette led the way, followed by Justine and Barrett. Ana waited on the landing and turned to head toward her room when they were all on the same level.

She opened the door and waved them in.

"Dibs!" Justine headed straight for the bed before anyone else could, sprawling out in a half-reclined position.

Barrett chose the armchair and Collette simply sat on

the floor, setting out the small bags she'd gathered from the others. Ana sat beside her.

She looked around expectantly. Collette got right to the point. "Basically, this is a do-it-yourself, super-duper spy kit. You get to choose."

"We're going to get searched," Ana said.

The ex-cop nodded. "Of course. That's why none of this looks like spy stuff."

"Does Ty get a kit, too?" Ana asked.

"Yup. Peter's taking care of that. Some items overlap. Carly wants you both to be prepared. But first . . . We never did get around to that mani-pedi," she said with a wink.

Ana gave her a puzzled look. She didn't get the other woman. She was dying. Why wasn't she more angry? "It's not a high priority."

"Most of this is ordinary drugstore stuff. But not all." With almost inaudible clicks, Collette demonstrated two small weapons disguised as manicure tools.

"Cool," Ana said with interest. "Like switchblades. Or shivs." She'd had blades in her street days, and in prison, a handmade shiv concealed in her bed frame. Women could be more dangerous than men.

"Use them only if you have to," Collette advised.

Justine yawned. "You know, in case your hero is flexing his muscles in the mirror at a critical moment."

They all laughed.

Barrett thought of something else. "Ana, keep in mind that we are maintaining high surveillance on the compound. The eyebrow thingy is actually a laser beacon."

"Got it. So what's in the little bottles?"

"Some are just nail polish. One has luminol," Collette answered.

"Which bottle?"

"The lavender-colored nail-polish remover, so you can

remember it easily. L for lavender, L for luminol. If you need to test for latent blood, use it."

Ana nodded.

"The others hold reagents for different tests—Ty knows how to use them. But we couldn't put all this girly stuff in his luggage."

"I understand." You didn't venture onto enemy turf unless someone had your back. An ex-cop knew that all too well.

"Thanks, Collette."

They all stood and Ana escorted them to the door. She hesitated, however, before opening it. After swallowing hard, she forced the words out. "Thanks to all of you. I—I appreciate what you've done and I . . ."

I'm glad I met you.

I'm glad we're working together.

I hope we'll get to do mani-pedis when this is all over.

It's what she wanted to say. What she *should* say. After all, if she was willing to fight for Ty, it made sense she'd be willing to fight for everything, and that included her place here. Among these women who, even though they were as different from her as women could be, had come here to support her. Who knows, their assistance could even save her life.

Even so, she couldn't get the words out.

Her eyes burned with frustrated tears until Barrett put a hand on her arm.

"Ditto, Ana," she said. Collette and Justine smiled and nodded.

They didn't hug her as they left, but it didn't matter.

They'd shown her what was important.

Somehow, some way, they'd become a team, one in which she mattered.

CHAPTER
THIRTY-THREE

Somewhere in the Sierra Foothills of California

The following day, after a luxurious ride in a private jet, Ana and Ty drove their rental car into Salvation's Crossing. The compound was rustic but beautiful, set in green rolling hills dotted with venerable oak trees, and orange poppies and purple lupine in the meadows. But despite the fancy plane that had flown them here, there was still something makeshift about the organization's headquarters. There were no paved roads, and Ana could see a clothesline with sheets and towels dangling off it strung between two cabins. Other than that, everything seemed orderly. A vast blue sky arched overhead, serene and somehow welcoming.

She could see how someone would feel at home here. Safe.

They hadn't gotten past the security gate of Salvation's Crossing without being thoroughly searched by armed guards. Fortunately, the manicure kit hadn't attracted a second glance. Justine had done Ana's nails with lavender polish just to be on the safe side.

Their luggage got a good going-over as well. Then they'd been given a pat down by uniformed staff and their rental car had been inspected with mirrors on metal wands, inside and out and underneath.

The closer they got to the main house, the more armed

guards she saw. Ana told herself the intense security was reasonable. After all Gloria had lived through, safety would be a huge concern. And if she and Miguel were indeed working with the FBI and vampires, their involvement had to be kept top secret.

As far as Ana could tell, the building layout and land under cultivation matched the satellite surveillance photos they'd reviewed. The compound was too big to take in all at once.

"Quite a place," Ana said. "How long have they been operating again?"

"About five years. Basic but not cheap. The communal buildings look like cinder block and stucco. Built fast but built to last. Miguel wants me to fund a new irrigation system, but some generous benefactor must have donated a few million already."

Ana's distracted mood gave way to excitement as they drove up to the main house. Her stomach quivered, nervous tension radiating through her. After years of searching, years of hoping, years of waiting, and years of grieving, she was finally going to see her sister again.

There was no predicting Gloria's reaction.

Ty reached over and stroked her hand. She savored the small touch. "Remember, we met at your coffee shop," he said. "I saw something in you I liked, and I swept you off your feet. The closer we keep to the truth, the easier it will be to play this role."

"Well, that's true enough. But you can't lie. So how are you going to explain having millions of dollars to spend on a worthy cause?"

"It's not a lie," Ty responded.

She turned her head to stare at him. "Seriously?"

"Not all of it." He waggled his eyebrows at her and smirked. "Watch your step."

Interesting. She'd thought the cover stories about his

wealth had been completely fabricated. How much did she really know about Ty? Besides his deepest, darkest secrets, that is—the everyday stuff hadn't been covered. She wanted to know more. She wanted to know everything.

They'd reached the front porch of the main house. Ty pulled the car into a graveled area at its side. Polished oak steps led up to a shaded veranda, with square columns made of river rock tapering up to the top. Wide windows were open, and soft music escaped from the inside.

"Ready?"

"Huh?" Ana caught a glimpse of a vehicle with black-tinted windows that must have followed them at a discreet distance turning off onto a different road. "I mean, yes."

"Is there a problem?"

A faint plume of dust rising at the turnoff was the only sign of the other vehicle. "I think we were followed."

"That's to be expected," he said curtly. "I'll help you out."

She waited for him to come around to play his assigned role. What a gentleman.

Only she knew even as she thought it that vampire or not, Ty *was* a gentleman.

Ty walked up the steps with her and knocked on the door. It opened to reveal an elderly Hispanic woman in a neat and tidy dress. Ana felt Ty's hand on her back, his thumb stroking her spine.

"Mr. Nunes? Ms. Garcia?" the woman asked. At Ana's nod, the woman gestured for them to follow her and come inside.

Ty kept his hand on her back, as if he knew she needed that simple connection, that acknowledgment that she was not alone. She stepped over the threshold and entered the building, seating herself on a bench the woman pointed out. Ty sat next to her, close enough so their shoulders, hips, and thighs were touching, the closeness both an emotional comfort and a sensual distraction. She clutched her handbag until he slid a hand underneath her forearm and tugged one hand loose, then wrapped it up in his.

He leaned in close and whispered in her ear, "Lovers, remember?"

She snaked her fingers between his and relaxed into him. Lovers.

The pretense should be a snap. They had slept together, yet that one explosive night hadn't been enough.

A cacophony of sound startled her—thundering footsteps, squeals, giggles, and high-pitched shouts. Children, having fun. A moment later, a stream of children from very young to almost teenagers ran into the house, excited and energetic. And all jabbering away in Spanish.

Ana thought she might have seen Ramona Montes in the group . . . with her daughter. But she couldn't be absolutely sure. It wasn't as if she and Ty had taken the blurry photos with them for comparison purposes.

A girl of about eight paused to stare at them before a woman's voice called her name. The girl gave an apologetic shrug, turned, and ran off down the hall, stopping at the end to turn and cheerfully wave good-bye.

"She seems happy," Ana said.

"Might be lucky to be alive," Ty commented, "if the coyotes smuggled her across the border."

"Her life will be far better now that she's here with us," a woman's strong voice rang out.

Ana's heart fluttered, and then pounded hard and fast. She stood, looking in the direction the voice had come from. Looking for her sister.

* * *

Ty stood. Suddenly pale, Ana had risen to her feet the moment she heard that voice. Even without having studied photos before coming here, he would have recognized the woman striding down the hallway as her sister.

Helena Esperanza—*Gloria*—was somewhat taller and more fair. Her light brown hair, though beautiful, could never match the brilliance of Ana's black sheen. Even so, her features, the shape of her body, and the expression in her dark eyes—defiant and vulnerable at the same time—were an exact replica of Ana.

He stepped forward, extending his hand to shake hers—and put some distance between Gloria and Ana, who he knew was trembling. "I'm Ty. I can see from the family resemblance you must be Gloria."

She stopped in front of him and placed her hand in his. Her skin, like his, had lost most of the chill that came with being a newly turned vampire.

He forced her to keep eye contact with him, allowing Ana a chance to regroup.

"Ana here has been telling me what a wonderful person you are. How much she's missed you."

"The pleasure is all mine." Gloria's gaze moved to Ana and her voice wavered ever so slightly. "I couldn't believe it when we found out Mr. Nunes knew you." She hesitated, bit her lip, then continued. "I'm glad you're here, Eliana."

"I'm just called Ana now, Gloria."

Gloria nodded and smiled. "Ana."

Ty wasn't sure what he'd been expecting. He'd thought she would be cold, even contemptuous. She wasn't. But he was puzzled by the friendly tone that didn't quite mask something underneath. Gloria had been turned. She couldn't lie. Was that why she couldn't say she'd *missed* her sister?

Ana drew in a deep, shuddering breath. Her gaze was

still firmly fixed on Gloria's face, her expression blank. "I'm so glad I've found you, Gloria." Ana reached into her bag and withdrew something. A doll. "I brought something for you."

She held it out to Gloria, whose eyes widened when she saw it. Slowly she reached out for the doll, caressed its yellow braids, then placed it gently on a nearby sideboard.

"She hasn't changed much," Gloria whispered. "Unlike me." Then she raised her gaze to meet Ana's.

"Doesn't matter. You'll always be my little sister."

"So you know?"

"That you're a vampire? Yes. And I don't care about that, Gloria. All I care about is seeing you again."

Ana stuck her right hand out as if to shake hands with Gloria. Odd, Ty thought. Why wouldn't she hug her? Was she afraid of being rejected?

Gloria slapped Ana's hand away with her own right hand.

Tension surged through Ty's body.

But then Gloria stuck out her left hand and Ana slapped that away, then both slapped the back of their hands together, clapped, and repeated the action again, only this time faster and more smoothly.

Gloria giggled, then said while slapping away, "Remember when we won the neighborhood competition?"

Still slapping and clapping, the rhythm growing faster, Ana grinned and nodded, her focus fully on her sister's hands. "Nobody could believe we could go this fast. We've still got it, Gloria."

"Now that I'm a vampire, I can go a lot faster. So, *andale, chica! Andale!*"

Ana kept up until finally one of them missed and the slapping pattern stopped. Then Ana wrapped her arms around her sister and held her tight.

They were just separating when a door behind them

opened. A man stepped out. Dark haired, dark eyes. Average height. Handsome in a feral way. Miguel Salvador.

He stared at Ana with the warmth of a former lover. "Welcome, Ana." He came forward, arms extended, and Ana allowed herself to be wrapped in the man's embrace. From his position, Ty could see that as Miguel held Ana tight, he closed his eyes. Breathed in the scent of her hair.

He'd been right.

Miguel still loved Ana.

The thought rankled. Ty had come here to protect her, not to control her. But something about this guy said *rival*. He didn't want to believe that she might be responding.

He'd fucking kill for her. He'd do much worse than what he'd done to Louis, the man at the nightclub, if anyone tried to hurt Ana now.

He gave himself a mental shake. *He* was the one who needed to be controlled.

He cleared his throat, and Miguel stepped back from the embrace, then came to stand behind Gloria, whose smile was patently false.

So Ty wasn't the only one affected by this impromptu reunion. There was an upside. If Gloria's jealousy got worse, it would make her impulsive. Careless. And that could only work in their favor.

Still, the need to mark Ana, to show everyone that she belonged to him, was riding him hard. He pulled her into his side.

She got the hint and melted into him, tipping her head up and gazing at him, rapt adoration in her eyes. Or was that lust? Didn't matter. She'd given him an opening. And he took it.

Swooping down, he placed his lips on hers, intending

to give her a polite brushing of the lips. Just enough to prove to Gloria and Miguel that he and Ana were lovers. But then her lips went soft under his, opening slightly, and his instincts responded.

Blood flowed to his cock. His pulse thundered in his ears, drowning out all other sound. Her scent filled his nostrils—sweet, spicy, all Latin and luscious—and he took her mouth with his.

All he wanted was her.

He tore his mouth away from hers and focused his gaze until her face swam back into view. She blinked, once, twice, her lids heavy but her eyes gleaming.

Ty stepped back. "Guess I got carried away," he said lightly. "I call it the Ana effect."

Miguel shook his head as he snaked an arm around Gloria's waist. Ty saw the tension in the lines around the other man's mouth. So he was jealous, too, because of what Ty supposedly shared with Ana. Love. Intimacy.

Eat your heart out, you rapist bastard. If Miguel could read minds, he'd hear that loud and clear.

But Ty didn't feel the telltale tickling in his brain. Either Miguel and Gloria didn't have the power, or the necklaces Ty and Ana wore were fully functional.

Good to know.

That kiss could have been too much, too soon. Given that Ana hadn't seen her sister in years and was probably longing to spend some time alone with Gloria—for one thing, to determine for herself whether Gloria was being brainwashed or coerced—it was time for some manly conversation.

"I bet these two would like to get reacquainted," he said to Miguel. "Let's discuss your plans."

Miguel looked at Ty with barely concealed contempt. "If you say so. Sure, let's talk."

CHAPTER
THIRTY-FOUR

"Want the grand tour of the compound?"

"I'd love to see it," Ana replied.

The garden stretching out before her in neat rows, the gentle California breeze caressing her skin, the robin's-egg blue sky—all of it should have had a calming influence, but instead, nerves danced under Ana's skin. Next to her, Gloria, the sister she hadn't seen in seven years, seemed equally nervous, twirling her hair the way she used to as a kid, but her eyes shone bright and her mouth was soft.

Ana needed to find out more. Even let Gloria know that she could help her escape the clutches of the cult, if that's what it was. First, she had to find out how deeply Gloria was embedded with Salvation's Crossing.

They wandered away from the main house, down a dusty path under the oaks. After several minutes, Ana had the official story.

"Salvation's Crossing functions as an advocacy group for those of Hispanic descent who can't catch a break. People like you and me."

"You've done okay, Gloria. So did I. Eventually."

Her sister didn't seem to want to hear about Ana's past. Not yet anyway.

"Yeah, well, for those who are about to lose everything—or *have* lost everything—we offer a work program on the farm. They can stay in ranch houses and we have an on-site school for the older kids and day care for the little ones. We provide training in a variety of fields for adults and then help them find a place to live and work. Help them assimilate into the community in a functional way. It's like we're their extended family."

Ana nodded. "You provide for them. Protect them. Just like the gang did for me. For us." She didn't pose that last part as a question, but she held her breath as if she had. She'd told Gloria she wanted out of the gang and her sister had resisted. Maybe she shouldn't have made that comparison.

Gloria visibly started, then seemed to take Ana's comment in stride. "We are like a gang in some ways."

An awkward few seconds passed. Ana wasn't sure how to reply. "Well, you turned your life around. I really respect that. I'm so proud of you."

At her heartfelt statement, Gloria turned and smiled. "I'm glad you see it that way. It was easier to turn my life around, as you called it, once I became a vampire."

She spoke so easily about having been turned. Ana figured she should ask more questions, but she was afraid doing so about this particular topic might appear suspicious. Instead, all she said was, "Oh?"

"We built Salvation's Crossing, and we want to expand. For that we need money. Lots of money."

"I'm sure Ty will do what he can to help," Ana said. "But he's just one person."

"Everyone counts. So do we. Too many Hispanic women have allowed themselves to be in the position of the downtrodden," Gloria snapped out.

Ana stopped, surprised by the sudden vehemence in her sister's tone. "Is that what you think you and I did? Allowed ourselves to be treated like dirt?"

Gloria snapped the blossom of a calendula off its stalk. She breathed hard for a moment, as if calming herself, then pushed her way through the field of flowers, letting her hands drift across the petals. "We were just kids. But our mother was an adult. She should have protected us. She bought into the whole women-are-worthless thing. Plus the belief that because you speak Spanish, or have an accent, that you're somehow sub-par."

"And the work you do with Salvation's Crossing stops that?" Ana asked.

Gloria turned around, opening her arms wide in a sweeping gesture. Ana took in the acre of edible flowers they stood in, the rows of corn and tomatoes and eggplant that lined the valley. As the hill rose to the west, an orchard of fruit and nut trees marched in lines like good little soldiers. Down at the compound, children ran and played in a large playground, the younger ones smacking a tetherball around a pole, skipping rope, or shooting hoops, the older ones crowded around some kind of touch-screen device. Women worked the fields, but none seemed overwhelmed by heat. Instead, the sound of their happy chatter rose to reach Ana—just not the words.

Everything was tranquil. Everyone seemed happy. Was this what cult life was like? Salvation's Crossing seemed more like a commune than a cult. Surely if these people weren't being allowed to leave, if they were being victimized by the cult leaders and sold off to vampires, she wouldn't be seeing joyful kids and women who found dignity in the hard work they did.

What wasn't she understanding here? What couldn't she see?

"Are you happy here?" she asked Gloria. "Even now that . . ."

Now that she was a vampire, Ana meant, but she couldn't bring herself to say the words out loud. Her sister looked the same. Maybe a little paler.

Gloria reached out to take Ana's hand. "More than

I've ever been. I have a purpose in life, finally. And I'm a lot stronger. Not just physically."

Ana was more curious than ever. "Gloria—I have to know: Why didn't you want to see me? Why did you send me that letter saying you didn't want anything to do with me?"

Gloria let go of Ana's hand. "After the shoot-out, when they took you away, I blamed you for trying to leave the gang and for not being strong enough to protect me." She shrugged. "I was just a kid. I've grown up."

"I'm so sorry." Ana hesitated for a moment. Had Gloria's words been chosen carefully? Because she hadn't said she *no longer* blamed Ana for anything.

"I don't want to talk about that night." Gloria moved away from her, headed back through the flower field to the compound. "As I got older, after you got out of prison, I was already involved with Salvation's Crossing. I needed to find my own path. And then after I was turned, it was glorious, Ana. I felt powerful and I still do, more powerful than you can ever imagine." There was a fanatical glint in Gloria's eyes as she repeated the word *powerful*. Then the glint faded and a softer look replaced it. "But there were times I did miss you . . ."

Unease rippled up Ana's spine, but she forced it away. "Same here," Ana said. "More than you'll ever know."

"Don't go away too soon," Gloria said, pulling her tight and holding her close. "Even if Ty leaves this place, I'd like for you to stay."

Ana breathed in deep, again wondering if Gloria's words had hidden meaning. *If* Ty left? Of course he was going to leave eventually. And did Gloria want her to join Salvation's Crossing . . . as a vampire? That might not be so bad, if it meant being reunited forever with Gloria and becoming Ty's equal in every way.

Gloria seemed content with her life here at Salvation's

Crossing and passionate about its mission, even if she
hadn't been able to explain it too well.

Was it because her sister had truly found peace and
helped to build a wonderful community that helped
others? Or because she was powerful and could do
whatever she wanted, even sell humans to vampires in
some kind of misguided attempt to empower her people?

Ana wanted to believe the former, but she couldn't
shake the feeling that had started to grow ever since
she'd first seen Gloria again, the feeling that maybe she'd
never truly known her sister after all.

Gloria continued to lead the way on their tour. Ana
suddenly realized something. There were plenty of
women and children milling around, but there were very
few men. Where were they? And was their absence one
more way in which Gloria had assured her own safety?

Ty gulped down a large glass of blood and wiped his
mouth. It was animal blood, thankfully. Not that Miguel
had told him so, but he recognized the taste now. Human
blood had a smoother and saltier taste. Far more addic-
tive.

He placed the glass back on the mahogany desk in the
inner office and met Miguel's curious stare.

The other man spoke first. "I've stayed away from
Ana all this time because I feared she'd never be able to
handle the fact that vampires exist or that Gloria and I
have been turned. Guess I misjudged her. She's stronger
than I gave her credit for."

"She's the strongest woman I've ever met," Ty said,
deliberately letting his admiration for Ana come
through.

"She knows what our mission is?"

"I've told her your goal is to strengthen the Hispanic

population by turning them into vampires. I wasn't sure how you . . . select . . . who is to be turned."

Miguel laughed. "Everyone who is turned volunteers. They do it so they can better the lives of their families. In exchange, they get something even more wonderful in return. Purpose. Wholeness. Power."

"Sounds almost too good to be true. But then you and I know what being a vampire is like, right?"

Next, they went over the financials for Salvation's Crossing. They discussed how the "nonprofit," as Miguel insisted it be called, had been formed when the Devil's Crew and Primos Sangre joined forces. He showed Ty spreadsheets and income/expenses documentation from countless files on his computer, all of which looked legitimate. It wasn't so much numbers Miguel was concerned with, however, as it was the land upon which Salvation's Crossing sat.

Salvation's Crossing had bought out the farmer who was the last in his family to run it. The fruit and nut orchards were mature and well tended, bearing heavy crops. The fields were rotated to maximize yields and conserve the soil. It was water that seemed to be the problem.

They went over blueprints of the existing irrigation system. Fortunately, Miguel didn't seem to know much more about the subject than Ty did. But then Ty, as a philanthropist, was mostly expected to hand out money.

Ty had a sneaking feeling that Miguel understood that the compound's need for a new irrigation system was merely a pretext, a way of getting Ana inside the compound. And the reason Miguel understood this was because he didn't give a shit about Ty's money or what it could do for the land, but because he'd cared a great deal about seeing Ana again. Because he actually thought, despite Ty's and Gloria's presence, that something was going to happen between them?

Only over Ty's dead vampire body.

Still, they played the game and talked shop. When they'd covered the business at hand in detail, Miguel offered him more blood.

Ty politely declined.

"I've made sure the fridge in your suite is well stocked. But if you're in need of more, please let me know." He tilted his head. "I wasn't sure . . . do you drink from Ana?"

Ty looked away as memories of his night with Ana flashed before him. "Yes. But it would be easy to deplete her. She can't fulfill all my feeding needs. I believe you have connections to human donors?" In other words, tell me if you're dealing in illegal blood slaves, you asshole.

Miguel looked slightly envious before his expression evened out. "If you don't mind me asking, are you born, or turned?" Miguel asked.

"Turned," Ty said automatically. "Why?"

"You made a face when you swigged the blood. I thought maybe, hombre, you find animal blood disgusting. Most natural-born vampires have an aversion to nonhuman blood."

No, he simply had an aversion to drinking blood, in any form. He gave Miguel a sly smile and said, "Nothing like that, believe me. The bottled blood was fine. I've just been spoiled by drinking Ana's blood. Now about those donors . . ."

"I can only imagine how wonderful Ana's blood tastes," Miguel said. "You are a lucky man." His gaze drifted away and his angular features seemed younger.

Memories, Ty figured. The man was lost in memories. And the way his pupils had dilated, those memories were pleasant ones, at least for him. Fucker. How dare he remember raping Ana as something that gave him pleasure?

Then Miguel's expression shifted. He turned to Ty. "You didn't know the connection between the sisters before you met Eliana?"

"Her name's Ana," Ty said. "And I—" He choked and fell silent. The question made sense, because if he'd known about the connection between the two females when he'd first contacted Salvation's Crossing, before he'd actually met Ana, it would of course make his current relationship with Ana suspect. Unfortunately, the question had also been too direct. He had no time to deflect, to work around an answer.

Miguel's expression hardened as he shifted position.

Fuck. Ty racked his brains.

"I only wish I'd known earlier. I could have brought them together sooner." There. Not a lie. A sidestep. Maybe Miguel wouldn't notice.

Miguel's gaze was shadowed. Ty couldn't read him at all.

"Speaking of those two, I guess we should get back to them," Ty added.

"Fine with me."

As they rose, Ty couldn't help wondering—had he succeeded in maintaining their cover, or had he blown it somehow? Had he inadvertently put Ana in danger?

They spent the rest of the afternoon touring the compound with Gloria and Ana. Miguel explained that most of the men were serving as migrant laborers, and were traveling up and down California and Oregon, picking fruit. In the fall, after harvest, they'd return to their families, having saved enough by then to start a life of their own, off the compound. By then, the women and children would know basic English, enough to get by.

Ty and Ana had also met more of the staff. Besides Mrs. Tobia, the housekeeper who'd opened the door for them earlier in the day, there were the brothers Esteban and Gustav Gutierez, both hulking ranch hands, and some of the teachers, Tessie Fuentes among them.

Ramona Montes and her daughter, Becky, their original reason for visiting Salvation's Crossing, were nowhere to be found. Even so, Gloria had mentioned the woman, saying she taught the preteen kids and teenagers. He knew Ana would keep her eyes open for the teacher. See if she could pull her aside and talk to her.

Gloria eventually brought them back to the main house and took them to their suite. The bed was the first thing they noticed. It was gigantic, heaped with pure white comforters against the chill of California nights, snowy pillows mounded against the antique headboard. A vase of heavy red roses had been placed on each nightstand, their natural fragrance filling the room. The simple decor was utterly romantic and sensual—and a marked contrast to the cinder-block practicality of the rest of the compound.

Their luggage was already there, the suitcases unlocked and left open on a long, low table.

"Oh, someone brought in your things," she said absently.

Ty and Ana exchanged a look.

"No need to dress for dinner," Gloria added. "It's communal and come as you are. Hope that's okay with you."

"Of course," Ana said.

"Most of the food comes from the compound's fields. See you in an hour."

Once settled and alone in their room, Ty turned to Ana.

And despite everything, despite the fact they were inside the cult, despite the fact they were on the verge of proving their intel true or false, Ty didn't give a shit.

Not at that moment.

Now all he cared about was taking Ana into his arms and making sure she forgot all about Miguel. That she thought only of him and the pleasure he'd brought her before. And could bring her again.

CHAPTER
THIRTY-FIVE

"So," Ty said. "Miguel seemed happy to see you."

"That's what we wanted, right?"

"Yes. But maybe he was a little *too* happy to see you. So much so that even Gloria noticed it."

Ana's eyes widened at his bold statement and he knew why. They were supposed to converse as if they knew they were being recorded at all times. Even if the little gizmo in Ty's smartphone that was supposed to detect bugs indicated the room was clear. Given that, it probably seemed strange that he'd speak so bluntly. But he saw no point in beating around the bush. A blind man would have been able to see how much Miguel had been affected by Ana's presence.

Ana seemed to search for the right words, then simply shrugged. "Miguel loves Gloria. I could see that for myself by the way he holds her. She has nothing to worry about."

Was her response for anyone who was listening? He didn't buy it and he wasn't letting down his guard for a moment. He'd seen the way Miguel stared at Ana. He still wanted her. He'd looked like he'd kill to have her.

For now, however, Ana was safe. She was with him. Ty just had to reach out and touch her.

He resisted doing so until she smirked and said, "You don't have anything to worry about, either, Ty. I'm so grateful you brought me here. You're the only man or vampire I'll ever want." There was just a hint of the dramatic in her voice, enough to tell him she was teasing without giving away her meaning to a listener.

He grinned and moved toward her. Her smile vanished and she took several steps back, but it was too late. He slid his hands up her back, then to her head, forcing her to remain still as he touched his forehead to hers. "Prove I have nothing to worry about," he whispered.

He claimed her mouth with his. Harsh. Without finesse. Showing only lust.

Desperation.

God, her lips were soft. Her breasts warm, pressed up against his chest. When she moaned, a shudder ran through him.

And then she touched the tip of her tongue to his lips. And the sexual desire he'd held at bay roared to life.

He released the hold he had on her head, but she wasn't going anywhere. Instead, she pulled him in tight, fusing her mouth to his, whipping her tongue in and out of his mouth. He slid his hands under her shirt and in a second had unhooked her bra, then moved his hands to the front and let her breasts hang heavy in his palms.

She came up for air and breathed out his name. "Ty."

No. No time for talking. Sex. Naked. Blood.

His hands moved, frenzied, sliding over her, tearing at the buttons at her top, grasping her ass and pulling her close when she edged away.

"Ty." Her voice. Strong. Emphatic. "Ty, come back to me."

He slowed. Controlled. Steadied. Holy fuck, he'd gone too far.

"Trying to prove you own me?" she whispered, her words holding double meaning. She was asking him if he was playing to any hidden cameras.

Damn her. How could she have thought that response

was for show? "I don't have to try and prove anything. You're mine. In every sense of the word. Whatever you had with Miguel is over, do you understand?" he said under his breath.

He slid his hands down inside of her pants, cupping her bare ass cheeks with his palms. Arching his neck, he exposed his jugular to her when she kissed him at the deep dip where his collarbones joined.

Ty tipped his head back even farther when she nibbled and licked her way up his neck. Groaned when she reached down and cupped his balls.

"You want me, but you're so angry. Why?"

"I'm not," he protested, not bothering to lower his voice. "Not at you."

"You're acting like you're jealous. Are you?" she asked point blank. Daring him to answer.

Time seemed to slow as he focused on her. The vulnerability in her eyes tore at him. Made him ache in places he didn't think could ever ache again. His heart. His soul.

She was waiting for him to deny it. To say that he wasn't jealous.

But he couldn't.

What *could* he say? That she mattered? That with her, he found some semblance of his former humanity? That she deserved to be loved and cherished and desired with passion and abandon—but not by a vampire?

Not Miguel. And not him. But Ty would stay close to her for as long as she would let him. As close as he could get.

"It's okay," she muttered, stepping back, putting distance between them. "I understand. I'll prove to you how much I want you. That no man can ever take your place." She heaved in a breath, closed her eyes for a moment, then opened them and stared blankly at Ty. That more than anything told him she was still playing to any hidden mics or cameras in the room. But what the hell. If there was going to be a show, he was front row, center, and already breathtakingly hard.

She stripped her top off, tugging her arms out of her bra straps, her breasts with their beautiful copper nipples standing proud and firm.

Suddenly ashamed of his insatiable lust, he put his hand out, stopping her. "What the hell are you doing?"

"Getting ready. For you." She said it with her chin thrust in the air, reminding him of what she'd been willing to do to prove herself in that alley with the man named Louis.

No. Not like this. He couldn't take her like two porn stars fucking for a potential camera. He wouldn't take her as others had. Under duress. "Stop," he murmured.

"Why?" she challenged, tipping her head to the side. When he didn't answer, she unzipped her pants and stepped out of them, leaving her clad in only a wisp of lace and silk between her legs. He caressed her shoulders. Kissed each of them. Kissed her forehead. Her nose. Her lips. Even the scar on her cheek. Although she stiffened slightly, she didn't push him away.

"I can't deny what I feel for you anymore, Ana. Not for another second."

Confusion spread over her face. She gave her head a brief shake, as if to order the tangled thoughts there.

"I'm jealous of your relationship with Miguel. Crazy jealous. And I don't know what the hell to do about that."

Ana was stunned speechless, but eventually, she tried to respond to Ty's bomb. She opened her mouth to speak, to clarify, but he didn't give her time. Instead, he covered her mouth with his.

His kiss was life-giving, so utterly sensual and so welcome that she wanted to weep with gratitude.

She remembered this. This feeling of rightness she'd

only truly felt once before—in his arms the night she'd found out what he was. A vampire. A man worth giving herself to.

Her mouth welcomed his tongue even as her hands reacquainted themselves with his body, shoving underneath his shirt to feel the muscles that rippled in his arms, chest, and back. She hitched one leg over his hip, gasping when he grasped her thigh and jerked it up higher while doing the same to her other leg until they were wrapped around his waist. He carried her to the huge white bed, then fell backward with her on top of him. Kissing frantically, they got completely naked and she tried to reverse their positions, but he held her down by her hips and shook his head. "No," he said roughly. "This time you take me."

She hesitated. He'd asked this of her in their shared dream, and she'd been able to do it. But now?

With all her experience, she'd never actually had sex with a man while she'd been on top. In a way, wielding that control and having to take what she wanted scared her.

Ty caressed her hip and whispered, "Do it. Just like you did in that dream. Take what you want. Take it how you want for real. I'm yours. Here. Now. I'm yours."

She blinked, both touched by his words and tormented by them. She wanted so badly for him to be hers.

Impatient with her momentary silence, he wrapped a hand behind her neck and pulled her down for a kiss. She sank into it even as she ground her pelvis against his. He'd brought her so much pleasure before. She wanted to feel that pleasure again and again.

He began to trail kisses down her throat, teasing her with sharp little bites that didn't break her skin even as he caressed her breasts and tugged on her nipples. The erotic sensation went right down between her legs. She wasn't sure anything could feel any better until he released her breasts, gripped her hips, and positioned her so her core was balanced right over the tip of his cock.

He swirled his cock through her moist folds, whispering, "Don't you want this? Don't you want to feel me inside you? Filling you with everything I have?"

"Yes, yes, yes," she chanted.

"Then take me, Ana. Please. Show me how much you want me."

Slowly, he released her hips, letting her balance herself on her knees with her arms braced against his chest. He folded his hands behind his head and stared at her in challenge.

One she fully intended to accept. After . . .

When she shifted away from him, his hands shot out to grip her hips again. She shook them off her. "Put your hands back where they were. And leave them there."

She was slightly shocked by the sexual commands that spilled from her lips . . . and how easy and erotic it was to say them.

His lips tightened and he looked ready to argue with her.

"Do it, Ty. I'll make it worth your while. I promise."

Swallowing hard, he did as she asked.

She gave him an approving smile, then kissed her way down his taut, muscular body. She played with his nipples. His abs and navel. His outer and inner thighs. Then she homed in on what she really wanted, keeping her touch light and teasing, even as his hips began to twitch and his fingers clenched the sheets.

"Do you still want me to take you? Do you still want to come inside me? Or do you want to come in my mouth first?"

His eyes widened at the promise in her voice. At her clear implication she'd let him do both. Then he said, "I want whatever you want, princess. This is about you, remember?" But even as he spoke, he tangled his hand in her hair and urged her face back to his cock.

She laughed with delight, her mission accomplished.

She took him deep and worked him with both her mouth and her hands. An invisible blanket of heat covered them, making them both pant and fight for air but she didn't stop . . . couldn't stop . . .

His taste was on her tongue, where it belonged. Ana suddenly wondered if tasting his semen would give her half the pleasure drinking her blood seemed to give him.

She was betting it did.

Her excitement nearly matching his, she sucked him harder, causing his hips to buck.

"Oh no. Oh fuck. I'm going to come. I—"

He tried to move her away from him, but she shook her head furiously, refusing to give up the chance to have all of him. To prove her point, she dug her nails into his thighs.

With a hoarse shout, he started coming. She swallowed his essence, something she'd never done for a man before. She'd always thought she'd hate it, but she didn't. Not with him.

She'd been right. It seemed she didn't care what Ty put inside her. If it was part of him, she'd always be greedy for it.

Carefully, she pulled back with a final flick of her tongue that caused him to jerk and shiver. She placed a close-mouthed kiss on the head of his erection, still ragingly stiff.

She remembered her promise to let him have her mouth and then her body.

With absolutely no hesitation, she climbed on top of him and pushed down, taking him inside her. She was vaguely aware of him gripping her tightly and moaning in ecstasy, and she was glad, but for once she was focused on what *she* wanted. In truth, she went a little crazy, driving toward her own pleasure, riding him even as she gazed into his dreamy eyes.

I love you, she thought. I love how you make me feel. I love how good and brave and strong you are, Ty. I love you and I know I can't have you. But I'm going to take what I can from you. Here and now. And I'm going to cherish the memory forever.

Her body tensed as her orgasm hit her. It rippled through her like an electrical charge designed to light her up for all eternity. In his arms, she was renewed.

"That's right—oh. Oh oh oh. Take it. Take me," he gasped, even as she felt him swell inside her, then shake with his own release.

Ana fell asleep in Ty's arms and he caressed her hair as he drifted toward sleep himself. Without warning, an ominous voice reverberated in his mind. Ty didn't recognize it but he knew one thing—it didn't belong to Miguel.

You have marked her. You took her. Now what are you going to do with her?

Next to him, Ana shifted. Whimpered. As if she could hear the voice, too.

Ty struggled to rouse himself fully, but he felt like his eyes had been glued shut. As if his limbs were weighted down with cement. It scared the shit out of him, because it was exactly how he'd felt after he'd been turned.

Helpless.

Helpless to save Ben.

Helpless to save Naomi.

Helpless to save himself.

But no, he wasn't helpless anymore. He *couldn't* be helpless. Not here. Not now. Not with this woman beside him. No matter what, he needed to protect Ana.

A great weight pressed upon his chest, pushing the

breath out of him. Ty wheezed and gulped for air but only for a few seconds. Before he knew it, he could breathe again.

Muscles tense, he opened his eyes but he and Ana were the only ones in the room.

The strange voice didn't come again, but neither did sleep.

Wide awake, Ty turned his head on the pillow and stared at the roses. Their scent filled the air. The petals of the heavy blossoms were wet.

And they looked like they were dripping blood.

Dark red blood.

CHAPTER
THIRTY-SIX

"Show us again!" A little girl named Elsa tugged at Ana's sleeve. Sitting on a grassy hill overlooking the compound, Ana was surrounded by six preteen and young teenage girls, each wanting to learn how to play Slide. When Gloria had suggested she take over after-school activities to give their teacher a break, Ana had expressed reluctance. Who was she to serve as a role model? After all, as much as she'd worked to protect Gloria, she'd led her own sister to a gang.

But Gloria had insisted, claiming the girls needed to see a strong Hispanic woman as a leader. Two teachers were in charge of the children. One was Ramona, whom Ana had finally met. She was the main teacher to the older girls, which had been perfect. Ana had already conversed with her several times. During those conversations, Ramona had made it clear she had escaped a bad marriage. That her husband had indeed abused her and their daughter, Becky, a beautiful sixteen-year-old who was very shy. Ana had told them she understood abuse, and that if they ever needed anything, she'd be happy to help. They'd just smiled and told her they were well taken care of. They were happy.

Now here Ana was, sitting on a hilltop, teaching young girls from countries as far away as El Salvador, Guatemala, and Mexico, part of American culture. So far, she'd taught them One Potato Two Potato, Rock-

Paper-Scissors, and Miss Mary Mack. She found herself enjoying the lessons just as much as the girls were.

"*Bueno,*" Ana said, encouraging Elsa and her friend Marcia as they slapped the back of their hands together, then the fronts.

Elsa flashed her a grin. "Speak in English, please, Miss Garcia. We want to practice. And you're such a good teacher."

Elsa's comment almost made Ana flinch. These girls were innocent. They had no idea that Ana was here under false pretenses. They didn't have to worry about such concerns, which was good. Gloria had created a place where they could be safe. Free. Granted, her sister had admitted that she was helping the FBI turn humans into vampires, and some would argue that was unnatural, but since all the humans were volunteers, she wasn't doing anything illegal or immoral, any more than the FBI was. She wasn't one of the Rogues Ty was looking for, going behind the FBI's back and preying on the innocent or selling humans as blood slaves. No, there was absolutely no proof of that.

In the three days Ana and Ty had spent at the compound, the only thing they'd observed was an idyllic life. The mothers and the children Ana had been fortunate enough to meet all were grateful for the help Salvation's Crossing had given them. Grateful for the work provided to their menfolk.

Still, that the husbands and fathers had to stay away for an entire growing season made Ana's heart ache. She'd never trusted men much—the horrific choices her mother had made in men had set her on a path of distrust. That Gloria's own grandfather—her flesh and blood—had sexually molested Gloria for so long had solidified her distrust. Oddly enough, Miguel had been the only male she'd trusted. Maybe because even though he'd led her to Primos Sangre, he'd done so with good intent. To protect her. And although she trusted Ty completely, he had an undeniable agenda, and was blind to the possibility that her sister and Miguel could be innocent.

She played with the girls for another half hour before they got bored and ran off. As they did, movement on the path up the hill caught her attention. Miguel. She smiled, though she felt herself tensing slightly. She was open to believing in his innocence, but she wasn't a fool, either. The longer they stayed here, the more she saw what Ty had—the way Miguel looked at her. With love. And sometimes with desire.

"Playing pat-a-cake?" he asked when he made it to the top of the hill.

"Something like that," she answered, forcing herself to grin and pat the ground beside her. He sat, stuck his legs out in front of him, and leaned on his hands behind his back. Close enough so their shoulders could touch. She tensed, unsure whether he'd touched her deliberately or not.

After making love to Ty the other night, the two of them had not touched except for a few displays of kisses and hand-holding. Even so, no matter how much she told herself it was impossible, she kept fantasizing about a future with him, one in which they didn't just fuck or work together, but gave each other everything.

Peace.

Happiness.

"You're good with them," Miguel said, nodding toward the chattering girls.

Ana blinked and refocused on the present rather than on her thoughts of Ty. "They're good kids, that's all."

"Be honest with yourself, *chica*. They like you for a reason. Don't sell yourself short. You always did before."

"*Gracias, mi hermano.*"

A flicker of movement appeared near the corner of his eye, then he smiled, but didn't look at her. "Is that what I am to you now? Your brother?"

"My sister loves you," she said carefully.

"Not as much as her cause," he bit out in response.

How could he possibly think he was second fiddle? Ana had seen the way Gloria looked at Miguel when she thought he couldn't see. The look of a woman completely in love.

"I've tried to talk to Gloria about what happened to her after I went to prison. She avoids the subject. I don't want to dig into her private business, but do you know what happened to her? After the shooting?" she asked.

"I never left her side, Ana. I took care of her, just as I promised you I would. We returned to the gang, but it wasn't long before Devil's Crew came to us. Shoved their way in, really. But not with disrespect. Just talked to the members about how bad our people were being treated. Gave legal options for how to get our families out of dangerous countries. Worked with us to find scholarships for our kids. Mostly, they talked to the women. The *cholos* at first ignored the representatives, thinking anything different was a threat. But the women—the mothers, the daughters—" Miguel cut himself off, his voice going thick with emotion. "The women knew how bad things were. How there was no hope. Salvation's Crossing offered hope. Some, like Gloria, listened. Some men, like me, listened to their women. Went against machismo."

"So you and Gloria were together by the time Salvation's Crossing came to Primos Sangre."

He looked at her sharply. "You were in prison . . ."

She patted his knee, automatically wanting to reassure him. But then she reconsidered . . . and kept her hand on his knee. If Miguel really did desire her, then perhaps avoiding him was taking the easy way out. She'd told Ty she'd do whatever the mission required, so what she should be doing was capitalizing on any feelings Miguel had for her.

"I don't mind that you're with Gloria, really. I want both of you happy. Always have, always will. But I must admit . . . seeing you now . . . I wish . . ."

A shadow crossed Miguel's face. "What do you wish?"

"I wish things could have been different for us. For all of us."

"What do you mean? Aren't you happy with Ty?"

She didn't have to fake her uncertainty as she looked away.

"Ana?"

She smiled as she turned back to him. Nodded. "Of course. Ty saved me."

"You love him?" Miguel asked.

Pain hit her midsection—tight and sharp. Love? There was that word again.

She did love him, but . . .

Love couldn't enter the equation. And thankfully, though she couldn't lie to herself about loving Ty, she could lie to Miguel—to see how he'd react. "No. I don't love Ty. Not the way I should. But I like him enough."

He looked away, but not before she saw a hint of a smile on his face. Another ripple of unease climbed up her spine.

"Is he good to you?" he asked.

"What does it matter?"

His head snapped around and anger flashed in his eyes, causing her to gasp. "It matters. Believe me, it matters. A man should worship you. Kiss the earth beneath your feet. Swear his fealty to you. End his life for you."

She stared at him in shock for a moment. The way he was talking, the intensity of his response, it was all consistent with a man who'd loved her so much he'd been doing whatever it took to keep her. Even kill her sister.

But what was she going to do? Ask him straight out if it was true?

Miguel stood abruptly. "I need to go now. The sun . . ."

Ana nodded and waved him off. "Yes. Go. I don't want you to get hurt. Besides, I'm supposed to meet Ty for a horseback ride soon."

He raised his brows. "That's right. He told me he wanted to check out our current irrigation system. But you? On a horse? I'd like to see that."

She crinkled her nose at him. "Well you can't. You've been in the sun too long, remember?" she said playfully.

He frowned, then nodded. "We'll talk later. But know this, Ana. I never forgot about you. I never stopped missing you. If you ever need anything, if Ty doesn't treat you right, you can always come to me."

"Thank you," she said finally, not knowing what else to say.

When he was gone, she got up and saw movement out of the corner of her eye. It was Becky Montes. How long had she been there? And why hadn't she announced herself?

The girl smiled and waved. "Hi, Ana."

"Did you want to talk to me about something, Becky?"

"No." She held up a ball. "I let it get past me."

"Becky! Come on!" a voice called. Three of the other girls waited down the hill.

Becky waved. "See you later, Ana."

"See you later," Ana said softly, then made her way toward the stables so she could meet Ty. During their stay he'd periodically disappeared to scour the property for anything suspicious. So far, he'd found nothing and she could tell his frustration was growing in proportion to her relief. Even so, as she walked Ana couldn't stop thinking about her conversation with Miguel. She went over everything he'd said and weighed it against everything she'd seen thus far. She tried to be objective and fair.

Nothing had changed. There was still no proof that Miguel or Gloria were involved in illegal activity or that anyone's human rights were being violated. Based on what Ramona Montes had told her, her husband was a complete liar.

However, she was another step closer to believing that Miguel wasn't the man she'd thought him to be. She'd never allowed herself to think of their one time together, the day he'd jumped her into the gang, as rape, but now that she was older . . . Now that Ty had classified it as rape . . . Well, that's technically what it had been, right? Statutory rape. Someone older taking advantage of someone younger, even if there had technically been consent. And if she could have been so wrong about him, wasn't it possible that maybe, just maybe, she could be wrong about her sister, too?

At the stables, Ty helped Ana mount a chestnut quarter horse before swinging up on his own palomino.

"They know their way home. Don't worry about getting lost," the stable hand said, about to retreat into the huge aluminum-sided barn. The stables were recently built and held multiple stalls, but there were only two horses besides his and Ana's. Why? To make it harder for anyone to leave?

"Thanks. I won't." Ty turned to look around at Ana, who lifted her head and gave him a nod.

Ty guided his horse out of the paddock, hearing the metallic clang of the gate closing once Ana had passed through, too.

Silently, he turned the palomino toward a path on the edge of the fields. Before them, the golden land was drenched in the long rays of the setting sun. The compound was many miles from the nearest town, nestled into a valley between hills that weren't as low as they looked. There was no view of anything else. Salvation's Crossing was a world apart.

Ana had balked at the suggestion of an evening ride, since she'd never ridden Western before and didn't know the first thing about neck reining. He'd raised his eyebrow at her and finally she'd understood: the twilight horseback ride was a chance for Ty to explore more of the land, but it would also serve as a cover so they could talk.

Soon into their ride, Ty spotted an aboveground valve for the irrigation system and rode toward it, with Ana some distance behind, going more slowly as she and her horse got used to each other.

She caught up with him by the time he'd dismounted. Ty was kneeling on the ground, using a fence slat to dig down.

"Whatcha doing?" she asked.

"Checking the system. That's the reason I gave for being out here." The slat hit metal. "Sounds like a pipe to me." Ty scraped at the ground and revealed a section of heavy, curved gray metal. "And it looks like a pipe."

"So you're an irrigation expert, too?"

Ty grinned and sat back on his haunches. "I do my homework."

Ana rolled her eyes, clearly unimpressed.

"I think Miguel's trying to scam me. My guess would be that the system works fine. You can hear the water gurgling." He dug a somewhat wider hole. "Now what is that doing there?" A section of white plastic pipe ran parallel to the metal one.

Ana dismounted by the fence and tied up her horse next to the palomino.

"Don't ask me," she said. "I'm from the Bronx. Water comes from water towers."

He looked at her blankly. "Those barrel things on top of the buildings?"

"That's right. And I have no idea how it gets up there."

Ty dug some more. He pressed his hand to the white plastic pipe. "There's no water in this one."

Ana glanced at the ground he'd opened up, her hands in the pockets of her jeans-clad hips. "Maybe there's something wrong with the irrigation system after all," she said. Then she looked up at the sunset sky, rocking back on her boot heels. "Let me know when you're done, Sherlock."

Ty stood and kicked the dirt back over the two pipes. "Let's keep riding while there's still light. I want to see where these pipes end up."

Ana shrugged and went to untie her horse. They rode single file for a while, then Ty made a right turn. After a while longer, they came out past tilled land that hadn't been planted.

Ty stopped his horse under an ancient oak whose massive branches nearly touched the ground, providing a perfect hiding place. "Look at that," he muttered when Ana stopped beside him. "I was thinking there'd be a pumping station."

There was a paved lot. And a nondescript cinder-block structure painted white, big enough for small trucks to drive into. There weren't any.

But there were several armed guards.

"Looks like a storage facility." She narrowed her eyes. "And that has to be a loading bay. Those doors roll up."

"I don't think Salvation's Crossing is selling spring water, do you?" Ty asked in a low voice.

She scowled. "They're not pumping blood through pipes that size, either," she said.

"Maybe not blood in its liquid form, but what about containers, vacuum tube propulsion—"

Ana's response was tense. "That's quite a theory. The question is can you prove it. The answer is no."

He glanced at her and sighed. Fuck. He'd known this was coming. Could see with every day that went by, each time he came back from a scouting mission without incriminating evidence, she was convincing herself she'd been right—that Miguel and Gloria were innocent of wrongdoing. That there was no cult. That Belladonna was wrong. "Give me a chance," he urged. "We haven't been here long enough to rule anything out. They're vampires. They work with vampires. Where there are vampires, human blood is bound to be a big business."

"I want to go."

"Ana, listen to me—"

Only she didn't. She dug her heels into the chestnut's sides and galloped away. It was Ty's turn to follow.

Once they were over the large hill and into a grove of oaks, he yelled, "Stop, damn it." When she didn't, he galloped up to her and grabbed her horse's reins, bringing it to a gradual stop. Both their horses' flanks were heaving from the hard run.

Ana immediately bounded off her horse and began walking back toward the compound.

Ty dismounted and grabbed her arm. "I need to tell you what I learned from Carly—"

"Fuck you. Fuck her."

He shook her. "You might be interested in what she had to say. She had news about Ramona and Becky Montes—"

"What? That Ramona's husband has been arrested for abuse? Because from what they've told me, he should be."

"He can't. He's dead. And so are his wife and daughter."

Ana froze then jerked away from him. "Wh—what are you talking about?"

"The women claiming to be Ramona and Becky Montes are imposters."

She backed several steps away from him. "You're crazy."

"I'm not."

"They look just like the pictures you showed me."

"Then they had damn good plastic surgeons. At least, that's what Carly suspects. I talked to her earlier via my satellite phone. The signal's encrypted." When she glanced at the horses, and more specifically their saddles, he shook his head. "No bugs. I checked."

"Fine. Then tell me—how can you and Carly know these women are imposters?"

"Because two women, burned beyond recognition, were ID'd from their dental records. Ramona and Becky were killed weeks ago, right around the time they left to join the Crossing."

"Oh, God," Ana whispered. "I didn't even know them and—" She shook her head and took a deep breath. "So fine. The Ramona and Becky I've been talking to are imposters. That doesn't mean Miguel or Gloria know it. Or that they're conspirators in anything illegal."

"No, it doesn't," he conceded, "but—"

"But nothing, Ty," Ana said. "I want out."

He'd suspected it was coming but her bald statement still shocked him.

"Gloria is happy here," she urged. "Salvation's Crossing is what she wants."

"And the vampire thing?"

She shrugged. "It's the new reality, right? Have you seen any vampires besides Miguel and Gloria? Even if some are hiding out here, that doesn't mean there's blood slave trafficking going on."

She was right, damn her. As far as he knew, Ty himself was the only vampire to have entered Salvation's Crossing since they'd arrived, and he'd only been served animal blood. But something was going on. They just needed to snoop around, find out more. The what and the where. And to do that, they needed more time.

Time she didn't seem willing to give him any longer.

"What happened, Ana?" he asked quietly.

"Nothing! That's the point. Nothing's happened. Salvation's Crossing is doing some good. You saw it for yourself. All those happy kids—"

"We saw what someone wanted us to see. People are surprisingly cooperative when guns get pointed at them."

"I haven't seen that happening, have you?"

Ty didn't have to mention the armed guards. She couldn't have forgotten them—or the car that had followed them. "Something's going on," was as much as he wanted to say. "I know it. And on some level, so do you. That's why you're scared."

She raised a hand to her forehead and rubbed it. "You're confusing me."

"No. I'm challenging you. You want so badly to believe nothing's going on here, but you're starting to have doubts. Why?"

"I—I don't know. Nothing concrete. Just a feeling. And I can't suspect my family . . . my *friend* . . . based on a feeling."

The way she emphasized "friend" had him narrowing his eyes. "You're talking about Miguel?"

She looked like she was going to deny it, then sighed. "It was what he said—or maybe the way he said it. It made me think . . . maybe he does love me . . . too much. Only nothing's happened."

"Let's keep it that way."

She seemed to think about what he was asking. "How long are we going to stay here if nothing shows up? How long is it going to take until you're satisfied?"

"I don't know. I—"

"Well, I do," she said. "I'll help you. We'll scour this place from top to bottom. And we're going to start with your theory about the pipes. If someone was going to take human blood, bottle it, and use the pipes to transport it to that loading bay, where's the most likely place they'd draw the blood?"

"The infirmary," Ty said immediately.

Ana nodded. "Then let's start there. We'll start tonight and I'll give you two days, Ty. If we don't come up with anything after that, we leave. Deal?"

Ty hesitated, then nodded. "Deal."

Ana turned to head back to their horses.

"Hold on a minute," he said with a hand on her arm. "We have a few minutes before the place locks down and we can search the infirmary, right?"

"Yes. So?"

He pointed to a patch of new grass surrounded by wild lilies. "Have you ever made love surrounded by nature?" He couldn't believe he actually had the gall to suggest it. They were both frustrated as hell. They'd been talking about underground systems to transport bottled blood for sale.

None of it mattered.

Two days. Ana had given him two days to find something or they were leaving. That meant he had two guaranteed days left with her and he wasn't wasting any opportunity he had to be with her.

She frowned. Then, just when he thought she was going to walk away, she asked him a question instead. "What exactly do you have in mind?"

*   *   *

It turned out Ty had a lot in mind. Not all-out sex, but close enough to it so anyone looking would think they had. By the time they returned the horses to the stables and got back to the main house, she hustled back to their suite in hopes of avoiding anyone in her state of flushed disarray. It was just her luck that she ran into Gloria.

Her sister looked her over and laughed. "Look at you, doing the Walk of Shame. Ty is hot stuff, huh?"

Ana cleared her throat. "Yeah. He is. I can't lie."

Gloria's gaze strayed to Ana's throat, where Ty had deliberately left his mark on her. To her surprise, Gloria stepped forward and lightly touched the small puncture wounds. Ana forced herself to hold still.

Gloria smiled. "He seems to make you happy."

But was it just her imagination or did Gloria's eyes harden?

"He does," Ana replied.

"So are you and Ty going to marry? You'd have cute kids."

The question floored her. She tried to imagine what a child of hers and Ty's would look like. All she could picture was a little vampire baby with silver hair and silver pupils. It didn't matter. It was still adorable. And Ana knew that if she was ever to have Ty's baby, vampire or not, she'd love it just the same.

Because she loved Ty.

Funny how Gloria didn't ask any questions about that.

Her sister reached toward her and Ana flinched. But all Gloria did was push aside the collar of her shirt and pick up the delicate gold chain Ana kept hidden beneath her clothes, the one that was supposed to prevent her or any other vampire from reading Ana's mind or exercising persuasion over her.

Gloria rubbed the chain between her fingers. "Pretty," she murmured before releasing it.

Ana tried to swallow past the guilt clogging her throat. She told herself there was no reason to be guilty. That her deception was for the purpose of proving Gloria's innocence to Ty.

Her sister turned when she heard Miguel calling her from downstairs. Then she looked into Ana's eyes and walked away without saying good night.

Later that night, Ty and Ana searched the infirmary but found no evidence of anything suspicious. Silently, they'd returned to their room and made love once again. Since then, a thin moon had risen and set. Ana had been sound asleep for a long time, her arm draped across his chest. Ty refused to disturb her, even though his body was half paralyzed by hours without moving. Even though he could still hear the echo of that strange male voice in his head.

I know your weakness.

It had only been said once, but Ty heard it over and over again. Because he knew exactly what the statement meant.

His weakness was the woman sleeping in his arms.

And someone—someone Ty suspected had to be a powerful vampire, maybe the same vampire that had been protecting Ana all this time and wasn't Miguel as Ty had initially suspected—knew it.

Beside him, Ana stirred and murmured his name. Ty turned his head and pressed a kiss to her sleep-flushed cheek.

"Shh," he whispered. "I'm here. I'll always do my best to protect you." He tried to say he'd keep her safe. That nothing would harm her. That he wouldn't let anything harm her.

But he couldn't say the words.

He wanted them to be true, but part of him doubted his ability to actually protect her.

How could he win a fight with a vampire powerful enough to invade his mind yet remain unseen? Unidentified?

Ty wrapped his arms tighter around Ana. He might not win but . . .

"I'd die for you, Ana. I love you."

CHAPTER
THIRTY-SEVEN

The next day, Ty sat at a picnic table across from the compound laundry facility. The wood was smooth and new. No carved initials, no emblems. He didn't know why he'd expected to see any.

The laundry workers seemed to be mostly women from what he could see through the steamy windows. Red bins trundled toward the low building on a noisy conveyor belt, holding what looked like towels and linens. The women shoving the bins from a truck onto the belt didn't look his way, calling to each other in Spanish.

He slipped the encrypted phone out of his pocket and checked his messages. Carly had texted him the results of the drone images he'd requested.

Second pipe inactive. Leads to portion of the main house next to kitchen. Check it out then plan your exit strategy.

That last part surprised Ty.

? he texted back.

Have a bad feeling. Need to regroup. Over and out. Which was Carly's way of saying the conversation was done.

Shit. She was spooked. Carly didn't spook easily. Now Ty was spooked even more than he had been.

But he also had a new lead.

An area next to the kitchen to check out.

He just needed Ana to help him with his cover.

* * *

"Cherry pie?" Ana said in an amused voice. "Honestly, Ty, you get the weirdest cravings." She turned to Mrs. Tobia and smiled. "Thank you so much for letting us use the kitchen. Cooking together is *one* of our favorite activities," she said in Spanish.

The older woman laughed at Ana's joke.

As she left, Ana fiddled with various supplies until she and Ty felt they were alone. Ty pointed to a hallway to the left of the kitchen. "Stay close," he mouthed.

She did. Methodically, they searched each room off the kitchen. Eventually, they came to the final room and still hadn't found anything.

After scanning the room for bugs with his smartphone, Ty cursed. "I was sure we'd find something!" Ty explained. "Those pipes . . ." He shook his head. "You were right, Ana. Maybe there isn't anything bad going on here. Let's get back to the kitchen and make that pie in case Mrs. Tobia returns." With a defeated sigh, he left.

Ana was about to follow him, but she paused to look around the room. The walls were bare, without pictures or a single piece of furniture or wall sconces. It was essentially wasted space. Why?

After a brief hesitation, she left, too, but the question stayed in her mind. She thought about it the rest of the day. By sunset, she still didn't have an answer. But she did have a plan. One that involved retrieving the bottle of luminol she'd brought with her.

Twenty minutes later, she and Ty were back inside the bare room by the kitchen, staring at what she'd discovered.

The luminol revealed latent blood on the room's floor. Not just traces of blood, but lots of it. The spatters outlined black squares, evenly spaced. Ty visualized the chairs that had been there. An irregular shape in one corner. He could almost see the curled-up corpse of a victim who'd bled out on the floor, neglected until it was too late by the ghouls in charge.

The outline was big and blocky. A man. Had he tried to pull out the needle draining every drop of his blood? Tried to escape?

Ty studied the unearthly scene in numbed silence. He saw more. An outline of a broken chain. A snakelike coil of surgical tubing. A scrawled word. *Ayudenos.*

Help us.

Ty blinked as the light came on again. Ana stared back at him, her face pale, her features pinched.

"You were right," she said. "About everything. You were right."

"Princess," he said, his heart aching for her. But as he stepped toward her, intent on folding her in his arms, she shook her head and stepped back. Whirling around, she ran from the room.

Ran from him.

Ty barely stopped himself from going after her. Give her time, he told himself. A few minutes to sort things out. Meanwhile, he searched the walls, something he cursed himself for not doing earlier. He found the secret compartment with the chute that propelled the bottled blood through the PVC pipes and to the loading bay. He was taking pictures with his smartphone when the wave of dizziness hit him and he blacked out.

Ty came to. For several moments, he didn't know where he was. The last thing he remembered was Ana spraying that room with luminol. Seeing the results. Finding the chute.

He didn't remember anything after that, but he felt

dizzy. Nauseous. Was he sick? Did vampires even get sick?

He was outdoors. Underneath some kind of tree, with moonlight shining through the branches.

Unable to comprehend the present, he cast his mind back to the recent past. What had he eaten? The fare at the compound didn't vary.

At breakfast, he'd had the same thing he'd had the morning before, and the morning before that. Animal blood supplied by—

His eyes widened, but he couldn't move any other part of his body. Had Miguel put something in the blood he'd given him? Had they been slipping him slow-acting poison a little at a time, so that he was only now feeling its full power?

Ty tried to sit up but he couldn't.

"Hey." A female voice broke through his racing thoughts. Ana's sister. "Are you okay?" Gloria asked. "Do you want me to get Ana?"

She was taunting him in a malevolent voice far different than anything she'd used before now. "Oh wait. I can't. She's going to have her own shit to worry about soon. But tell me. What hurts? Because I really, really want to know."

Nothing, he wanted to say. Everything. And it was true. Technically, he wasn't in significant pain, but the knowledge that he *had* been poisoned, that Gloria had known about it, and that Ana was going to be defenseless without him, made him want to roar with agony.

He strained to move. Could feel his muscles tensing and the veins in his neck bulging. He tried mentally commanding her to let him go, hoping he could exercise some kind of mind control the way he had seemed to with Bobbie Hernandez.

None of it did him any good.

He was utterly paralyzed. His mind wasn't working right.

He hadn't felt this helpless since he'd learned his sister was dead. That had almost killed him. If anything happened to Ana—

God, Ana.

After fleeing that horrible room, Ana had immediately jumped into the shower, but no matter how hard she scrubbed, she couldn't wash the stink of betrayal and despair off her.

Oh, God, those people. Those poor people, she thought.

She needed to get dressed. Needed to get back to Ty. Needed to get out of here—

Ana was drying off when she heard Ty moving around inside the room. He's back, she thought. He came to check on me and I'm going to tell him. I'm going to tell him that despite the fact he was right, I don't hate him. I'm not going to be a coward. Not this time.

Wrapping the towel around herself, she entered the bedroom. "Ty—"

She stopped abruptly as she saw the tall, dark-haired man standing in the bedroom. Fear washed over her.

"Miguel? What—what are you doing here?" When he didn't answer, she dared to take a step closer. "Are you okay?"

Because he didn't look okay. He looked ill.

As if he was going to puke at any moment.

"What's wrong? You're sick?"

Miguel shook his head and stared at her with glassy eyes. "I'm sorry, Ana. I—don't want to do it. But we have our orders. Gloria was so close to changing her mind. So close."

"What orders? What are you talking about?" She

clutched the towel tightly, afraid she might drop it. She couldn't run away stark naked. And where was Ty? Where the hell was Ty?

"You and Ty being here—it's a setup. A trap. You thought you could stop us, but it's the other way around. We're supposed to get rid of both of you."

There it was. Miguel had just laid it out, plain and clear. And now he was going to make sure she couldn't tell anyone.

She had to stall him.

"So everything we saw—the compound, the good you do—that's all a lie?"

"No. Vampires can't lie. But we can hide the full truth."

Once again, she saw that luminol-stained room. She thought of the women and children she'd met. She thought of her foolish hopes of being reunited with her sister.

"The men who are supposed to be working in the fields? Where are they really?"

"They work the fields, just as we said. Some also provide human blood. A worthy service."

"As blood slaves?"

"Slavery implies they had no choice. The men sacrificed themselves for the greater good. We've kept our part of the bargain. We're providing a better life for their families. A better life than they could ever provide."

A flicker in his expression caused her eyes to narrow. "That's bullshit. Why do you do it, you and Gloria?"

He shrugged. "Why else? Money. Perks. Like being turned into a vampire. It comes with such amazing powers, Ana. You can't know—"

"Oh, I know," she said, backing away from him. She'd seen the vampire power firsthand when she'd seen Ty tearing into a man's throat, but that had been self-defense, not cold-blooded calculation and self-interest. "Where's Gloria? Why isn't she here? She's my sister and she can't even grant me the privilege of killing me herself? Because that's what you meant by doing 'it,' right? You're going to kill me?"

"Gloria is taking care of Ty, but I asked her to let me have you. I'll make it fast. I'll make it painless, *m'ija*."

Miguel stepped toward her and she held out her hand in an instinctive attempt to ward him off.

With an anguished look on his face, he stopped. "Please, *m'ija*. Don't fight me. It will only make things worse."

"You can't, Miguel. You can't kill me. *Te quiero*. I loved you and I know you loved me."

At first he looked confused, then angry. "Yeah? You left me, Ana. And you love Ty now, no matter what you say. You asked me to stay with your sister, to protect her, and you fell in love with someone else."

"Did you put a hit out on Gloria?"

"Of course I did," he shouted. "That's how much I loved you. That's how much I wanted to keep you with me. But you screwed it up. You saved her, the way you always saved her, with no thought for what it would cost you. And then you went to prison."

Her mind was spinning. All she could think was she'd been too late. She'd realized she loved Ty too late. She hadn't told him she loved him, his vampire side included. He was good. Kind. He'd taught her so much. Not just to fight, but to feel again. She didn't want to stop feeling again. She wouldn't. Not if there was a chance of him surviving.

She was going to do whatever she needed so that if he came looking for her, she'd still be alive when he found her.

"You wanted to keep me with you, Miguel. So do it now. Please."

"What?" he asked, his expression stunned.

"Don't kill me. Turn me instead. You know how it's done, don't you?"

She reminded herself that he couldn't read her mind as her thoughts tumbled over each other. *Please know how it's done, Miguel, please. But don't pick up what I know—that by turning me, you'll be sacrificing your own life.*

"Why—why would you want me to turn you?"

She forced herself to do it then. She walked up to him and kissed him. She kissed him the way she kissed Ty. As if she loved him. As if she'd die without him. And when she pulled back, she knew he'd felt exactly what she wanted him to feel. He looked dazed. Elated.

"So we can be together," she urged. "Finally. The way I've always imagined."

"What about Ty?"

"You're totally wrong about him," she forced herself to say. "I don't love him, and I see now you don't love Gloria. It was always us who were meant to be together. Just be with me, Miguel. Please."

The last traces of hesitation left his expression. With a look of determination on his face, he came for her, fangs unsheathed.

She felt his fangs plunge into her throat. There was none of the pleasure that came with the act when Ty did it. This time it hurt. It hurt so much she screamed.

In her mind, she called for Ty. She told him to fight for his life. To fight for her.

To fight for their love.

And then, just before everything went dark, she saw something move behind Miguel.

CHAPTER
THIRTY-EIGHT

Ty grunted and instinctively tried to reach out and grab Gloria's ankle, surprised when his fingers actually responded by curling infinitesimally. Not enough to actually grab hold of anything, but enough to tell him he wasn't completely paralyzed anymore.

"How's the moonlight feel, Ty? Good, yes? Enjoy it while you can. In a few hours, the sun will rise and the real show will begin."

Ty was silent. He licked his cracked lips.

"Ohhh. I love it when you do that," she taunted. "By the way, I saw your fingers move. Feeling coming back? Believe me, it won't be enough to matter. Try turning your head toward me . . ."

He did as she said. It was like slogging through hardening cement. He didn't know how long it took him to actually turn his head a couple of inches until he could see her, sitting beside him, but eventually it happened.

She waggled her fingers at him.

"Hi there. That took you about fifteen minutes, just so you know. Soon, Miguel will be finished with Ana and he'll be able to join us."

Inside, Ty screamed with rage. Was it true? Was Miguel killing Ana while Ty lay here helpless? He wouldn't believe it. He *couldn't*. Maybe Gloria thought her lover could actually murder her sister, but Ty knew exactly what Miguel had done in an attempt to keep her with him seven years ago . . .

Only Gloria didn't know Miguel had actually put a hit out on her back then. If he could just tell her, get her upset enough that she left him . . .

Maybe she'd attack and the two vampires would be locked in battle long enough to give Ana a chance at escaping.

It was a long shot.

Ty tried to form the words. Tried to speak. *The man you love tried to kill you so he could have Ana. You've always been second best to him.*

Nothing came out.

But Gloria saw him struggling to speak and laughed. She came closer and cupped her palm over her ear, pretending to strain to hear him.

"What is it? Are you trying to beg for mercy? Go ahead. Beg."

"Read . . . mind," Ty breathed.

Her eyes narrowed. "No such luck, *mi amigo*. I've been trying to do that since you got here. Strange, since it's something I'm quite good at."

He gritted his teeth and tried to speak again. It took several tries before he got out, "Off . . . chain."

"For God's sake, I have no idea what you . . ." Her eyes widened and her gaze bounced to Ty's throat. "Take off your chain? Your necklace? Is that why I haven't been able to read your mind? Or Ana's?"

Ty didn't bother responding. Gloria chewed her lip. Finally, she crouched down and ripped the necklace off him. Ty immediately felt a tickling sensation in his brain. He saw the moment Gloria read his thoughts in the widening of her eyes.

"No, you're lying. You're lying. You're. Lying!"

She'd started to scream. "Miguel loves me. I know he

loved Ana, but he said he always loved me, too. He wouldn't have hurt me."

She'd read the truth in Ty's mind but still denied it.

"You're wrong," she said. "You're wrong and I'm going to prove it. Then I'll be back to see you burn and suffer, you son of a bitch."

With that, she was gone.

He's drinking too much.

One moment, Ana felt her life draining out of her and in the next, she sensed Miguel being ripped away. Something wet splattered on her face. Her torso. Instinctively, she knew it was blood. As she crumpled to the ground, she heard muted screams. She tuned them out, struggling to breathe and get her pounding heart under control.

In the next instant, a shadow hovered over her. A face and form came in and out of focus, one she didn't recognize. It wasn't Ty, she thought sadly. Even though someone or something had just killed Miguel, she was still going to die, and she was going to die without seeing Ty again or telling him that she loved him.

"Ty . . ."

Her savior pulled her into a sitting position, propping her up against the wall. He caressed her face. "You're hurt and bleeding, but your sister has him, *m'ija*. I must go if I'm going to save him. I'll bring him to you. You wait here. Just wait."

Instinctively, she tried to reach out and stop him from leaving. She wanted him to get Ty, just as he said he would, but she was cold, so cold, and she knew the specter of death was near. She didn't want to die alone. It didn't seem right. Didn't seem fair.

Once he disappeared, however, she began to think maybe she wasn't going to die after all. Her throat

burned where Miguel had bitten her but the pain was
easing somewhat. The more she blinked, the more her
vision cleared. She could make out distinct shapes now.
Colors.

A few more blinks and she saw Miguel, lying on the
floor in front of her.

His blood pooled around his body from a mortal
wound to the chest.

A knife, she thought. It had to have been dipped in
liquid nitrogen. Whoever had saved her had known how
to kill a turned vampire, per the instructions of the Vampire Queen.

Had the queen sent a vampire to help them? Had
someone from Belladonna broken into the compound?
Maybe Peter?

Not him. Her rescuer was someone who'd known her
before, she thought confusedly . . . someone who'd
called her *m'ija* . . . but only Miguel had ever called her
that . . .

Miguel and Gloria.

Gloria.

Had she already killed Ty?

Ana.

She heard her name, spoken in Ty's voice. Muffled.
Barely there. But yet . . . there.

*Ana, Miguel and Gloria want to hurt you. They're
coming for you. Run!*

Fear ripped through her. Fear and doubt.

Was that really Ty in her head, warning her that Gloria was coming for her?

She wouldn't believe it . . . except she knew he'd been
in her head before. When they'd had sex. When he'd
heard her screaming no even when she'd let Louis paw
her outside that club. But where was he? Why wasn't he
coming for her?

I love you, Ana. I can't live without you. Save yourself.

Her body jerked upon hearing Ty's confession.

He loved her. He was trying to save her.

And as much as she'd wanted to believe her sister would never hurt her, she knew that was a lie now. She loved Ty. And she believed him.

But she couldn't wait for him to save her. For some reason, he knew that wasn't possible; that's why he'd inserted himself into her mind.

She couldn't stand. She couldn't run.

But somehow . . . she had to save herself.

A rabbit was sitting not six inches from Ty's outstretched hand.

If he could just grab it and bring it to his mouth, he could drink its blood. The influx of fresh animal blood might counter the effects of whatever poison or drug was still running through him.

Might give him some hope of getting to Ana and saving her before Miguel or Gloria harmed her.

His fingers moved closer toward the rabbit. Just three inches away now.

He could see the rabbit's damn nose twitching.

Help me, he thought. Help me help Ana.

Ty almost had it . . . almost had it . . .

With a burst of strength, he lunged out, frantically grasping for the rabbit, but it bounded away.

Ty groaned, an inhuman sound of frustration and despair that was cut off as suddenly as the fleeing rabbit was picked up. He hadn't moved his fingers more than an inch.

He blinked when someone grabbed his shirt and yanked him into a sitting position. A man who looked vaguely familiar stared back at him even as he brought the rabbit to his mouth and tore open its neck. Then he held the carcass over Ty so the rabbit's blood dripped down on him.

"Drink. Ana needs you."

Ty already had his mouth open and was swallowing the rabbit's blood, but the man's words caused an influx of power all on their own. They meant everything to him because they told him Ana was still alive. And that he could still save her.

The more blood he swallowed, the more his head cleared. The more his muscles awakened. The more his rage promised vengeance.

He recognized who the man was in front of him. Ty had seen him talking to Miguel inside Bobbie Hernandez's head. He'd been the one who had sent Officer Southcott after Ty. He'd been the one protecting Ana. And now he was giving Ty the chance to save her life.

I'm coming, Ana. Hang on, baby. I'm coming.

Though she'd tried to prepare herself, Ana couldn't help it—she jolted when her bedroom door was thrown open and Gloria walked in. Their gazes immediately met and held, just before Gloria's eyes dropped to the floor where her lover lay in the center of the room. Ana had positioned herself in the corner farthest away from Miguel, her back protected by the wall.

Shock flooded Gloria's expression, followed swiftly by grief. With a feral shriek, she flung herself at Miguel's body, her screams growing louder as she realized he was indeed dead. She cradled him in her arms and rocked back and forth until her anguish faded away.

After several minutes, she looked up at Ana.

"Eliana?" she whimpered, her voice that of a little girl seeking comfort. "Eliana, what happened? Are you—are you okay?"

Her words and tone immediately drove Ana back in

time. Despite what her mind was telling her, they made her drop her guard. This wasn't an evil creature bent on killing her or exploiting others out of greed. It was her sister. Gloria. Someone who needed Ana's compassion and help, not her suspicion.

"Eliana, why are you looking at me like that? I need you, sister." Gloria reached out a hand. "Come to me."

Ana straightened slightly, wanting to go to her so badly. Wanting to trust her. But Ty's warning played in her head, making her hesitate.

That's when she saw the expression that flickered across Gloria's face.

Hatred.

Utter hatred.

Ana saw it clearly then.

But she still couldn't move. Couldn't throw the knife she'd dragged out of Miguel's dying body, hoping there was enough liquid nitrogen left on it to kill her sister.

She stood stock still until Ty called her name and staggered into view in the doorway.

Gloria didn't even turn around. She just smiled and her muscles tensed as she prepared to lunge for Ana.

And Ana knew at that moment that she had to make a choice.

Her sister or her life. Her last chance at happiness with Ty.

Silently, Ana didn't flinch from her feelings of betrayal or grief. She accepted them. Embraced them. And threw the knife the way Ty had taught her.

The blade pierced Gloria in the heart.

Her sister gasped even as she stumbled closer.

"Eliana, you hurt me. Eliana . . . why?"

She was almost to Ana before she dropped to her knees.

And died.

With a sob, Ana collapsed next to her.

CHAPTER
THIRTY-NINE

Ty stepped over Gloria's body and gathered Ana in his arms. She stared numbly at her sister, clearly in shock. Her skin was cold, so cold.

He recognized that chill. He'd felt it himself. Every hour of every day since he'd been turned. It had only been in the past few months that the chill had begun to dissipate . . .

It had left him completely the first night he'd made love to Ana.

Ty glanced up at the man who'd saved him and accompanied him to Ana's room. "She's freezing."

"When I came in, Miguel had started to turn her. I stopped him, but not in time. Her body's cold because the turning process has begun. There's a chance I can stop it if I feed her my blood, but I have to do it soon. Even then, it might already be too late."

"How soon?"

"Within the next ten minutes."

Ty growled. "You should have fed her your blood instead of coming after me!"

"She loves you. And I knew if I didn't save you, she wouldn't want to live anyway. This way, she has a choice, but it's one she must make. Otherwise, I'll make the choice for her. I believe she'd want to be with you, not just for a human lifetime, but for eternity. So unless she tells me herself to stop the turning, I'm not going to do it."

Ty looked frantically down at Ana and he saw it clearly then—the possibility of a life with her. No, infinite lifetimes. The idea of being what he was, even the idea of living forever, didn't scare him when he thought of spending that time with Ana. But he couldn't be selfish. Couldn't consign her to becoming a creature like himself, a being she would loathe as he had loathed himself for so long.

No matter what the other vampire said, she hadn't chosen that. So he shook her.

"Ana. Ana, goddamn it, listen to me. Tell him you don't want to be a vampire. Ana!"

Ty was calling her, and he sounded panicked. Frantic. That realization finally enabled her to look away from Gloria and search for Ty. He was right beside her. Holding her. The first thing she did was smile. He looked so worried and she wanted to reassure him but the words wouldn't come. She raised a hand to his face to caress it, but her hand froze and fell when she saw the man standing beside him.

At first, she thought it was Miguel. Then the past—everything in the past—came rushing back at her. What he'd said. What he'd done. Her hand flew to her neck, but before she could touch it, Ty grasped her wrist. "Shh. You're okay. Don't touch it. Don't—" His voice broke and he quickly looked away, as if he was ashamed to look at her.

But what did he have to be ashamed of?

"Listen to Ty, Ana. Everything's going to be okay."

How? was her first thought. *My friend and my sister are dead.* But she was again too distracted by the other man to get the words out. She studied him more closely, and was immediately struck by that powerful sense of recognition. This time, however, pieces to the puzzle drifted closer together.

She'd seen his face before. A long time before. But despite the passing of years, he looked exactly the same as he had back then. Not a single wrinkle marred his skin. Only his hair and eyes were different. Silver.

A vampire. But what kind? Born or made?

"Pablo?" Ana asked, her tone laced with disbelief . . . and fear.

"Ah." He smiled widely. "You remember me, even after all this time. That's good."

She tried to stand, but her legs wobbled and Ty gently pressed on her shoulders, keeping her sitting on the floor. She glared at him, even as she snapped, "Of course, I remember you. You're the one who gave me this scar. The one who came in with the others, guns blazing, the night I tried to jump out of Primos Sangre."

Her voice was a shaky whisper, not the scathing retort she'd intended to make. But Pablo heard her anyway.

"Both things I truly regret, *m'ija*. All I can say is that you and I didn't know each other then. I had no reason to know what a beautiful creature you were, inside as well as out. But when I learned what you were willing to do to get your sister out of the gang, when I read your mind after the shooting, well . . . that changed and I've been with you ever since. Watching you. Protecting you. It's why I came here. To help you . . . and the vampire you love."

Her head ached. She tried to think it through. Carly had said Devil's Crew had been made up of Rogues. Likely he'd been a vampire even then and was simply no longer hiding it. But he'd said he was here to protect her, which made no sense. "Why me?"

"Because of what you were willing to do to protect your sister. Anything and everything. You let yourself be beaten to get her away from Primos Sangre. And you were willing to do whatever it took to be reunited with her. I've seen it all. Everything that's happened. And your loyalty and goodness is what tells me you're beautiful. Deserving of the protection I've given you. You remind me of my Carolina. My love, my wife. I lost her hundreds of years ago and I'm growing so weary without her. You've helped fill a void in me."

"Were you—were you turned, too?"

"No, *m'ija*. I was born this way. Even born vampires can love. Can care."

She remembered what Ty had said about someone following her. Someone protecting her by killing off anyone who had hurt her.

"I cared about Téa Montgomery, too."

"Yes. Unfortunate. An associate of mine—you remember Officer Southcott, don't you?—getting a little too carried away. She was supposed to be given a warning, not killed. I apologize, but rest assured, Officer Southcott got what was coming to him."

"And that's supposed to make it okay? Your apology? The fact you killed another man? Because it doesn't."

Pablo nodded sagely. "I understand if you feel that way."

"What about Bobbie Hernandez? Is it true that he's been working for you? That he wants to be a vampire?"

A look of regret flashed over Pablo's face.

Ana shook her head. "Bobbie, too? Did you—did you—?"

"No, *m'ija*. He was doing a job for me. Talking to a few men who were in the bar before Ty killed Louis. I wanted to be sure what Ty meant to you, and Bobbie was helping me with that. Unfortunately, Louis's friends were stronger than Bobbie thought. They killed him. But I took care of them. For you, but also for him. Bobbie was loyal to me. I owed him that. I should have protected him, but I'm happy I didn't fail you, Ana. I want only for you to be at peace at last. Happy."

Had he protected her? She supposed he had in some way. But he hadn't been in time to save her. Nor had Ty. Not to save her from Gloria. She'd had to do it herself.

"Ty . . . I heard him." "In my head, just like before . . ."

Pablo smiled and nodded. "It's a rare talent, even for vampires, the ability to connect minds with someone, even from a distance. I can do it. Obviously so can Ty."

Yes, she thought. A very powerful thing. She looked down at Miguel, then her sister, but strangely, she felt no grief.

How could she not feel grief for the boy she'd once loved? For her sister, who'd meant everything to her. It was as if her heart had frozen over. Even hearing Pablo refer to the vampire she loved—*Ty*—felt strange. Distant. As if that love was still there, but encased by layers and layers of ice.

She shivered and shook with cold, and thought of how cold Ty had been when she'd first met him. Was that what was happening to her? Was her body temperature dropping as she lost her humanity?

She turned to Ty. "Miguel was going to kill me," she said slowly. "I—told him to change me instead. He bit me. Am I—?"

"Pablo stopped him," Ty said in a low voice. "But not quite in time. The process has already started. He says he can still stop it, though, Ana. He just needs you to tell him to do it."

He said it with relief but no hint of envy. As if he were glad she could regain her humanity. But what had being human given her? Nothing. It had left her a victim to the whims of fate. Why shouldn't she want to be something stronger? Something more powerful?

Her thoughts shamed her. Reminded her that Miguel

and Gloria had coveted that power, too. But even through her shame, she couldn't deny she wanted something more than her humanity could give her. "Do you hate what I am now?" she asked him.

Ty looked shocked by her words. "No. No, I could never hate you. I'm only thankful that you'll live."

"How can you suddenly lie? You hate yourself." Her gaze went to the knife she'd used to kill her sister. Could Ty still use it? Would he?

He gripped her chin and brought her gaze back to his. "I'm not going to kill myself, Ana. I haven't wanted that for a long time. You've changed so many things for me. You showed me my life is still worth living. That I—that I can still love. And if I can still love you as I am, then I'm not the monster I thought."

"You really love me?" she whispered.

"I can't lie, remember? But ask Pablo. He's been in my head. Isn't that right, Pablo?" He glared at the other vampire, who merely nodded.

"He loves you more than himself, Ana. More than his next breath."

"That's right," Ty said. "But you don't need to hear *him* say it to believe it. You heard my thoughts before. You know I love you. That I don't want to live without you."

The ice surrounding her heart seemed to melt slightly. "I did hear you. I just wasn't sure if I'd been imagining things."

He took her hand. "You weren't. You heard me and you did the right thing. The only thing you could do. You saved yourself. And in doing so, you saved me, Ana. Because as long as the world has you in it, it's a place I never want to leave."

She couldn't quite feel joy, not with the carnage that surrounded them. But she knew what she wanted to do.

She turned to Pablo. "I love him, too. I don't want you to stop the turning process."

"Ana, no!" Ty said, but she saw what he couldn't hide. She saw his hope.

"I want to live forever if I can. With Ty."

Ty grasped her hand tighter, then lifted it to kiss it. "Are you sure, Ana? The turning process is . . . I mean, it won't be easy."

"Will you stay with me? Help me with it?"

"Of course."

"And afterward? Will you want me for an eternity?"

"Forever will never be long enough."

"Then I'm sure," she said. "I've never been surer of anything in my whole life."

Ty's face lit up. She'd been wrong. It was possible to feel grief and profound joy at the same time. She was feeling it now.

Because she had a chance at a future with Ty.

She kissed him then. They kissed for a long, long time.

When they finally pulled apart, Pablo was gone. And so were the bodies of Miguel and Gloria. He'd taken them with him, once again protecting her, this time from the pain of disposing of their bodies.

"Do you think we'll see him again?" Ana asked.

"I don't know. He came when you needed him, but odds are he's been working with Gloria and Miguel. He could have been giving the orders." If that was true, then Pablo was a Rogue, and it would be their duty to take him down.

"Now what? Because Miguel said this was a trap, Ty. They knew we were coming here and why. They were supposed to kill us."

"I read Carly's mind, Ana. Whoever is playing us played her, too. We just need to figure out who that is."

"And the people here? The children?"

"We'll call Carly and the rest of the team. They'll help

us talk to everyone, and we'll make sure we bring them someplace safe. Then we need to call in the Strange Phenom brass from the FBI."

"Even though you don't know who to trust?"

He nodded. "We have to pretend we're still operating in the dark. Belladonna must continue its work. That's the only way we're going to find out the truth behind why we were sent here and why we were set up. It's the only way we're going to be safe. Because even though vampires are immortal—"

"They can still die," she said, automatically thinking of Miguel and Gloria again. Someday she would be able to grieve for them.

But for now . . . for now she was going to focus her energy on what mattered.

Surviving.

Only this time, she didn't have only herself to rely on. She had Ty.

CHAPTER
FORTY

An Undisclosed Location

Ty's eyes flew open and he jerked to a sitting position. It took a moment to orient himself. To realize that he'd been having a nightmare again. Not about being turned or tortured. No, his nightmares were about Ana's pain now. And how helpless he felt because he couldn't spare her from it.

Right now, however, Ana's naked body was curled slightly away from him, her expression soft and relaxed. Her breathing was steady, her body enjoying a much-needed respite from the difficulty of her transition. The tightness in his chest unraveled and he gently reached over, smoothing her hair back from her face, smiling when she instinctively burrowed closer. He stared at her for several more minutes before pulling the sheet over her and then standing.

He was acutely aware of the stiffness of his muscles and the ache in his joints as he dressed. His mind was equally sluggish, insisting on returning again and again to the memory of Ana lying on the ground, bite marks at her throat, choosing to give up her last chance for humanity in order to spend an eternity with Ty—even if that meant spending it as a vampire. And even though he didn't think of himself as a monster anymore . . .

Despite the fact that she was still in bed and sleeping

peacefully, guilt assaulted him. Seven months ago, he'd experienced suffering firsthand. This past week, he'd witnessed hers. How she'd been sure, despite his assurances otherwise, that there would never be enough blood to sate her hunger, never be enough sex to appease her lust. How she'd cried, certain she was being eaten from the inside out. Time and again, he'd cursed himself a hundred times for allowing her to put herself through such torture, certain he wouldn't be able to stand it for another second . . .

But now . . .

Now, thank God, most of her pain had eased. Even with the worst of it over, the next few months would still be difficult—for both of them.

He made sure she got what she needed to drink—bottled animal blood, since giving her human blood risked her becoming addicted to it. And he made sure she got what her body needed in other ways.

Sex . . . God, they'd been going at it until he was raw. He'd given her orgasm after orgasm, exhausting both of them until they were unable to move. She'd be satisfied for a while, barely enough for them to rest, and then it would start all over again. It wasn't easy. It wasn't pretty. But it wasn't the same kind of transition he'd experienced, either. Ana had him, and thank God, that seemed to be enough for her. He hoped it always would be.

He loved her more than he'd ever thought possible. She was his. Whatever happened next, they'd work through it together. After all, their reward would be an infinite future in one another's arms. Included in that future, however, was the need to finish their work with Belladonna.

Above all, to find the person who had set them up by sending them to Salvation's Crossing.

Until they found him, stopped him, he would always be a threat. And they *would* find him.

Swiftly, in case Ana woke and needed him again, Ty called Carly.

"How's she doing?" she asked.

"She's strong. She's handling it."

"And how are you doing?"

He swallowed hard. "I'm doing the same. Waiting for her suffering to ease. Praying that she never regrets the choice she made."

"Give her more credit than that, Ty. She's seen first-hand what she's going to have to deal with. She obviously thinks you're worth it. And she's right, of course."

It was a rare compliment from Carly and sure enough, before he could even attempt to respond, she kept talking. "So you found hard evidence of human blood trafficking. Looks like a vampire sex ring is up next."

"Based on what?"

"The Russian women who posed as Ramona and Becky Montes have been identified via a DNA match through Interpol's Most Wanted. Their real names: Oksana Kaptsova and Daria Tkachuk."

"Who played whom?"

"Oksana impersonated Ramona, Daria impersonated Becky. Even though Daria passed for sixteen, she's actually twenty-one."

"Did they kill the Montes women?"

"Maybe. They have a string of prior arrests but none for murder. Oksana practically raised Daria. Encouraged her to join a cult."

"Another cult. Just what we need," Ty spat. "What kind this time?"

"Pseudoreligious crap, dark and deep," Carly said. "With ties to vampire cults in Eastern Europe. Their mystical leader saved lost souls, cash only, but he did admit young women for free if they were pretty."

"I get the picture."

"Anyway, Oksana and Daria signed up new members.

They cleaned out the cult's bank accounts and fled to America. But not before they founded a multimillion-dollar whore factory in Odessa."

"Nice way to put it. What happened?"

"The Russian mafia muscled in."

"So how did you find all this out?"

"They're looking to strike a deal and they're willing to talk to get one. Daria met Miguel online and they hit it off. Posing as Ramona and Becky, they volunteered to be a part of Salvation's Crossing. To work with the teenagers."

"Of course. Full access to innocent and vulnerable girls. They couldn't know Miguel and Gloria were vampires."

"Oh, they knew," Carly said. "And common sense tells us Oksana and Daria had partners on the outside. I'm betting at least one was a vampire, too. They're not talking."

"You think they're scared?"

"Of us? No. Of whoever they were working with? Definitely."

"So who's handling it?"

"Barrett. She helped find trafficked children in foreign countries while she was in the army."

"She had support in the army. Miguel told Ana we were set up. Have you decided about Rick Hallifax? Mahone? Queen Bianca?"

"Until we have time to check it out, I'm not giving anything away. Our intel stays within Belladonna. Same for the fact that Ana's been turned. And your current location."

Ty nodded even as he heard movement in the other room and Ana's voice softly calling his name. All concerns fled but one.

"I've got to go. Ana needs me."

* * *

Gloria had been so busy playing with her new doll that she hadn't even noticed their mother had left and they were alone in the house with nothing to eat but left-over cake. Eliana, however, had known the moment her mother had left, taking the man with the slicked-back hair and shiny leather jacket with her. She'd seen that look on the faces of her mother's "friends" before when they looked at her, when they looked at Gloria, and it scared her. She knew what they wanted, and it wasn't what Prince Eric wanted from Ariel, or Prince Charming wanted from Cinderella, or Prince Phillip had wanted from Sleeping Beauty. Luckily, however, Gloria seemed oblivious to such realities, and was content to play with her baby doll, brushing her yellow hair and smoothing her gingham dress while feeding her her "bottle."

"I'll take care of you, baby," Gloria crooned. "I won't ever let anything happen to you. We're going to have a wonderful life together—you, me, and Eliana. I'll protect you the way Eliana protects me."

Eliana smoothed Gloria's hair. "That's right, Gloria. I'll always protect you."

Gloria smiled up at her, the dimple in her cheek flashing, but then she frowned. "But if I'm taking care of my baby, who's going to take care of you, Eliana?"

Eliana shook her head. "I can take care of myself, Gloria. You know that."

"But everyone needs someone to take care of them. When you work so hard, who's going to take you to the ball? And if you sleep too long, who's going to kiss you awake?"

No one, Eliana thought, thinking once more of her mother's "friends." "I have you, that's all that matters to me."

Biting her lip, Gloria stared down at her doll. When her eyes filled with tears, Eliana hugged her.

"Why are you crying? It's your birthday, Gloria. Mama got you a beautiful doll. She loves you. I love you. Be happy."

"I love you, too, Eliana. Do you think that someday, when you don't have to worry about taking care of me anymore, you'll find your prince?"

Eliana had thought about it, but even with all her fantasies about being a Disney princess, she couldn't lie to Gloria. She didn't have a fairy godmother, after all . . . "True princes are hard to come by," Eliana said. "But anything's possible. Now come on. Let's have some of that cake."

Giggling, they dug into the leftover birthday cake. Afterward, Eliana and Gloria climbed into bed and snuggled, just as they had for years. Just as they would for the months to come, until the day that Gloria would leave Eliana for a better life . . .

"Gloria!" Ana jolted awake, disoriented and confused. At first, she didn't recognize where she was; part of her was still in the small bedroom she shared with Gloria in the Bronx.

Then reality settled into her bones and her confusion faded.

Gloria was dead.

Along with the hopes Ana had for a happy life with her baby sister.

Alone in the dark, her throat parched and her bones aching, grief overtook her . . . until she suddenly heard Gloria's childish voice, "All those nights I prayed for you, Eliana. For you to find *your* prince. And now you have. You're Ana now and you have."

A soft giggle followed.

Automatically, Ana's gaze darted around the room.

Nobody there. But . . . she'd heard the words clearly. The happy giggle still vibrated in her ears.

Gloria.

Maybe it was just a figment of her imagination or wishful thinking or a delusion aided by her turning . . . but vampires were real, for God's sake. Who's to say that really hadn't been Gloria's voice. Not the voice of the person Gloria had become after she'd left to live with her father's parents, but the voice of the innocent and loving little girl she'd been before that.

To that girl, Ana whispered, "I'll always love you, Gloria. Always."

In the past, she'd had to take care of herself. She'd also taken care of Gloria as best she knew how. The ache that she should've done more would probably never dissipate, but her life had changed. There was another person determined to take care of her.

A man. A vampire.

"Ty," she called out.

In seconds, he was there. He immediately climbed into bed beside her, whispering words of reassurance and thanking her for choosing a future with him.

Ty had turned out to be her prince, after all. He'd changed her. Turned her in a way even Miguel hadn't.

He'd awakened her from the evil spell that had imprisoned her for her whole life.

As he kissed her, the hunger inside her grew—the yearning for blood and sex—but at the same time, her soul was nourished by being in his arms.

She hurt. She grieved. She needed.

She loved.

In other words, she *lived*.

ACKNOWLEDGMENTS

I can't thank my editor, Sue Grimshaw, and the Random House publishing team enough for believing in me and this series. I'd also like to thank my agent, Holly Root, for her continuing support. Susan Hatler, Cyndi Faria, and Rochelle French, I adore you. A special shout out to Rhyannon Byrd, Tina Folsom, and Virna's Vixens, and Danielle Gorman, Vanessa Romano, Karin Tabke, Grace Chow, Vanessa Kier, Kristin Miller, and Joyce Lamb for reading this manuscript during the early stages. Thank you to my fans, friends, fellow writers, and family, too many to name here but you know who you are—whether you write a review, message me on Facebook, provide brainstorming help, or lend me a hand during difficult times, I appreciate you all. Finally, as always, much love and thanks to my boys, Craig, Joshua, Ethan, and Zachary, who mean everything to me.

Read on for a sneak peak at

AWAKENED

by

Virna DePaul

Published by Ballantine Books

Barrett regained consciousness with agonizing slowness. She was lying down. Her head banged like someone was hitting it. Hard. Over and over. She willed the pain down, but it didn't go away, interrupting her awareness of the rest of her body and her surroundings. Bit by bit she got it back.

Her wrists were loosely bound. She was alive, but she wasn't sure why.

The decaying smell of the unseen creature that had nearly killed her still hovered in the air. It could be near. Watching her. Its captive.

Waiting to kill.

Vaguely she thought of working her hands free and running for her life . . . but . . . she was someplace inside now, no longer surrounded by stunted trees. It seemed to be night. The air coming in through a reinforced window was cool. She forced raw breaths in and out of her swollen throat.

A face swam into view. A man was leaning over her. He smelled nice. Like the outdoors. The sun. Trees.

She took in a few details. The shadowy light in the room didn't help much. Dark brown hair, messed up. There was a leaf in it. He had rugged features that were somehow familiar and a strong jaw. Dark eyes, serious. He was strongly built with broad shoulders, wearing faded jeans and a camo shirt with the sleeves rolled up.

Brawny arms lightly dusted with dark hair reached out to her. He drew back when he saw her flinch.

She blinked, forcing herself to focus. Who was he?

"You got a hell of a knock on the head." He reached out a hand and brushed his fingertips over an aching lump on her temple. The gentleness of his touch made her even more confused.

"Huh?"

He shook his head. "You fell. Do you remember?"

The effort of thinking made her head throb painfully again. Automatically, she tried pulling herself to a sitting position.

"Stay still," he commanded. Something hidden in his other hand gave off a steely glint and Barrett cringed. "I'm not going to hurt you. Let's get these off." He clipped through plastic zip ties, by the sound of it, and released her hands.

She didn't have the strength to hit him.

"Did you . . . why . . ." Barrett thought maybe it was better not to ask.

She had no idea who'd attacked her, but as the man got closer to the light and memory returned, she knew with absolute conviction that it hadn't been him.

She didn't know how and she didn't know from what, but Nick Maltese had saved her. More fleeting memories came back to her. He'd drawn back the mechanism of the crossbow and aimed. The arrow flew. She'd heard it sing. After that, nothing.

"Sorry," he said. "Had to tie you to get you across my shoulders and run back here. Two miles, uphill."

Barrett blinked, summoning up a memory of stunted trees and scattered rocks. Seemed to her she'd been closer to the top of the hill than that. Nick was just as strong as she remembered. Maybe stronger. "I didn't know when you'd come to or how you'd react." He sat next to her on the bed and examined her wrists. Then he let her go.

"You carried me here?"

"Like a little lost lamb."

He'd said that about her once before. During one of their arguments about whether she was suited to military life and working with refugees. He'd never said it again, probably because she'd ripped him a new one and then hadn't spoken to him for over a week.

Despite everything, Barrett managed a weary half smile. "I wasn't lost. And I'm not that little. But thanks." She touched her neck.

"You could have called or texted." He held up her smartphone.

"Give that back. You never were reachable unless you wanted to be."

Nick grinned as he handed back her phone. "So shoot me." He reached into a pocket and came up with her gun. She noticed that the holster was lying on the bed.

"Would that get your attention?" she asked. "I did think about calling you when I was driving up, decided not to at the gate."

A minor lie. She hadn't wanted to give him the chance to tell her to go away, that was all. She'd just wanted to knock on his door and see his face when he opened it.

Hello, Nick. Imagine finding you here all alone.

Stupid fantasy. He didn't seem inclined to pursue the subject.

Barrett's sigh hitched roughly in her throat. "So who or what tried to strangle me?"

"I'm not sure," he said after a fractional pause. "Whoever he was, he was big." His gaze moved to the crossbow he'd left leaning against the wall, then back to her. "I took aim the second before you moved. Threw me off."

"I didn't see you," she murmured. "I was fighting for my life."

He gave a curt shake of his head. "No shit. Good thing I got there in time."

"Yeah." She cleared her throat. It hurt inside and out.

"Anyway, not a total miss. The arrow took a chunk out of his ear. He let you go and ran. I thought it best to stay with you rather than give chase."

"I appreciate that," she said softly.

With more determination this time, she once again tried to sit up, bracing herself on wobbly arms. With an impatient sigh, Nick helped her until her back was braced against the wooden headboard. Other than that, the whole room seemed to be made of stone and furnished in steel. Taking shallow breaths to keep the dizziness at bay, she asked, "Are we in a safe location?"

"For now. I've got satellite tracking. It's how I knew someone was heading up. But I had no idea it was you until the last second."

"Oh."

"I think the video feed from the gate cam broke down or got whacked. Did you park down there?"

"I was looking for a camera. Didn't see one. And yes, I left my car."

"The camera's hidden in the poison ivy. One of my better ideas. Low maintenance and no one goes near it."

"Kind of low tech for you." Tiredly, she closed her eyes, then jerked them open again when she feared she was dozing off. What had she been talking about? Oh, right. His gizmos. "So you're currently doing the type of research and development that requires you live on a mountain?"

"For some projects, yeah."

She watched him carefully.

"Projects designed to identify vampires for the feds?" she asked. "Meaning the FBI."

Given Mahone's report to Carly, that was Barrett's best guess at the moment. Why dance around the subject?

Rather than appear confused or deny what she'd said, he narrowed his eyes at her. "Then this isn't a social call. And you still haven't learned to stay out of trouble, I see. What happened to going back to your privileged life and taking up painting again? Wasn't that part of the plan?"

"Maybe in your mind. Never in mine." And he'd effectively avoided her question.

For the next few minutes, the tense silence pulsed between them, but she refused to go any further into their past, what he'd encouraged her to do, and what she'd known immediately upon stepping back onto U.S. soil was never going to happen. She also wasn't going to bring up the mistakes she'd made and would make again if she had to, even knowing it would end the same way. She prayed he wouldn't bring them up, either.

Nick finally sighed, then said, "So I guess you're working for the feds, too."

Thankful he wasn't going where she didn't want him to, she relaxed slightly, not thinking about why he'd assumed so, just that Mahone had been right. Nick knew about vampires and freely admitted he was working with the FBI. And he didn't seem overly surprised by the fact she did as well. "In a manner of speaking."

He cocked a brow. "Meaning?"

"Like you, I'm an independent contractor. I like my freedom."

"I remember."

Her gaze flew to his. Had that been bitterness in his tone?

He hadn't seemed to mind when she'd ended things. But his next words seemed like another dig. "You never liked following orders, even if they were there for a reason."

So she'd been wrong. He had no intention of letting sleeping dogs lie, but he couldn't force her to talk about it. "Let's not get into all that. It's in the past, Nick."

Clenching his jaw, he stood again, massive as a statue. For a moment he seemed to be listening to something outside that she couldn't hear. Then he returned his dark gaze to her. "Okay. Then let's get into something new: Why you're here, how you knew where to find me, and whether anyone knew you were coming."

The last part of the question confused her but only for a second. Then she realized why he was asking it. Her attacker . . .

It hadn't been some random assault by a maniac wandering in the woods. He'd been inhumanly strong. What if he was a vampire who'd been instructed to follow her and kill her? If so, who had sent him? The FBI? Tash? And why had he smelled like a rotting corpse, unlike every other vampire she'd ever met or heard of?

She looked sideways at Nick.

Was it totally crazy to think he'd sent that thing after her? That he'd only pretended to save her?

She shivered at her thoughts and shook her head. She hated this. Being suspicious of everyone around her, including the man she'd once trusted enough to welcome inside her body. She'd come here for a reason; she had no choice but to trust Nick again. It shouldn't be such a difficult task.

She answered him slowly. "There's a lot I need to fill you in on."

"Including what you know about vampires and what it is you need from me."

At her slight nod, his mouth twisted. Something disapproving radiated from him, and he didn't even bother to hide it.

"What's on your mind?" she asked him. The Nick Maltese she'd known hadn't gone in for displays of

emotion. But he was older now. His eyes showed it—
and revealed more than he probably wanted to.

"I wish you were here for a whole different reason,
Barrett. A personal one. But I've wished for a lot of
things that never came true, and something tells me
nothing's changed."